SANTA FE
RICHES

To
Mark and Jeannette Neal
May God bless you
as you read this.
Mel Stevens

SANTA FE RICHES

MEL STEVENS

TATE PUBLISHING
AND ENTERPRISES, LLC

Santa Fe Riches
Copyright © 2012 by Mel Stevens. All rights reserved.

No part of this publication may be reproduced, stored in a retrieval system or transmitted in any way by any means, electronic, mechanical, photocopy, recording or otherwise without the prior permission of the author except as provided by USA copyright law.

Scripture quotations marked (ᴇsᴠ) are from *The Holy Bible, English Standard Version*®, copyright © 2001 by Crossway Bibles, a publishing ministry of Good News Publishers. Used by permission. All rights reserved.

Scripture quotations marked (ᴋᴊᴠ) are taken from the *Holy Bible, King James Version*, Cambridge, 1769. Used by permission. All rights reserved.

Scripture quotations marked (ɴᴋᴊᴠ) are taken from the *New King James Version*. Copyright © 1982 by Thomas Nelson, Inc. Used by permission. All rights reserved.

This novel is a work of fiction. Names, descriptions, entities, and incidents included in the story are products of the author's imagination. Any resemblance to actual persons, events, and entities is entirely coincidental.

The opinions expressed by the author are not necessarily those of Tate Publishing, LLC.

Published by Tate Publishing & Enterprises, LLC
127 E. Trade Center Terrace | Mustang, Oklahoma 73064 USA
1.888.361.9473 | www.tatepublishing.com

Tate Publishing is committed to excellence in the publishing industry. The company reflects the philosophy established by the founders, based on Psalm 68:11,
"The Lord gave the word and great was the company of those who published it."

Book design copyright © 2012 by Tate Publishing, LLC. All rights reserved.
Cover design by Matias Alasagas
Interior design by Mary Jean Archival

Published in the United States of America
ISBN: 978-1-62147-578-1
1. Fiction / Christian / Western
2. Fiction / Westerns
12.10.29

CHAPTER ONE

"I'll not have a Mexican brat make as much as I do out of this deal," said Lud Fuller. "I've been roaming those hills for years, and he ain't hardly been out of Santa Fe his whole life. I don't think he's got anything worth taking along, nohow."

Grandpa said, "There are two things wrong with that, Lud. First, Carlos is *not* a Mexican. Carlos is Spanish—in fact, he's related to the king of Spain. He's not a brat, either. If you want someone who can find gold, he's worth taking with you. He's found gold for us for nine years."

Grandpa's a sergeant in the Army. When he speaks, he gets your attention.

"What's your name, boy?" asked Lud.

"Carlos Rodriquez, sir."

"Well! Did you hear that? First time I've been called *sir*. We may need this kid, after all."

"Would you come with us if we agreed to pay you a full year's wage for the three or four months we'll be gone?" Pierre DuPlette addressed his remark to me, the boy Lud had referred to.

"No. Grandpa and I've done better than that, and we've never spent more than two weeks each year. I'm planning to spend this summer working the same area and figure I can bring home at least six or seven times that much. Grandpa's in the Army and won't look for a mine. He says the king of Spain considers that all mines belong to him, so if we found one, it'd have to be given to the king. I think I can do enough to get all I want without anyone learning that I have a mine. How much do you think a full share from your deal would be?"

Bud Remington responded, "I'll be disappointed if I don't come away with at least ten times what most men make in a year."

"I'll have to think about whether I'd go for even a full share," I said.

"You've never seen what a dowser can do when it comes to finding gold," said Pierre DuPlette. "The only other dowser in Santa Fe is this boy's grandmother, and we can't take her. That leaves us no other choice than this young fellow. I say we take him. If he's good, he'll be worth a full share."

"Why don't we take him along and see what he can do? If he can't produce, we'll cut him out next year." This from Bud Remington.

"Seems reasonable to me," said Pablo Romero.

Juan Ortego added, "Yep."

There I was, thirteen years old, skinny as a stray pup, five feet six on my tiptoes, as confident as a mouse facing a mountain lion. The men were as friendly as a pack of wolves. I weighed a hundred pounds—with a few rocks in my pockets—and could lift half that much on a good day. The smallest of them was twice as heavy. I was ready to run. Lud Fuller was as rough and tough as anyone I had ever met—a tall, raw-boned, bearded, buckskin-clad man with a hint of red in hair that hung to his waist. His beard was stained with juice from the quid of tobacco in his cheek. His red-rimmed eyes were always on me, and a scowl was his constant expression. The other men didn't look as mean, but each of them was two or three times my age, and full of confidence in his strength and abilities.

The only men in my life were my grandpa, an uncle, and the priest. My father had walked out when I was five days old. My mother had borne me in her forty-second year and lived five days after my arrival. If she hadn't come back to her parents' home to give birth, I would have been left to die alone. My grandparents had given me a good home. I was aware from an early age that I was blamed for the death of my mother.

This conversation took place in 1755. Santa Fe was an insignificant settlement in the midst of a huge territory claimed by the king of Spain. Surrounded by numerous Indian tribes, the town survived only because of the presence of a detachment of soldiers. My grandpa was a builder by trade and was over a crew that built the fort, a home for the governor, and several other buildings that formed the town square.

Grandma was a relative of the king of Spain. She was better educated than most of the officials in the New World. She had been disinherited by her parents when she married a "common soldier." She had no regrets because she had "the best husband any woman could ever want!"

Grandpa accepted her love with joy. He had learned quickly that she was a lady who knew what she wanted and would allow little interference with her plans. She took over the job of preparing me for life in Santa Fe.

It was from her that I learned to dowse for gold. As a devoted follower of Jesus Christ, she learned the science, or art, from a priest in Mexico prior to moving to Santa Fe. I've never forgotten her words when she started my training.

"The key's in knowing that you have nothing to do but carry the gold. God causes the gold to move so it will tell you where he's put *his* gold. The only thing you can do by your efforts is to cause the gold to misbehave. All you have to do is watch what God does with it. If he chooses to show you where he's put his treasure, you'll find it. If you try to force anything, it will just spoil the message. You're sort of along for the ride and get the privilege of looking like you've found the ore. Just remember that and stay out of his way, and you'll find more gold than any man in all of this country."

Each August when the Army gave Grandpa leave, the three of us would go into the Sangre de Cristo Mountains and search for gold. The first year, when I was four, she handed me a strip of leather with a nugget tied to one end and a loop on the other end. She said, "Put this loop on the middle finger of your right hand, like I have this one on mine. You may watch me some, but you need to watch your nugget most of the time. You need to understand what's happening. God has placed gold in the ground, and he'll show you where it is if you let him."

"How will he do that?"

"Move your hand and cause the nugget to swing straight ahead of you. Start walking up the bank of the creek. Walk as smoothly as you can so you don't change the direction the nugget is swinging. When you walk close to where God has put some gold, the nugget will swing toward that gold."

"Will he do that for me?"

"Do you love God?"

"Yes."

"Does he love you?"

"I think so."

"Why do you think so?"

"You say he does."

"Do you know why I tell you that he does?"

"No."

"The Bible is God's word. He had men write it so we can know what he said. We believe the Bible's true because God said it. I've read in the Bible that God loves you. That's why I tell you that he loves you. Do you believe that I love you?"

"Yes."

"I do love you, but God loves you more than I do. Do you think I want you to find gold?"

"Yes."

"Why?"

"I guess it's because you love me."

"That's right. Do you believe that God loves you?"

"I hope so."

"Do you believe me?"

"Yes."

"Can you believe that God loves you because I tell you he does?"

"Yes."

"He loves you. Let him show you that he does."

"Will he show me gold to help me believe that he loves me?"

"Let's find out."

I walked up that creek bank convinced that God loved me and was going to show me exactly where he had put a big bag of gold. I scrambled over rocks, jumped over bushes, and soon had that nugget jiggling like a leaf in a strong wind.

"You need to slow down, Carlos. The way you're tearing around, God can't do anything with the nugget because you're making it jump around so much. You need to walk so you don't cause it to do anything but swing straight ahead of you. He'll show you, but the way you're acting, he isn't able to control anything. Calm down and walk so you don't get in his way. Let me walk with you."

She walked slower than ice melts, and our nuggets just swung back and forth ahead of us. I suppose it was a hundred yards, but that can seem like a mile to a four-year-old boy.

My nugget started swinging toward the creek!

"Keep walking, but watch the nugget. It'll show you what to do."

I hurried up the bank. By my sixth step, the nugget was swinging wildly. "What's it telling me?"

"Come back to where it started swinging differently. Stand there until it's doing what it was before you ran ahead."

"I didn't run."

"You almost did. This is a time when you need to wait and see what the Lord does. When you take control, he has to wait until you slow down and watch him work. Is the nugget swinging like it did before?"

"Yes."

"Walk slowly and watch closely. Try to not cause any movement. This is the most important time, when you're allowed to watch and see what God does. You're being shown that if you do anything other than watch him work, it'll spoil everything.

He wants *you* to *carry* the tools so *he* can use them *for* you. How much work do you do when you're riding your horse?"

"The horse does all the work."

"Let the Lord do the work now, just like you let your horse do the work."

"I'll try."

"That's all he asks of you."

I started walking, and Grandma said, "Slow down. God isn't in a hurry."

The nugget continued to swing, and as we moved slowly, it was soon swinging straight across in front of me. I stopped and asked, "Is the gold out there? Where this is pointing?"

"It may be, but see if you can find out for sure. Keep walking and see what happens."

As I moved forward, the direction of the swing continued to change. Each change indicated that the gold was in that same place. After I had gone another ten feet, Grandma said, "Turn around slowly and walk back downstream. Stop when you think you know where the gold is."

When I stopped, she said, "Walk toward where you think it is. Walk slowly and watch the nugget."

I waded into the creek and followed the nugget. It was swinging straight ahead of me. There was no change until I was close to the bank on the other side of the creek. At that point the swing changed quickly and swung farther than previously, then swung to my right. The swing back toward me was stronger, and the next move was to the left of center. I stopped because the action was confusing to me.

"Walk forward slowly and see what happens."

The action continued to confuse me as I took four small steps forward. The nugget continued to swing in a manner that I didn't understand.

"Keep walking. It'll tell you something pretty soon."

After two more steps, the nugget was swinging in a complete circle and was getting faster.

"What does that mean?" I asked.

"What do you think it means?"

"I must be standing on the gold."

"It'll be directly below your hand."

We took out several sacks of high-grade ore during the next few days. The sale of that deposit exceeded Grandpa's earnings for that year. The following years were even better. My grandparents were generous, and I was given my choice of a horse along with a nice saddle and bridle. Grandma also made certain that they found a tutor so I was taught how to read, write, and do fairly complex mathematics.

The tutor was a young priest, so the principal reading was from the Bible. The priest was a strong advocate of peaceful co-existence and did his best to persuade me that any violence was a sin, all of which was poor preparation for spending several months in the company of a rough, tough crew of older men like the five with whom I was at that time.

"He'll go with you, and we know he can find gold if it's there," said Grandpa. "He'll receive the same share as each of you does. Is that the agreement?"

"Lud's furnishing all of the horses, mules, and equipment, so he'll get a double share. Everything will be divided into seven parts. Each of us will get a share, with Lud getting an extra share for what he is providing," said Pierre.

"What will he be expected to do other than locate the ore?"

"He'll need to help as much as possible, but we won't ask him to do a man's work. He'll need to help in camp and do some of the work in the mining. We don't need another miner. If he finds gold, we'll see that he's taken care of, and he'll come home in as good condition as any of us. In fact, if he really can find gold, I'll personally see that nobody bothers him. I guess if he can't, he'll not be given any special care, though," said Bud Remington.

"He'll find gold if it's there. He's taken us to gold not far from here. We're expecting his part to be pretty big, or we wouldn't let him go with you."

"All right. We leave a week from now. Have him here by sunup next Monday. We've got a long trip," said Lud.

The next few days were filled with apprehension. I finally went to Grandma and said, "Do I have to go with those men? I'm scared of that Lud. He's a hard man and will probably find all kinds of things to shout about. I've never been on a trip like this and don't know what they'll expect me to do. What'll they do if I can't understand what they want?"

"Grandpa said that Bud Remington's a nice man. You're old enough to be away from us. Remember that you aren't alone. Jesus is always with you. Do your best, and he'll make sure you're all right."

"How about Indians? Will they bother us?"

"That man Lud says he knows the Indians, and they won't be any trouble."

"I wish it was someone else who told us that. I don't like Lud, and he surely doesn't like me. Can we believe him?"

"The other men seem to like him, and they're depending on him. He's spent a lot of time there and should know what he's talking about. Quit worrying and go make us rich. You can do it."

"Do I need a gun? I've got enough gold to get a rifle and probably a pistol, too. I'd feel a lot better if I had something besides my knife for protection."

"Ask Grandpa. If he thinks you should, he can take you to get them."

Grandpa thought it was a good idea. I bought the finest firearms that were available in Santa Fe. They were used but in excellent condition. A trooper had obtained them on a campaign in Mexico and needed some extra money.

Grandma made sure I had clothes that were too big for me, as well as some that fit me.

"You're going to grow into them this summer. You'll be glad for them by the time you come home."

CHAPTER TWO

The sun lacked an hour of rising when Grandpa and I arrived. I was riding my pinto horse, and my gear was in the cart driven by Grandpa.

"What're you doing with that horse?" demanded Lud.

"Riding him," I said.

"I've got a horse for you."

"Nobody said anything about not bringing my own horse."

"What difference does it make, Lud?" asked Grandpa.

"Well, I was just figuring he'd ride one of mine. I guess he's got to be pampered, though. This is just like I figured it'd be. We got to take care of the baby."

"Hey, Lud, I've got my own two horses, so quit bellyaching," said Bud Remington. "You never said anything about any of us having to use your stock."

"When his fancy spotted pony wears out, I've got one that'll last the whole trip. I never saw one of those pintos that could handle the tough going. Makes me think we've got an Injun in camp. Those red boogers love their pintos."

"I've never been able to see that color made much difference in how good a horse is," said Pierre. "Let's get on with business and forget about personal opinions."

"Have you ever loaded a pack on a mule, kid?" asked Lud.

"No, sir, but if you'll teach me, I'll appreciate it."

"I'll show you once, and you better get it right that time."

"That'll be nice of you. Thanks."

"Get your stuff over by that last mule. Somebody had sense enough to wrap your duffel, anyway. Get it stuffed in these panniers. If it won't all go into the panniers, we'll put it up on top and tie it in place."

When I tried to place the stuff on the mule, the animal stepped away so I couldn't reach the pack. This was repeated four times. I led my horse around the mule and tied him close beside him then picked up my pack and approached again. When the mule tried to move, the horse stood firm, and I quickly shoved the bundle in place, slapped the mule on the shoulder, and said, "We'll get along fine if you'll just behave."

"Hey, you may make a hand yet," said Lud. "I figured he'd buffalo you. If you'd got rough with him, he'd have probably ended up kicking the daylights out of you. I like the way you handled it. Finish on the other side, and I'll show you how to tie everything together."

It took about ten minutes to complete the lashing of the packs, and I even got a half grin out of Lud when he put the finishing touches on the rope and stepped back.

"All right, you're on your own," he said and walked off.

It took another half hour to get everything ready. Grandpa came and gave me a final hug and a pat on the back along with an assurance that everything would be fine. We were under way when the sun was barely visible on the eastern horizon.

I expected someone to tell me what to do when the mule train started but was left to make my own decision. I stayed at the rear. The other riders, twelve mules and three spare mounts were ahead of me. I was content with that arrangement because it allowed me to observe everything. I found it all quite interesting. The first mule was led by Lud. Each of the other mules had its lead rope tied to the pack on the mule in front of him. The spare horses were allowed to roam free.

Lud led almost due north out of Santa Fe and set a pace that would cover a considerable distance each day. The mules had been loafing all winter and seemed glad to be on the move. They were frisky enough to nip at each other, kick at anything that was a likely target, and shy from anything that gave them an excuse. After an hour on the trail, all the playfulness was worked off. Each of them was packing at least two hundred pounds, which soon used up all the fun of being on the trail. By the time the sun had the men warm, all the animals were settled into the routine of getting up the trail with a minimum of effort.

By midmorning we were in country that I had never seen. I was fascinated by the different types of grass, brush, and trees growing at the higher elevation. There was a beauty in the pines that I had never seen, and early flowers were blooming alongside banks of snow. I had always thought my horse was a gentle, dependable mount. He took on a new character in the wide open country. He was more alert, his ears forward, head high, and his step much quicker than it had ever been before. He was glad to be on the move. I was forced to tug on the reins to keep him from moving toward the front of the procession. My concern about the trip was dissolving with each turn of the trail. I spotted a herd of elk across a clearing from us and several times saw deer moving through trees on hillsides not more than a hundred feet away. Birds flew by almost continually, and I saw rabbits and squirrels frequently. None of the wildlife was afraid of us, which seemed unusual. All the animals around Santa Fe had avoided contact with humans.

When the sun was almost directly behind us, we rode into an open grassy area with a small creek running along one side. Lud pulled up and dismounted. "We'll stop and rest the mules a while, and we can eat a bite and check all the gear to make sure nothing's come loose. There's some food in the right pack on that black mule. A couple of you can get it out while the kid and I check the mules. Come on, kid. I'll show you how."

I was ready for a rest, and when I stepped off, I discovered that my legs were stiff and my rump was getting tender. I moved as quickly as I could to where Lud was checking the mules.

"Make sure the cinch's tight and the rope hasn't worked loose on any of the packs. A loose cinch makes for a sore back and will maybe let the pack slip. The ropes need to be tight, or we'll lose the load. Be sure you look close. Don't be gentle. Yank on stuff good and hard," Lud said.

I did everything the best I could. Lud followed and checked each mule after me. "You didn't check this one enough, kid," he said on the fourth mule. "Come here, and I'll show you. See, that cinch isn't tight. Grab hold and show me how you check it."

I grabbed the cinch and pulled on it. Nothing moved. Lud said, "Take hold here."

I took hold, and Lud grabbed my wrist and jerked it toward his body. My hand came off the cinch.

"Take hold again. Now, hold on this time. See there, see how that moves? That's loose. Now do it yourself."

I tried again, and the cinch gave some, but only by exerting all my strength.

"Now, loosen that latigo and tighten it."

I tried but could get no movement from the strap.

"Take the strap, turn your back to the mule, put the strap over your shoulder, and squat down some. Pull the strap tight then stand up under it. Hang on tight and keep lifting as far as you can. There now, see how much you got that time? That's the way to do it. Tie the strap again and check it. Let me check. Good. You did it. That's your job every time we stop to rest or eat from now on."

I finished checking the rest of the mules and found one more loose cinch and one loose rope. Lud followed and found nothing more that needed to be fixed. The two of us walked to the place where the others had built a fire and were making coffee. There were biscuits and jerky laid out along with some dried fruit. As simple as it was, nothing had ever tasted better.

After finishing the meal, Juan and Pablo each rolled a cigarette, and Pierre filled a pipe. Lud cut off a sizable chunk from his plug, and we all settled back and relaxed for a while. It wasn't long before Lud said, "Okay, time to go. I want to be up by those hot springs in three days, so we can't tarry."

In a matter of minutes, we were back on the trail. Even though I thought of it as a trail, there wasn't any visible path. Lud led off, and the rest seemed happy to let him choose the way. It was still quite early in the season, and as we proceeded into higher elevation, there were frequent patches of snow in the shaded areas. When the sun was close to the western horizon, Lud rode into a fairly level clearing with a creek running down the east side. He turned toward the creek and pulled up.

"This's the best camp spot for the next thirty miles. We'd best make camp. Kid, you'll help me get the stuff off these mules and put all the critters on grass," he said.

"I'll help all I can, but I'll probably drop some of the packs."

"I reckon you would. Don't worry. I'll get the packs off. You take care of the rigging. I'll show you on one of them, and then you can finish the job. There's more to a pack saddle than one like on your horse, especially when you're using mules. They're built without much withers, so you've got to not only keep the saddle from moving back, but you need a strap around the rear so it won't slip forward onto the neck. Start by loosening the breast collar then unbuckle the rump strap before taking the cinch loose. Then pull the whole rig off. Stand it on end and lay the saddle blanket on top upside down, so it can air out and let any sweat that's in it dry. Be sure and put them in order, because in the morning you need to get the same outfit back on the mule it's on now." Lud worked while he talked and soon had the pack and saddle off the mule at the back of the line.

"How'm I supposed to tell which mule's the right one?"

"You'll picket them in the same order as they line up here. Before long, you'll know them by name. Always *unsaddle* this back one first and *saddle* the front one first. That way they're lined up and ready to go when you're done. Pay attention to how you take the gear off, because you'll be putting it on in the morning."

When we had the packs and saddles off the two mules at the back of the string, Lud said, "The picket ropes and pins are in this pack that came off the left side of the back mule. We'll lead these two over to water then put them out to graze. They'll want to roll on the way, too."

When the pair of pack animals were well watered and had rolled as much as they wanted, Lud said, "These ropes have this strap here on the end. Fasten that to the left forefoot then move out to the end of the rope and drive that pin in the ground with this hammer. Pound it in solid, or it'll come loose before morning, and we don't want to have to chase any mules. Be sure to leave enough room between the critters, or they'll get tangled up and won't be able to eat."

By the time the mules were all settled for the night, Pierre had a meal ready. The other three men had put up a lean-to and gathered a supply of firewood after taking care of the saddle horses. When the meal was over and the smokers in the group had finished with their after dinner light-up, Pierre heated water and invited me to help with clean up.

"We'll all bed down under the lean-to, else we'll have wet beds in the morning," said Ben. "It's not going to rain, but there'll be plenty of dew. If I was you, I'd get as far under there as I could."

"Thanks," I said. "I didn't know where I should make my bed."

"I'll sleep over here close to the fire. I usually wake up during the night and can keep the fire going. It'll be cold in the morning, and I hate to have to build a fire in the cold."

The moon appeared in the east shortly after we had eaten. It was almost in the full phase and lit up the area so it was easy to see the animals spread across the clearing. Soon after that, the howling of coyotes filled the air.

"Will they bother the animals?" I asked.

"No, they never mess with anything that big. They go after rabbits and other small animals. They'll try for a young deer or any sick or wounded critter," answered Juan. "I saw a pack of them kill a big bull elk that had a broken leg. It took them a while, but they ran him until he was totally worn out then moved in for the kill. One of them went for his nose, and while he was fighting that, the others hit his throat, and he was done for. They're a pretty smart animal. The Indians mostly figure he's the smartest of all critters, and some of them seem to worship him."

I learned during the night that a couple of my companions were hearty snorers. One of them not only filled the air with his snores but added snorts periodically. Even so, I was able to sleep quite soundly. The day's ride, coupled with the stress of learning new duties, had tired me thoroughly.

When I awakened the next morning, I was greeted by Pierre, who was busy with breakfast. "You sure know how to saw logs, boy. Better get around so you can help Lud with those mules. He doesn't like it when anyone isn't on the job on time. He's over by the gear."

I dressed quickly and hurried to where Lud was working.

"Better get those mules in here. The sun'll be up by the time we get them packed and ready. Do you remember which ones to bring first?"

"I'll bring the two closest to us first."

"Get it done then."

I got the animals in place and started getting them saddled and cinched as tightly as I could. It was difficult to keep ahead of Lud, who put the packs on as soon as the mules were saddled. When everything but the items needed for cooking was in place, Lud said, "Now we'll check to be sure you got those critters cinched up tight enough."

On the fourth mule Lud checked, he said, "You need to give this one some more muscle. That pack'd come off in a couple of hours."

I fixed the problem, and Lud was waiting by the seventh mule. "Here's another loose one," he said. When that one was tightened, Lud was walking back to the campfire. As I joined him, the big man said, "I can maybe make you a packer by the time we go home this fall."

"Thank you. I want to learn all I can, and you're a good teacher."

"Don't go making a teacher of me. I can hardly sign my own name, and reading's way over my head."

"Maybe I can teach you, if you want."

"Do you know how to read?"

"Yes, sir."

"How'd you learn?"

"Grandma arranged with the priest to teach me. He also taught me to handle numbers, too."

"Do you really think you could teach me to read? And maybe how to do some figuring, too?"

He sounded excited at the thought of being able to read. This could be a way to make him like me!

"I could sure try. Do you have any books?"

"No, of course I don't. Why would I carry a thing like that around? Do you have any?"

"All I've got is my Bible, but there's a lot of reading in it. Grandma wouldn't let me leave it at home. She wants me to read some every day, and I try to do that most of the time."

"You don't reckon a miserable sinner like me'll ruin it, do you?"

"I reckon it'll stand up to most anything and still be going strong. When do you think we can start?"

"It'll be a while. I'm not sure I want to tackle something as tough as that. My old brain isn't too quick. You'll probably want to quit before we get very far. I don't figure to be easy to teach. I'm sort of like those mules—stubborn and not too bright."

"You've taught them to do exactly what you want them to, so you must be smarter than they are. I'll bet you'll be reading better than most school teachers before very long. You let me know when we can start."

"I'll think on it. I'll just say, you're tougher than I thought you were. I'd not want to tackle something like that. We may make a pair yet."

"I'd really like that."

CHAPTER THREE

During the next two days, we traveled through some more beautiful mountain regions followed by a section that was primarily open, grassy areas surrounded by dense forests of yellow pine. We encountered frequent snow drifts inside the pine forests, and the temperature at night was cold enough to put a skim of ice on water. It was late the third afternoon that we dropped down to a river. Lud followed it to the left for half a mile and stopped near a spring that gushed hot, steaming water close to the river.

"This here's the San Juan River, and the Injuns call that Pagosa Spring. Got no idea what it means, but they claim it'll heal most anything that ails a person," said Lud. "Don't try jumping in up here close, or you'll be scalded. Follow it down a ways, and there're some pools where it won't burn you too much. Sure's a nice spot to clean up and soak away any aches and pains. We're not far from where we'll start prospecting. From here on, it'll be pretty much work from sunup to dark, so enjoy this while you can. We'll probably not see it again till we're headed home."

There was an hour of sunlight left after the camp was set, and a supply of firewood was in place, so everyone took advantage of the hot water. All the men except Lud shaved, and Lud and I joined in cavorting in the hot pools where the cold river water was warmed by the inflowing springs. The men were satisfied after an hour, but I continued until they hailed me for supper.

During the meal, Lud said, "We're here now, so where do we start looking for gold?"

Pablo Romero said, "Our best chance is to get on a creek, start panning, and when we find anything, we'll turn the kid loose and see what he finds. I figure I can locate as much with my pan as he can with his witching, but we'll soon know."

Pierre responded, "It won't be long before you'll learn what a good dowser's worth. I'm guessing that within a week, we'll be starting a mine. Have you seen better country for finding ore?"

Juan Ortega said, "It's pretty, but I have yet to see scenery weigh much on gold scales. Some of the richest mines are in desolate country that isn't pretty in any language. I'd like to find it here instead of in some desert, but gold's where you find it. If we find anything with pans, there'll be deposits nearby."

"We can't depend on having water close to a deposit of ore," said Pierre. "The biggest mine I was ever in was twenty miles from water. All the gold that washes down a stream comes from some deposit, but that doesn't mean that every body of ore's going to show up with water anywhere close. I'll be surprised if Carlos doesn't find the best ore away from any stream."

"He's got to show me that he can locate anything with that string and glob of gold," Pablo responded. "Not that I don't want him to. I don't care who finds it, just so we get it out and get it sold. If you can find it, kid, I'll sure enough mine it. Juan, you know this country. Where do you think we should start looking?"

"I've taken quite a few pans out of a creek about a mile west, on that mesa yonder. It runs up into some pretty rough country where I think it'd make sense to find a body of ore. That's where I had in mind to start."

Pierre said, "Carlos, how long does it take to find out if there's gold in an area?"

"It's never taken more than half a day to find what little we've dug. We weren't looking for a mine, though. We always worked a couple of weeks in the summer and were happy with any bit of gold regardless of the size of the deposit. My Grandma had worked that area for several years, so she knew where to start looking. I guess it won't take more than a day or two to work an area a mile long and a quarter mile wide. If we find some indication, we might decide to extend the search to be sure we don't miss the big body. We should know pretty quickly whether or not we want to stay in an area. I hope I can understand the sign when I get close to a big ore body."

"How're you supposed to know if it's big or little?" asked Bud Remington. "I've never heard of dowsing before."

"It's just a matter of watching the gold nugget swinging on the end of the string. Gold's attracted to gold, so it swings toward any gold that's close to it. When there's more gold, it swings farther, and I've learned how to pinpoint the location so we don't have to dig many empty holes. It tells me pretty accurately how big the ore body is as well as how rich it is."

"Your grandma taught you all this?"

"Yes, sir."

"And could you teach someone else?"

"I don't know. Why would I want to? We don't need more than one person to do my job. I'll probably try to teach my son if I ever have one."

That was the shortest night I'd ever spent. We had finished breakfast before the sun was more than a glimmer in the east.

Lud said, "It's time to get under way. We'll not find gold setting here chewing the fat. Come on, boy, let's get those mules loaded."

CHAPTER FOUR

It seemed to me like a lot of work went into moving a mile or so from the previous camp. I thought it would've made sense to stay where we were and ride the mile or so to the area they wanted to start looking for gold. I wasn't ready to start making suggestions, though. The move took until midmorning, at which time Pierre and I started walking upstream along a shallow creek.

Most of the others attacked the creek with pans, hoping to find signs of mineral. Had anyone asked me, he'd have learned that I was about as comfortable as a frog in a skillet. I felt the full weight of responsibility and wished, as I had every day, that I hadn't been forced into this situation. I knew better than anyone that I wasn't prepared for the responsibility of guiding these men to a gold mine. I'd never been in a situation where Grandma hadn't been available to assist if I encountered a problem. She *had* always encouraged me to solve them without her help, but she'd always been there in case I needed her.

There was no one to whom I could turn for help now, so I slipped off into the trees where I could see nobody and knelt down and prayed for guidance. Feeling somewhat better, I got out my equipment and walked to the creek bank. I placed the leather thong over my right forefinger, moved my arm so that the nugget was swinging like a pendulum ahead of me, and walked slowly upstream. I had done this frequently and soon was quite comfortable about what I was doing. I'd gone less than half a mile when the nugget veered to the left toward the creek—a definite indication of a deposit of gold!

I continued upstream until the nugget was swinging back toward my left hip then waded across the stream and walked downstream, watching the nugget all the time. When I was almost exactly straight across from where the nugget had first changed direction, it was indicating that the gold was once again to my left. Altogether the actions had shown that there was a fairly decent deposit of ore in the stream.

I went into brush that grew along the bank and cut three branches about four feet long. Returning to the stream, I trimmed the branches and sharpened the larger end of each so it could more easily be pushed into the ground. I placed one on each bank where I thought it was directly out from the deposit and the third one in the stream bed where the ore seemed to be.

I hadn't asked what I should do if I made any discoveries, so I continued to search upstream. By the time the sun was setting, I had covered approximately four miles and had made four more discoveries. If the men believed that I was correct, each of them would have a spot to work tomorrow.

When I reached camp, it was dark and the others had already eaten.

"Thought maybe a bear had got you, kid," said Pablo. "You must've got away from him all right. Did you find us a mine?"

"No mine, but there're five pretty good spots."

"What do you mean when you say 'pretty good spots'?" asked Lud.

"I think there're twelve to fifteen ounces of gold in each of them."

Pablo asked, "How many of us can work on each of them?"

"I think it's best if one person works alone. Otherwise you get in each others' way."

"Are they along the bank?" asked Juan Ortega.

"No, they all seem to be out in the stream."

Pierre said, "You'd better eat while we talk. You've been out all day with no food. We need to keep you healthy if you're going to find that much gold every day."

"Thanks. I doubt that it'll happen every day, no matter how well you feed me."

Juan said, "If the gold's in the middle of the creek, how do you get it out to pan it? I've never worked the middle of a stream."

"We've always diverted the water around the deposit. I brought some deer hides that we've used to build dams above the ore. With no water to deal with, it's easy to dig it out and pan it. I can show you in the morning."

"How many hides did you bring?" asked Pierre.

"I think there're twelve of them. We sometimes used two or three at a time, so we had a pretty good supply. You'll see. It isn't hard to handle the water if it's done right."

Lud said, "I can see that we'll not be sleeping late in the morning. I'll be anxious to see just how much we actually find. It sounds like a lot for one spot. If there's really ten ounces in each of them, that's enough to make the trip worthwhile already."

"We'll know something by this time tomorrow," Pierre commented. "My guess is that Carlos isn't telling us how much he really thinks is there. I'll be surprised if there's less than a hundred ounces in those five spots. I think we've got ourselves a full-fledged dowser, and it'll just keep getting better. I'll make another guess that we'll have a mine in a couple of weeks."

"Now you're really putting pressure on him, ain't you?" said Lud. "Let's back off some, or he may get all nervous and start trying to force his equipment to do more than it can, which just might put a stop to everything. Kid, as far as I'm concerned, you're doing fine. Just keep it up like you are, and I'll be plumb tickled."

There was a chorus of comments expressing agreement with Lud's statement, which took a lot of tension out of the moment. I was able to enjoy my meal after that. Even so, I lay awake quite a while that night, thinking about how much the success of this venture depended on my ability to locate gold in big quantities. I had never before felt that I was important to any undertaking. I was afraid that I'd forget to trust the work to the Lord without any interference, even though I knew that all I could do was diminish the results if I did anything other than allow the gold to show where any deposit was. I was amazed at how tired I was, and was soon sound asleep. I was embarrassed when everyone else was fully dressed and starting to eat when I woke the next morning. I dressed quickly and was through with breakfast as soon as most of the others.

"Okay, kid, where are those hides you've got?" asked Lud.

"Right here in my pack. I'll need help carrying them."

"I reckon each of us can carry a couple of them."

"We'll need some axes and shovels, too."

"I suppose we'll all need our pans, too, but we should be able to handle all of it."

"Pierre, is it all right if I make a sandwich to take with me today? I sure got hungry yesterday."

"Sure, you do that. The rest of us came back at noon, but you were a long way up the creek and didn't come back. No wonder you got lanky."

CHAPTER FIVE

We were at the first location an hour later. Pierre said, "Tell us what to do."

"That stick out there's in the center of the deposit. We'll need two logs, four feet long and a foot thick. We'll place them upstream of that spot in a sort of wide, upside-down V. We'll put the hides above them with the upper edge of them covered with rocks to hold them in place and the hides stretching over the tops of the logs. That'll carry most of the water away from the deposit. Then it's fairly easy to shovel the sand and gravel into a pan and wash it. Each of the sticks out in the water's in the middle of the deposit that's there. If a couple of you'll get the logs, I'll start getting this place ready for them."

"Okay, Lud, let's go get them."

I said, "Give me a shovel and I'll prepare the area where we'll put the logs." I made a place five feet upstream from the gold. That left an outline in the shape of a low-pitched roof above the stick. Upstream from that, I moved six inches of gravel next to where the logs would lie.

"This creek'll start getting pretty wild soon and we won't be able to do this. We need to locate a mine before that happens. I plan to work upstream until I find it. I'll help each of you get ready to work a spot; then I'll go ahead and look for the mine."

"That sounds like a good idea," said Ben.

"It'll take most of today to get all of these places ready, so I won't get much done today. In a couple of days we'll know more about how much we have in the creek and we'll have a better idea about the possibility of a mine being close," I said.

We stayed at that spot until it was ready for working. We decided that Pierre should stay and work there while the rest of us went to the next location.

Lud said, "Bud, can you and Pablo get this spot and the next one ready? That way Juan and I can go on and set up the others. Carlos can hunt a mine."

"We can do that, can't we, Pablo?" answered Bud.

"If we can't, we'll holler for help."

CHAPTER SIX

I was sure there was a lode from which the gold had come. That gold couldn't have washed very far from the source. I located two deposits before dark. I could reach camp by going over the hill east of the creek. Starting at a brisk pace, I saw evidence that the creek had flowed the way I was going. I got my equipment and was rewarded with a reaction. The reaction was so intense I worked until it was too dark to see the nugget. My heart was pounding when I was forced to quit.

I was convinced that there was ore there. I got landmarks before leaving so I could go back the next morning.

"Did you find our mine?" asked Bud.

"I don't think so, but I'm sure there's a deposit along a hillside. It looked like a bigger deposit than I've ever encountered."

"How big do you think it is?" asked Pierre.

"It's ten to fifteen feet from end to end. I couldn't get any idea about the width or depth of it, but the nugget was practically pulling me toward it, so it should be bigger than anything I've ever worked with. I can't give you any definite answers until morning. How'd you do?"

Pierre said, "I dug a hole four feet deep before reaching gravel and sand, then it was too dark to pan. I'll probably start seeing something in the morning."

Bud said, "That's what I hit, too. Gold won't be in that top layer of rock."

"There's gold there, but it may be hard to get." said Lud. "We'll know a lot more tomorrow. I hope you've found a big bunch on your way back. We could do a lot of panning and not end up with much. You need to prove you can find a bunch of ore, Boy."

Pablo asked, "How'd you figure out that there might be gold up on the side of the hill?"

"I was taking a shortcut to camp, and it looked like the creek had run along there sometime, so I checked. The nugget started almost jumping, so I spent as much time as there was light. It got me sort of stirred up, I'll say that. It wasn't anything I can take credit for. I guess God just led me."

"You'll have all of us figuring God's your partner if this keeps up," said Pablo. "Maybe I'll join up with you."

"I hope you all join me."

Shortly afterward we all settled down for the night. We were all tired.

Lud had the fire ready for Pierre to cook breakfast when the sun was just starting to color the eastern horizon. Nobody wanted to lie in bed; they wanted to find gold.

"Do you need help with that spot you found last night?" Lud asked.

"I don't think so."

"If it's as big as you think, we'll all want to see it before we come to camp," said Bud. "I didn't plan to just pan in cold water."

"If you have anything, come let me know," said Lud. "I reckon the others'll want to know, too, so report as soon as you know what you've found."

I wished I'd said nothing about my latest discovery. Now they'd all be expecting it to be something big, and I had no real idea if it was even worth working. However, I'd never had a reaction as powerful as what I had experienced last night.

I rode my horse that morning. I was certain I would cover a lot of territory before evening. I also wanted to see if it would be possible to dowse on a horse. I rode away from camp before taking my equipment out. I was pleased to see that there was almost no difference between the action of the gold when riding and walking. This would allow me to cover more area each day, and it might make a big difference in the success of the operation.

I wasn't surprised when there was no response until I was a hundred feet from where I had expected to see the nugget indicate the presence of gold. Once I got that reaction, I picketed the horse and proceeded on foot.

The nugget swung six inches toward the hill as I approached the deposit, then widened to a foot. When I proceeded along the bank, the swing increased to a maximum width of two feet. The swing became less and continued to decrease until it was indicating that I had gone beyond the gold. I walked to the point where the swing was the most dramatic and tried to measure the height. There was gold to the bottom of the slide, and the nugget swung the same as I moved four feet up the side then settled down as it was raised higher. At six feet, there was no response. I was unable to get any indication of how deep the deposit was because the hill was steep and it was over a hundred feet to the top. The nugget showed five spots of bigger deposits, and the height appeared to vary from four feet at the deepest to nothing at each end. I spent all morning trying to get a mental picture of the size.

By noon I was convinced it was big but was scared to tell the men how big it looked. I assumed that my relationship with them would depend on the accuracy of my report on this deposit. My heart was thumping and my mind running wild. The nugget said that this was a major find, but the possibilty of being wrong scared me. When I finally took time to pray, it calmed me. I thanked the Lord and was able to trust him to control the outcome.

I got my horse and rode to where Lud was working. The big man heard me coming and was standing on the bank when I arrived.

"How's it look? Did you find us a good one?" he asked.

"I think it's good but will feel better when you've seen it."

"Do you want to get everybody?"

"I want everybody to see it before we go back this evening, but if you want to go now, we can get the rest of them later."

"Let's go see what you've got."

"All right. It isn't far. I'll picket this horse, and we can walk."

At the location, Lud said, "It don't look like much. Where's the gold?"

"Behind that slide rock. It starts here and runs down to that tallest bush. I can't tell how far it goes into the hill, but it's four feet deep in the middle and tapers off toward the ends."

"How much're you guessing is in there?"

"I've never worked with anything this big, but I'll be disappointed if there's less than fifty pounds."

"How many ounces is that?"

"There're twelve ounces to a pound, so it'd be six hundred ounces."

"I thought a pound was sixteen ounces."

"Gold is measured in troy ounces, which are different. There are only twelve troy ounces in each pound."

"Oh, all right. So there'd be six hundred ounces. That would give each of us a hundred ounces. Most people make twelve ounces in a year. Do you really think we might have that much?"

"I'm not going to tell anyone else, but that's what it looks like to me. I've never dealt with anything this big, so it's a guess. Let's tell everyone there could be twenty-five pounds."

"If they aren't happy with that, it'll surprise me. I would be. But golly, if there's as much as you think, we'll be rich. How do we find out if it's like you think it is?"

"The only way I know is to clear off enough of that rock to get some of it exposed. We'll need to pan some of it."

"Have you tried to get to any of it?"

"No."

"Let's see if we can get a look at it," said Lud, and he started moving rock.

Every time we moved a rock, it caused others to slide down. The hill was steep, and the slide went nearly fifty feet above the deposit.

"We're going to have to get rid of that slide before we can get the gold, kid. Let's stop and eat. Then we'll get the others and see if anyone can figure something out.. I'm fresh out of ideas."

"If we go after them now, they won't finish working the spots in the creek. Let's wait. We know there's gold. I don't want to ignore what we have in those other spots."

"I'd better finish my spot then. What're you going to do?"

"I'll ride up the creek and see if anything more shows up. I'll be back here about sundown."

When I got back the sun was just going down. The rest of the group was standing at the base of the rock slide.

"Have you figured out how to get to it?" I asked.

Pierre said, "We can remove the rock at the top, install timber to keep stuff from coming down. We can work our way down and haul away the loose stuff as we go. It's going to be a big job. How sure are you there's a big deposit?"

"I've never found anything that caused the reaction this does. There's a lot of gold in there."

Bud asked, "How much?"

"I guess at least twenty-five pounds, maybe as much as forty."

Juan said, "If there's ten pounds, we can spend a lot of time here and be better off than working spots in the creek. I'm convinced you can find gold. We should do what it takes to get it."

"Let's go to camp and discuss this," said Lud. "We can't do any more here."

CHAPTER SEVEN

It took three more days to pan all of the locations in the creek. Each of the men then went to the slide area and began removing rock.

After three weeks, we had four shelves above the area where gold was indicated, with all of the rock removed.

Juan said, "You'd better be right about how much gold's there."

Bud Remington said, "We're going to need a sluice down by the creek with a way to direct the water through it, too. We can't just pan all that we're going to be dealing with here. Some of us had better start work on that, too."

Lud said, "If you'll tell us how to do it, the kid and I'll take care of that."

"I'll draw you a plan for it tonight. In the meantime, you can cut a bunch of poles at least twenty feet long and six inches in diameter. We'll need ten of them."

"Okay, let's go, kid."

It took four days to build and place the sluice, and the men working on the rock pile finished the next day.

That evening Lud said, "We're almost out of meat. If nobody objects, Carlos and I'll take off in the morning and take care of that. We need to get in touch with those Injuns, too, so we'll see if we can shoot a buck and take him to them. That should put them in a good mood. They can give us lots of grief if we start wrong. Later we can slip away and shoot a bull for our use."

We left early with our saddle horses and two pack mules.

"Do you know where the Indians are?" I asked.

"Oh, sure. They're over west and a little south of here. We'll amble along and wait until we're close before we look for that buck. That way it'll be nice and fresh when we get there."

We followed the creek down to the San Juan River and then took a trail through the valley. It was a clear day with just a couple of clouds in sight. The temperature soon warmed up so we tied our coats behind our saddles.

"We'll likely need to get up in the timber to find any deer, but it's nice in this valley," said Lud. "This'd be a great place to run cattle or horses, wouldn't it?"

"I've never been on a ranch. The only times we left Santa Fe were when we went for gold each summer. It sure is pretty here, with all this grass in the valley, and brush and trees up higher."

It was mid-morning when we crossed the Piedra River. The valley curved off to the northwest at that point. It was late afternoon when Lud said, "We'd better move up into that timber and see if we can kick out a buck. It's not over five miles to the Indians' camp."

He led off and was soon moving through tall, yellow pines. It was but a few minutes before he stopped and dismounted. "You a good shot?"

"I've never shot at anything but a target. I did all right then."

"See if you can put that buck down."

"I don't see him. Where is he?"

"Under that tallest tree. He's bedded down, looking at us. He'll be up and running in a minute. See him?"

"I think so. Is he a four pointer?"

"No. I only see three points. Where's the one you see?"

"Just to the left of that big pine. He's looking right at us."

"Can you get a clear shot at his heart?"

"No, but I can hit his neck."

"Have at it, then. I don't see him, but he should be bigger than mine. Go ahead."

I sat down and assumed the traditional Army position for shooting. Carefully sighting at a point just behind the buck's ear, I took a deep breath and slowly let it out as I squeezed the trigger. The buck's head jerked up then fell forward. I watched carefully for any other movement. When I saw nothing more, I reloaded then walked toward the buck.

Lud said, "I never did spot him, but you nailed him as slick as anyone could have. That was good shooting, kid. My buck high tailed it quick when you shot. Do you know how to take care of your meat?"

"I've never seen an animal butchered. If you'll tell me how, I'll try."

"You keep an eye out for anybody sneaking up on us, and I'll take care of your buck. You might watch me a little bit, and you can help with our elk on the way back."

It took the big man but a few minutes to clean the buck. His knife was razor sharp, and there wasn't a wasted motion. When the entrails were laid out with the liver, heart, and kidneys back in the body cavity, Lud said, "Bring those mules over, and we'll divide the load. Either of them could carry the whole thing, but it'll be more impressive if we take two loaded mules."

Lud did everything with no effort, and within minutes the deer was divided with the head and front quarters on one mule and the hind quarters on the other one. I doubted that it'd ever be that easy for me, but I enjoyed watching.

"Do you suppose I'll ever be able to do that as easily as you?"

"I reckon you'll be doin' it by the time we have all the gold we want. That could be several years, but practice is what it takes. Let's try to get to the Indian camp in time for them to cook some of this for supper."

CHAPTER EIGHT

The camp was alongside the Los Pinos River in a valley bordered on three sides by mesas and on the south by foothills covered with brush and pinon pines. We were greeted by a pack of dogs followed by a bunch of kids. It was late afternoon, and there wasn't much activity. The noisy dogs and kids brought several adults out of tipis, and we were met by four men and a girl who was ten to twelve years old.

"We're looking for the chief," said Lud. He spoke Spanish.

The girl answered, "He's in the fourth tipi over there." She pointed toward the largest one.

"What's his name?"

The answer was a word that neither Lud nor I could've repeated.

"What does that mean?" asked Lud.

"It means something like Smart Coyote, but that isn't exactly what it means. You probably know that the coyote's almost worshipped by the Utes. It's difficult to say in any other language."

The girl wasn't an Indian, but she was allowed to speak without concern on the part of the men.

"Why're you the only person who talks with me?" Lud asked.

"No one else speaks Spanish."

"You don't look Spanish, and you're no Indian. What's the situation?"

"It's a long story. You should see the chief. If there's time later I may be able to explain."

She led us to the chief's tipi. She slapped the opening. There was a response from inside, and she spoke in Ute then backed away. A stocky Indian came out.

He spoke Ute. The girl then said, "He wants to know what you want."

"First, we brought a deer for him. Then we'd like to talk with him."

The chief listened as Lud's response was translated. He gazed across the camp as she spoke then said something in Ute.

The girl turned and said, "He thanks you for the meat. He'd like to have some of it prepared so you can enjoy it while you're here. If that's all right, I'll have some men remove it from your animals."

"Of course. We'll be honored to eat with the chief."

"I'll need to be with you so you can communicate."

"I'll be delighted with that arrangement," Lud responded.

"And I will, too," I said. Santa Fe had never contained more than twenty girls my age, and I had never seen one as pretty as this one. I felt compelled to be a part of the exchange and hoped I'd be able to talk with her in private. I'd be disappointed if I was unable to learn how and why she was here. Her complexion was much lighter than an Indian, and she was slimmer by far than any of the Utes. She was taller and walked more gracefully than anyone I'd ever seen. I was amazed that she was allowed to talk freely with outsiders.

"What shall we call you?" I asked her.

"I'm Molly O'Hara. You may call me Molly."

"Thank you. I'm Carlos, and this is Lud."

"I'll inform the chief. Please join us inside."

When the four of us were in the tipi, the chief sat on what appeared to be a tanned elk hide. He motioned for me to sit beside him with Lud next to me, which placed Lud in a position facing the chief. Molly sat between Lud and the chief, facing me.

Lud and I were wearing buckskin clothing, but I felt that we were shabbily dressed when I examined the clothing of the chief and Molly. Both of them wore buckskin, but theirs was adorned with beads, shells, and porcupine quills in patterns that made

Lud's and mine appear plain. The chief's shirt depicted coyotes in various poses, all easily recognized. Each showed the animal in a pose that made the animal look wise and helpful. Molly's was less elaborate, and hers was pictures of birds and animals like deer, elk, and buffalo, along with the sun, moon, and stars. While Smart Coyote's was obviously a personal depiction, Molly's was the more beautiful. Around each of their heads was a band of buckskin entirely covered with porcupine quills.

The chief sat with his buttocks flat on the floor with his legs bent so his ankles were crossed, and the sole of each foot faced the opposite thigh. Lud managed to position himself in almost the same manner, as did Molly. I had difficulty getting in position. I wondered how long I'd be expected to stay like that and hoped it wouldn't be long. Every muscle from my waist down was stretched to the limit. As far as I could tell, the others were quite comfortable.

Smart Coyote picked up a long-stemmed clay pipe and filled it with something that looked like coarse tobacco. He lit it, puffed several times, and handed it to Lud, who lifted it in what I assumed was a salute to the chief. He took a long pull on the pipe and blew a series of smoke rings, each smaller than the previous one. He then looked at the chief and waited for some indication of where he should pass the pipe. After a long wait, the Indian reached for it, and Lud passed it back to him.

The chief started speaking but I didn't understand a single word. When the chief paused, Molly spoke in Spanish.

She said, "He welcomes you to his lodge and wants you to join him for the evening meal, when we'll share the meat you brought."

Lud said, "We thank him for the invitation and will be happy to eat with him."

The conversation was continued with each man using his own language and Molly translating.

"Why're you here? Do you want to trade with us?" asked the chief.

"No. We're seeking gold. This is your land and we don't want to do anything that'll disturb you. We're working near the Piedra River. We're camped near where the Piedra runs into the San Juan with our animals along the banks of the San Juan. We think we'll need to stay there at least one moon. We've discovered a fairly large deposit that will take at least one moon to mine."

"There are six of you. Where will you hunt?"

"We haven't hunted yet but plan to do so on our trip back. We'll go half a day into the mountains before we kill any animals."

"I thank you for coming to tell us what you plan to do. We don't object to you mining as long as you don't bring any more people. We need all the deer and elk we can find. There aren't enough animals to feed any more people."

"We don't expect to need more men. Do you ever look for gold?"

"No."

The chief looked at me and said, "Why do you carry gold on a piece of hide?"

"The Lord God uses that to show me where he's hidden gold."

He asked Lud, "Is he your medicine man?"

"Yes. His medicine is strong. He gets it from his grandmother."

Smart Coyote looked at me again. "Can you find water or tell us where elk sleep?"

"I'm still learning what power God's given me. I've not tried either of those things. He can give wisdom to anyone. I'm happy to learn about this gift. I talk with him every day. He tells me what to do."

"What does he sound like? Is his voice loud?"

"I've heard his voice only once—the first time he spoke to me. Every other time he's spoken to my spirit, silently. That one time he sounded powerful. It wasn't loud, but he spoke with authority."

"What did he say that first time?"

"I was praying about an important thing. He said, 'It's all right. I've taken care of it'. Although I knew who had spoken, I looked to see if there was someone beside me. I saw nothing."

"How does he speak to your spirit?"

"His spirit's in me. Our spirits talk all the time just like you and I do. Then my spirit tells me what he's said."

"I'll consider this. I've never known anything like this. I spend lots of time seeking the voice of my spirit and don't always hear it. Yours is powerful if you can speak with it any time you want to. We'll talk more about this, but we go and eat now."

The Indian simply placed his hand on the floor, straightened his legs, and stood. Molly did likewise. Lud was almost as nimble. I felt like a clumsy oaf when I had to straighten out then get onto my hands and knees before standing. No one seemed to notice that I had any difficulty, but I promised myself that I'd practice until I could do it like they did.

CHAPTER NINE

Molly asked Lud and me if there was anything we'd like to do until the meal was ready.

Lud said, "I'll take care of our horses. If you'll show me where we're to spend the night, I'll get it ready to use."

"The tipi over there's empty, so you may use it," said Molly. Turning to me, she said, "What would you like to do?"

"I've never been in a place like this. Can you show me the camp?"

"I'm to entertain you, so I'll show you anything you want to see."

She showed me three-sided structures that were open on the south side to take advantage of the sun yet provide shelter from rain, snow, and wind. They called them *wickiups*. She also showed me how hides were tanned and made into clothing or other useful items. The two of us moved through the camp and out to the river. There was a shady spot with a log where we sat and watched the water.

I said, "How'd you become part of this tribe? You're obviously not Indian, so you're apparently a prisoner. Can you tell me about that?"

"It's sort of a long story."

"Do we have enough time for you to tell it?"

"I think so. My family lived in an area with many lakes and rivers, a long way from here. When I was three years old, the Sioux killed my father. They took my mother and me captive, and took us to their camp in the Black Hills. Mother was placed in a building where women were kept as prostitutes. Any man was allowed to use the women. It was a bad situation for the women, who were abused. The women were miserable. It was apparent that they had been treated horribly.

"Mother said she hated what was required of her, but the Lord Jesus was still in control and would give her what was needed to change things. She asked to be taken to the chief. When that was granted she told him how the women were treated and asked for permission to teach the men how to act with the women so there'd be less fear and more willingness to be with the men. She also wanted to instruct the women in how to make it a pleasing experience for both parties. She told him that she would also instruct couples of the tribe in ways that would make their marriages more fulfilling.

"The chief agreed to give her three months to accomplish her goals. She made such progress that he got more involved with her, and before long Mother was one of the most respected women in the camp. The captive women were still required to serve as they had, but there was no ill-treatment, and they enjoyed liberties that had never been given before. Mother made several rules that prevented pregnancies. She told me that we can't control everything that happens to us, but we can control how it affects us. When I was captured by this tribe, I remembered that and have tried to act in a way that would make my situation better."

"How long have you been here?"

"Let's see…I was three years old when the Sioux took Mother and me, and it was four years later when I was brought here, so I've been here five years now."

"Have you been able to do things that have made a difference in this tribe like your mother did with the Sioux?"

"I was exposed to things that most children don't see, so I learned a lot about what both men and women want. I told those things to the chief's wife, and she's taught other women things that have brought changes. I think Smart Coyote's told the other men what their wives like, and that's helped, too. I guess the answer would be that I've been able to help some.

"I've also learned the Ute and Spanish languages. I knew Sioux and English when I came, so I'm able to interpret for Smart Coyote. That's given me freedoms that other captives don't enjoy. You'll not be allowed to talk with any other captives."

"What'll happen when you're an adult?"

"I suspect that I'll be required to marry someone in the tribe."

"Will you be allowed to choose your mate?"

"Marriages are arranged by the father with the girl having almost no voice in the matter."

"How's the marriage arranged? I've heard that the bride is sold. Is that practiced here?"

"It's not quite that way. When a man wants to marry a girl, he approaches her father and offers things he thinks the father would like to have. It may be horses, a rifle, hides, or something unusual that the man hopes will be considered valuable. If the offer's attractive to the father, he'll agree to the marriage. I've seen the bargaining continue for several weeks with several men making offers. Fawn Heart, Smart Coyote's squaw, has told me that the father will usually make sure that the girl's choice is the one whose offer's accepted. That's not always true. If the father's offered something he considers to be valuable, he'll accept that. I've seen some girls who weren't given to the men they wanted."

"I guess Indians're not too different from Spaniards," I said. "What you've described is like what I've seen in Santa Fe. The men make decisions, and the women are expected to agree. It hardly seems proper, and I'm certain that Grandma would fight for her rights. In fact, she told me that she married Grandpa against her father's will. I've seen her oppose Grandpa and she almost always wins."

"I think I'd like your grandma. She sounds a lot like my mother. Is your mother like your grandma?"

"She died giving birth to me, so I didn't know her. Grandma's told me that she and Mother were very much alike."

"You haven't said anything about your father. What kind of man is he?"

"I don't know him. He left when Mother died, so I've always lived with my grandparents. Grandma's a kind woman, but she's never spoken kindly of my father. She's told me that I'd have been left to die if Mother hadn't insisted on returning to my grandparents to deliver me. My father's never mentioned."

"What's the term for a person who has no parents?"

"*Orphan.* That's what we are, but I have someone who has acted like they were my parents. You've been taken from your mother, and your father was killed, so you're in a much worse situation. Would you like to be able to leave here?"

"That would depend on where I went. I'm treated well and have the protection of Smart Coyote. If I could arrange Mother's freedom and the two of us could be free together, I'd really like that. It'd also be nice to choose the man I marry. There's little chance of that, so I don't worry about it."

"I'll ask the Lord to give you those things. He's able to do anything."

"Mother always told me that, but I find it hard to believe. Many things aren't the way I'd have planned."

"Don't give up. I think he's got something special for you. He may let me be part of it. If I understand the Bible, he doesn't need any help, but if I let him, he'll give me the privilege of being part of what he does. That's how it is when I'm looking for gold. Grandma told me, when she first started teaching me, that all I had to do is stay out of God's way and he'd find the gold. After all, he put it there, so it's no trouble for him to find it. If I try to do it for him, it gets all messed up. If I relax and let him do it, the gold appears. When I approach anything else the same way, it works. Let's both pray that he'll give you what you want."

"I'll try. I've never thought it was worth asking for anything. If it works for you, I'll try it. How soon should we expect an answer?"

"I can't tell you that, but don't stop praying. It seems like it's important that we believe that he'll answer in a way that's best."

We were interrupted by a dark, muscular Ute with long hair held in a dirty headband. He had the meanest scowl I've ever seen. His voice was harsh and guttural. He stood facing Molly and said something in Ute. She replied and she didn't like what he said. He didn't reply but continued to scowl at her. She said something else, and he stalked off several feet, stopped, and looked back then continued toward the camp.

"He seemed to be upset," I said. "Is anything wrong?"

"He's decided he wants to have me as a squaw and is angry anytime he sees me with someone else. If it gets bad enough, I complain to Smart Coyote, and he leaves me alone for a while. I told him I was instructed to entertain you, and he should talk to Smart Coyote. He didn't like that but won't pursue it. Don't worry. We should go eat."

"Will I eat with you?"

"That's what's been planned."

"Good. You can help me avoid doing anything improper. We want to have a good relationship with the tribe. They could make it difficult for us to mine. If you can advise me about that, I'll really appreciate it.

"The chief apparently doesn't call you *Molly*," I continued. "What does he call you?"

She said something that I felt would be impossible to pronounce. There's no way I could spell it.

"Does that mean something?"

"It means something like 'Dawn on the Mountain,' but that's not an exact translation. It's a description of first light in the morning when everything's fresh and bright with a light breeze blowing. I can almost see a doe and her fawn feeding in a meadow when he says it. It is a lovely name when it is pronounced correctly."

"That's beautiful. Maybe someday I'll learn to say it well enough so there's a lake with a trout jumping in it. Who chose the name for you?"

"Fawn Heart, the chief's squaw."

"I think I'll like her."

"Smart Coyote likes you. He's interested in the way you find gold. He's gone with the men he has watching you so he could see how you do it."

"Does he have men watching us all the time?"

"Yes. He usually won't allow anyone to stay in this area. He lets you stay because he thinks you have some special gift. He wants to learn more about that."

"I'd like to be his friend."

"I think he wants that, too. He's good at judging men. I've never seen him be mistaken. He's never had me spend time with a stranger before."

"I feel honored."

"You should. He's treating you differently than I've ever seen."

"Will you help me so I won't do something wrong?"

"Of course. I'm enjoying this."

"So am I. I've never been alone with a girl. Does he have someone watching us?"

"I doubt it. He said I'd be safe with you, which means that he trusts you."

"You're a prisoner, but seem to have a lot of freedom. Are all prisoners treated like you are?"

"No. You wouldn't be allowed to spend time with any of the others."

"So, he trusts you too."

"He treats me like a daughter. His sons are all married, and there are no girls in the family."

"Do you live with him?"

"Yes, with him and Fawn Heart."

"Do you remember living anywhere other than an Indian camp?"

"I remember a few things about our home before we were captured by the Sioux. I've lived with Indians for nine years, though."

We talked for a few more minutes; then she said, "We need to go back. We'll eat soon."

We walked back to the chief's tipi and met him as he came out. The two of them talked briefly, and he nodded to her then motioned for me to follow him. Molly walked beside me. He led to a central area surrounded by tipis. There was a table loaded with food with the hind quarters of the deer we had brought laid at the end with steam rising from it. Smart Coyote took a dish from a pile, cut off a thick slab of venison, and walked on along the table, adding other food as he went. I cut a slice and put it on a plate for Molly and did the same for myself. We walked together along the table. I had never before seen most of the items, so I asked Molly to help me select things she thought I'd like.

She said, "You'll be safe if you take some of everything I do. I'll be careful to take only things you'll probably enjoy. Don't ask too many questions, though. You'd not like the way some things are prepared."

"I don't think I'm a finicky eater, but I'll just hope whatever we eat doesn't bite back."

She laughed and said, "I've never seen that happen, so you should be safe. Someday I'll tell you how some of these things are prepared. It's quite interesting if you aren't squeamish."

We joined the chief, his squaw, and Lud in an area higher than the rest of the camp. I decided that it was all digestible. There were several berries and nuts, including pinon nuts and acorns. There was fried bread, which was tasty with honey on it. The venison had been seasoned with herbs and was as good as any meat I had ever tasted.

Smart Coyote asked some penetrating questions about both Lud and me. He wanted personal information, but I saw no reason to withhold anything. It was an interesting evening. I was surprised when the chief suggested that we should go to bed. I checked the stars and found that it was quite late, so we thanked him for the meal and went to the tipi assigned to us.

"You sure managed to keep that Molly gal busy," said Lud. "You never let her out of your sight. It's a wonder that brave didn't challenge you. He was mad as a wet hen and wasn't careful to hide it. I'm surprised that he didn't complain to the chief."

"He complained to Molly, but she told him to take it up with Smart Coyote. She had been instructed to entertain me, and that kept him in his place."

"You'd better be prepared for him to try to get you in a fight every time you're in camp. He'll find something to make you take him on, and he'll keep at it until he finds something the chief can't overrule. Are you a fighter?"

"I've never had to fight anyone."

"You walk careful around here. Next winter you'd better learn how to fight a killer. He'll most likely come at you with a knife, so you need to learn how to handle that."

"You're serious."

"I've never been more serious in my life. That brave'll spend every minute he's awake figuring out ways to get you. He's figured that Molly's going to be his. You're his target from now on."

"Can you teach me what I need to know?"

"I can teach you some, but you need to learn things that I don't know. Maybe some of the soldiers know how to handle things like that. All I can show you is how to use a knife and a gun. We'll look for someone who can do something else. That Indian's an experienced fighter and will have his own ways of trying to kill you. Don't think he'll be like anybody else you know. He might hide in the brush and shoot you from there."

"All I did was talk with Molly, and she chose what we did. She told him that she was doing what the chief told her to do and said he should talk with Smart Coyote about it. I knew he didn't like it but didn't think he'd be mad enough to kill me."

"Anybody could see that you were enjoying yourself. You were like a pup with a fresh bone. Keep an eye on any place where he could sneak up on you. He'll prob'ly try for you soon. I'll watch your back. He'll maybe cool off if you don't spend any more time with her. You might live out the summer if you stay away from their camp."

"I don't know why he's so upset. All we did was sit in plain sight and talk. She's only twelve years old. I can't imagine what he'd think gives him the right to say who she's to spend time with. The chief treats her like a daughter. If anyone should be concerned, he should be."

"You'll probably never understand how a redskin thinks. That old boy's mean enough to scare off all the other guys in the tribe so he thinks she's already his. I'll bet he's let everybody know he's staked his claim and he figures she's his."

"Wouldn't she have anything to say about it?"

"I don't know. If Smart Coyote says he can have her, that'd settle it. You'd better assume he's going to try to do you in."

"Okay, I'll be careful. He looks mean enough to try most anything. I'm going to try to come up with a plan to get her away from here."

"Be ready to fight that guy if you start to take her out of here. He'll not let her leave without making a fuss."

"I'll probably just try to buy her from the chief."

"I don't think they sell women to outsiders."

"Well, it won't be a problem for a couple of years. By then I should be able to learn what it'll take to get her."

"I wish you lots of luck. You're not going to find it as easy as you think."

CHAPTER TEN

We found and killed a big bull elk. An hour after that we reached camp.

We were pleased to find that the others had almost finished getting the rocks off the slope above the gold. By midday we were able to dig a pile of the sand and dirt from the spot. We put it on a mule and went to the sluice. We placed the sample at the top of the structure and diverted water so it washed it down through the grooves that allowed the dirt and gravel to wash away while the gold settled into the bottom of the grooves.

Pierre examined the sluice and collected the gold. The sluice allowed the particles of gold to be removed. It took as long to collect the gold as it had to wash it.

Juan said, "What do we have? Did the kid find gold?"

"If the rest of it's like this, we're in for a great summer. We have at least twenty ounces here."

I said, "Remember that we took this from the richest part."

Lud said, "If that part continues to produce we'll have a good summer."

I said, "It won't take long to work this location. I'd better see if I can locate a mine. We need something to go to next. I'm more confident now, so I should be able to find where this washed from."

Juan said, "Go find it. I didn't think anyone could find gold the way you do, but this proves it works."

Everybody joined in the encouragement, which made me feel good. After lunch, the others went back to work, and I headed up the creek. I walked less than a half mile before there was a strong pull toward the creek. The pull was so strong that I felt compelled to investigate. I had no difficulty finding the deposit. The action indicated that it was rich. I marked it but decided to not mention it to the others. If I could find a time to work it myself, I'd come back and pan it. We needed a mine rather than more small pockets.

I continued up the creek, and in less than a hundred feet, there was an extremely strong pull to the right. I made a circle up the bank and the nugget started swinging in a complete circle. I stopped and it swung faster still and was soon going so fast it was almost straight out from my hand. I was directly over a rich body of ore!

I was too excited to think straight, so I walked fifty feet away and sat down to pray. I said, "God, you're showing me something I never even asked for. This's much richer than what we're working below. Please show me what to do. I feel dumb as a rock, and the men are going to expect me to tell them more than I know. I need your wisdom, Lord. Please tell me what to do and say."

Time meant nothing to me. I stayed there at least an hour before I was calm enough to go back to the deposit.

The base of the area touched the creek bank, and I was unable to go up the bank far enough to find the other side of it. I decided it was probably the mine we were looking for. I spent most of the afternoon trying to find out how big it was, but the bank extended uphill for almost a quarter of a mile, so there was no way to learn how far it went into the hill. It was ten feet wide, and the nugget indicated a rich body of ore. The creek flowed along the base of the hill, so it could have never run any farther in that direction. It seemed reasonable to assume that it hadn't washed down from another place.

"Now, calm down," I said. "This may not be as big as you think. There's no doubt it's a nice batch of ore, but don't tell anybody how big you want it to be. It's worth digging here, but make it show you how big it is. Don't get all worked up. You could have a spot of really rich ore. You've never worked with anything like this. Tell them you've found it but that you can't tell how big it is. When they see the location they'll understand. Don't get excited and tell them more than you know."

I talk to myself at times like that. When I'm riding I say it's talking to my horse. I continued to carry on until I was almost back to the other men.

Lud spotted me and called, "Did you find it this soon?"

"I found a mine. I can't promise how big it is, but it looks richer than anything I've ever seen. It's ten feet wide, but I can't tell how deep because the bank's steep. It's worth working, but it could be small."

Pierre said, "You're sure it's rich?"

"My gear shows that it's richer than anything I've ever been around. Based on what we have here, it's got more gold than this has. I have to admit that it got me excited, but let's make it show us what's there."

"That makes sense," said Lud. "Take a look at what we've already taken here. If you've found something better than this, we're going to get rich."

"How much do you think's in that sack?" I asked.

Pierre said, "I'm guessing it's at least forty-five ounces. We've only washed four sacks of rock, and there's a lot more than we first thought. We haven't found the bottom yet, and we've dug at least four feet down. We'll have to go clear to bedrock to get the richest part, and that could be another five or six feet down. We may need to split up and work both spots. How far away is it?"

"You can almost see it from here. It's a quarter of a mile, around the point of that ridge. We should be able to work both spots at the same time, using the sluice where it is."

Lud said, "That'd be handy. We'll look tomorrow and see what we need to work that spot. We may need to do a lot of blasting if it's in solid rock. I say it's time to call it a day."

CHAPTER ELEVEN

They insisted that I tell them everything I'd done at the new location. I didn't tell them about the spot in the creek or the time I spent praying. Some of them got some rather strange expressions when I talked about the times I spent talking with Jesus, so I avoided the subject whenever possible. I thought that a few more successes would convince them it was all right.

There were plenty of questions so it was after our normal bedtime when they stopped asking. I was excited after our conversation and lay awake thinking about the possibility that we might be wealthy.

We rode our horses the next morning. The men thought it would take most of the day to determine the type of rock containing the ore. That would dictate the method of extracting it. I knew we had brought explosives but was surprised that we were prepared to handle extensive blasting. I learned that most gold mining's done in solid rock that resists intrusion. It makes you think the ore's treasure is precious to the rock.

"We'll get plenty of time using a double jack and drill steel," said Bud. "How much experience have you had with a sledge hammer, kid?"

"I've never used one, but if you'll teach me, I'll do it. How much does it weigh?"

"Most of them weigh ten pounds. After you've spent a summer swinging one of them, you'll have some new muscles, and those shoulders'll be wider. We'll let you off easy and only have you swing one a half a day to start. In a week or so, you'll be ready to do it ten or twelve hours a day."

"How many of us will be able to work in the same area?"

"Just one. Some of us'll work part of the day while you're getting used to it. It shouldn't take you long to get where you can handle it by yourself."

"Who'll find the next mine?"

"You can have a day off after a couple of months. You can go find the next mine then."

"You expect me to always find a mine in a day?"

"Sure. You can pray while you're swinging that sledge. You don't have to think while you're doing that. The fellow holding the steel will want you to pay attention, though. If you don't, he'll lose at least his hand, so you can't go to sleep. If you hurt someone, you have to hold the steel while they swing the hammer until you're injured."

"I don't remember this being discussed before we left Santa Fe. I didn't expect all of this."

"You find the gold, you help mine it."

"Who's going to hold the steel while I learn?"

"We'll draw straws for that. We'll do that every morning. You'll probably cripple two or three of us."

"I think you're having fun with me. I don't think anybody wants to risk losing a hand trying to teach me how to do it right."

"We'll find out soon enough. I'd be getting the feel of that hammer."

The trouble with that conversation was that nobody smiled. I figured that at least one of them would be laughing if it was a joke. It wasn't until we actually were mining that I learned it *was* a joke.

I was able to do enough lifting the bags of ore so that by summer's end, my upper body was noticeably larger. I also used an ax chopping wood for camp as well as cutting timbers for the mine. Grandma was wise when she sent clothes that were larger than I had needed in the spring. I also grew some three inches in height.

Both deposits proved to be rich. It took thirty-eight days to extract all the metal from the first place, and a few days after that, Pierre said there was no more ore in the mine. I got a strong signal that there was more gold farther in. We continued mining. There was nothing during the next ten days.

"You still say there's gold farther in?" Lud demanded. "We've done lots of work for nothing so far."

"My equipment still says it's there. In fact, it's looking better all the time. It's never been wrong before."

When there was still nothing after five more days, they were all looking at me in a manner that showed they doubted if we were going to find anything.

Pierre said, "Have you ever failed to find gold when that nugget said it was there?"

"No, but we never did any mining. All we did was work in creeks with pans."

"We only had to go four feet to get to the first of this. We've already gone ten feet, and there's nothing yet. Are you sure that stuff'll find gold that far away?" Juan asked.

"It shows that there's gold here when I'm fifty feet away."

Ben said, "He's done good so far. I say we should give it another week. If there's nothing by then, we'll decide whether to go farther or not."

Juan said, "Can you tell how far it is to the gold?"

"No, but I have a feeling that we're awfully close."

"What's that mean? I've thought I was close to a house when I was a mile away," Lud said. "I want something better than that."

"I'll guess it's not more than three feet. That's just a guess, though."

"We'll make that in less than a week. We can decide what to do then," Ben said.

"All right, we'll go another week. You'd better pray we hit it by then, kid," said Lud.

His suggestion was good, but I was already on my knees at least three hours a day. It was almost noon the second day after that conversation when I felt a tremendous surge of relief. It seemed like seconds later, Lud came out of the mine, followed by the others.

"We'll blow at least two feet this time, kid. If you're right, we should see some ore," Lud said.

"We'll see gold," I said. "God told me it's all right."

We had to wait until the smoke cleared before we could enter the mine. When we could see the face, Lud said, "Let's go, kid. I want you to see what we've got."

We walked into a hole still filled with a strong odor of dynamite. Within two feet, tears were running down our cheeks, but we went on. Almost half the face was visible above the rubble from the blast, and gold showed clearly over most of what we could see. Lud grabbed me by the arm and ran back outside.

"By gum, he did it! It looks richer than we had before. Kid, you're all right."

"Praise God," I said. "He's the one who did it. I get to watch him do it."

"That's likely the way of it, but you're the one he uses. I reckon we should take your word when you say there's gold someplace."

"Thanks, Lud. I hope there's enough to make it worth the effort it took to get to it."

"We can't work in there anymore today. Do you feel like going after a ram?"

"I sure do. Do you feel like celebrating?"

"I do! I got pretty wound up the last couple of weeks. I guess I got on you pretty hard, didn't I?"

"We all got sort of tight, so don't worry about it."

"Maybe I'll not be so worried if we have to wait to find gold when you say it's there. I was frettin' some, though. If it happens again, remind me."

"I was starting to worry, too, but God made me sure about it this morning."

"Let's go shoot a ram."

We did, and he was delicious.

It took twenty-three days to work that batch of ore. I got a strong indication that there was more gold either above or below the area we had worked. We decided to drill below the section we had just completed. The deposit was located eight feet down. It was a lode measuring five feet in each direction. When we had extracted all of that, I got no more action from the nugget.

I spent ten days searching for other deposits upstream from that mine and found one about a mile away. I got the signal that I was close to gold but couldn't find where it was. It was the afternoon of the second day before I realized I needed to stop and pray. Within fifteen minutes, the mystery was solved. It was in a cliff face fifteen feet above the creek. We built four ladders and a scaffold to make the entrance. We lowered the ore to ground level then to the sluice. We constructed a crushing area, where we broke the ore into small chunks so the gold would wash properly.

I went exploring again. I worked upstream for three miles without finding anything in the creek or on either side of it, so I went downstream and rode west to the next creek. I soon got indications of gold in the creek, and some three miles upstream, there was good action by the nugget. After marking it well, I went back to the mine to report. The night after we felt we had cleaned out the mine, a storm laid down a foot of snow, so we decided to head for Santa Fe.

Lud and I decided to visit the Ute camp while the others were getting camp ready for the winter. We made a door for the mine and arranged it so it could be secured against entry and covered it with rocks.

Lud warned me again about the Indian man who had been so upset the last time we were in the Ute camp. "Don't do anything to get him mad. If possible, stay away from that girl. That fellow's big trouble."

"She'll need to be with us so she can interpret. Should I stay here?"

"Smart Coyote told me to bring you if I came back. I don't want to do anything that'll make him mad."

I had thought a lot about Molly but didn't realize how much I wanted to see her until we were almost to the camp. I was looking for her above all else. We were greeted by the kids and dogs and they raised such a racket that the whole camp knew we were there. While Lud gave his attention to the kids, I kept my eyes on the chief's tipi. I feared she'd not be happy to see me.

We were almost to the tipi when Smart Coyote came out. He turned and spoke to someone inside the tipi. Molly came out and her smile was the prettiest thing I'd ever seen. She started toward us, but the chief blocked her way. He said something to her, and she looked startled and stepped back. She looked me in the eye, and the smile returned. I must have been grinning from ear to ear, I was that glad to see her again. I decided that I'd do whatever it took to get her away from there. She was no Ute, and I'd not rest until she was in Santa Fe with Grandma.

Smart Coyote spoke to her, and she stepped back. We dismounted and approached him. He held up his right hand, palm toward us, and we returned the greeting. He motioned for us to enter his tipi.

Inside, he seated us in the order we had been on the previous meeting. He filled his pipe and lit it. After puffing three times, he passed it to Lud, who took three puffs and looked toward the chief. He closed his eyes, raised his face toward the top of the tipi then motioned toward me. Lud passed the pipe to me and nodded twice. I took three puffs then passed it to the chief. He took it, held it up with both arms raised full length toward the top of the tipi for at least a minute with his eyes closed. He then placed the pipe by the fire.

He then spoke to Molly in Ute. She translated to Spanish as she had done previously. "We welcome you to our lodge again. You've stayed away a long time. Has your God given you success?"

"He's been good to us. He's guided Carlos to much gold."

He looked at me and said, "You're Carlos?"

I said, "Yes, sir."

"You found the gold?"

"Yes, sir, but I don't really find it. God shows me where it is."

"That is good. You'll show me sometime?"

"I'll be happy to do that, but we're finished for this season. It'll please me to show you when we return next spring."

"It'll be good to watch this thing. Your medicine's strong, or your God wouldn't show you what you want. My god sometimes tells me where deer, elk, buffalo, and lions are and shows me where to take my braves to steal horses, but that doesn't happen often. Are you telling me your God tells you where the gold is whenever you ask him?"

"He's never refused yet, but this trip he's been especially good to me. You know that we didn't leave the area these four moons. He's been very generous. I'd like to go on a hunt for elk with you next summer and watch you find the game. We had difficulty finding enough game to feed us. It appears that you've been successful in your hunts."

"We've found the game to be plentiful and are grateful for that. Do you need some to use as you go home?"

"I think we have enough to last the three days we'll be traveling. We thank you, though."

The chief turned his attention to Lud, and the two of them discussed the weather and other things of common interest. That gave me an opportunity to watch Molly. She had the most expressive face I had ever seen, and her voice was low-pitched for someone her age. It had a rich tone that filled the tipi without being loud. Her hair had been in braids on the previous visit but was hanging free that day. It reached six inches below her shoulders and had a natural wave in it. When light shined through it, there was a red tint. I learned it was called auburn.

We talked until the evening meal was ready. This time there was no large gathering, but we were joined by four braves and their families. The meal was simple—some kind of meat, a vegetable, fresh and dried berries, and a tea made with herbs.

After the meal, Molly said, "Would you like to take a walk? It's nice down by the stream."

I said, "I'd like to, but I don't want to get that fellow upset again—you know, the one who got so mad last time?"

"Oh, you mean Dark Dog. He isn't here now—he's still out hunting."

"I'd like to walk, then."

When we were alone, I said, "Lud warned me to not try to be alone with you. He's afraid Dark Dog will try to kill me if he sees us together."

"He very well might do that. Dark Dog's an exceptionally good fighter. No one would challenge him, so he could get what he wants."

"Would you consider going with me to Santa Fe to live with my grandparents?"

"You mean that you'd try to buy me from Smart Coyote?"

"I'd try to buy your freedom. You'd be able to make your own choices if you were free."

"If I was free I'd want to get my mother from the Sioux. Do you think you could do that?"

"Could it be done during the winter?"

"That would be difficult. It took two weeks to travel from there, and it'd be harder in the winter."

"My summers are going to be filled. I'd like to help get your mother as soon as I have enough to stop mining."

"What's your grandmother like? I don't want to go from what I have here into something that could be worse."

"Grandma's kind to everyone and helps people when there's a need. She's often at the church helping teach children, and she plays a guitar and sings. Grandpa says that if it wasn't for her, church would be the dullest place in town, but she makes it worth going. You wouldn't need to worry about her making your life worse.

"We need to learn whether Smart Coyote would let you leave the tribe."

"I'll try to learn how he feels about that."

We went back to Smart Coyote's tipi, where we parted. I joined Lud in the tipi we were assigned for the night.

"I warned you about going off with that girl. Can't you understand that it's worth your life to do that?" he said.

"That fellow isn't here. He's out hunting."

"You be careful. Our whole mining deal depends on you."

We thought we'd leave early the next morning, but Smart Coyote wanted to show us a new travois he had designed. It wasn't a fancy rig but was better than anything they had before.

After that he said, "We should smoke the pipe again before you leave. You're the first white eyes we've not had trouble with."

We entered the tipi and got seated when there was a commotion outside, and there was soon a hand slap on the flap to the tipi. Smart Coyote called out, and a brave entered. The two of them carried on an excited exchange.

Molly said, "This man's saying that a man from your party and another man who wasn't with you stole all of the horses and mules and left. They also apparently took all of the gold."

Lud said, "Does he know which way they went and when all of this happened?"

"They didn't go toward Santa Fe. It happened during the night."

"We've got to get back. Please explain to Smart Coyote."

We were on our way within a matter of minutes.

CHAPTER TWELVE

No one was in sight at camp.

Lud called out, "Anybody here?"

We hurried to the tents. I found Ben and Pierre in their tent, both sound asleep. I shook Pierre, but all he did was turn over and groan. Ben did open his eyes when I shook him, but he closed them again and didn't say anything.

I rushed to the other tent, where I heard Lud talking. I found him holding Juan in a sitting position, trying to get him to drink some water.

"What happened?" Lud asked.

"I don't know, but I feel awful," said Juan. "I was all right when I went to bed last night. What time is it?"

"It's after noon," Lud answered. Turning to me, he said, "What did you find?"

"The others are asleep and didn't pay any attention to me."

"Pablo and the other guy must've put something in the food last night. It knocked everybody out. I hope it wasn't some kind of poison. Let's go see what we can do for the others."

Ben was trying to get up when we got in their tent.

"What happened?" he asked. "I can't get Pierre to answer me, and I'm sick as a dog."

"Can I get you anything?" I asked.

"No, I'll be all right. Just see about Pierre."

We finally had all three of them on their feet. When they started walking, they all started vomiting, and it wasn't long until they were all hit with stomach cramps and diarrhea. Lud dug around in his pack and got out some herbs, which he used to make a tea. When the others came back, he had each of them drink some of it. None of them liked it, but they all said it helped them feel better.

"Where's Pablo?" asked Ben.

"A couple of Indians told us that he and another man left with all the horses and mules loaded and were heading over the pass. Carlos and I had best get after them."

"What're you going to do with them?" asked Ben

"Whatever it takes to get our stuff back."

"You'll have to kill 'em," said Juan. "I'd love to get Pablo in my sights. I've never been this sick."

"We'd better get on our way."

Lud took off at a fast pace and had no difficulty following the trail. They had crossed the river near the hot springs then had gone upstream.

"That's a high pass," Lud said. "If they plan to go over it, we'll catch up soon. Those mules won't go as fast as we can."

That was a beautiful valley, with grass rubbing our stirrups all the way. The river was lined with cottonwoods, willows, and pine trees along with brush of several kinds. I could have wished for time to loaf along and enjoy the scenery, but we had a serious task to handle and needed to move as quickly as we could without wearing out our horses. The tall grass made it easy to see how the others had gone. It was knocked down in a fairly wide area by the horses and mules. We could see their path for at least a half mile ahead. It took us almost three hours to reach the foot of the pass, and the trail was much fresher. The valley ended abruptly, and we were soon riding through a mixture of yellow pines and brush with occasional open areas.

"We can't follow any farther now," Lud said. "It'll be dark in half an hour, and we can't see their trail. Let's camp here and get after it again tomorrow."

We located a cut bank where we could have a fire that wouldn't be seen from above with a decent place to picket the horses. We doused the fire and bedded down as soon as we had eaten.

It was cold the next morning, with frost on the ground, which would make tracking more difficult.

"We'll have to slow down," said Lud. "If they hear us or glimpse us, they'll try to ambush us. Go over there two hundred feet, and we'll go up apart. Watch for anything that looks like a horse or mule. If you see anything at all, stop and wave your hat. I'll do the same thing, so look over this way once in a while. We'll get together then and check out what we've spotted. We're dealing with men who'll shoot you if they have any chance, so don't rush into anything. This is every bit as serious as the thing with that Indian brave, maybe worse. A man who pretends to be your friend and then steals from you won't hesitate to kill you if he gets a chance. Do you understand?"

"Yes. Is it all right to be scared?"

"That's the best thing you can do. We just can't let being scared keep us from doing what needs to be done."

We slipped up through the timber, and neither of us saw what we were looking for. The sun was touching the tops of the mountains off to the west when I saw Lud waving his hat. I stopped and watched for some signal of what he wanted me to do. He motioned for me to ride over toward him.

"They're just ahead of us. It looks like they've found a spot to stop for the night. We'll try to get above them. We'll settle in for the night and wait for them to come up to us tomorrow morning."

We rode back and found a trail toward the west. We followed that then took a game trail northwest. It veered farther to the north.

"We're above them now. Let's see if we can work our way east and settle in. We'll need to be really quiet from now on. Be careful where you ride, and if your horse acts like he's going to nicker, jerk him up short."

We were three thousand feet higher than our camp near the mine, and we could have no fire. We drank cold water and ate dry biscuits and jerky. It didn't help that we could see the campfire below us.

"Seems unfair when crooks are comfortable and we sit up here, shivering and wishing for a cup of hot coffee. Maybe crime does pay," said Lud. Then he added, "You know I'm not serious, don't you?"

I answered in a voice barely more than a whisper. "We must make sure it doesn't pay this time. Who do you suppose the other man is?"

"I have no idea. We've seen no one all summer. Pablo must've planned all this from the beginning. It's hard to think that a person we worked with and planned with was just waiting to rob us. He fooled all of us completely."

"What do you plan to do in the morning?"

"We'll take them prisoner if possible, but if they fight, we'll have to shoot them. I know you don't want to kill anyone, but you need to be ready to if they don't throw down their guns."

"I hope I can do what 's necessary."

We were bedded down almost as soon as it was dark. I lay awake and asked the Lord for wisdom and courage. I remembered the stories of how the Israelis were instructed to destroy everyone when they entered the promised land. God destroyed hundreds of thousands on occasion when the enemy invaded Judah. I eventually went to sleep at peace about the possibility of shooting a thief.

CHAPTER THIRTEEN

The stranger came into the park. He was mounted on a beautiful *grullo* stallion that was sixteen hands tall with black mane and tail and a black stripe down his back. The *grullo's* head was up and his ears forward, eager to see what was ahead. His mane and tail had a slight wave in them, and his step was just short of a prance.

The man was plain in comparison. His clothes were wrinkled and dirty, his hat the remains of a handsome sombrero. His beard was thick, black, and matted, as was his hair. Food and tobacco stains were by his mouth. I had heard Grandma's remarks about men like him, "There goes a man who doesn't care about himself or anything else. Thank the good Lord you don't have to live with something like that."

He was leading the pack string. The horses followed the mules, and then Pablo followed.

When they were all in the park, we stood up, our rifles covering them.

"That's far enough," said Lud. "Drop your guns slow and easy, or we'll shoot."

I thought they were going to do it. The stranger eased his pistol out and dropped it. Lud headed back toward Pablo. The stranger reached across his body with his left hand and started taking his rifle out of the boot. It looked like he was going to drop it, but when he had it out he switched it to his right hand and shot me. I saw the muzzle blossom, felt a tremendous blow to the left side of my head, and felt myself falling. I hit the ground with the other side of my head.

I woke up with a headache like I had never experienced. It was black as pitch. I had never seen it that dark, even the time I ventured into a cave when I was five years old. I got in a couple of hundred feet until I couldn't see the entrance. Looking farther into the hole, there was no light at all, and I had no candle. That blackness wasn't as deep as what I was in now. I could hear horses' feet and their breathing, and something scraping the ground. I could tell that I was lying on something moving and decided a horse or mule was by my head while the scraping sound came from beyond my feet.

I tried to sit up but stopped because it increased the pain in my head. I also discovered that I was bound in a way that prevented movement. I groaned, and the horse stopped.

"You all right, kid?"

It was Lud.

"I don't know. My head hurts. What time is it?"

"Probably two or three o'clock."

"At night?"

"No. You've only been unconscious five or six hours. We're on our way to camp."

"I must be blind."

"That guy just about blew your head off. It's lucky you aren't dead. You can't see?"

"Not a thing."

"Can you handle a drink?"

"I'd like that."

"Open your mouth so I can pour some of this in it."

I almost drowned before we got that drink in me. We finally had a routine worked out, and I was no longer thirsty.

"You better?"

"My head feels like a drum with a Ute hammering on it. It just about busts every time my heart beats. You got anything for that?"

"Not a thing."

"Let's get on our way, then."

"I hope you can get some sleep."

Getting to camp was no Sunday school picnic. I either went to sleep or passed out.

When I woke up again Lud said he was going to keep going all night. I assumed it was dark when it got colder. Lud felt it too and added a blanket or coat on me while we continued on our way.

It was a blessing that I was unconscious most of the time. We reached camp late the second day. Ben carried me into the tent Lud and I shared.

"How do you feel?" he asked.

"I'm afraid this headache isn't going to stop, but other than that I feel all right. It'd be nice if I could see, though."

"You've got a nasty wound on your head. It's no wonder it hurts. That'll probably stop. I don't know about your sight," he said.

"You think I'll be able to see again, don't you?"

"I've never been around anybody who lost his sight. I don't know. Most things heal after a while. It's probably a good time to do some of your praying. I'd think it might do some good."

"I'm doing that."

"Keep it up. We don't have anything else to give you."

Lud came in and said, "I'm going to hit the hay. Do you mind if I stay here, kid?"

"No. I'll try to not bother you."

"If you need anything, here's a stick. Jab me with it."

Bud said, "I'll get out of here so you can sleep."

Lying there in total darkness, a lot of questions came to me, but there was no way to get answers until Lud was awake. I heard him get undressed and get into his bedroll. He took a deep breath, and when he exhaled, it was a snore. I had known he was tired, but that's the quickest I've ever heard anybody go to sleep. He didn't make another sound for what seemed like hours.

I found that I didn't hurt any place except my head, but every movement caused that ache to increase unbearably. The constant pain seemed minor in comparison when I tried to do anything other than lying absolutely still. I guess it was night, and it was the longest one I'd ever lived through.

I spent a long night there in that tent, wondering if I'd ever quit hurting, hoping and praying that I wasn't blind for life, and wondering what had happened to Pablo and the man who had shot me. I thought there was shooting after I hit the ground, but I wasn't sure about it. I was certain that Lud had done what needed to be done, and I assumed that meant he had shot the others. Lud wasn't hurt seriously, or he wouldn't have been able to bring everything back, but that didn't mean he hadn't been injured some. There had been very little talking among the others before Lud came in and went to sleep, so I assumed that nobody else knew much either. I thought I had heard Pablo's voice, but that didn't seem likely.

Lud's first question was, "How you doing?"

"I hurt a lot and need a drink of water."

"I've got a canteen here."

It was easier this time. I only strangled three times.

"Thanks, Lud. That was good. How are you? Were you hurt?"

"No. When I heard the shot, I took care of the guy who shot you. Pablo gave up and helped me bring things back here. He's tied to a tree now. We have to decide what we're going to do with him."

"Who was the other man?"

"I don't know. I'm sure Pablo can tell us, but he's not a problem anymore. The buzzards are probably taking care of him. How are your eyes?"

"I still can't see anything. What if I'm blind for life?" I was as scared as a deer with a cougar jumping at him. I had never thought about not being able to see. I'd be of no value to my partners unless I could see the nugget. I had seen only one blind man, and he was a beggar.

"I won't try to fool you. I don't know if you're blind or not. I promise that we'll take care of you either way."

"I guess all we can do is wait and see. I'm going to need a lot of help as long as it lasts."

"Don't you fret about that. I'll see that you get what you need. Are you hungry?"

"I don't think food would stay down with this headache, but I'd like a cup of coffee."

Every movement caused terrible pain, so we got me sitting on the floor with a pack bchind my back. Lud put a box beside me as a table. I spilled parts of three cups of coffee while I learned how to drink. The coffee was good, and it brought a slight improvement in the headache. I didn't sit very long.

I slept until Bud woke me and said, "We're deciding what to do with Pablo. What do you think we should do?"

"He stole from us, and we'd have been in serious trouble without the horses. We'd have worked all summer for nothing, too. He's earned whatever punishment he gets."

"Even to killing him?"

"Lud killed his partner, so I guess he deserves the same. I may be blind. Maybe that makes me a poor judge, but I don't feel any pity for him."

"Do you want to take part in the discussion?"

"No, you can tell the others how I feel."

"You sure you don't care if we kill him?"

"I'm ready to agree to anything."

"I figure it's just a matter of how we do it. Nobody wants anything but executing him."

They decided to hang him. I was glad that I didn't see it. There were no law officers available, so it was the usual way to handle situations like that.

I awoke in the morning with a little less headache. I tried to get out of bed, but pain shot through me like a flaming arrow. Being out of bed would've helped very little, since I was still blind as a bat and had no idea how to get so far as the tent flap.

Lud came in and asked, "Can you eat something?"

"I'm hungry. What is there?"

"We got an elk yesterday, so I can bring you a steak."

"That sounds good, but you'll have to cut it. I can't handle a knife."

"Do you want anything else? There're some biscuits."

"Just the meat and some coffee, please. I don't think my stomach's ready for much, but it's been growling, so I'd better eat something."

We got me up in a sitting position, with the food in my lap and the coffee on the box beside me. The coffee was hot and tasted good. I ate the steak with my hands. It was delicious, but when I started chewing, it felt like my head was going to explode. I quit chewing, but the pain continued for several minutes.

I was finally able to say, "I can't chew. It hurts like fury."

"I can cut it into some tiny pieces," Lud offered.

"We can try that. Don't cut much of it in case I still can't handle it."

I was able to swallow pieces that were small enough, but any pressure to my jaws literally disabled me. It took a long time to get that one piece of steak into my stomach. I wondered if it was going to stay down. Every time I moved the headache reared up, and my stomach rebelled. Within a short time, my belly was growling, and I was on the point of losing everything. I tried to stay absolutely still, but the turmoil in my stomach caused retching, so it was impossible to not move.

It's impossible to tell how much time has passed when you're in total darkness, but it seemed like several hours before my body adjusted to the food and I was able to go to sleep. I had barely got to sleep when I was awakened by loud voices. I recognized

Molly's voice and wondered what she was doing in our camp. Then I heard Smart Coyote talking.

Molly said, "We heard that Carlos was injured. Is he all right?"

Pierre answered, "No, he's pretty sick. He was shot in the head and is blind and hurts. We finally got some food in him, but it made him sick. He's either asleep or unconscious now."

"May I see him?" asked Molly.

"He's in that tent."

I was able to hear her progress as she approached the tent and then came inside.

"Carlos? Are you awake?"

"Yes. What're you doing here?"

"Some braves came and followed you so we'd know what happened. They returned and told us about you getting shot. I talked the chief into bringing me here so we could be sure you're all right. What can I do to help you? Oh, good heavens, you have a terrible wound on the side of your head. Does it hurt?"

"Yes, it does, but the worst part is that I can't see. I'm scared of being blind the rest of my life. Every time I move, it makes my head just about explode."

"How do you eat?"

"Lud brought me some elk meat, and when he cut it into tiny pieces so I didn't have to chew, I could swallow it."

"What have they done for your head?"

"There's not much they can do. The bullet just grazed me, I guess, so we don't have to get it out."

"That side of your head's swollen terribly. They didn't even put a bandage on it. Did they give you anything for the pain?"

"We don't have anything like that."

"I got our medicine man to come with us. He'll have something. I'll go get him now."

I heard her talking in the Ute tongue; then she came back.

"He's making a tea that he says will help. I'm going to crush some jerky and make it into a broth so you don't have to worry about chewing or swallowing chunks of meat. I'll put some herbs in it, too, so it'll taste better and be more nourishing."

"That's mighty fine of you. Thanks."

"There's not much more we can do. Is there a doctor you can see when you get to Santa Fe?"

"There's an Army doctor. I don't know if he'll do anything for me. What can he do about my being blind? I figure the headache will stop eventually, but will my sight come back? That worries me."

"We'll see if Star Gazer has any ideas about that. He's taken care of a lot of injured braves. He may have seen some that were injured like you are. Here he comes now with the tea."

"I'll need to sit up to drink anything, and I need help to do that. You'll have to go really slowly because any movement really sets off the head pain."

Molly chattered in Ute then said, "We'll lift you carefully. Let me know if we're doing anything wrong."

"All right. I'll need a pack to lean on. There should be one close."

"There's one right here. Are you ready?"

"Yes, let's do it."

I have an idea that a man with a broken jaw might have some glimmer of how it felt to sit up, but I've never felt anything that came close. We got it done without destroying any mountains. I suppose I was learning somehow to handle it, but it really didn't seem to be any better than it was the first time.

"Are you all right?" asked Molly when I had stopped sweating.

"I'm all right. What do I need to do?"

"Drink this. It's really hot. Star Gazer says it needs to be this hot, so don't take any longer than you have to."

"What's it supposed to do?"

"I think it's for the pain. Why don't you drink it and see what happens?"

"How long are you going to stay here?"

"Do you mean how long before we go back to our camp?"

"Yes."

"Tomorrow morning, when you leave for Santa Fe."

"I wish I could see you. It's hard to sit here useless, not able to get out of bed and blind as a new-born pup. I don't know if my eyes'll ever be any good."

She didn't say anything for quite a while then said, "You'd better drink that tea. It's only good when it's hot."

I took a sip. That was the worst-tasting stuff I had ever had in my mouth. I must've made an ugly face because Molly sounded like she was trying to keep from laughing.

"You should try this. I don't know if I can get it down," I said.

"Drink it as fast as you can. Star Gazer said it'll make you feel better. He helps the Utes when they're sick or injured."

I managed to drink all of it and almost immediately, the headache was a lot easier to handle. I was soon comfortable enough to try moving.

"That really *does* work. I wonder how long it'll last."

"He said you'll need some of it each morning and again at night."

"Does he have enough of it to last until I get to Santa Fe?"

"I hope so."

"That makes a difference. I think I can even get up and walk."

"Don't try until I talk to him. You could hurt yourself if you do too much. I'll go talk to him now."

I said, "Will you see if you can learn who the man was that Lud shot?"

"All right."

She was gone quite a while, so I tried moving, and it hurt very little. When I tried to get on my feet, I didn't have any strength. I was as weak as a baby. The pain was still present, but I was sure I could handle it if I could get some strength. I was able to move the pack and lie down. After a bit I sat up and put the pack where I could lean against it.

Molly returned and said, "Star Gazer says you shouldn't try to stand up, but it'll be all right for you to try to lie down and sit up."

"I just did that, and it worked fine. Did he say how long it'd be before I can try anything more?"

"He said he'd see how you are in the morning. If you're improved a lot, you may even be able to get on your horse and ride home."

"I hope I can."

"They've fixed a bed attached to a mule in front of you and another behind."

"I'd rather be in a saddle. Being hauled in a bed's no way to travel."

"But you can't see. How're you going to guide your horse? Are you sure you could even stay in the saddle?"

"I could. I've ridden at night when I could hardly see and didn't have any trouble."

"Star Gazer will decide in the morning. You had better get some rest now. Oh, I learned the name of the man who was shot. It was Pedro Gonzales," she said.

"*Pedro Gonzales?* That was my *father's* name!"

"What? Do you think it might've been him?"

"I don't know. My grandparents will be able to tell me when I get home. I'll tell them what he looked like, and they'll know."

"Don't you know what he looked like?"

"He left when I was a few days old, and I never saw him again, so I have no idea what he was like."

"I hope it was someone else with that name."

"It doesn't matter. Whoever it was, he deserved what he got. It *would* be a shame if he was the one who shot me. I know it'll please Grandma if he was killed. She was really bitter about what he did."

We sat in silence for quite a while, and I fell asleep. It must've been the medicine, because there was almost no pain.

When I almost fell off the pack at my back, Molly said, "Let me help you lie down so you can sleep comfortably. It's time to go to bed anyway."

"Would you get me some more water, please?"

"Of course. I'll be right back, and then I'll help you."

While she was gone, I moved the pack and was sitting without any support when she returned.

"You should have waited and let me help you. You'll hurt yourself trying to do too much."

"There's hardly any pain now, and I need to do something to get back my strength."

"Well, here's your drink. When you're ready I'll help you lie down again. And don't tell me you don't want help."

"I'll be glad to have you help me any time. I just wish I could see you. You're the prettiest thing I've ever seen, and now I can't enjoy it."

"You must be feeling better if you feel like flattering me."

"Sometime I'll argue whether it's flattery or not. Just take my word that it's true."

"You'd better go to sleep. I'll see you in the morning."

"All right. Good night, and thanks for all you did."

"You're welcome. I'm glad I was here. Good night."

She took both my hands in hers then placed them on my chest and pulled the blanket up over them. She made hardly any sound, but she left a huge empty spot in that tent. The tea Star Gazer had fixed was strong enough to take care of my headache, and it also made me sleepy. I must have slept like a bear. The next thing I knew was when I heard someone chopping wood for the breakfast fire. My headache was back in full force, but I had enjoyed the best sleep I'd had since getting shot.

I heard someone come into the tent, and I asked, "Is that you, Molly"

"I ain't hardly Molly," said Lud. "She wanted to be sure you were decent before she came in. You're a lucky guy to have that little gal taking care of you. I may shoot myself and see if she'll take care of me."

"I think she'd take care of anyone if they needed it, but you're right. I wish we could take her with us."

"I reckon that chief'd say no to that. He seems to think a lot of her, bringing her over here and bringing the medicine man, too. You have a friend there."

"I hope so. I plan to try to get him to let me take her to Santa Fe."

"You're too young for that."

"I don't mean that. She should be with someone like Grandma. She needs to learn to read and write and how to take care of a home and cook with a real stove. A white girl shouldn't grow up with redskins."

"You've got to get well before you try to get her away from them. I'll tell her to come in. We're going to leave after we eat."

"I'll do what I can to get ready. I need some more of that tea. My head's as bad as ever."

Lud left and Molly came in.

"Did you have a good night?" she asked.

"Yes, but I need some of that tea."

"I have it. Let me help you sit up so you can drink it."

I was surprised at her strength. She lifted me and it didn't seem to be difficult for her.

"You're strong. You did that easier than Lud does."

"I know more about doing things like that. I'm certainly not as strong as he is. Here's the cup. Be careful. It's hot."

It was, and it didn't taste any better. She had also brought some more broth.

"I wish you could go to Santa Fe with me."

She said, "I'd like to go with you, but Smart Coyote wouldn't allow that. I'm sure he knows that if I went to Santa Fe, the officials there 'd never let him bring me back."

"If I recover from this injury, I plan to see if I can buy your freedom."

"Do you have any idea what you'd offer him?"

"I've been praying about that, and I think he'd like to have a stallion and some mares. There's a shortage of horses. If he had more mares and a stallion, he'd be able to take care of that problem. What did you ride over here?"

"I rode on Smart Coyote's horse with him."

"Will you ask Lud to come in here, please?"

"All right."

Lud came in and said, "What do you need?"

"Did you bring that *grullo* that the fellow helping Pablo was riding?"

"Sure. He's quite a horse."

"I suppose you brought the saddle and everything, too, didn't you?"

"Yes. Why?"

"I want the whole outfit. Do you think anyone will object to my having it?"

"I reckon it'd be small pay for what he did to you. Shall I ask them?"

"Yes. I want to give my horse and saddle to Molly."

"I'll do it. We're almost ready to leave."

"Ask Molly to come back in here, please."

"I'm here. I can't take your horse, Carlos. What'll you ride when you're well?"

"Didn't you hear me say I want that *grullo*? If they let me have him, I'll have a lot better horse, and you'll have one, too. Did you look at that *grullo*?"

"Yes, he's quite a horse. He acts like he'd be hard to manage. Are you sure you want him?"

"I wanted him as soon as I saw him. He obviously hasn't been taken care of properly, but it won't take long to get him looking like a parade horse with his coat shining like brass buttons. I can clean up that saddle and bridle, get a good saddle blanket, and have a horse to be proud of. He might get to be almost as pretty as you are."

"You shouldn't be saying things like that to me. I don't have any clothes that would make me look like he does."

"You don't need any fancy fixings to make you pretty. Just don't strut too much in front of that brave who acted so mean last spring. It wouldn't take much to get him worked up to the point he'd haul you off and make you his squaw."

"Don't even talk about that."

"You'd better pray the chief'll accept my offer. Will you do what you can to get him in a good mood, so when I make my proposition he'll accept?"

"Do you think your grandma would like me? She might not want someone like me in her home."

"She'd love you. Why, she'd keep you so busy teaching you how to be a Spanish lady that your head would spin. I can just see her getting you rigged up so all the men in town would flock around, just trying to get a look at you. You can't imagine how glad she'd be to have you to dress up and curl your hair, paint your lips, and teach you how to flirt with all the guys. She'd have more fun than four pups chasing a squirrel."

"That sounds like a lot of work."

"Oh, she'll make it fun for you, too. She'll have you so excited and happy you won't know what to do. She knows how to keep folks glad to be doing what she wants. I can hardly wait to get the two of you together."

"We've got to get you well first. Here comes Lud, so quit all that foolish talk."

"You wait and see how foolish it is."

"Hush."

Lud came in and said, "You've got a horse and outfit. Nobody had any objections. You sure you can handle that horse?"

"I'll need to be able to see. I'll just have to give him something to be proud about, and he'll do whatever I want."

"We'll see."

"I need for you to get my horse saddled for Molly. She'll be riding him back this morning."

"Ben's taking care of that now. I heard what you told Molly and went ahead and got that taken care of. Here's your gal. Don't dally. We've got to leave soon."

"Thanks, Lud. Molly, did you hear that?"

"Yes."

"Now, will you take that horse of mine? He's really too small for me now."

"Yes, I'll be happy to take him. I'll have something to remind me of you. How'll we know if you recover from this injury?"

"We'll be back next spring."

"I'll be worried all the time until you come back."

"Just don't worry. Assume that everything's all right," I said, hoping she'd be able to do it. "It won't hurt to ask the Lord to work on it, too."

"I'm already doing that."

"I think it's in the book of Mark where the Lord said we should trust God, and when we pray, we're to believe that we *have* what we ask for and we *will receive* it. If that was good for the folks he was talking to then, it should be good for us now."

"I'll try, but I'm afraid my faith isn't very strong. When I was with Mother, she kept it strong, but it's difficult when I'm all alone."

"One of my favorite parts of the Bible's in the letter to the Galatians. Paul said something like this, 'The life I now live, I live by the faith of the Son of God,' so I guess we don't have to depend on our own faith but can draw on the faith of Jesus. That's what I try to do when my faith gets weak."

"Does it really say that?"

"It surely does. You don't have to worry. I'll be fine."

"Tell me that again, so maybe I won't forget it."

"Paul said, 'The life I now live, I live by the faith of the Son of God.' It's in the letter to the churches in Galatia."

"That sounds too good to be true."

"Isn't the whole story of what Jesus did too good to be true? But it *is* true. We just have to believe it."

Lud interrupted then, saying, "You two need to get your good-byes said. We're gonna tear down this tent."

"I hope you're going to take him out first," said Molly. "If you'll take him over by that tree, I'll stay with him until you're ready to leave."

"All right. Pierre, grab that end of his rig, and we'll haul him over there," said Lud.

They were fairly gentle in the way they handled the move, and since the tea had already taken effect, I didn't hurt too much. When they put me down, Molly said, "We're where everyone can see us and hear what we say. I liked it better when we were in the tent."

"It's all the same to me, since I can't see, but we don't have much time. Will you go with me if I can make a deal with the chief next year?"

"Yes, but I'm afraid he won't let you take me away from the tribe."

"The life that I now live, I live by the faith of the Son of God. That works for things like that, too. My friend, who's a priest, says something like this, 'Believe God and leave all the results to him.' It seems to work."

"I've never heard things like that. Is God really in charge of everything?"

"You bet he is. And he can do more than you think he can. Just trust him, Molly. He loves you and will give you what you need. That's a promise he makes over and over in the Bible."

"I'll try to believe. What if I can't believe enough?"

"That's when you tell him about it and ask him to give you some of the faith of Jesus."

"That's all?"

"That's what it says."

"I'll try. Will you pray, too?"

"You can depend on it. I want you to be free, and I want my sight back."

"Here they come, so I'll have to leave you. Please get well and come back next spring."

"I will. I've got a great reason to do that."

"Good-bye," she whispered, and I felt her lips on my cheek then heard her run away.

Pierre said, "There she goes on your horse. She's quite a girl. If you can hang on until she grows up, you'll have a real woman."

"She doesn't act like a twelve-year-old, does she?"

"It seems like she was the reason the medicine man came and brought the stuff that helped your pain. I don't think many prisoners are able to talk a chief into something like that. Yes, she's a special little lady.

"We're almost ready to leave. Do you need anything before we put you in your swing?" he continued.

"I was hoping to ride that *grullo*. Molly was going to see if the medicine man thought it'd be all right, but she didn't say anything."

"He said you need to ride in the sling. You'll probably enjoy it."

"I don't have a choice. Is there something I can do to help?"

"Just lay there and don't try to do anything. We'll load you pretty soon then we'll be on our way."

I was surprised at how soon Lud and Ben came and picked up my bed. They told me everything they did so I had some idea what they were doing.

Lud said, "You're hung between a couple of mules. You've seen how they stay in line and don't crowd together, so you should be all right. I'll ride along beside you for a while so we can be sure they're handling it all right. It'd be pretty nice to lay there and get rocked like a baby in a cradle. Enjoy it."

I suppose it was the medicine, but that along with the motion of the bed swaying between the mules put me to sleep almost immediately, and I was awakened when I felt the bed lowered when we stopped at midday. Lud brought me water and later some of the broth Molly had prepared, and shortly afterward we were on our way again. Everyone was busy when we stopped that evening, so it wasn't until suppertime that I was able to talk with any of them. There was little conversation then, and it seemed like a very short time before everyone settled down for the night. The medicine man's tea took over again, and I slept through the night as well.

Since everyone was experienced in what needed to be done, things were done quickly each time we set up or tore down the camp. As a result we were underway early the next two days and were in Santa Fe the third day. I slept almost all the time, so it was an easy trip.

CHAPTER FOURTEEN

Lud went to the Army post as soon as we arrived in Santa Fe. He found Grandpa and told him about my situation. Grandpa sent a trooper for Grandma and came to Lud's barn.

When Grandma arrived, she was more upset than I had ever seen her. She wanted to know every detail, but Grandpa intervened and they took me home.

Grandma said, "Can we get the doctor here tonight?"

Grandpa said, "I'm sure he won't come at all. We'll have to wait and go to his office tomorrow."

"You *will* go talk to him, won't you?"

"You mean now?"

"Of course. We don't know if he'll come if we don't ask him."

Grandma won as usual. But Grandpa was right.

The doctor instructed Grandpa to have me in his office at ten o'clock the next morning, and we were there earlier than that. We were escorted into an examining room, and a robe was put on me. I hadn't drunk any of the tea, so the pain was back.

I heard the doctor come in. He said, "Let's see what we've got here. You say he was shot?"

Grandma said, "Yes."

"How do you feel?" he asked.

"I feel all right except for a bad headache. But I can't see."

"Can you tell if it's light or not?"

"No. There's nothing. The last thing I saw was when I was falling after I was shot."

"How long ago was that?"

"It was five or six days ago."

"And your head's hurt all that time?"

"No. A Ute medicine man gave me some kind of tea that kept the pain down. I didn't drink any this morning, so it hurts like crazy now. I can't even chew."

"How'd you manage to get to the office?"

"The tea was still working. It's almost completely stopped working."

"It was a medicine man who gave it to you?"

"Yes, sir."

"Weren't you afraid he might poison you?"

"No. There was a white girl there who helped with all of it, and the chief was there, too."

"A white girl? What was she doing there?"

Grandma said, "Does that matter? Is that going to help you fix Carlos?"

"All right, but we're going to have to talk about her later. I'm going to have to do some reading in order to determine what we can do. The brain's swollen, and that's what's causing the headache. It may also cause the blindness. My first thought is to remove some of the skull to give the brain room, so the pressure's reduced. That's a touchy procedure, though. I want to take time to read up on doing that before even considering it. I'm going to give you something to take care of the pain. It may not be as effective as what you've been taking, but at least I know it's safe. I'll try to make a decision today. If there's time, we'll go ahead and do what we decide this evening. I want to relieve that pressure. I'm surprised there's been no other problem from it. I've seen men who appeared to be injured a lot less have severe seizures and more serious effects."

I asked, "Do you think I'll get my sight back?"

"I can promise nothing, but it'll surprise me if you don't."

All I can say is that that painkiller wasn't as effective as the Ute tea.

When Grandma came and asked how I was feeling, I said, "Do you think it'd be all right to take some more of the tea?"

"I don't think so," she answered. "He said this medicine is certainly safe, and he isn't sure about the Ute tea."

"When can I take some more?"

"You may have some more in a half hour."

"That means there'll be no relief for over three hours."

"I'm sure if he's able to get rid of the pressure on your brain, the pain'll be gone."

"That *would* be nice. I hope it brings back my sight."

"You'd better see if you can sleep now."

Grandma had hardly left the room when I heard a knock at the door, and she came back.

"We need to go. The doctor's ready."

Grandma took charge, which was to be expected. "Have you decided what to do?" she asked.

"I think so, but it's a very dangerous procedure and not something I'd undertake except in an emergency. I'm willing, if you understand exactly what's involved and ask me to do it. I don't want that unless you're willing to risk his life."

"All right. Please explain what's involved and what the dangers are," said Grandpa.

"I'd need to remove a section of his skull so there's more room for the brain to swell and to allow blood to dissipate. The skull we remove would need to be placed under the skin by his stomach, or it'll deteriorate. We have nothing to keep this from hurting, so we'll need to bind him so there's no possibility of movement during the operation. The head must remain absolutely still, or we'll injure the brain. It'll be very painful, so everyone, including Carlos, needs to be prepared to endure it."

Grandma asked me, "Are you willing to go through this?"

"I'm willing. How long will it take?"

The doctor responded, "I don't know. I've never done anything like this. You'll probably lose consciousness after ten to fifteen minutes. The difficult part is cutting through the bone without damaging the brain. Any slip on my part could cause permanent damage or death."

Grandpa said, "What are the other choices?"

"We can wait and see what develops, and he may recover without any damage. That happens rarely. There are severe lasting consequences in almost all cases—permanent blindness, frequent seizures, idiocy, and a list that goes on and on."

I said, "What are the chances that I'll get my sight back?"

"Son, I can't guarantee anything. If we do it, it could make things worse. If we don't, things could get better. I feel that the chances are better if we do it, but I can't tell you what to do— you have to decide for yourselves. I wish I could get someone to take my place. This type of operation's been done for centuries, but there are no good records of how successful it was. All of the evidence shows that the patient had a permanent hole in the head. I think we can keep the bone alive by placing it under the skin in the abdomen. If so, the bone could be replaced. I don't know if that's ever been tried. If we do this the bone may be rejected. We'd be doing something few people have tried. I have a sense that it's the thing to do. Only the good Lord knows."

"How soon do you have to start?" asked Grandma.

"I wouldn't dare start later than a half-hour from now."

"I want to pray about it," she said. "I won't take more than thirty minutes."

"That'll be fine."

We all prayed, and I've never heard anyone get so serious with God as Grandma did. When she finished, we all felt she had placed all the responsibility on him, and we agreed that we'd do the surgery.

"Are you sure you want to go through the pain?" asked Grandpa.

"If God has ever heard anyone, he heard Grandma, so let's trust him to do what's best. Let's go ahead."

That doctor stripped me and put a blanket over me up to my armpits. He put straps around my feet and across my knees, thighs, waist, chest, and shoulders. When he got to my head, he warned me then placed four straps so I wouldn't be able to move. He then put something in my mouth to bite on when I hurt. I remember a lot of pain before I passed out. When I woke up, there was a lot of noise but it didn't hurt. I must've done something to let the doctor know I was awake.

He said, "Are you doing all right now, Carlos?"

I was fixed so I couldn't talk, so I grunted.

"Take that stick out of his mouth so he can answer me. Now, can you talk?"

"Yes, and I'm fine except for the noise."

"I'm sorry about that. Is there much pain?"

"Not except for the headache."

"I'm really sorry about that, but we have to continue cutting. You'll just have to be tough."

"That's fine. Just make me well."

"Carlos, I'm not too smart, but I do know that only God can make you well."

I woke up to silence. I had just a hint of a headache but no other pain. I was still blind.

"Are you done?" I asked.

It must have been a nurse who answered. She said, "Ah, you're awake. Yes, we're done, and the doctor did a good job. How do you feel?"

"Sort of tied up. Why am I still tied?"

"You have a hole in your head. We have to be sure you don't hurt yourself. I'll go get the doctor."

I was in absolute darkness. The surgery had done nothing about my sight. The headache was still there but was almost gone, so there had been something good from it. That'd be enough to justify the pain and effort.

The same voice said, "He's with another patient. Do you need anything—a drink, perhaps?"

"I'd like some water, but how can I drink in this position?"

"I'll give you a straw."

"How'll that help?"

"I'll show you."

She put something in my mouth and told me to suck on it. I did and water came into my mouth.

"Be careful or you'll choke. Coughing would be painful."

The first sips were difficult, but I was soon able to handle it.

"What time is it?" I asked.

"Almost nine o'clock."

"Is it night?"

"No. It was almost two o'clock this morning before we finished your surgery. You've slept almost seven hours since we finished."

"Have you been here all that time?"

"Of course. We didn't dare leave you alone."

"You must be tired."

"I think the doctor'll probably close the office soon so we can rest."

"Did you help during the whole thing?"

"Yes."

"Did I do all right?"

"What do you mean?"

"Did I act like a man, or was I a baby about the pain?"

"I was really proud of you. You bit on the stick and made no sound."

"I prayed that I could keep from acting wrong."

"Well, your prayer was answered. I'll be sure your parents know about that."

"I don't care if anyone knows. I appreciate what you said. Thank you."

"You did fine. I hear the doctor."

"Thanks again."

"How're you doing, Carlos?" asked the doctor.

"I'm fine, except I don't see anything."

"I'd be very surprised if there was any change yet. We need to give your head a chance to get back to normal size and let some blood leak. It'll be a month before we can expect much. You'll have to be careful for the next two or three months. I'm delighted. The surgery was a success. I expect you to recover completely. I think you're going to be able to do whatever you want by next spring."

"Do my grandparents know how well it went?"

"They left after we finished the operation. They'll be back soon. You can tell them more than I can."

When my grandparents came they made a fuss over me, and I didn't mind. It was wonderful to be free of pain.

"You're going to be fine," said Grandma. "I just *know* you are. How do you feel?"

"I'm fine."

"Does your head hurt?"

"There's almost no pain."

"I think they'll let us take you home today, but we'll need to protect your head. I'm sort of glad you can't see yourself."

"I have a lot of confidence in that man. He'll know what we need to do."

"I had no idea he was such an accomplished surgeon."

Grandpa said, "I don't think he is. God stepped in and took charge."

"You're right," Grandma answered. "Let's thank him for it."

"That's a good idea," Grandpa said. "Father, we want to thank you for giving Doc the ability to perform this delicate surgery. We're sure that you did it and want to give you the glory. Thank you."

Grandma continued, "Lord, thank you for giving the doctor confidence in you so that he was willing to do this. He was a frightened man, and I'm sure we have you to thank for leading him to do it. You guided his hands or he'd have damaged the brain. You're wonderful, and we give you all the praise and all the glory."

"Thanks, Lord," I said. "I'm still scared that I'll be blind, and I ask you to let me see again. Lord, I want that soon. Thanks for what you've done, Lord."

Grandpa said, "Amen."

The doctor came in. "Well, folks, what do you think?"

"We're thankful you performed the surgery. It seems to be successful." Grandpa said.

"Everything seems to be going well, but it's too soon to call it a success. With that skull open, we could have an infection, and the brain's exposed, so it can be damaged. We must figure out how to protect it and still give it room to heal. We're not out of danger. We definitely have made a good start and need to praise God for that, but there's a lot that we have to do."

Grandma said, "I know you have to warn us about the dangers, but I'm so happy that I refuse to stop rejoicing."

"If possible, I'm even happier than you. I know how blessed we are to have everything turn out this well. But it *is* my responsibility to make you aware of the dangers we still face."

Grandma said, "I apologize for that outburst. We want all the advice you can give us."

"I wasn't offended, ma'am. I want you to continue to be able to rejoice."

Grandpa said, "Tell us what we need to know and how to do it, and I give you my word of honor that we'll follow your instructions."

I fell asleep at that point and didn't hear all the instructions. When I woke up and asked about the time of day, the nurse told me I had some visitors. It was Lud, Ben, Pierre, and Juan.

"You mustn't get him excited. You may stay ten minutes. Don't disturb other patients."

Lud spoke so softly I hardly recognized his voice. "How're you doing?"

"I'm fine. How are you?"

"We're a lot better now. We wondered if we'd ever see you again."

"I still can't see you, but the doctor thinks I may get my sight again. He says it could be a couple of months before it happens."

Pierre said, "That's a long time, but he should know."

"He did a good job," I said.

"How much did it hurt?" Ben asked.

"I guess I wasn't a crybaby, so it must not have been bad."

"No, I'm serious. Was it really bad?"

"It was bad enough to put me out. I woke up after he had taken my scalp and was cutting bone. There's almost no headache."

Lud said, "We rented a place north of town. There's a set of corrals, a pasture, and a barn where we can finish working the ore. The barn's set up so that one or two of us can live there, too. We don't want folks snooping around out there. How does that sound to you?"

"It sounds fine. I hope I can be out there helping soon. Are we going to be able to sell any gold?"

Juan said, "I can get rid of some of it without any trouble, but probably not more than we'll need to get equipped for next year. We need to find out where we can sell all of it, and none of us has any ideas about that. We've never had this much before. We could take it to St Louis."

I asked, "Does anyone need more than we can get from what you can sell, Juan?"

"We've all agreed that we can wait, but if we find the big one, we'll need to find a way to sell a lot of gold. We have to learn how to do that. We're all right unless you need a lot to take care of this doctor bill."

"He's the Army surgeon, so my care's been covered because Grandpa's in the Army."

Lud said, "That doc tackled something that not many men would've dared to try. I'm going to find something special and get it for him. Most men would've taken one look at you and said he couldn't do anything. When I see that hole in your head and think how much nerve it took to do that, I'm amazed."

"Does it look really bad?"

"You may be lucky that you can't see it. It *is* some spooky," Pierre said. "I don't know how long it'll be until they close that up, but I'd be scared I'd move wrong and spill all my brains out."

The nurse came in and said, "I'm sorry, but you've been here twice as long as you were supposed to be."

They left, all quietly voicing their apologies. They left a room full of a warmth that I had never felt before—a warmth that I learned came from people who cared about me. The visit had made me very tired and I was soon sleeping again. The doctor told me that sleep was one of the most important things in the healing process and that I should sleep a lot each day.

The next month dragged by a few hours at a time. I wanted to see improvement every time I woke up. At least one of my partners visited every day, and the doctor came by every week. I had an ongoing battle with the lack of change in my sight. Every time I awoke, I expected to see again.

CHAPTER FIFTEEN

I t was two weeks before I thought about the man who shot me. The next time Grandma came in, I said, "I just remembered, the man who shot me was named Pedro Gonzales."

"It was *what?*"

"Pedro Gonzales."

"What did he look like?"

"The thing I remember most is that he was dirty. His hair was black and wavy and hung half way down his back, and it looked like he'd never washed it. His beard was also black and dirty, and it reached almost a foot down his chest. He had a scar on his left cheek that went clear up into his hair, and at least two of his front teeth were gone. He had the bushiest eyebrows I've ever seen. His beard was dirty from food and tobacco juice. He was wearing a blue hat with a red feather on each side. The only thing I liked about him was his horse, which is now mine. It's a beautiful *grullo* stallion and has the greatest gait I've ever seen. He walks as if he's in charge of the world."

"It sounds a lot like I remember him, and he had a horse like that. If it's the same horse we'll know it. If it is, you were shot by your own father. Did you recognize the name?"

"Yes. I don't know why I wanted to know but made sure we learned his name before they hung Pablo."

"Good night! We've got a lot of things to learn about what happened up there. I don't even know if you got any gold. You apparently met some Indians, and I want to hear about that white girl who had something to do with the medicine man. You must've had quite a summer."

"It was great. I was scared of all the men when we left here, and now they all treat me like a friend. I met an Indian chief, and the girl's his prisoner. She's twelve years old and was only three when she was first taken by the Sioux. Her mother's still held by them. The Utes captured Molly. I think the chief would've let her come with us so she could take care of me, but he knew the Army would never let her go back to him. I want to buy her from him and bring her down to live with us."

"That's something we'll talk about, but I think anyone who helped you would be welcome. I want to know everything about your summer. I can tell that you're not the boy who rode away last spring."

Grandma asked me several questions about the mining and the Indians, and we talked until I had told her most everything.

"My word," said Grandma. "I have lots of questions, but that's a start. The first thing is to learn if you were shot by your father. I'll ask Grandpa to go look at the horse as soon as he gets home. If it was your father, I'm glad he was shot."

"I told Molly you would be, and I understand. I was glad when I found out Lud had killed the man who shot me, and it hasn't changed."

"He was never a father to you. He'd have let you die the day you were born. I wouldn't be surprised if he knew who you were when he shot you."

"Maybe we should assume that he was the one who did it. Will you be disappointed if you find out he wasn't?"

"Did I sound like I was enjoying the thought that he was dead? I was, and I'm not proud of it. We need to learn whether or not he was the one. I can't imagine that another man with the same name would have a horse like that. I hope he was the man who was shot. I'll cook a big steak for the man who shot him."

"I don't think you should tell him what it's for. He earned a reward for taking care of me the way he did. He taught me a lot of things that made it easier when we were working the mines and took me to the Ute camp. We hunted together and shared a tent. I was scared of him at first, but he soon let me know he wanted to be my friend."

"I guess we'd better give him that steak even if he didn't shoot the right man."

"I'd like that. He helped me the most."

"We'll make sure he gets some extra attention. How'd the other men treat you?"

"They were all fine. They never quarreled, but neither did they talk except about the mining. The work in the mine was divided so everybody had a job. There wasn't much reason to talk. They all treated me fine."

Grandpa went to check the *grullo* and told us that there was no doubt it was the one my father had owned. Grandma and I talked about it enough to satisfy her that I wasn't disturbed, and it was never mentioned again.

Grandpa came into my room one morning and said, "The doc says it's time to put that piece back in your skull, so we have to go to his office. I'll help, but you need to walk to the cart and into the office. Can you do that?"

"I can if someone guides me."

"I'll make sure you don't run into anything. We'll start teaching you how to get around by yourself. He may put the piece back in your skull today, and then we can let you start walking around the house."

It was a half mile to the office. We were led to a room, and my clothes were exchanged for a gown. The doctor came soon.

"Any pain?" he asked.

"It's tender," I responded. "How does it look?"

"I'd say it's a nice hole."

"I'd rather have a head without a hole."

"I think we'll give you that today. Are you ready for me to cut your belly and take that hunk of skull out?"

"I'd cut it myself. I want to get up and walk."

"You'll be on a short rope, but you'll be able to do more than you have been. It'll be at least a month before you can go outside alone. That skull won't be knit before that."

I was still blind. Grandma was my support as we attempted to make me self-sufficient while moving around the house. She spent as much time as I could endure each day, teaching me where each piece of furniture was and where the doors were. She had learned about people who used a special type of cane with which they were able to gauge how close they were to objects, even to the extent of being able to walk freely in strange places. They were able to walk unattended in towns and in open areas. She talked Grandpa into making the cane with a strap at the top and proceeded to train me to use it in the house.

It was quite interesting as I learned how to tell, from the sound made by the cane striking the floor, when I was approaching an object. She insisted that we work with it every day, and we usually continued at least an hour. When I told her I was coming close to an object, she'd tell me what it was, and before the month was up, I was able to tell quite a bit about it. I could always identify a wall and was fairly accurate in my ideas about the size of other things.

It became more difficult when we moved outside. The cane didn't work as well in making identifiable sounds when it was striking dirt. When we were in an area where there were boardwalks, it worked almost as well as inside; in fact, sound was louder and somewhat easier to identify after I learned each individual sound. I learned to walk fairly fast but had to remember to keep the end of the cane ahead of me to detect things that would cause me to trip and also had to keep tapping the surface to miss holes.

I soon learned that mud and snow muffled the sounds and made the cane ineffective. Since there was much more danger of slipping, I was confined to the house during much of November. That made me even more frustrated about the lack of change in my vision. Not only was I handicapped in moving about and couldn't do many simple tasks, I couldn't imagine how I'd be of value to my mining partners if I couldn't see my dowsing equipment. I hadn't asked any of the men how much gold they weighed but had no doubt that my portion would be the equivalent of at least twenty years earnings for the average person. That was considerable wealth, but I had come to realize that having the gold wasn't as fulfilling as finding it.

I hadn't given up hope of my sight returning, but each day made it more difficult. Father Manuel advised me to trust God to enable me to overcome the handicap. I became more determined to seek complete healing.

I reminded God of what he said in Galatians 2:20, and every night I recited, "I am crucified with Christ, nevertheless, I live; yet not I, but Christ lives in me, and the life that I now live in the flesh I live by the faith of the Son of God, who loved me and gave his life for me."

On the night of December first, while I was praying, I was given this message. "Don't worry about it. I've taken care of it." It was the same message he had given the first time he had spoken, and I wondered if I had thought it because I wanted it so badly. As I continued to pray, he made it clear that he had said it.

It was so definite that I felt around me to be certain there was no one in the room. The confidence that I'd soon see surpassed anything I had ever experienced.

I awoke early and was in the kitchen when Grandma came in. "You're up early. Didn't you sleep well?" she asked.

"Yes. I want to tell you what happened last night."

"What happened?"

"I was praying for Jesus to heal my eyes, and he told me to not worry about it, that he had taken care of it."

"You heard him?"

"No, it was spoken to my heart. I heard it as clearly as if it had been shouted. I think it'll be my Christmas present."

"You'd better talk this over with Father Manuel. I don't think Jesus goes around healing folks."

"Did he stop speaking to people?"

"I don't know. Why don't you just keep this to yourself?"

"I know I'll see again by Christmas day."

"I'll pray for it, too, but I have trouble believing like you do."

"I'm not sure Jesus hears if you don't believe. I asked Jesus to give me his faith. Paul said that he lived by the faith of Jesus, so I thought that'd be a good thing to ask for."

"You know more about that sort of thing than I do. I want it as much as you do."

The days that followed proved that I was still a fourteen-year-old boy. I expected to see every time I awoke.

I went to bed Christmas Eve fully expecting to be able to see the next morning. I got up early and went to the kitchen. Grandma had taught me how to make coffee, so I set about doing that.

I made noise enough to rouse Grandma.

"Well?" she asked.

"Not yet. It can happen any time today."

"What if it doesn't?"

"I've been mistaken about lots of things, but not this time. I remember the story of Shadrach, Meshach, and Abednego when they were threatened with being thrown into a burning furnace. They said something like this: 'Our God can save us from the burning, fiery furnace, but whether he does or not, we're not going to bow down to your idol.' They were put in, and the fire was so hot it killed the men who threw them in, but Jesus went in with them. When they came out, nothing was burned, and there wasn't even the smell of fire on their clothing. I serve that same God, and he hasn't changed. He told me himself that he had taken care of my problem, and I believe him."

I don't want anyone to think it was easy to drink that first cup of coffee then have breakfast in the same way I had for almost three months. It's not easy to see absolutely nothing when you've been so sure that you'd have sight. I'd be lying if I said it was easy to believe at that time. I could sense that everyone was feeling the same way. Lud and Pierre were there, and there were gifts for each of us. My partners brought me a sheepskin coat, which fit me perfectly. My grandparents gave me a saddle and bridle. Grandma had helped me find a leather hat for each of my partners and a finely made ax for Grandpa. Lud and I found a necklace made of silver and turquoise with bear claws encircling the gem for Grandma.

Everyone appreciated the gifts, but no one was as joyous as they usually were. I was sad because my eyes were still useless.

Grandma had prepared a bountiful meal. When we gathered at the table, the aroma of roast wild turkey, dressing, freshly baked bread, potatoes, gravy, and fruit pies surrounded us. Grandpa said, "Carlos, why don't you thank God for all this food?"

"Lord, we thank you that you've brought us together to celebrate the birth of your son. We thank you for the many ways you've blessed us. You enabled Grandma to prepare the food that you provided. Now we ask that you'll bless the food as we eat it. We pray this in the blessed name of your Son, Jesus. Amen."

When I opened my eyes, I could tell that it wasn't dark.

"Is it especially bright today?"

Grandpa said, "No, in fact it's cloudy and looks like it might snow at any moment."

"I can see that it's light in here. It was dark when we sat down."

I'd have caused less excitement if I had exploded some dynamite on the table. Everyone forgot about eating. Grandpa finally reminded us that dinner was getting cold. It was a joyous meal. We assumed that my sight would be restored.

The light was brighter, and I saw color when the sun set. I lay awake a couple of hours, just praising God. As I talked with Jesus,

I was given an assurance that I'd see by New Years Day. I said, "Thank you for giving me back the use of my eyes," and he gave me the faith to believe it.

I hurried downstairs, awaiting the sunrise. I watched it get brighter, and could almost see the sun when it came over the horizon. It was so bright that I had to close my eyes. I felt like shouting.

The next day I could see large items, and the following day I could make out large trees. The improvement continued until by New Year's Eve I could see most things. Small items were still without definition, but I'd be able to serve as dowser.

Lud shared my excitement. When I could look him in the eye on New Year's Day, the two of us did a jig around the room.

"By gum, it happened!" he shouted. "Your God came through. I guess I'll have to let you introduce me to him."

"I can do that right now, Lud. John three sixteen says, 'God so loved the world that he gave his only begotten Son, that whoever believes in him should not perish, but have everlasting life.' It's that simple—believe that Jesus died and paid the penalty for your sins and he gives you the privilege of becoming a child of God. Would you like to do that?"

"I could never find a better deal than that. Sure, I'll do it. What else do I have to do?"

"You believe and ask Jesus to save you, and he does it."

He didn't answer for quite a little while. Then he said, "Is it really that simple?"

"Yes. Jesus said, in Matthew eleven thirty, 'Come to me, all who are weak and heavy laden, and I'll give you rest, for my yoke is easy, and my load is light.' Why don't you ask Jesus to save you?"

"Why don't you tell me what to say and let me repeat it?"

"All right. Jesus, I know I've sinned. I want you to come into my heart and be my Savior. I believe you paid for my sins and have given me eternal life. Thank you, Jesus."

Lud repeated it. He closed by saying, "God, I want to thank you for letting me see what you did for Carlos. That convinced me you're able to do what you say you can. I believe in you now."

I said, "That was great, Lud. I know God liked that. We'll read the Bible, looking for parts that will help you be sure that you have eternal life. In First John we read something like this. 'These things are written to you who believe in the Lord Jesus Christ, that you may know that you have eternal life, and that you may believe in the name of the Lord Jesus Christ.' He says we already have eternal life. In the Gospel according to the same man, we're told that whoever has Jesus has life, and anyone who doesn't have him shall not even see life. There are lots of places in the Old Testament as well that tell us in advance that Jesus was going to come and give himself that we might be saved."

<hr/>

The next few days were stormy, and we endured snowfall almost the entire time. Friday dawned clear. I had asked Lud to come and take me out to the facilities we had rented.

At nine o'clock, I complained to Grandma, "Lud said he'd come this morning and get me. Do you think he may have forgotten?"

"Good night, son, the day's hardly started. Give him some time. He's never failed to do what he said he would, has he?"

"No."

"The coffee should still be hot. Get yourself a cup and sit there and fret if that makes you happy. Otherwise, enjoy the beauty of snow on everything. It's cold. Lud may have decided to wait until it's more comfortable."

He arrived and had brought my *grullo* stallion.

I said, "Someone's shined him up. Who cleaned his mane and tail? They were matted and tangled like a bunch of brambles."

"We all worked on it. We wanted you to know what a good horse you have."

We put my new saddle and bridle on him, and I mounted him for the first time. Riding him was as I had imagined it would be if I was a knight mounted on a warhorse headed for battle. He responded to the lightest touch of the spur or rein. I decided to name him *Raton* (Mouse, in English) because of his color, which is mouse-colored.

Lud started his horse at a trot, and I held Raton to a walk, which was much faster than most horses. I had to slow him to keep from getting ahead of Lud.

"That critter can really walk, can't he?" Lud commented. "I've never seen a horse walk that fast. Give him his head and see what he does."

I loosened the reins and touched him with a spur. Within a quarter mile, we were two hundred feet ahead of Lud's trotting animal. I barely touched him with a spur, and he went to a faster gait that was the smoothest ride I had ever enjoyed. I knew it was neither a walk nor a trot.

"What was he doing at the last?" I asked.

"That was a single foot. I've only seen two other horses do it. Only one foot's off the ground at any time. The back goes even with the ground even more than when he's walking. As you could feel, it's a much smoother ride than a trot or gallop. That horse is worth a lot. You're lucky to have him."

"I'd change that from lucky to *blessed*. With Christ you no longer depend on chance or luck."

I learned that he was a well-trained horse. We passed some cattle, and he handled them easily. He was quick and agile and, given his head, he'd be at the front of any string of horses. He was even better than I had expected.

I liked our facility. The barn was large enough for all the livestock. It was of adobe brick construction with walls twelve feet high and a roof of dirt with grass growing on it. The living area would allow all of us to stay there. Pierre, Ben, and Lud were doing that. Juan was there only about half of the time. The corrals were spacious, with four enclosures. Each area contained a shed. The pasture was fenced into three sections. There was another shed where hay was stored.

Pierre asked, "How do you like this setup?"

"It looks excellent."

"We leased it for a year with the option to extend it another year."

"That's great. If we continue to have success, maybe we can buy it next fall."

"We're hoping for that," Lud said.

"Have you worked all of the ore?"

"Yes, there wasn't much."

"Are you all right, or is there a lot more healing needed?"

"The doctor says I need to be careful for a while, or I can have trouble with the hole he cut in my head. The groove where I was shot's still tender, but otherwise I seem to be fine. I want to find a good stallion and five or six nice mares to take up with us. I plan to try to trade them for Molly's freedom."

Lud said, "You'd better get ready to fight that ugly brave. I reckon it won't make any difference to him if you buy her from Smart Coyote. You'll have to fight him to get her out of camp."

"If I deal with the chief, nobody else will have anything to say about it, will they?"

"Unless they're different from any Indians I've ever dealt with, the chief won't interfere. Any brave'll be able to challenge you. That brave'll cause trouble."

"What should I do?"

Juan said, "I heard that there's a soldier who's teaching a form of fighting that he learned from a Chinese man. Maybe your grandpa can get him to teach you. Why don't you talk to Grandpa?"

"I suppose I'd better do that."

CHAPTER SIXTEEN

G randpa was able to get me into the class. The sergeant who was teaching the class had learned from an Oriental, and he was teaching a form of karate. It was soon apparent that he'd be able to overcome an unarmed opponent quite easily. He could choose to leave him without injury, with an injury, or take his life.

A person armed with a knife presented almost as little problem. The methods were fairly easy to learn, and within a month I had reached a point at which the sergeant felt that I'd have little reason to fear an attack from anyone in face to face combat.

The second phase involved the use of hands to break bones and other objects. He took four boards that were two inches thick, placed them one on top of the other, and drove his hand through them, breaking all of them with a single blow without injury to his hand. He explained that his hand never touched the boards, but he mentally placed energy ahead of his hand, and that energy was what broke the boards.

I had no peace of mind about that phase and stopped participating. I would trust God to give me wisdom in any conflict.

We spent a lot of time going over the tools and equipment, buying dynamite and caps, and reviewing our list of food and supplies. I bought every good mare that I could find. There was never a surplus of horses, and good brood mares were hard to find, so I was able to buy only seven. I expected to pay premium prices, but few buyers had gold to offer, so the sellers were willing to bargain. I also bought four iron kettles and had an iron plate built. It had a hole in one corner, drilled at an angle so that a rod could be driven in the ground and the plate could be placed at different heights above the fire and could be swung around the rod to place it in the best position for cooking. These, along with the horses, were items to be offered Chief Smart Coyote in exchange for Molly's freedom. I also intended to breed the mares and offer the use of the *grullo* stallion to breed the mares owned by the Utes. I liked the iron plate for cooking so well I had another one built for our use.

We were able to leave the morning of March sixteenth. There was snow along the way, and the site we had chosen for our camp was covered with about six inches. We selected an alternate site and were settled in the fifth day.

CHAPTER SEVENTEEN

We examined the mine I had discovered the previous fall, and while the others began to open it, Lud and I started moving the sluice to the new location. Mining was started on the fifth day, and by the time the sluice was in place, there was a nice accumulation of ore.

I visited the Ute camp two weeks later. I rode the *grullo* and took two mares with me.

The youngsters and dogs alerted everyone, and I rode to Smart Coyote's tipi. The chief was the first person to come out. I could only guess what he said, but his face assured me that it was all right.

Molly came next, and she left me with no doubts about her welcome.

"Are you all right?" she asked.

"I'm great now that I see you."

"Are your eyes well?"

"Yes. You've grown and are as pretty as I remembered. I could hardly wait to get here. I want to try to reach an agreement with the chief."

"Don't begin discussions for a while. Will it be all right if I tell you when to begin?"

"I'd appreciate your help."

She talked with Smart Coyote; then we entered the tipi. I was given the spot facing the chief with Molly on my left. We proceeded as we had on the other visits, with Molly translating.

"Tell us all that happened since you left us," Smart Coyote said.

It took two hours to satisfy them. They insisted on a detailed description of the surgery. I tried to leave out no detail about the return of my sight, and they were properly amazed. I made every effort to give God the glory he deserved, and the Indians seemed to understand. Smart Coyote sent for Star Gazer so he could hear about the surgery.

I wanted them to understand how delicate the removal of the skull had been.

I had to go over some of the details several times. Even the medicine man seemed to be open to my insistence that it was God who had given me back my sight.

We talked about the ways that Star Gazer would be able to treat similar injuries and the use of herbs, berries, and animal tissues to treat illness and injury. I came to the conclusion that it'd be beneficial for the doctor who had treated me if he could spend time with Star Gazer.

We talked the sun down.

"How soon will I be able to try to make a deal for your freedom?" I asked as Molly walked with me to where we'd eat.

"I'll let you know as soon as it's all right. You may need to wait until another time."

"I want to breed the tribe's mares. We should start that right away."

"He'll not consider any offer if you do it too soon. Does prayer help in something like this?"

"Yes. I've been praying."

"Pray that I'll know the proper time."

"I'll do that. Is Dark Dog in camp?"

"Yes. His tipi's the last one beyond the chief's."

"Has he bothered you?"

"The chief's made it clear that he'll not allow anyone to harm me. Dark Dog will possibly challenge you if the chief says that I may go with you. Are you prepared to fight him?"

"Of course. I've already discussed it with God, and he'll take care of me."

"Has he told you how he'll do it?"

"No. He killed two hundred thousand men one night, so a Ute brave'll not be a problem. He made an army blind so they couldn't hurt a prophet. Another time he confused an army so much they killed each other. All God's people had to do was pick up the treasure the army abandoned. He doesn't need to tell me any details."

"You are ready to fight Dark Dog?"

"Yes."

"I don't want that. He's an experienced fighter, and you aren't."

"I'll do what's needed."

"Please pray for me. I'm still frightened."

"I'm not confident in *my* strength or ability but in *God's* power. I'll pray that he'll enable you to believe."

When we had eaten and were going back to the tipi, Molly talked to the chief then said to me, "He wants to see the horses you have with you. After that, you can discuss your proposal."

We inspected the mares and the *grullo*, and he was impressed favorably. I said, "I have five more mares as good as those you saw. All seven are with foal by my stallion. I also have some cooking utensils that'll make it much easier for Fawn Heart to cook. I want to take Dawn on the Mountain to Santa Fe this fall. I'm offering you the seven mares, the metal pots, and will leave my stallion so you can breed all of the mares. Dawn on the Mountain would live with my family. She'll never lack for anything but will become like a princess. I'll bring her to visit you at least once each year for the next five years.

"I intend to try to find and rescue her mother so they can be together. I know that you're fond of Dawn on the Mountain and truly want what's best for her. Dark Dog expects to take her for himself. You know she doesn't want that.

"Please consider this and give me an answer tomorrow."

"Will you breed our mares other years?"

"I'll do that for three years, as long as the stallion's able. After that, you should use a different stallion, or the foals won't be as good."

"I'll think on this. Go now."

Molly went outside with me. "I'll make it obvious that this is what I want, Carlos."

"Good. You're not an ordinary prisoner to him. I can't imagine that he wants you with Dark Dog."

"Pray hard."

"God knows what's best. I'm prepared to accept his decision."

"I'll pray, then."

"Good. I'll see you in the morning."

"Good night, Carlos. Thank you."

"Good night, Molly."

I went outside the next morning. Molly was a delight to see. She wore a buckskin dress that was dyed a bright red. It was decorated with bear claws, elk teeth, and porcupine quills. Her hair was in braids.

"You're beautiful."

"You shouldn't flatter me."

"It isn't flattery. If that skin came off a buck, I hope he can see you. He'd gladly give his hide for such a pretty dress on a lady with your beauty."

"That's definitely flattery. You must stop."

"I'll wait for another time. I meant every word."

The look she gave me made it a moment to remember. It carried me through some lonely times.

We ate a leisurely meal and talked about a lot of unimportant things. I had to wait until he was ready to talk business.

"I've decided," he said at last. "Dawn on the Mountain must marry a member of this tribe."

I had been so certain he'd accept my offer that I hadn't considered any other possibility. I was speechless.

Molly said, "You must respond."

"What can I say? I have the mares and the utensils, and they'll be a burden if I keep them in our camp. I must go somewhere and pray. Tell him I'll be back soon."

I went to the log by the river. I said, "Lord, I'm sure that you led me to do this. I never doubted that you'd have Smart Coyote accept my offer. What can I do?"

I lost track of time. There was no response from God, and I was desolate. The disappointment was overwhelming. It kept me from talking with the Lord. I wandered outside the camp, completely empty spiritually. I had never faced such a difficulty and had no solution. I was unable to corral my thoughts. I'm sure the Lord finally intervened. I returned to the tipi. Smart Coyote and Molly were waiting.

"I want to give him everything I mentioned. He's my friend, and I bought the items for him. I ask for nothing in exchange. Please tell him that."

Molly sat and looked at me. "You're offering those things and ask for nothing in return?"

"Yes."

She sat for long moments and then spoke to the chief. Her voice broke, and tears flowed. I didn't need to understand. The message was clear.

He spoke, and she turned to me. "He said, 'He's a wise man. I accept his gift'."

"That's good. We need to decide how to get the other mares here, as well as the pots. If you'll loan me a horse and will send someone with me to bring everything back here, we can start."

"I'll take another man, and we'll go with you. You can ride your horse, and we'll bring him back."

"That'll be fine. Have you bred mares?"

"No. You will need to tell me how to do that."

"If we can find a mare that's ready, I can show you. Otherwise, we'll discuss it as we ride to our camp. It'd be good if we can actually breed at least one mare this morning."

"That's good. Let us smoke to make it right."

We did the ceremonial smoke then took the *grullo* out to the pasture. It took but a few minutes for him to discover a receptive mare, and they were soon coupled. We found four more who were ready and were on our way within a half hour.

If he had been allowed to set the pace, Raton would've been a mile ahead of the other horses when we arrived at our camp.

"One of you may want to ride him back. I'd prefer that either you or the chief ride him," I said to Molly. "I'm sure you'd enjoy riding him."

"Do you think I can handle him?"

"It'll be easy to find out. I'll switch horses with you."

"Would we need to change saddles?"

"No.."

"I'd like to try it. I think anyone would be excited at the thought of riding Raton. He walks like a big chief leading his braves into battle. I love to watch him. He appears to be proud of having you on his back."

"He'll be even prouder with you there."

"Flatterer. You need to stop doing that."

"I hope to tell you things like that until you know it isn't flattery. It's nice to be able to do it now because nobody else understands and you aren't embarrassed by it."

"I want to say the same sort of thing to you, but I don't know how. I've never had any experience."

"I've never wanted to say those things to anyone else. I've never seen anyone like you. I can't keep from saying them to you."

"I like it. Maybe I'll be able to say what I feel sometime."

"I can't resist saying again that you're beautiful today."

"Thank you, but let's talk about something else."

"All right."

"You said last night that you want to see if you can rescue my mother. Were you serious?"

"Of course. I can imagine how concerned you are about her. If we can get her to Santa Fe, it'll be great for both of you. Lud wants to go with me. We can't do it until we're through with the mining, so it'll be at least a couple of years."

"I'd like to go with you. She'd not leave with someone she didn't know. I know how the camp's arranged and where she's kept."

"I'd love to have you along but don't want to put you in danger."

"I'd be safe with you."

"Lud would make it a lot safer. I plan to discuss this with Smart Coyote. He can give us directions."

"I've longed for this but never imagined that it might actually happen. Do you think we can do it?"

"Yes, I do. God wants his children to be happy He tells us to keep asking, and he'll provide what we need."

"How do you know all of these things?"

"The Bible was almost the only book available, and my teacher was the priest, so we spent a lot of time in it. Father Manuel's convinced that we're to accept the things in the Bible literally and to believe it absolutely. The more I watch God work, the more I believe his word. The priest says we should listen at least as much as we talk and God will tell us what we should do. I'm not as good at that as I want to be, but when I do it, God always comes through."

"I've never heard of that before. Does it really work?"

"It does for me."

"I've got a lot to learn. Will you teach me?"

"I start out telling him what a great God he is. I thank him for blessings, and confess. Then I ask for what I need."

We arrived at our camp, which was near the mine.

"You can't stay here," Smart Coyote said. "This's one of our horse pastures, and your animals will eat all of the grass. You must leave immediately."

"Will you please go talk with Lud?"

I caught the mares and managed to attach the pots to two of them and then went to the mine.

I heard Lud say, "You're giving us fifteen days to finish here?"

"Yes, but only fifteen days," answered Smart Coyote.

"We can do that."

"All right."

I went to Molly and said, "We need to transfer your saddle and bridle to Raton."

"Oh, yes. I may not let you have him back."

Pierre and Molly prepared a meal, then the Indians and Molly left. I helped Molly mount Raton, which gave me another moment with her. She was only thirteen years old but was mature beyond her age.

As they rode off, that *grullo* made it plain that he liked having her in the saddle, and her smile was evidence that the feeling was mutual. She turned and waved just before the trail went into some trees. I stood and hoped for another glimpse even though I knew there was no possibility of it.

Lud came over and put his hand on my shoulder. "She's quite a lady. You need to go find us another mine. We've got two weeks to finish this one, and then we'll have to move."

"I'll get a horse and do what I can this afternoon."

"Good idea."

CHAPTER EIGHTEEN

I was really discouraged before that dowsing nugget indicated any ore worth mining. I had learned a lot the previous summer and was able to cover a lot of area by staying in the saddle and riding slowly. I worked along each stream and was far west of our camp before anything of interest appeared. I was on Vallecito Creek when the nugget finally made a move.

It started swinging to my left, increased as I rode toward the creek, then diminished when I rode beyond it. I got off and searched afoot. It took ten minutes to determine that the gold was in the bank of the creek where it burst out of a small, steep canyon. The nugget's swing carried it above the level of my hand as I walked beside the creek. The movement decreased when I moved in either direction and was strong along the same area every time I reversed direction. The creek bank was steep, but the face was rough enough to climb. The nugget was active over a surface five feet wide and six feet high. The pull was sufficient to cause it to swing in a complete circle between my hand and the face of the bank. I had experienced that action when I was standing above ore, but never when the gold was on the same level as I was.

The men were in camp when I arrived. Ben was the first to spot me.

"Did you find it?" he asked.

"Yes, but it's way over west. I've been riding since daybreak to get here."

"That's all right."

"It looks better than this one."

Lud said, "We're through here, so we can get things ready tomorrow and leave the next day."

"That's good. The Utes'll be here soon to make sure we're leaving. I hope they don't object to the place I discovered."

"We'll probably know right away if they don't want us there."

"That Ute'll have someone watching our every move," said Juan.

Pierre said, "We're in country they've always counted as theirs. Let's try to get along with them."

We all felt that he was right. The next morning we were on our way at dawn.

It took until late afternoon of the second day to reach the site.

There was time enough to make our first excavation. We hit the first ore three feet in, and we knew it was rich. It was embedded in crumbly quartz, so a blow with a pick loosened chunks a foot in each direction. We found that it was one-fourth gold. It took three days to accumulate fifty pounds of gold. Some nuggets were a half inch across.

The Utes arrived on day six. We had found a favorite hunting ground, and they insisted that we leave within a week. We were able to get the richest ore out in that time. We left no evidence of the mining.

Smart Coyote, Molly, Star Gazer, and three others stayed overnight.

Molly said, "Smart Coyote wants to talk with you alone. We can walk and talk."

The three of us walked downstream a hundred feet, and the chief said, "We'll sit on this log."

We sat for ten minutes before he said, "Dawn on the Mountain didn't smile from the time you left until she saw you today. Her eyes were wet all the time, and her face was sad. She changed as soon as she saw you. She looks different when she's with you. Give me your hand."

I extended my right hand.

"The other one," he said.

He turned my hand so the wrist was on top and then cut a slit in my skin. He did the same thing to his wrist and placed it against mine, with the slits touching.

"You're part of me, now. Since you're now of our tribe, Dawn on the Mountain is allowed to go with you."

I silently asked God for the right words. As I waited, I looked into his eyes. His was the most penetrating look I had ever seen.

"You honor me. There's nothing greater than this. I'll always be grateful. You've given me a full heart."

"When will you take her?"

"We'll mine until the first snow."

"You may come then. I leave you now. You have things to say to each other."

"Thank you, sir."

He walked away, his head high, looking straight ahead.

Molly almost jumped into my arms.

"Did you know he was going to do that?"

"No. He's been quiet, and I saw him watching me often, but this's a total surprise."

"We need to pray."

"Shall we kneel?"

"I'm not ready to turn loose of you. God understands. Jesus, you've given me the greatest gift I've ever received. Thank you for making Smart Coyote understand how important this is to us. We'll never stop praising you for it. You're wonderful."

"Forgive me, Lord. I didn't even pray that you'd do this. Please teach me to trust you."

"Amen."

"I'm probably bleeding all over you," I said as I released her.

"Your blood will remind me of you. I won't wash it off."

"Where will you go next?" Molly asked.

"I don't know. Does anyone have a suggestion?"

She discussed it with the Indians then said, "Several of them think you should follow this stream into the higher areas."

"Is there a trail?"

Smart Coyote answered, "There are some game trails. You'll have no trouble getting there."

"Is there water?" Lud wanted to know.

"There are springs in the area."

Ben said, "You've seen how we use water where we wash the ore. Will we be able to do that?"

"No."

"We'll decide after we finish here," Pierre said. "We appreciate your help."

Molly had ridden Raton, and they were getting along well. The stallion made her appear regal.

She said, "You may have lost your horse. He seems to enjoy taking care of me."

"We'll have to find an outstanding horse. I'm sure we can do it. I'll probably have to steal him. It's almost impossible to talk a man into selling a good horse."

"I know. You had to get shot to get Raton. We may be forced to share him."

"You and he make a picture together. I've never seen anything to compare with it. I can hardly wait to see you on him, dressed the way Grandma will fix you, and with the rigging she'll have for you. She's going to have the time of her life."

"I'm sort of scared about that. I'm sure I've never known anyone like her, and she may not want me."

"You can forget about that. She's the nicest person I know, and you'll fit right in with her. If there's any hesitation, Grandpa'll take care of it. They both have done everything they could to see that I've been happy, and they'll see that treating you really nice is what I want, so that's what they'll do. As soon as they get to know you, they'll do it because they like you, too."

"It's exciting to think about it. This is going to be a long summer."

"Yes."

"Have you told them about me and what you hoped to do?"

"Oh, sure. They helped get the mares and cooking gear. In fact, Grandma's the one who suggested the pots. She said any woman would like to have good equipment in her kitchen, and if I brought something that she'd want, the chance of getting a good decision from a man would be much better. She's a truly wise person."

"Then they won't be surprised when I come with you?"

"Not at all. In fact, Grandma promised to pray for that every day. I wish there was a way to let her know that Smart Coyote has agreed. She could start praying about Dark Dog. I still have to take care of him some way."

"That's something I'll pray about. What do you think he'll do?"

"I'm sure he'll want to fight me, and from what I've learned, no one will interfere with that. I'm prepared to fight but hope to avoid it. I'm praying that God will show me another solution. I'd much rather become his friend."

"He's used to having his way and has planned to make me his next squaw. He's not likely to want to be friendly with anyone who stands in his way."

"God's able to do all things, even to changing a man's heart. I'll trust him to handle this in a way that's best. The Bible tells us that he causes all things to work together for good to those who love him and are called according to his purpose. I just need to wait and see how he does it."

"I have so much to learn about God. Do you think I can do it?"

"Of course you can. I remember reading about a woman named Lydia. It says that God opened her understanding so she could believe. He'll do that for anyone who seeks him."

"You amaze me. You're still young, but you know so much about the Bible and seem to really know God personally. I've never heard of anybody who knew him like that."

"You'll get to know him before this time next year. I'll get the two of you together, and he's a friend who sticks closer than a brother. That's from the Bible, too."

"I can hardly wait."

"We'll be riding toward Santa Fe before you know it. Just keep praying."

Smart Coyote came and said they were leaving.

"I'll see you again as soon as I can get away," I promised. "Maybe I can arrange a visit to your mine."

"I'll hope for that."

"Me too. Good-bye."

I watched every move until she was out of sight.

Lud said, "All right, kid. Come help us finish this mining. You and I'll be working nights. We'll need to work around the clock."

The next week, Lud and I slept days and mined nights. Pierre, Ben, and Juan worked the day shift, and we were able to get the richest ore out by the deadline.

The lower section of Vallecito Creek came through a rocky canyon that was narrow and too rough to take horses and mules that way. Instead, we went over the ridge and came back to the stream ten miles upstream.

The creek ran through a valley a half mile wide.

The valley narrowed rather quickly with the steep flanks closing on both sides until they met in a slope that forced us to go up a much steeper, tree-covered hillside. At that point, the creek was only five or six feet wide and six inches deep and continued to diminish in size.

Juan said, "Let's stop here. It's almost level, so we won't need to tie ourselves to a tree. I think I can get us a meal of trout out of that creek."

I was riding a horse that plodded along with an even, steady gait. I could dowse as I rode. If I used a large nugget, I wouldn't detect small deposits but would find larger ones. We were approaching timberline when the nugget started responding to something.

"There's gold here," I said. "I'll let one of you take this horse, and I'll try to pin down the gold."

"I'll take him," Lud volunteered. "We'll stop at the first decent spot. We need to stop anyway."

I followed the nugget for a hundred feet. It suddenly indicated that there was gold off to the right, so I followed its lead. After another fifty feet, there was a strong indication of ore farther to my right. Before I had gone that direction ten paces, the nugget showed that there was gold in an entirely different spot.

I spent two hours there and found nothing. I concluded that there was so much gold in the area that as I approached a deposit, another one gave a stronger indication. I never located a single thing. I continued to get signals until I was in camp.

I explained to the others how the nugget had acted. We discussed it through our meal, but no one had a solution.

I prayed but went to sleep with no progress. I slept well but woke the next morning with the problem still unsolved. The next eleven days brought nothing but frustration. I felt like that nugget must have felt the first time I tried to find gold, when it was bouncing like an aspen leaf. I searched over an area at least two miles square. Each signal was superseded by another one. It was a terrible time for me.

As we were eating the eleventh evening, Lud said, "Kid, we need to be mining. If you can't find it, we'll go down below. I'll give you two more days."

I prayed most of that night and had the answer when I awoke the next morning. I needed a heavier nugget that would be affected only by a large body of ore. It seemed so simple, but none of us had thought of it. I put three more nuggets on my string. Each of them was larger than what I was using. It took but a few minutes to learn that there was no difference. I finally sewed a buckskin bag and filled it with nuggets. It weighed at least a pound.

I decided to see if there was any response from something that heavy. I went through the area I had covered. There was no reaction. I was rewarded with a definite signal four hundred feet above the camp. It continued and became stronger until I was another hundred feet to the left of the direction I had been going.

I proceeded on foot. Within minutes I had pinned down the exact location of the deposit. It was in a gully at the base of a steep hillside. It was ten feet across and about the same height. It was rich, and I estimated that it extended into the hill a considerable distance.

"What do you think, Carlos?" Pierre asked.

"It's bigger than anything we've found before. This could be the spot we've been looking for. It's either extensive or rich—or both. I can't tell how far it is to the ore, but it's big."

Lud said, "I'll go get some equipment, and we'll see what we find."

We all accompanied him and were soon making the first excavation. We encountered nothing but dirt for five feet then found a face of crumbly quartz. The rock was easy to handle, and we soon saw the first gold. Ben grabbed a pick and soon had a six inch cube. It had gold on all surfaces. When it was broken, none of us could find words for our emotions. It was laced with gold. It came apart easily, and the gold literally fell out of the rock.

Juan gathered a handful of gold and said, "We've hit the mother lode, men. If this goes into that hill twenty feet, we're richer than King Solomon. If it goes only five feet, we're rich. Kid, you've earned your share."

Before we quit that evening, we knew that the face of the deposit was twelve feet wide and ten feet high.

Ben said, "If it's only a foot deep, we'll have more than any of has hoped for. Carlos, I reckon you'd better lead us in prayer."

I knelt down and said, "We're grateful for what you've done for us, Lord. We don't understand why you did it, but we want to praise you for it. We want to serve you with it. In Jesus' name, amen"

Ben said, "That's the first time I ever prayed, but I agree with every word. You've convinced me that your God's the real thing."

"Ben, that's worth more to me than this gold. We may find that we've taken out all this spot has for us, but what you just got from God's more precious than every ounce of gold in the whole world. You just received eternal life, available only through Jesus, the Son of God. We'll dig this hole as deep as the gold goes, and I want to dig into the Bible with you, so you'll learn what you've been given."

Pierre said, "We need to be careful, or we'll make you into a preacher. We still need you as our dowser, so don't get too involved in teaching us the Bible."

"We need to mine as fast as possible," said Lud. "Summer doesn't last long up here. We'll be lucky if we don't get snow in September. I'm interested in learning about the Bible, but we'll have lots of time to do that when the snow won't let us mine. We need to figure how we're going to get this gold out and down to Santa Fe."

Juan added, "We need to find a shorter way down from here. It'll take an extra four days' travel if we go back the way we came. We want to get things ready so we can fix the mine entrance so no one can tell what we're doing. We need to be able to stay out of sight."

"We need to learn more about what we've got," I cautioned. "This gold may only be a couple of feet deep."

"Don't you think we've found the big one?" Lud demanded.

"Yes, but I want to see some more evidence before I start spending any of it."

Pierre said, "I'm going to assume we've got what it looks like we have. I'm going to celebrate. Lud, do you figure you can find an elk or a bighorn sheep? If you can get us some fresh meat I'll make a pie out of those dried apples. I brought a bottle of wine to top it off."

"Come on, kid. You can find gold, so a ram shouldn't be a problem. Let's go!"

We rode below timberline, and Lud spotted a pair of full-curl rams. There's no more beautiful animal in this world than a Rocky Mountain Bighorn ram. He's king of his domain and walks so you know that God designed him for that high mountain region. If you've watched a herd of bighorns navigate the face of a cliff at full speed, you've seen a feat that defies description.

I dropped to my belly, took a deep breath, let out most of it, squeezed the trigger, and saw hair fly from the neck of the bigger ram.

"You don't waste meat, do you? That didn't ruin five pounds."

"You gave me good instruction, and he was standing still in a perfect position. A good gun helps, too."

"You still have to make a good shot. I couldn't have done better."

"It's been almost a year since we had a ram. Pierre makes a good apple pie, so it'll be a real treat. He'll probably have some potatoes. I get tired of eating cornmeal all the time."

"You'd better not complain, or you'll be cook for a while."

"Yes, and I'll admit that cornmeal's better than eating my cooking, so I'll be quiet."

We had the ram field dressed and were on our way back to camp in less than thirty minutes. It was a beautiful day with hardly a cloud in the sky. It seemed to me that we could see at least a hundred miles to the south and west. We were higher than anything but the high peaks, which were north and east. We were between Rio Grande Pyramid and the Window, which would always give us something to watch for as we came from Santa Fe. I wished for Raton. He'd fit the majesty of the mountains. I thought that if I was mounted on him, I could imagine being from a royal family. Then I realized that Grandma was truly royalty, and it caused me to sit a bit straighter and make the horse walk with a bow in his neck.

"Do you have any idea how we're going to separate the gold from the rock?" Lud asked. "We're a long way from enough water to justify making a sluice, but we don't have enough mules to haul everything home with us."

Juan said, "Why don't we do what we did today? It was easy to get the gold out by breaking the rock."

"That'll work fine if all of it's like that," said Ben. "I doubt that much of it'll be that easy. Eventually we're going to need to either bring a couple hundred mules or figure out a way to melt the gold and make bricks. We can't do that now."

Pierre said, "Let's wait and see how the ore is as we get deeper."

I said, "We'll need timbers. Are we going to cut them around here?"

Lud said, "We don't want to cut live trees anywhere. We want to keep this mine hidden. We need dead logs. We'll also need to pack all the overburden off and throw it on rock slides away from here."

"You think it's that big?" Juan asked. "We may have the whole thing dug out this summer."

"What do you say, kid?" asked Ben. "How big is it?"

"I think we have a much bigger deposit than any we've had before. What we've seen shows that it's rich."

"We won't get it out in less than four years," Pierre stated. "I think we've found all we'll ever need."

"I'll dream with you, but if we're still working on it when the first snow falls, we'll all be richer than I've ever hoped for," said Lud. "We may not need to come back next year."

Juan added, "I'll come back until there isn't any more. If it's there, I'll keep digging. When we don't find anymore is soon enough to stop."

"What do you suppose the Utes'll think about our bringing a lot of people with us?" Lud wanted to know. "I think we've been treated mighty well, but we can't expect them to let us bring half of the folks in Santa Fe up here without making a fuss."

"Why would they care how many we have up here?" Ben asked. "They don't hunt or pasture horses this high. They shouldn't care how many people are up here for three months."

Lud said, "They usually won't let anyone mess around in their country."

"We're making a lot of assumptions, aren't we?" asked Juan.

Pierre said, "That pretty much covers it, doesn't it?"

That put an end to the speculation. We were all bedded down within a matter of minutes. I didn't go right to sleep and doubt if anyone else did. I had a good talk with the Lord, then let my thoughts wander to Molly. I wanted to ride down and tell her what we had found.

CHAPTER NINETEEN

Our partners had learned more about our mine. The width was over twelve feet. The height didn't change. The quartz continued to break easily. They had excavated four feet by evening. The rock around the ore was solid, so we wouldn't need many timbers. Safety wouldn't be a problem if that continued.

Only two men could work at the face, so one man could break up the ore. He wasn't able to keep up, so there was quite a pile when we got there. We were able to break up all that was mined before we quit for the day. We estimated we had fifteen pounds of gold.

Pierre said, "If we do this for even a month, none of us'll need to worry about money as long as we live. None of us will wonder if we need a dowser now. There's no way we'd have found this without Carlos."

Ben said, "We knew that last fall, but this beats anything I ever dreamed of."

Lud said, "Don't brag too much, or he'll be trying to get an extra share. No, I'll be the first to say he's earned his keep. If we can keep him away from Molly, he may be worth keeping."

Juan said, "If he gets Molly, he'll get more out of this than any of us does."

"He's got her already if he can get past that brave," Lud commented. "That Ute'll do everything he can to keep her for himself."

"Maybe we can make a man out of him this summer. I figure we can give him all the hard jobs. That should get him ready to fight that red Indian," said Ben.

I said. "It's gettin' deep here."

And so ended the first day at our new mine. The moon was barely up when we went to our bedrolls. We labored without a break for the next thirty-five days. The weather was nice most of the time, broken by only three rains, when the sky became a display of the power of God. Lightning filled the air followed by thunderclaps louder than dynamite. The smell was so pungent it crowded out the scent of the pines. At times the electricity caused every hair to stand straight out from our bodies. Even the horses and mules looked like porcupines ready for battle. At those times we retreated into the mine but stayed close to the entrance so we could watch the display. It was magnificent. We were awestruck. Each storm left the world fresher than I thought possible.

After each storm, we were quiet around the table. I knew how fortunate we were to watch such a demonstration of God's might. My time with God was always richer after each storm.

The mine continued to amaze us. We kept a record of each day's production and our total came to six hundred pounds of gold on the thirty-fifth day.

We had decided to celebrate with another feast when we reached that amount of production. It was easy to find a young bull elk not far from camp. Pierre baked an apple pie again and made a batch of biscuits. We had a supply of honey, which converted them into a delicacy.

Ben said, "A pound of gold is what the average man earns in a year. We each have about one hundred twenty years of wealth in our cache here in addition to what we have in Santa Fe. We've earned a rest. I'm going down to those hot springs and take a bath."

"I'll join you, then I'll head for that Ute camp. I can hardly wait to see Molly," I said.

"I'll join you," said Lud. "Somebody needs to keep that brave off your back. You'll not see anything but that gal. Not that I blame you. But we still need you."

"I'll be glad to have you along."

Juan said, "You'd better find a way to shave, too. You've grown up some the past few weeks."

Lud said, "He won't have any trouble shaving. He keeps that knife sharp enough to shave with—even with no water. We'd better trim his mane or she'll think he's that stallion. We don't want her to put a saddle on him."

Ben added, "You're some taller, too. You got any clothes that'll fit you?"

"Yes. Grandma said this would happen, so she sent some clothes that were too big for me."

"You reckon you can get your stallion back?" asked Pierre. "Molly may feel he's hers."

"She likes him," I said. "This is a good time to see if she wants to be spoiled."

Ben said, "You need to feel your way along and then let Grandma teach you."

"Grandma'll probably teach her more than she does me," I answered.

CHAPTER TWENTY

It was another bright day when Lud and I rode to the Ute camp. We shot a four-pointer and took him along for them. The kids and dogs welcomed us and led the way to Smart Coyote's tipi.

Molly was the first one to come out, and she was a sight to behold. She had such natural beauty and grace of movement that no adornment was needed. I wouldn't have noticed, anyway. I was given a smile that almost stopped my heart as she rushed into my arms.

"Carlos! I wasn't expecting you."

We spent a couple of hours swapping tales with Smart Coyote, Fawn Heart, and Molly. The sun was on its downward slide before I was able to get Molly away so we could talk.

"You're taller. We were almost the same height. Now I have to look up at you."

"You're taller, too, and you've grown in other ways. The clothes I wore last spring don't fit anymore. I'll bet you grew out of yours as well."

"Yes, that's true. I like the way you've changed."

"Your changes look good to me. I'm looking forward to our being together. I'll get to watch you become more beautiful. You need to be prepared for Grandma to make some changes."

"Will she make you change?"

"I won't guess what she'll do."

"I'm sort of scared. I may not be able to do all the things she wants."

"Don't worry. She's the kindest person I've ever known. Where's Raton? Has he finished with the mares?"

"Yes. Smart Coyote thinks every mare's carrying a foal. He's really excited about having a pasture full of babies next spring. They'll have the best horse herd in this region. He says that within a few years, we'll have a horse for every member of the tribe."

"I'm glad. That may be the reason he's willing to let you to go with me."

"I'm sure that helped, but he likes you well enough that he might have accepted any offer you made."

"I don't care what his reasons were. He agreed to let you go."

"Dark Dog knows about it, and is angry. Have you decided how to handle him?"

"I'm confident the Lord'll take care of it. Jesus said in the Book of Matthew that we're to seek first the Kingdom of God and his righteousness, and he'll provide the things we need. I'm sure that includes what we need to deal with Dark Dog."

"Did God tell you he'll take care of it?"

"No, but he's given me great confidence in him. You should see the mine he's given us. It's so rich we'll never need to worry about needing money. My portion of what we have is enough to hire more than one hundred men for a year. It's more than any of us ever imagined we'd find." I told her about the difficulty finding the mine and how rich it is.

"Is there a large block of it, or do you have to work in a small hole?"

"The hole's ten feet high and twelve feet wide. It's convinced all the men that God's real. They've all accepted Christ. I'll teach a lot this winter. There's almost no spare time while we're working, but we had a bunch of loafing time last winter. I expect that we will this year, too, so I'll have plenty of time to teach."

"Do you think I can be in that class? You said you'd teach me."

"I might be selfish and teach you alone. I'll want to spend as much time as possible with you. We'll need to see how it works to have you and the men in the same class. You might distract them so they don't learn as well as if they study alone. I'd love to have you there, but we'll need to do what works best."

"I want to learn everything you can teach me. I want to reach the point that I know God as well as you do."

"I can't do that for you, but he can. When Paul went to Ephesus, he taught some ladies who were meeting for prayer down by a river. Lydia was among them, and the Bible says that God opened her understanding so she could believe. He'll do that for anyone who honestly seeks him. He tells us to draw near to him, and he'll draw near to us, indicating that he'll let anyone have a close relationship with him."

She sighed and said, "I want that. I hope you never stop telling me about him. It's so exciting to think that God wants me to know him."

"He does for sure. We'll never be able to really comprehend how much he loves us, and it's all in Jesus."

"I talk to him every day, and it gets easier to think that he hears."

"We'll do a lot of practicing together this winter, and you'll see how he works. I do a lot of listening, too."

"Did you bring any gold with you?"

"Yes, I wanted to show you some of it. It's in my saddle bag."

We walked to where my tack was, and I took out a small bag of gold. "Hold your hand so I can pour some of this into it."

She did, and as the chunks and nuggets went into her palm, she said, "Oh, Carlos, it's beautiful! Did you polish it?"

"That's the way it is when we get it."

"I've never seen this much and certainly not any as pretty as this."

"Do you want to keep it?"

"The whole bag?"

"Sure."

"I'd love to keep it. Won't it be missed?"

"That's a tiny bit out of a huge store of gold. Nobody's going to complain if you have it."

"How much is this—how many ounces?"

"Probably five ounces."

"How much is your share of what you've mined?"

"About one hundred twenty pounds. We took about forty pounds down lower. We've really done well."

"I know almost nothing about gold. Is one hundred twenty pounds a lot?"

"Most men make no more each year than what a pound of gold's worth."

Molly's mouth flew open, and she said, "You mean you've already mined more than it would take most people one hundred twenty years to earn?"

"Yes."

"How much did you get last year?"

"Not more than half as much."

"Do you think you'll get much more this year?"

"We're getting fifty pounds each week. We'll need to leave as soon as it starts snowing. If the snow doesn't come too early, we'll get another two hundred or three hundred pounds."

"Do you have any idea how much more there is?"

"We can only guess. If it continues the way it's been, I'll not need more than what we can get this year and next year. Then we can go try to find your mother."

"Do you really think we can do it?"

"I think the Lord will help us find her and get her free. I plan to see if Smart Coyote will make us a map, or he might even send someone with us who was there when you were captured."

"Wouldn't it be wonderful if he'd go?"

"Do you think he might consider doing that?"

"Can God help in that?"

"He can if he chooses to."

"Let's both pray. If we do everything right we'll succeed. If he's the person who suggests helping, it'll be even better than if we try to persuade him,"

"You've already received wisdom, haven't you?"

"Is that the way it works?"

"Sometimes it's that simple."

CHAPTER TWENTY-ONE

The ride back up that mountain seemed to last forever. It must have been obvious because when Lud tried to talk to me, he ended by saying, "I guess I'd better wait until you get used to being away from Molly. You're sure not enjoying my company. Well, it won't be long before we get snowed out and the two of you can ride together. I can't say I know how you feel because I never knew a girl like her. Maybe I'm the lucky one."

I didn't bother to answer; I was that much down in the dumps. We rode along, and the sky got darker with clouds, which fit my mood just fine. When the wind came up and it smelled like rain I looked at Lud and saw that he had already put on his slicker, so I hurriedly got mine from behind my saddle to get ready for a storm.

The wind caught that slicker and blew it over my head so it was flapping and whipping above Raton's ears. It may have been the first time he had ever seen anything like that, or it may have been that the impending storm gave him an extra measure of meanness. Whatever it was, he broke in two under me. I was entangled in the slicker and was totally unprepared for his action. Just at that moment a bolt of lightning struck a tree not more than twenty feet from us.

I must depend on Lud's description of what followed. It must have been instinct because I had no experience or training to draw on, but somehow I managed to stay in the saddle and get the slicker down around my body and controlled. That apparently took away the reason for bucking and we settled into a gallop into camp.

"That saddle must have glue on the seat," Lud said, laughing. "I've never seen anybody stick that tight on a horse bucking that hard. I was guessing whether the slicker'd come off first, or you'd come loose and hit the ground. I have no idea how you managed to keep everything together and get that horse settled down."

"Neither do I. I didn't know which way was up. Maybe he just isn't very good at bucking."

"He was doing a first rate job of bucking. I'd say you had somebody holding you in place. You didn't even grab leather."

"I had my hands full with that slicker trying to sail me off the mountain."

"It looked like you were flying. You wouldn't have been hurt if he had bucked you off. I think you'd have just floated to the ground."

"Somebody got here first. Maybe they have something cooked."

"Now I know how to get you in a good mood. Just put you on a bronc, let him try to get rid of you, and it changes things completely."

"Maybe you could just *threaten* to do that and I'll change."

"I'd like to see if you could do that again. I may not wait until you get grumpy to try it."

The storm continued until we had our horses picketed and the gear under cover. It ended just as we entered the cook tent.

Pierre looked up from where he was cooking and said, "Don't you bring a bunch of mud or water in here. We've got everything clean, so don't mess it up."

Lud said, "Good day to you, too, friend. I'm glad you're happy. We brought a buck, but maybe we'll put his hide back on and send him home to his wife."

"We'd like to keep him," Ben said. "The weather's sort of got on top of Pierre. How was your visit?"

"The kid had a great time. I didn't see much of him or Molly, but he was happy as a lark all the time we were there. I got to watch some kids and dogs play. When did you get here?"

"This afternoon. We just finished getting things put away maybe an hour ago."

"I guess we're ready to get back to mining, then. What's for supper, Pierre?"

"We got some grouse on the way back and found a bunch of berries, so we've got a pie, some biscuits and the birds."

CHAPTER TWENTY-TWO

The next two weeks were days of mining from dawn to dark with no change in the ore. On the fourteenth day, things showed a difference, and by the seventeenth, the change was complete. The rock containing the gold was then much more typical, the gold less concentrated and more difficult to separate from the rock. It required us to drill and use dynamite, and the ore-bearing rock narrowed and shortened. On the twentieth day, the vein split into three sections. Although the ore was still very rich, it was much more difficult to mine. We were no longer able to extract the gold by easily crushing the ore-bearing rock. We awoke the twenty-second day to a light snowfall.

"We need to get down off this mountain," Lud said. "If we don't, we may spend the winter here. The kid and I'll close the mine while the rest of you get things packed. We need to be gone by noon."

We had prepared a frame that fit rather tightly inside the mine entrance, along with logs to complete a tight door that would hold substantial weight. Since the entrance was at the base of a slope, all we had to do was loosen rocks above it and let them accumulate and cover the door. The mine was thereby sealed and hidden. Our care in removing all traces of activity paid dividends.

"Get your stuff packed while I get that black mule," Lud said. "You've got to go almost twice as far as we do to get to those hot springs. Neither of us'll make it there today, but we'll plan to meet you tomorrow. We'll stay there tomorrow night and go on the next day. I hope you don't have to tackle that ornery brave, but if you do, you're on your own."

"He wasn't in camp the last two times we were there. Maybe he's left the tribe. I think I'm ready for him if he's there. The Lord'll show me what to do."

"At times I wish you didn't have such faith. On the other hand, I wish I did."

"I'll have quite a while to talk with him as we go down there. He'll let me know exactly what to do, and then he'll take care of it. He's never failed yet. Remember how he gave me back my sight just like he said he would. Look at the mine he gave us. We have every reason to trust him."

"I need more practice. Maybe I'll get to the point of believing like you do. In the meantime I'll worry about you."

"Why worry when you can pray?"

"I've had more practice worrying."

"I'd rather you prayed."

"All right, I'll do it. You be careful and avoid a fight if you can."

That mule and I knew each other well by then, so he didn't fight much, although he let me know he'd rather be with the rest of the mules than with me. After half a mile he quit fussing and we made good time. My gear was a light load, and there was little to distract him. Raton kept the lead rope tight, which allowed him little time for pranks. After a couple of miles he was giving all of his attention to keeping up, and we had no more trouble.

The Utes had seen the snow, so Molly was packed and ready to go when I arrived. It was late afternoon, so we wouldn't leave until morning. There was a dance that night with Star Gazer providing the most significant part. The purpose was to have Star Gazer put good medicine on Molly and me.

We rose early the next morning, added her stuff to what was on the mule, saddled her pinto, and went to say her farewells. There was quite a crowd who came to give her a good sendoff, so it took almost half an hour to give everyone a turn. Smart Coyote said, "I'll ride with you. I want to be alone with Dawn on the Mountain when we say good-bye."

His horse was standing ready, so we all mounted and left. I watched for Dark Dog and spotted him as we were riding past the outer tipis. He was in the brush at the edge of the horse pasture close to camp. I had just a glimpse of him slinking along with a bow almost as though he was stalking an animal.

The chief rode with us at least half way to the hot springs. He stopped three times to examine something off the trail. Each time he managed to return in a way that would allow him to see the trail we had just traveled. He was making sure we weren't followed.

It must've been somewhat awkward for him to talk to me with Molly interpreting, but he didn't hesitate.

He said, "You're taking from me the only person other than Fawn Heart who has kept my heart. She's as precious to me as my sons. If I had a daughter, she'd not be any more mine than Dawn on the Mountain is. I've agreed to let her to go with you because you're the person she's chosen. I trust you to care for her as you would your mother. You hold her happiness in your hand. Care for her well."

I was deeply moved by the emotion, a thing seldom seen in an Indian. I asked for the perfect words for the occasion and received these: "You've extended the hand of friendship in a way that I could never expect. I thank you. I'll place her under my canopy of love. I'm taking part of your heart with me. As my God is able, I'll not fail you or her."

"You'll be a great chief among your people. I'm glad she'll be with you. Your sons will walk beside you and make your way smooth. Your home will be warm and filled with laughter and joy. I bless you. Go in happiness."

He turned his horse, and with a yell that echoed again and again, he raced back the way we had come.

Molly watched him until there was nothing but a wisp of dust to show he had passed. Her eyes were leaking tears when she looked at me.

"He's like a father to me,"

"He *is* your foster father."

"He rarely shares his feelings like that. You were given the gift of his friendship as well as his trust. I really can't tell you what that meant to him. He's a wonderful judge of a person's character, and I've never seen him like he was now."

"What a blessing to have him for a friend. I wonder if he realizes how he's honored me."

"I doubt that he considers it that way. I thought I knew him completely, but this is something entirely new," she stated with tears streaming from her eyes. "You see, he was telling me how much he cares for me, too."

I dismounted, helped her from the saddle and took her in my arms. "Does it make you sad?"

"No. These are tears of joy and wonder. I love him. He gave me a wonderful gift by allowing me to be involved in his conversation with you. Normally the woman wouldn't know what was said by the men. It was a special privilege for me to be here and listen."

"We'll discuss this at length, but we need to do it as we ride. We have a long way to go before evening," I hugged her and helped her back into her saddle.

We rode quietly for several miles. I was considering all that had been involved in the exchange with Smart Coyote.

"Where would Smart Coyote have usually had that conversation with me?"

"I think it would've taken place in his tipi with at least Star Gazer present. I've been thinking about that and feel there must've been a reason for doing it out here away from his home. Why do you ask?"

"There was some reason for it. I wonder if he was protecting me from Dark Dog."

"Yes, his riding with us would prevent an attack. No one would bother us while he was with us. You've probably figured it out." We were quiet again for quite a while, and then she added, "That makes the whole morning more unusual. He was informing the whole tribe that he had made you a member of his family."

"What a special man he is. We need to somehow let him know we realize what he did and that we appreciate it."

"We must be very careful about that. He is sensitive about showing any emotion. If we make him think he made his intention obvious, he'll consider that he's done a dishonorable thing. It was exactly opposite, and that's the way he wanted it, but a careless act on our part could easily spoil it for him. I'm glad we'll have all winter to decide how to let him know we understand and appreciate what he did. It was a very, *very* special act."

"We'll pray about it often, and not do or say anything until you're absolutely certain it's proper. He not only did something outstanding but placed considerable responsibility on us to handle it correctly."

When we arrived at the hot springs the others had things ready for the night. Pierre was broiling a mess of fish and grouse.

"Where is everyone?" I asked.

"They went swimming. They called it 'taking a bath,' but if you stroll downstream a ways, you'll see them having a great time. If you want to clean up, you can join them, but I don't think they'd like it if Molly's with you."

"We'll wait until they come back."

We left at sunrise the next morning. We were at the southern end of a long park with a grove of aspen closing in on both sides. I was watching the grove on the right, hoping to see a deer or elk that would give me a decent opportunity to add to our supply of meat.

I saw a gleam of sunlight on metal followed by a flash. I recognized it as a gunshot and fell off my horse, falling to my left, away from the flash. I heard the gunshot while I was falling and was able to see the black powder floating up from the place the flash had been. I can't take any credit for my actions. I was immediately surrounded by the others of our party. I stayed where I had landed beside my horse.

"I'm fine. I saw the gun and fell off before the shot. Let's make it appear that I was shot so the shooter will leave. Let's make sure he's gone."

Juan was quick to gallop toward the place from which the shot had come. While he was gone we discussed what to do next.

Lud said, "Let's put you across the saddle and tie you so it looks like you're dead. We'll be out of sight in about a mile. Then you can get loose and quit pretending."

"That's a good idea. If he thinks he killed him he won't follow and try again," said Ben.

Everyone but Molly liked the idea. She finally agreed, so that's what we did. It was difficult to stay completely relaxed and let them do all the work, but we were underway soon. It took fifteen minutes to get over a hill, and I was able to get back in the saddle and ride normally.

"Do you think it was Dark Dog?" Molly wondered.

"I don't know of anybody else who'd want to shoot me. Since Smart Coyote prevented any action yesterday, he must've watched until he had a good close shot at me. The Lord took care of me again, and then he gave Lud the idea of making him think he killed me."

"Was he sure enough leaving the country, Juan?" Pierre asked.

"He was in a hurry to get out of here, and I figure he thinks he did what he wanted and we won't see him again. He wasn't going to let any of us close to him," was the response.

"Let's get on down the trail, then," Lud suggested.

CHAPTER TWENTY-THREE

The animals seemed to understand that we were going home, so we traveled more miles than usual each of the following days. We reached Santa Fe before noon the third day, and I was able to introduce Molly to Grandma by the middle of the afternoon. The clothes she had worn looked fine to me, but she wouldn't wear them for the meeting. She had packed a truly beautiful dress made of buckskin dyed a bright yellow with a wonderful example of bead work covering much of the area above the waist. She had woven some feathers into the braids of her hair and wore a pair of white moccasins. The dress was circled by a belt of elk hide with six bear claws on each side. Her head was uncovered, but she wore a beaded band around it, which covered almost half of her forehead.

"You don't need anything to make you beautiful," I said. "But dressed like that, you'll convince everyone you're a princess."

"Do you think Grandma will like it?"

"She'll *love* it. You chose *exactly* the things she'll adore. Nothing would please her more."

"Is there anything I should change?"

"Absolutely not. It's perfect."

"I'm scared."

"It's perfect. Trust me. Grandma's probably expecting someone in rags with her hair dirty and tangled. You could easily meet a king in his court looking the way you do."

"You look nice, too."

"These clothes fit perfectly. I had never worn them since you made them. Nobody'll notice me while I'm with you, but I feel really dressed up."

"You look like a chief ready for a big powwow."

"Thanks. I had to dress up some so I wouldn't embarrass you."

"I can't ride in the usual way in this dress."

"I have a saddle that you can use, and you'll ride Raton."

I had a sidesaddle, and it was fancy enough for her. It took her about a minute to understand the proper posture and get used to the differences from an ordinary saddle. When we had ridden a hundred yards, she was completely comfortable in the rig, and when we arrived at our house, she looked like she had used that saddle for years. Being mounted on that *grullo* stallion added to the appearance of royalty.

Everyone who saw us stopped and watched as long as we were in sight. She had used some Indian paint to accent her eyes and cheeks and put some red berry juice on her lips. When we were fairly close to our house, I paid a boy to run and tell Grandma that she had some company coming.

We rode through the front gate and up toward the house. Raton was home, and he knew it, which put a special prance in his step and a deeper bow in his neck. Molly sat a little taller, her head high and shoulders back. I had watched them for three miles, but the difference was so dramatic that I dropped back so I could see them better. They were an impressive pair.

The youngster I had sent ahead was standing at the front door with Grandma, and they both stood as though entranced and watched as we approached. Their full attention was on Molly and that stallion.

Grandma finally moved. She wore a very ordinary dress with nothing special about her hair, but she looked as much like the mistress of a royal house as she would have in the full costume of a queen. Molly's bearing brought an automatic response. They reflected each other. I was amazed and elated by what I saw. They connected immediately, and each obviously saw in the other a person with whom they could relate. It was a truly magic moment for me.

Grandma met Molly at the edge of the porch, reached up, and said, "You'll be Molly. I'm glad to have you come to our home. Please come inside so we can get acquainted. Carlos will care for your horse."

I was finally able to move and hurried to assist Molly to dismount. I took the animals and put them in the barn before I joined the ladies inside. I found them in the parlor, each with a cup of tea in hand, as friendly as two long-lost sisters. Any concerns I had about them getting along were dispelled with one look. Molly was sipping her tea, completely at ease, with not a sign of the fear she had expressed earlier. Grandma left no doubt that she was already captivated by Molly. I went to see if there was a cup of coffee in the kitchen, thanking the Lord for creating a miraculous connection between the two women. When I had my coffee, I returned to the parlor.

"Your Molly's lovely, Carlos. Your description lacked a lot."

"I knew that I could never tell you what she's like. She's changed tremendously since I saw her last year. In fact, she's become more lovely as we approached Santa Fe."

Molly said, "I felt that I had to do this for our first meeting. Carlos has told me so much about you and how wonderful you are. I couldn't come in ordinary clothing to meet such a special person. This is the first time I've worn these clothes and will seldom wear them again."

"And Carlos put you on that fancy stallion to give you that advantage. I must say, I *am* impressed."

"I hope I didn't offend you by doing too much. Honestly, I was afraid I'd seem like a plain Indian girl."

"You'd never be mistaken for a plain *anybody*. I'm honored that you wanted to impress me. It'll be four or five hours before

Grandpa comes home, but I'd like for him to see you the way you are now. Are those clothes uncomfortable?"

"Not at all. I'm enjoying wearing them."

"Good. I suppose there's no way we can arrange for him to see you the way I did. I must say, you were the most striking thing I've ever seen. I'll remember that as long as I live. I'd *really* like to have Grandpa see you like that."

I said, "We can leave shortly before you think he'll be here. Then we can come back so he can see her like you did."

"That'd be a lot of trouble, but it'd be worth it," Grandma stated.

Molly said, "We'll be happy to do anything you want us to. I want to make a good impression on him, too. Riding Raton is so pleasant that I'll do that every time I have the opportunity. Carlos let me keep him for almost two months, and it spoiled me for any other horse."

We sat and talked an hour. The conversation lagged, and Grandma said, "Tell me about being a prisoner in a Ute camp."

"It's the only life I recall clearly. Mother and I were taken by the Sioux when I was three. I don't remember much before that. I was seven when the Utes took me from the Sioux. Smart Coyote, the Ute chief, has kept me in his tipi and treated me like a daughter. I knew I was a prisoner but was never treated poorly by him or Fawn Heart, his squaw. The other Indians knew I was under his protection, so I was never mistreated. Carlos wants to free Mother and bring her to be with me. We're praying for that."

"You've had a horrible life. It must've been awful. How'd you cope with it?"

"The Indians all treat children well, so in both tribes I did well. Most girls marry before they are fifteen years old, so I was concerned as I got close to that age. Carlos tried to buy me this year, but the chief said that I couldn't leave the tribe. Carlos gave the horses and pots to the chief as a gift. Three weeks later, the Chief agreed to let me come with Carlos. He had seen how sad I was when he refused earlier. He's a father to me."

"He certainly not a crude person. I know of few men who would've been that concerned about you."

"I hope you can meet him and Fawn Heart. They're good parents. He's a powerful man."

"Can you tell me about your mother?"

"She's like Carlos. She has a close relationship with Jesus and is able to do things that no one else would try. I haven't seen her for almost six years, but she taught me that Jesus will provide what I need. Carlos has shown me much more. We plan to study the Bible this winter."

We talked the afternoon away then left to wait until Grandpa was home. We rode to a high spot half a mile away, where we could watch the way he'd follow as he went home.

"Grandma's everything you told me she is," Molly said as we rode away from the house. "She makes me feel as though she's truly glad that I'll be living with her."

"That's exactly the way she feels. You'll learn that she's seldom careful about the feelings of those she's with. She's not afraid to let you know if she isn't pleased. You won her heart immediately, and after you were together a couple of hours, she was convinced you're the greatest person she's ever met."

"I think it's wonderful that she wants me to make a good impression on Grandpa, too. I've never known anyone who cared that much about how another person responded to me. *That* isn't true, is it? You did a lot to make sure that I'd look all right to them."

"It's important to me that they like you. You'll live with them for quite a while, and if they don't like you, things'll be unpleasant."

"It appears that we don't need to worry, but we still need to win Grandpa's heart."

"He'll be won the moment he sees you. After he's been with you ten minutes, you'll have him hooked completely. He's fairly old, but he's still mightily impressed by a pretty lady, especially when she'll sit and talk with him for a while and seem to enjoy his company."

"Do you mean I should expect to not enjoy sitting and talking with him? And that if that *is* true, I should act like I do anyway?"

"You just act natural, and he'll like you, no acting required."

"I guess I'll believe you. Grandma was at least as nice as you said she is."

"We won't have long to wait. There's Grandpa down there. We'll wait another ten minutes and follow him. Just relax. You'll do fine. By the time we sit down to eat, you'll know you're welcome."

Grandpa was properly impressed, and by the time the three of them were inside the house, he had fallen in love with Molly. When I got the horses put away and joined them, they were all in the parlor, and Molly was telling them about the Ute camp and what it was like to be a prisoner. We had an enjoyable evening, and by bedtime there was no doubt in any of our minds that we were going to fit together beautifully.

"How was the mining this year, Carlos?" Grandpa asked.

I told him about the summer and the mines we had found. He was as impressed as I was with our success.

"We need to find at least fifty men to help us mine since the material changed so much."

"You won't have any trouble finding fifty men who'd be willing to go with you for the right wages, but there aren't any experienced miners in Santa Fe."

"Ben says he can teach them what they need to do, but we aren't sure how we should go about hiring them. We need to be careful to not let anyone know about the mine."

"You have all winter to work out the details," Grandma said. "I'm sure Juan will have friends who can help find the men you'll need."

"Pierre and Lud both have friends here, too, so we should know fairly soon if we need to look for men somewhere else."

Grandpa said, "I want to see that saddle you had made for Molly. Can we go look at it now?"

He had helped me design it and knew more about that saddle than I did, so it was obvious that he just wanted to get alone with me, so I agreed.

"That little gal's really special, Carlos," he said as we walked to the barn. "I never dreamed a girl who'd been a prisoner in a Ute camp would be so mannerly and able to carry a conversation as well as she does. She could have spent the last ten years in a fine home and not be much different."

"She's a really bright person. I know she speaks at least four languages and learned most of them with no instruction. She made her clothing and the things I'm wearing. She acts like a lady as well as anyone I've ever known. I want to teach her to read, write, and do mathematics. The main reason is to make it possible for her to read the Bible, but it'll help in many other ways, as well."

"What kind of relationship do the two of you have?"

"We've spent maybe five or six hours alone together, not counting the time we rode to meet the other partners. That isn't much time to find out what relationship we have. She's made a couple of comments that indicate she thinks I own her because I made a deal with Smart Coyote so he'd let her come with me. As far as I'm concerned, I bought her freedom. She may understand it differently. I need to talk with her about that. I guess I'm probably in love with her and more than likely will want to marry her. We've not had a chance to discuss any of that. I want to try to get her mother from the Sioux first, anyway. I mentioned that once, and she's really become excited about that possibility. I'm sure she won't want to make any major decisions until we do that."

"When are you going to have time for something like that? You can't do it in the winter, and you'll be busy mining the rest of the year."

"I don't plan to continue mining more than a couple more years if we continue to do as well as we did this year. I don't want to be away from home that much. Also, why would I want more than I should have by then? So we could go look for her mother maybe two years from next spring."

"Is she willing to wait that long?"

"Yes. She had never considered the possibility of seeing her mother again until I mentioned it, so she says she'll not fret about the wait."

"I'm going to need to retire from the army soon. I can't stay in there, knowing that you're committing a crime as far as the king is concerned. My duty would be to report what I know, and I'm not willing to do that."

"I have enough already, so you won't have any financial problems. You can retire as soon as you think it's appropriate."

"I'm not worried about that. We've saved quite a large amount. I'll work with your uncle, building houses, so we'll be fine," he assured me. "I just wanted you to be aware of what'll be happening."

"I want to build us a nice place, so I'll need to make arrangements for that. What I have in mind may keep you busy quite a while."

"You shouldn't plan to ask your uncle for any special pricing. He needs to make a profit on his work."

"I'll want him to at least do as well as he would with anyone else."

"Good. There'll be no problem then. We'll need to make those arrangements before you leave next year."

"Do you really want to see the saddle?"

"No. I wanted to talk with you privately. We can go back now."

We returned to the house and found that the ladies were cleaning up the kitchen and getting things ready so we could retire for the night.

Grandma said, "Carlos, please take Molly and her things to the room next to yours. That's where she'll be staying. I'm tired, and so is Grandpa. We'll say good night and leave you now."

Both Molly and I said, "Good night."

I picked up her bundle and said, "If you'll carry that candle, I'll show you where she wants you to sleep."

When we were in her room and I had helped her put some things away, I showed her where things were kept.

She said, "I'm delighted with your grandparents. They're even nicer than you said. I hope I can make them glad to have me live with them. I want to thank you for bringing me here. But I'm still scared that I'll do something that they'll not like. I've never lived in a home like this or with people like they are."

"Let's pray about it, then," I said.

"All right. Will you hold my hand while we pray? I don't want to feel alone right now."

"Of course. In fact, come here and face me. I'll hold both your hands."

She seemed to like that idea, and we were soon standing facing each other.

I said, "Lord, you've given us a really good day. Grandma and Grandpa have made it clear that they already love Molly, and she's learning to love them. We now need your wisdom so that nothing will cause even a tiny problem. I pray that you'll give Molly your peace so she can sleep really well tonight. Take her fright and concern away and replace it with your assurance that you're in control and will guide all of us so we'll not only be pleasing to you, but also pleasing to each other. We know that you're able to do that and even want it more than we do, so we thank you in advance for doing it. We ask this in the name of Jesus. Amen."

She looked up into my eyes, a beautiful smile on her lips, and said, "Thank you. I believe God will answer that."

"He'll do more than that. He loves you."

She took her right hand from mine and reached up behind my head, pulling it toward her. I had no resistance to that but took her in my arms and kissed her. It was a new experience, but the results were completely satisfactory to me.

It was a very brief kiss. I said, "I'm sorry if you didn't want that, but I couldn't resist the opportunity. Please forgive me if I offended you."

"Oh, Carlos, I wanted you to kiss me. In fact, I initiated it."

"I know, but only because I was scared to try."

"I liked it."

"So did I. Shall we try again?"

Her answer was to draw my head down again with her hand caressing my neck. I drew her close, and we kissed. It was the most exciting experience of my life. I was finally able to pull away.

"I'd better leave. We need to talk about this tomorrow. I love you, Molly."

"Oh, Carlos, I love you," she whispered.

"Good night. Please have sweet dreams."

"I know I will."

I've never done anything more difficult than walking out of that room. I knew at that moment that my life would never be the same and that Molly was the person who could make me complete. I also knew that I'd have to resist embracing and kissing her. That would have to wait a couple more years. It brought a time of delight in remembering as well as a period of prayer about how to keep from doing the wrong things. We had declared our love and had demonstrated the attraction for each other. Now we must keep it pure in God's eyes.

The next morning we had an early breakfast, and Grandpa prepared to go to the army post. I said, "I'll ride along with you and go talk with the other men. We need to make some definite plans about several things. I'll be back before evening."

We saddled up and rode toward the army post. I told Grandpa about the development with Molly.

Grandpa said, "She's a right pretty girl, Carlos, and you're both healthy, normal kids. You do need to set some definite boundaries for what you do. If you just let things happen naturally, you'll do things you'll regret because you'll be sinning."

"What can we do?"

"I'd say you're more than likely going to kiss each other, but when you do, don't hug each other. Now, that's not near the fun it would be otherwise, but it's fairly safe. We can talk about other things as we go along, but that's a start. I'm glad you're concerned about it. Most young fellows would be trying to figure a way to go as far as they could, and that's not good."

"I want what's best for Molly, and if we don't make some good plans, I'll hurt her."

"You keep that thought on the top of your mind, and you're apt to come out all right. If I can help any time, you call on me. I'm not the greatest fellow at giving good advice, but I'll try to steer you in the right direction."

"Thanks, Grandpa. You've helped already. I'll try to keep you aware of how we're doing."

"If you'll be honest with God, yourself, Molly, and me, you'll do fine. Just keep on track and trust God," he said. "Well, here we are, so I'll leave you now. See you this evening."

"All right. Thanks again."

I rode on to the facilities we had leased. The men were sitting around the table, coffee cups in their hands.

"How'd it go, kid?" asked Lud. "Did your gal get chewed up pretty bad?"

"No, and she didn't chew anybody up, either. She and my grandparents hit it off really well. With her in that dress, up on Raton, she sort of knocked their eyes out, and they fell in love right off. She took to them like a baby calf to its momma. Things are off to a good start."

"I guess that's no surprise," said Pierre. "We know what they're all like, and that's the way it should have turned out. Are your folks well?"

"They're fine. Grandpa told me he's retiring from the army, so he won't feel guilty about knowing we have a mine. He's going to help my uncle build houses, and I plan to have them put up a place for me, which will keep them busy for a while."

"That's good," said Ben. "You'll need a place of your own, and you don't have to worry about the cost. In a couple more years, we can all quit working and loaf for fifty or sixty years."

"I can just see you sitting around town, getting fat and sassy," said Juan. "You'll be back out looking for another mine or hunting elk or fishing."

"I'll try lying around for a while, like maybe ten years, first."

Pierre said, "Two more good years, and I'll go back to France."

I said, "You lived in France and came over here?"

"Yes. I've been here twelve years and am getting homesick. I might even go if we have one more good year."

"I don't blame you for wanting to see your family. Do you have brothers and sisters?"

"I have one sister and two brothers and of course my parents and several aunts and uncles. They all have kids, so there are quite a few of us."

"How about a sweetheart?" asked Bud. "Is there someone waiting for you?"

"No. My family's poor, so I had almost no opportunity to meet any girls. Poor men often die without a wife."

"You'll not be a poor man when you return," said Juan. "You should have a woman in a short time."

"After meeting Molly, I'll be hard to please. There aren't many like her. Do you have any idea how lucky you are, Carlos?"

"I know better than anyone how *blessed* I am. It wasn't luck that brought us together. God's in charge of those things, and he chose to bless me. Nobody knows as well as I do how much he blessed me. I know it better today than I did yesterday morning. The best is yet to come. I'm going to marry her if she'll have me, and it looks to me like she will."

"If you marry her, you'll move up several notches," Lud exclaimed. "She'd make a king out of a beggar who couldn't put food on his table even if all he seemed good at was siring a string of brats."

"Carlos has already taken care of the food on the table. I don't know how he'll be about the other part," Pierre said. "I'd guess he'll do all right there, too."

"I don't know that I want to sire a bunch of brats. Molly ought to have nothing but kids who behave well. If they take after her, they'll be fine."

"If they take after you, the town had better start finding a place to hide," Lud added.

"You'll have to wait a few years to find out," I said. "I haven't even asked her to marry me yet, and she may not like the idea at all."

"Maybe you didn't see how she was when she thought you were shot the other day," Pierre said. "You'd have thought she was the one that brave had shot. She'll not turn you down."

"If I asked her today and she said yes, it would still be a long time before we married. I want to get her mother from the Sioux before we do anything about marriage."

"You *do* dream big, don't you?" Ben stated. "Getting a prisoner from the Sioux's about as easy as eating an elk in one meal—you'd better have lots of help."

"We won't try for at least a couple of years, so we may be able to figure out how to do it. Molly plans to see if Smart Coyote will give us some help. He knows a lot about the camp and could at least give us a map so we can find our way without a lot of trouble," I said. "She hopes he may even go along and help."

"That might make all the difference," Lud commented. "I'd like to go watch that fellow handle something like that. I'll bet he's something when he's in action."

"He might do it for Molly," I said. "When he talked to me as we were leaving last week, he made it clear that she's like a daughter to him. She can probably talk him into most anything."

"That's not going to happen for a while. Let's figure out what we need to do to be ready for next spring," Pierre interjected. "How many men are we going to need, and how many mules?"

Ben said, "I figure at least fifty men and a hundred burros. We can use burros instead of mules. They eat a lot less than mules. There are more of them available, too."

Pierre said, "I'd really like to have twice as many of each. If we have that many, we can find a place down lower where we can dig a storage cave. We can haul a bunch of ore down there and go back next winter to bring it down here after we can't get up to the mine. We're going to need to rig a place here in Santa Fe where we can finish working the gold. I don't think we can plan to do all of that up there. The ore we have now will need to be melted and made into bricks. The rock it's in's too hard to plan to break it up and wash the gold out."

Juan asked, "Where are we going to dig that storage area? Have you got a place picked out?"

"No, but we can go up earlier next spring and find a good spot. We can also leave a crew there to melt some of the gold. We can also do some of that at the mine. We've got a lot of ore to work, and there's no way we can do it without a lot of help. It's sort of like that elk dinner Ben was talking about—we need a lot of help."

Lud said, "I'll need some time to think about all of that, but we've got a couple of months before we need to start putting together a crew. I think the first thing we need to do is figure out how we're going to get the gold out of the ore we brought with us. Ben, you said you know how to do that. Can we do it here?"

"Yes. We'll need to make charcoal first. For that we need probably ten logs ten feet long and a foot in diameter, one hundred adobe bricks, a three-foot piece of small stove pipe, three or four feet of metal pipe at least an inch in diameter, and a brick with a spot dug out of a side that's three inches by eight inches and two inches deep. Charcoal is wood that's heated enough to burn, but it has to be in a place where it can't create a flame. That leaves a fuel that'll burn with no flame or smoke. We then need a place to heat the ore enough for the gold to melt and a way to transfer the melted gold into the mold to form the gold brick. We'll also need a hole in the ground about three feet square and two feet deep."

Lud asked, "If we get you all that stuff, can you build the contraption?"

"Yes. I'll need to decide where to put everything, but the rest's fairly simple."

"I'll get the bricks," I said.

Lud volunteered to get the logs, and Juan said he'd get the stove pipe and the one inch pipe.

Pierre said, "I guess that means I get to dig the hole. Where do you want it?"

"I don't know yet. I'll pick a spot after we have some lunch. We're moving awfully fast, considering that we have at least six months to do all this."

I said, "I guess we want to see your rig work. We'll need at least two more for next summer."

"Why two?" asked Juan.

"We'll want one at the mine and another at the lower storage spot."

"All right, I suppose we will."

Pierre asked, "Can we do all of this here at the barn?"

Ben said, "I think so, but I haven't looked for the exact spot. We can do that this afternoon. We need a place that's not visible, but it can't be in the barn. We may have to *make* the charcoal someplace else, because that'll require an open fire. We can burn the charcoal here, though."

Juan said, "It'll take a day or two to get all the things we need, so that'll give you some time to figure all of that out."

We eventually decided to make the charcoal in a valley north of town. It was situated so almost no one would see us, and a fire in that area wouldn't cause concern. The melting setup was installed in a shed in the corral closest to the barn, which was concealed from the view of anyone in town. The pasture kept people at a considerable distance in the other direction. It was ten days before we melted the first ore, and on the thirteenth day, Ben was satisfied with the entire arrangement. After that things moved smoothly, and it took only another eight days to melt all the gold from the ore we had brought with us. We were all pleased and confident that we could process a lot of ore the next year. We took an elk to my grandparents' home and celebrated the night following the last melt.

I took the meat over as soon as we completed the melt, which gave Grandma and Molly time to prepare the meal. It was typical of Grandma that she wanted to make a grand affair of the occasion.

She said, "You go back and tell those men to be prepared for a formal dinner. If they don't know what that means, tell them to come dressed as though they're visiting the king of Spain. I want to make this something we'll all remember."

I rode back quickly and warned the others. When they arrived, they were an impressive group. They had all shaved or trimmed their beards and hair. They each wore a buckskin suit complete with fringes and fancy belts. Their hats were either good beaver or leather. Ben had a necklace of elk teeth while Juan's was of bear claws. Pierre wore a headband of porcupine quills with a beautiful design depicting a coyote howling at the moon.

Grandma and Molly were each wearing a silk gown with turquoise belts and necklaces. Grandpa wore his fancy dress uniform and was as stiffly military as if he had been a general instead of a sergeant. I had nothing better than the outfit Molly had made for me that I wore the day I brought her to Santa Fe, but it was fine even for that dinner.

Grandpa knew how to host such a meal, and Grandma was truly a grand lady. Molly acted as though she had attended hundreds of such affairs. I admit to being biased, but the two of them were as beautiful as any pair of ladies you'll ever see. If it had been a royal dinner, the dress would've been different, and the dinner would've been served by a staff of servants supervised by a professional, but none of us wanted more than we had, and everyone enjoyed it more than we would have in a grander setting. It cemented the relationship between my family and my partners as well as placed Molly in the center of things.

The men didn't stay long after the meal, which allowed Molly and me to spend some time together.

"That was a lovely dinner, Carlos," she said. "Whose idea was it?"

"I think Lud was the first to mention it, but the rest of us started adding ideas until it grew into what we suggested to Grandma. I guess it was sort of a group scheme."

"I hope we can have more of them, although they wouldn't need to be as elaborate as this was. It was really fun to have a dress-up party. I like having the men at their best, all sort of slicked down and behaving tame. It caused all of us to be more mannerly and considerate of each other."

"Your dress was almost exactly the same as Grandma's. When did you make them?"

"Last week. Grandma's an excellent seamstress, and she showed me how to work with cloth instead of leather. It was easy."

"It was a work of art. Did you make both dresses?"

"We each made our own."

"They both looked perfect to me. I'm amazed that you were able to do so well in such a short time."

"It was easier than it would've been using leather. We didn't add any decoration, either. Grandma said that silk is almost never sewn with anything added. The material's rather delicate and any addition would tend to pull it out of its natural shape. The most difficult part was stitching it in a way that left everything smooth and even. Grandma had to show me several times before I was able to do that correctly."

"A beautiful lady ought not be so bright and capable. Your beauty would be enough to please anyone. You've shown over and again that you're also able to do things better than most other people. I'm sure that you'll continue to amaze me even when we're old and gray."

"You're accomplished at flattering me. I enjoy it but don't want to be given more credit than I deserve."

"I've never told you anything that isn't true. Please believe me. I'd love to try to impress you with flattery, but it isn't necessary. You can believe everything I've told you."

"I admit that I like having you tell me things like that. Coming from you makes it special. I want to please you."

"You could sit and smile at me, and it'd please me, without doing anything else."

"I'd love to do that, if you'd return the smile."

"I'd enjoy that more than you can imagine, but it would never be long before I'd need a kiss, and then things would get dangerous. You have no idea how those kisses the other night stirred me. I love you and want only what's good for you. We need to be careful to keep our love pure before God. I'm afraid that we can't do that if we kiss like that. You're a truly beautiful, desirable woman, and I'm a normal, healthy man. If we embrace and kiss the way we did, I'll respond in ways that're wonderful between a married couple. That's not pleasing to God if it's between a man and woman who aren't married. Our love is precious, and we mustn't let our emotions and physical needs cause us to step over that line. I hope you understand when I tell you that I'll not embrace you the way I did that night except on very rare occasions. I want to kiss you often but will try to do it in a decent manner. Do you understand?"

"Mother often talked with me about how she hated being with men, and it was because she knew what the Bible says about it. The Utes feel much the same. If a woman in the tribe is unfaithful to her husband, her nose is cut off. It leaves her looking horrible. A man can be exiled from the tribe or even killed.

"I'll try to do nothing that'll cause us problems. Have you thought of some way we can kiss without placing ourselves in a dangerous situation?"

"We need to act as though there's a fence between us. It's a fence that extends up to your shoulders, so we can hold hands and kiss without our bodies touching. We'll need to limit the number of kisses, too. I'm sure I won't be happy with that arrangement but would like to try it."

"It'll be better than nothing, won't it?"

"A kiss from you will always be wonderful. I'll take every one I can get."

"Well, let's see if we can make it better than you think it'll be."

We practiced for half an hour, and it was amazing how nice it was. I finally said, "I love you and could do this all night. We'll be well off if we stop for now."

"It's great to kiss you any way I can. I'll remember this night, darling."

"Sweetheart, you're not only beautiful and brilliant, you also know how to fill my heart. You'll never know how happy and blessed I am to have you as my lover."

"Yes I do. I feel the same way. I love you deeply, Carlos."

"I love you, Molly, darling. Good night. I'll have wonderful dreams."

"I look forward to tomorrow when I'll see you again. Good night, my love."

CHAPTER TWENTY-FOUR

We gathered at the barn the next day with the intent of planning the things we needed to do the rest of the winter.

I said, "It seems to me that we need to find a way to sell quite a bit of this gold. We surely can't use those bricks. We'll need to purchase lots of equipment and supplies. A crew of fifty'll need much more than we've had. Somebody at the Army base'll get suspicious if we spread a bunch of gold around. Does anybody have any ideas?"

Juan said, "We'll probably be able to buy the burros with gold, and the people we'll get them from'll be happy with that arrangement. We'll need to have money for the other things as well as to pay our crew. The only way I know to do that is to take the gold to St Louis, up east of here. That fellow who has the trading post down town is running a bunch of wagons up there and back on a regular basis. If we handle it right, one or two of us could go with his outfit and sell gold there. He should be able to tell us how to get the money in a form that's acceptable here. We could probably buy a lot of what we need there and pay him to haul it back for us. If he won't do that, we can get him to buy it and sell it to us. Either way, we'd get what we need in exchange for the gold. Do any of you know that man?"

Lud said, "I do. He's a good business man and deals in almost everything we'll need. The simple way to handle it may be to just order everything through him and give him gold for it. He can get rid of gold easily on the other end of his trail, and we can negotiate a decent price. We'll need what would be a sizable order, so he should be willing to give us a somewhat reduced price."

Pierre said, "I like that idea. It's something we could do every year. Otherwise we'll be getting involved in things we know nothing about."

Ben asked, "Will he accept gold for his stuff and not report it to anyone?"

"I'll talk with him about that. He's undoubtedly doing it all the time, and nobody expects him to not accept gold in payment for his goods. He's always been dependable about everything when I've dealt with him," Lud said.

Ben said, "Why don't you talk to him and be sure he can get all the things we'll need. If he can, and you're satisfied that he'll not report the gold, we'll try to work out a deal."

"I'll try to talk with him tomorrow."

Ben said, "All right, Lud'll talk with the trader about supplies. I'll get things together for the gold melting rigs. We need to get the gold stored, so some of us will work on that. None of this is going to take a lot of time, so we'll not be very busy this winter. Does anybody have any ideas about how we spend the rest of the time?"

I said, "Some of you want me to teach you things about Jesus. We can set up a schedule for that. Molly wants to be involved in that, too. Does anyone object to that?

Lud said, "Anyone who does, come to me. We'll have a real short discussion. If we have her around, the job of learning will at least be fun."

"Will you study with her around?"

"Now, I'll say things will go lots better with her around. She's a distraction, but we'll need to behave, too. I say she'll be a big help," Juan said. "I vote for anything that'll cause her to spend time here."

Ben said, "How do you feel about it, Pierre?"

"You know how I feel about her. She's welcome anywhere and any time. If there was any possibility that I could win her, I'd make that my full-time job. I'll settle for being around her as often as I can."

Ben said, "There's no question then. We all want her in the class. What do you have in mind for a schedule?"

I said, "Why don't we all think about it? I'll talk with Molly tonight and see if she'll join us tomorrow. We can all discuss it and decide then."

We were able to arrange all of that. I asked Molly to be ready at ten o'clock when I rode to the house and accompanied her to the barn. Pierre had lunch ready when we arrived, and we discussed the possibilities as we ate.

I started the discussion by saying, "It'll take me a while to prepare a plan of study, so we can't start until next week. I think it'll be hard for us to have classes every day, so we can plan for two or three a week. We'll need to study together, but you'll each need to work on this alone, as well. I think an ideal arrangement would be to hold the classes on Monday, Wednesday, and Friday. We can study together from ten o'clock until noon, have lunch, and study another hour on those days. You'll have assignments to study between classes, which will take another three or four hours. That means you'll spend about twenty to twenty-five hours a week on this. Is that too much?"

Lud said, "How long'll it take to teach us what we need?"

"I have no idea. This is a new thing for me. I've been studying for ten years and still haven't learned all I want to. My classes took forty to fifty hours a week nine or ten months each year. We'll need to adjust as we progress. This might be more than we want, or we may decide to add some time. I want this to be enjoyable but serious enough for you to learn as much as possible."

Ben suggested, "Let's try that and see how it works. We'll know fairly soon if we need to change anything."

"All right," said Pierre. "Can we start next Monday?"

I said, "I can have enough ready by then for us to start. I'll be as busy as you because the lessons will have to be planned as we move forward."

Molly and I left shortly after that for the ride home.

"Are you sure the men all want me in the class?" she asked.

"That was discussed fully, and there was complete agreement that you'll not only be welcome, but some of them'll probably drop out if you aren't included."

"I don't want to interfere with your teaching them. You and I can do my lessons at a different time if that would help."

"I'm sure they'll all rebel and refuse to study if you don't come. They all love you. You have no idea how much they like to be with you. They're totally different when you're there compared to the way they are when the five of us are alone. Your influence is so noticeable that it would probably shock you if you could see, and especially hear, the difference."

She was quiet for several minutes then said, "I remember how the men worried and fretted when you couldn't see and the way they acted when Dark Dog shot at you. I suppose they feel something like that about me. I can understand why they feel like that about you because I love you. Maybe that helps me understand their feeling about me. I'll think on it."

"I can understand their feelings with no difficulty. When I compare that with the way God loves us, it almost overwhelms me. We've done nothing to cause him to love us, but he sent his only Son who gave his life so that we can be his children. I can imagine doing something like that for you and maybe for children that we may have, but to do it for *everybody* is beyond my ability to conceive."

"I don't even understand the way people seem to feel about me. God's love is totally beyond my ability to understand. I need to keep reminding myself that you love me, that's such a marvelous thing."

"I'll try to remind you until you have no doubt about my love. I can't imagine not loving you. I think everybody should love you."

"I'm not used to hearing you tell me you love me. I always thought a man would only say things like that to a girl when the two of them were alone, and in the dark. You're telling me here in broad daylight, and it seems that you wouldn't care if others heard you."

"I'll shout it if you'd like. I want *everybody* to know that I love you."

"I'm not ready for that yet, although I want others to know that we love each other. They'll surely be able to tell that without you shouting, though."

"All right, I'll try to not embarrass you. I'd be delighted to demonstrate with a kiss, but it'd be somewhat difficult to do that now."

"We're almost home, so we should behave. I'll try to be patient."

We told Grandma about the schedule of classes, and she approved immediately. "We'll arrange things here so you'll both have time to study. It'll be easy to allow you to attend the classes, Molly. You'll need to be ready to go with Carlos on those mornings, and you could stay to do your individual studies before you come home. That'll allow you to ride with Carlos as you come home, too."

"Are you certain you won't need me those days?"

"I'll miss having you here, but the studies're important, so we'll manage. You help me a lot, but I managed without assistance until you arrived. You can still help on the other days."

With that settled I got paper and my Bible and retreated to the patio to start work on the lessons. I spent from daylight until dark the next few days getting ready for our first class. That may have been the most difficult work I'll ever tackle, but almost two hours of each day were spent in prayer. The results were better than I had thought they'd be. Lud appeared the third day.

"We were afraid something was wrong," he said. "You've never failed to come to the barn before."

"I'm sorry, I've been getting ready for next week and have been so engrossed that it never occurred to me that you'd expect me. I'm surprised that Molly or Grandma didn't ask me about it. Please forgive me. You had to make a trip for nothing."

He spoke softly so that no one else would hear. "You'll maybe notice that I came close to time for a meal. This isn't a wasted trip. I'll bet Grandma asks me to eat with you, and I'll get to visit with her and Molly. The other men wanted to come, but I made sure they were all busy before I left."

"If you'll tarry awhile, maybe Molly and I'll ride back with you and see the others. I'm sure your problem is that you haven't seen Molly for a few days."

"I told them you'd figure that out. We're all getting anxious to have her up there. You'll be ready to go Monday, won't you?"

"We'll start Monday. However, since you're all so antsy, why don't we all saddle up and ride in the hills tomorrow? We can take some grub and have a picnic."

"We've all been pretty busy, so I'm sure all of us'd like that. Can your grandparents come, too?"

"We'll need to go where they can take a cart. Grandma hardly ever rides anymore."

"I'll get back this afternoon and pick a spot for it. We'll get the food ready tonight, so that'll not delay us. I'm assuming that you'll talk everybody into it, and I don't worry about the other men. They'll jump at the chance."

"All right. I'll tell Molly first, and with her help Grandma and Grandpa'll be easy to convince."

Our assumptions proved to be correct, so we all went about an hour north of town the next morning. It was midmorning when we arrived at the spot Lud had chosen. It was at the edge of a cedar covered ridge. We had a view of Santa Fe and the surrounding area. It was a mild, clear day with no wind. As long as we were in the sun, we needed no coats. Shade brought the temperature down so a light jacket was comfortable. Pierre had fixed a venison roast and boiled potatoes and had baked some cookies. We built a small fire, made coffee and heated the meat and potatoes. Lud had dragged a couple of logs into the clearing for us to sit on. They were located so we could enjoy the view. It was a day of pure joy for me. My family, Molly, and my partners seemed to become a unit in a way that was like an extension of our family.

When the food was ready, Grandpa said, "I usually ask God to bless a meal, but this is Carlos and Molly's party, so I want him to lead us in praising the Lord."

It was something I did all the time, so I lifted up a prayer straight from my heart. When I looked around afterward, it seemed to me that everyone had joined in the prayer. We ate a leisurely lunch, then most of us strolled along the ridge and pointed out things to each other. The others elected to find a cozy spot to take a nap. The horses were picketed on a nice patch of lush grass where they munched and loafed. It was a time that would have seemed dull and uninteresting to some but for me it was very special. That group was never able to duplicate that day. We were undoubtedly more closely knit than we'd ever be again, and I thought it was more important to me than to any of the others.

When Molly and I were allowed to go off by ourselves, she reached for my hand and said, "I *love* this! You've made that group into a family. Who would've imagined that people so different would come to a place like this and make it a banquet hall? There's no way it would've happened without you."

"Who's flattering now? There were so many things that made this day what it is. I just had the privilege of participating in it. God does that to me often, and it reminds me that if I allow him to he'll let me share in what he's doing."

"Are you saying that this is all a gift from him?"

"Yes. None of us could've touched the hearts of all of us the way it's been done today. We had no control over the weather, and we could never make the sky this color and the air clear enough to see that mountain as clearly as if it was a mile away. It's at least twenty-five miles from here, but it looks as though we could walk to it and back in a few minutes. I don't want the credit when he deserves all of it."

"You make him seem so real, I find it easy to believe what you tell me. I'm beginning to understand more about how you think, and it's delightful. I'm trusting that the classes will bring all of us to a point of belief that's beyond what any of us can imagine now."

"Remember Lydia?"

"Is she the woman you told me about whose mind the Lord opened?"

"That's *amazing*, Sweetheart. I hardly mentioned her. The Bible calls it *opening her understanding*, but you were really close to saying it exactly. Now I see how you could learn all those languages. You have a phenomenal memory."

"You haven't told me about many people in the Bible. It's easy to remember each of them."

"I'll need to be careful. When you learn to read, you'll be able to teach better than I can."

"That'll never happen. I'll always want you to teach me. I'd never want to take your place as the leader. It might cause you to resent me."

"I'll always rejoice when you succeed, whatever it involves."

She pulled me toward her, put her arms around me, pulled my head down, and kissed me. It was a gentle kiss, with our lips hardly touching. We were careful to keep it safe. Her right hand caressed the back of my neck while her other one gently rubbed my cheek. I had my right hand under her chin and my left on her waist at her back. When we finally ended the kiss she placed her cheek against mine, moving it while barely keeping contact.

"You're the most wonderful thing that's ever happened to me," I said. "I love you with my whole heart."

"You're the answer to my prayers. You've changed my life so completely I can hardly believe it. I'd never dreamed of anything like this until I met you. You've already given me more joy than I could ever hope for. I love you so much it won't stay inside. I must show you how intense it is."

"I could stay here forever, telling you how much I love you, but we must stop. I'll be overcome soon and do something we've agreed to not do. We must go back," I whispered. "I love you and will forever, my darling."

"Kiss me again."

My answer wasn't with my voice. What a woman she was, even at fourteen. It was easy to forget her age and that I was only two years older.

CHAPTER TWENTY-FIVE

When we assembled Monday morning, we each had a copy of the Bible, a supply of paper, a pen, and a glass of water. We were seated around the table in the barn. It was just after ten o'clock, and we planned to study until noon, stop for lunch, then have another hour of study.

I said, "We need a starting place, and I don't know of a better place than the first page of the Bible. When you turn to the first page, you'll see a bunch of numbers along with the words. The Bible is arranged into books, then chapters, and then verses. That allows us to refer to any place in the Bible by naming the book, and then within that book, we can find the chapter and finally the verse. The first book is Genesis, and it starts at chapter one, verse one.. That's for convenience, and it'll make it much easier for us to all get to the same exact place we want to study. You'll want to learn the order of the books so you can find them easily, but that'll happen as we go through them. Don't be concerned about it yet. I'll explain where the books are for quite a while until you're more familiar with the way they're arranged.

"The first verse is Genesis one, one, and it says, 'In the beginning God created the heavens and the earth.' I want us to think about those first four words, 'In the beginning, God.' Try to imagine what it was like before there was anything except God—no earth, no sky, no sun, no moon, no stars, no darkness, nothing but God. But God is three persons, the Father, the Son, and the Holy Spirit. Yet he tells us he's one God. I can't explain that because I don't understand how it can be. The closest I can come is to say that he also tells us that when a man and a woman marry and know each other intimately, the two of them become one flesh. If the marriage is ordained by God, there will be a unity that cannot be explained by comparing it with anything else.

"Time hadn't yet been created because that first verse says, 'In the beginning,' which indicates that was when time began. We're trying to place ourselves before that. It was then that God chose each of us and determined what would be done to make it possible for us to become his children, in spite of what we'd do to offend him. Any questions?"

Ben said, "You're telling us that God knew about us before he made anything?"

"Yes. In Paul's letter to the church in Ephesus, he says that he chose us in Christ before the foundation of the world. Now, I want us to get a picture of what things were like before anything had been created."

Molly said, "Did God look like we do?"

"We're told that God is spirit and must be worshiped in spirit and in truth. We aren't told anything about his form, although there are lots of places in the Bible where he talks about himself as if he has bodily features. I think that's to help us understand what he's telling us rather than giving a description of himself. When Jesus chose to become a man, he was all man but never stopped being all God at the same time. His body was just like any other man's. After he came back from death in the resurrection, he was able to walk through walls, appear, and disappear when he wanted to. We aren't told anything definite about what God looks like, but he's always existed and will continue forever. That's how he's able to offer us eternal life."

Molly asked, "Is it all right if we ask questions?"

"Of course. The purpose of the classes is to give each of us a better understanding of God and his Word. What's your question?"

"Where is he now?"

"He's in a place he calls heaven. However, he also tells us that he's always with us. The Bible says there's no place we can go to be away from his presence. When we accept Christ as our Savior, the Holy Spirit comes into us somehow, and he lives in us forever. But we're also told that both Jesus and the Holy Spirit are with the Father, encouraging the Father to do things that are for our benefit. I can't explain how they do that, but the Bible says it is so, and I believe that the Bible is entirely true and completely dependable."

Ben said, "Then God's here in this room now?"

"Yes, he is, and it pleases him that we're studying his Word."

"How can he be everywhere all at the same time?" Lud asked.

"That's just one of the things he can do that I don't understand. That ability or characteristic is called *omnipresence*. That simply means that he's everywhere. He's also *omnipotent*, which means that he's all-powerful. There's nothing too difficult for him. Another characteristic is that he is *omniscient*, which means that he knows everything with no exceptions. So we serve the God who's *everywhere* all the time, *knows everything* all the time, and is able to *do anything, anytime*. He created everything we can see and another dimension that we can't see. He keeps this whole world operating just like he designed it to function. If he stopped doing that, everything would simply disappear."

Juan said, "You're starting out with things I don't understand. Will it get easier?"

"I think it will. I feel that unless we have some idea who God is and how he works it'll be much more difficult to understand what he's done, what he's doing now, and what he'll do in the future. Unless we know how powerful he is and know about his wisdom and have some grasp of his presence at all times, we'll never be able to understand that he gives us the opportunity to establish a close, personal relationship with him. He actually wants to be close to us, even to the extent of coming to live in us. That's hard for us to believe, much less understand."

"I just don't get it," said Lud. "I'm going to need some time to figure this out."

I said, "Let's stop and pray about it. I'd really like it if some or all of you would join in the prayer. I want each of you to become active in praying, not only when you're alone, but when you're with other people."

I asked God to do for us what he did for Lydia by enabling her to understand his Word. I also asked that if any of us hadn't accepted Christ as Savior that it would occur that day. I continued, asking something for each of the men and for Molly. When I finished, it was but a few moments before Molly prayed, which didn't surprise me, but when Lud joined in, I was delighted, and Juan's prayer was a real bonus. The others didn't enter in, so after a fairly long period of silence, I prayed briefly again and made it obvious that we were through.

Pierre then suggested that we pause for coffee. I said, "I'll try to answer any other questions now. Please don't hesitate to ask about anything you don't understand. I'll often have to tell you that I can't explain something, but we can talk about anything. God isn't worried when we ask questions. However, there's a difference between asking questions because we don't understand something and questioning God. By that, I mean that we mustn't say, 'That can't possibly be true', when the Bible says it's true. The Bible is God's Word, and it's without error. When we read something in the Bible, we're to accept it as completely true even though we can't explain it."

Molly said, "Now we know how it all started, so what do we study next?"

I took them through the story of the six days of creation, the creation of Eve, and the sin that occurred in the garden of Eden.

I said, "When Adam and Eve sinned, we're told that it caused a situation in which each of us is born with a sinful nature. In the letter to the Church in Rome, Paul tells us that all of us have sinned and fallen short of the glory of God. He further says that sin brings separation from God and eternal or everlasting punishment. But he also tells us that God requires a payment for every sin, and the payment he requires is the death of a sinless person. That's why Jesus, the Son of God, who is God himself, became a man, lived a perfect, sinless life, and submitted to being killed. That was the sinless sacrifice God required. Everyone who accepts Jesus as his savior is forgiven for all the sins he has committed and will ever commit. That's the only way to escape the punishment for those sins. Christ himself said that he is the way, the truth, and the life, and that no one comes to the Father except through him. Then he tells us that we who believe on the name of Jesus have eternal life right now, not some time in the future."

There was silence for several minutes, then Molly said, "You mean we don't need to do anything other than accept Jesus as our savior for all the bad things we've done to be forgiven?"

"That's exactly what the Bible tells us, and it never tells us of another way to get that."

"I always thought I had to be good enough, and then God would let me into heaven," she said. "Is that wrong?"

"In the letter to the churches in Galatia, Paul says that if we can get to heaven by doing good things then Jesus wasted his entire life and his death on the cross wasn't needed. He makes it absolutely clear that there's nothing else that will satisfy God."

After another lengthy pause she said, "I think I accepted him when I was really young, but how can I be sure?"

Juan said, "Yes, tell us what we need to do. I can't imagine anyone not wanting to do something that simple in order to be sure of going to heaven."

"You just need to tell God that you believe him that Jesus died for your sins and ask him to forgive you. Then you'll probably want to thank him for doing it. I'm going to close my eyes and pray for all of you. After awhile, if any of you don't think you did it right but want to be sure, I'll tell you what I'd say and you can repeat it. It isn't necessary that your prayer be spoken aloud.

You can speak to God with your mind. I'm closing my eyes and suggest that you all do that, too."

I heard several of them moving, so I looked up. The sight brought a lump to my throat. Every one of them was kneeling. The men all had their heads bowed, but Molly's face was in the position to look toward heaven, and her arms were lifted with her hands spread, palms up. I have no idea where she'd have learned that, but it was a beautiful posture of praise and supplication. Her lips moved silently, and her face was a picture of joy. I had to close my eyes again to keep from going to her and taking her in my arms. I may never again see a sight that moving and beautiful. She needed no instruction about worship. It was undoubtedly given her by the Holy Spirit.

When everyone was seated again, I said, "Does anyone want to tell us what you just did?"

Juan said, "I did the best I could to say what you suggested. Is there anything else we need to do?"

"I'll answer that soon. How about the rest of you? Do you want to share anything with us?"

The other men each said he had done the same thing.

Molly said, "I asked God to tell me if I was already saved, and he told me I have been his child for most of my life. It was the most exciting thing I've ever experienced. I had never heard God before, but there was no doubt about it. He spoke as clearly as anything I've ever heard. Thank you, Carlos, for telling us how to do that."

I could wait no longer. I went to her and held out my arms. She took my hands and came into my embrace.

I lifted her face so we were eye to eye. I said, "If we don't get anything more from these classes, this is more than enough to make it worth our time. I praise God for giving us this."

"It's wonderful. Now I know what you've told me about when God's spoken to you. I hope it happens often. It was as clear as if he was here so we could see him. There's really no way to describe it properly."

I was finally able to release her and look at the men. They were smiling broadly, obviously delighted for us.

I said, "I want to do one more thing. I want to be sure we all understand what happens when we accept Christ. God forgives us of all sin and adopts us into his family. The Bible says that we're children of God and even *joint heirs with Christ.* When we sin from now on, all we need to do is confess it, and he forgives and cleanses us. We don't need that to keep our salvation. It's to keep our relationship with him clean and complete. Any questions?"

Lud said, "Kid, you sound so sure of all this. I'm going to need to have you remind me a lot because it sounds too good to be true. I've never had anybody make me this kind of offer. It doesn't seem natural."

"It isn't natural—it's *supernatural.* Only God would devise a plan like this."

Ben said, "I'm confused. You use the name *Jesus* sometimes, and other times you say *Christ.* Can you explain that?"

"That's a good question. I'm glad you asked. *Jesus* is the name given by an angel before Mary had conceived him. *Christ* is a title. In the Old Testament, God promised a deliverer whom he called the *Messiah. Christos* is the Greek form of the word *Messiah.* If we were to use it fully, it'd be *Jesus the Christ* or *the Messiah.* It would be similar to saying *King Ferdinand.* You'll often hear it said, '*Jesus Christ*'."

We all got some coffee and sat quietly for several minutes. I said, "We've covered some really important things today. I think we need to call it enough for one class. I hope you'll each spend some time talking with God tonight. Some people seem to be really particular about how they pray, but I feel free to talk to any or all of them. I sometimes talk to the Father, sometimes to the Holy Spirit, and more often to Jesus. I hope you all understand that the Holy Spirit is living in you after you accept Jesus as your savior, so it's really easy to talk to him. He's apparently the one who speaks to us, but it often seems like it's Jesus. Since they're one, it shouldn't make a difference, anyway. Be sure you thank him for what he's given you and ask him for anything you need. I like to wait quite a bit and listen to see if he has anything to tell me."

Pierre said, "I've learned more today than I ever thought you could teach me. My mind's a whirlpool. It's going to take me until Wednesday for sure to take all this in. I hope you don't have anything for us to study."

"No, this has been a really full day. I had no idea we'd cover all that we did. I didn't follow my plan at all, but this is what God had for us today. We'll go slower most days, so don't expect as much. I'm trusting that you'll each review what we covered today, and I'll plan to have a summary for you next time. I'm tired and ready to stop for this lesson."

There was immediate agreement, so we had another cup of coffee, then Molly and I headed for home. We were barely away from the barn when Molly said, "You're a *wonderful* teacher. I didn't expect anything like this. You made God so real it was almost as though I could see him. I know the Holy Spirit is within me now, ready to guide me and show me what I should do and say."

"That's great. The Bible says that the Holy Spirit witnesses to our spirit that we're children of God. He's always ready to give us the wisdom and direction we need."

"I agree with Lud when he said this is the best deal I've ever heard about. I knew enough to accept Jesus but had never learned what that achieved for me. I never dreamed that all the sins I'll ever commit have already been forgiven. That's almost too good to be true."

"The whole plan of salvation is that way, isn't it?"

"Yes."

"The only thing close to it is that he brought you into my life. That's another wonderful blessing he's given me."

"Oh, Carlos, you'll never know what a blessing that is for me. When I think of what a difference you brought into my life it almost causes me to cry. When I dwell on it and think of what my life would've been if you hadn't come, it makes me wonder how it could happen to me. When you bought me from Smart Coyote, I was afraid of what you'd require of me, but it was soon apparent that you wanted only to help me. Smart Coyote told me that I was being chosen by a special man, and he was right."

"As you know, I never considered that I was buying you. I purchased your freedom. You're free to choose anything for yourself. I'm blessed that you're willing to become my wife, and that it's not because you must do it."

"I'd be delighted to marry you if it was required of me, but I'm happy that you asked me, and I'm able to tell you that it's exactly what I want. I'd be terribly unhappy if you didn't want me."

"There's not a man who's ever seen you who isn't envious of me. Those who know you are even more wishful that they were the one with whom you'd spend your life."

"I'm glad you feel like that. It makes me feel special. I can't imagine any woman not wishing she was in my place, but she'd have a battle to face if she tried."

"We must be the most blessed people in the world."

"I am, anyway."

That sort of thing went on all the way home. I had the pleasure of watching her seated in that saddle, making it look like a throne, her face showing every emotion, her eyes like two pools of welcome, into which I felt I could dive and float in her love. We arrived at the house more quickly than I wanted. I lifted her from her saddle and stole a hug that was entirely too brief.

She whispered, "Thank you for a wonderful day. I love you."

"It was wonderful because we were together. I adore you, my darling."

"I guess I must come back down to earth and go help Grandma."

"I'm going to stay on the moon awhile, just thinking about you. I'll put the horses up."

CHAPTER TWENTY-SIX

The teaching was more difficult after that first day. Ben was the only one of the others who could read, so they needed to learn that along with the teachings of Christ. I decided to teach them to read by having them read the portions of Scripture we studied, which served both purposes. They might have learned each of them faster some other way, but the combination of the three hours of class work and another period of individual study worked quite well. By spring they were all reading fairly well, and a couple of them had started reading the Bible in its entirety. I was really encouraged when they started asking questions about how to tell their friends about Jesus.

Our studies were interrupted when we started the search for men and pack animals. There were many lengthy discussions about the numbers we needed. We settled on a hundred men and at least two hundred burros. I cautioned them that the Utes would have serious objections to our taking that many of either into their territory, but the others thought it'd be all right since we'd be in the high country.

Another matter of discussion was regarding how much we'd pay the men and the method of payment. I suggested, and we finally agreed, that the men should be paid for a full year even though they'd work only half that long. The wives of married men would be paid each month with Molly and Grandma handling that. Molly devised a method that would allow them to be certain they paid only the correct women, which was a real bonus. The men without families would be paid in the fall for the time they were on the job. Each man would be paid monthly during the time they were idle. That gave us some assurance that our crew would be available the following year. They'd all be on call and would do anything we needed during the idle months.

I was afraid that we'd have to travel to find that many men, but the men we hired in Santa Fe knew of others living elsewhere. Two weeks after we started hiring locally, we had a surplus of applicants who came from other areas. We had to travel to eight ranches to acquire the needed burros. We made arrangements with one of the ranchers to care for the animals when they weren't being used. We were careful to keep our activities quiet and unobtrusive due to the Army. If the officers became aware of what we were doing, we'd lose the mine, and be thrown in prison until a decision from Spain was forthcoming.

Lud and I went together to meet with the trader who brought merchandise from St. Louis. He was a Mexican rather a Spaniard. His father was Spanish and his mother an Aztec. Those of mixed parentage were given the designation of Mexican. He was a bigger man than was usual for either, and his skin was quite dark compared to the Spanish but lighter than most Indians. He took us into his office, which was a large, well-furnished room. The primary light came from a window in the ceiling along with two large windows along one wall. He asked us to join him in chairs made of an attractive wood covered with dark leather. They were arranged around a small table upon which were glasses and a container of water.

"How can I help you?" he asked.

Lud said, "We're mining a long way north of here, and we need supplies and tools. We'd prefer to buy what we need locally rather than undertake going where the items might be readily available. We understand that you're able to supply almost anything and want to give you the chance to take care of our needs."

He said, "That's my business. Do you have a list of what you want?"

I said, "Yes, here it is."

"Well, this is unusual. Most of my customers tell me what they want, and I have to make up a list for them." He looked at the list and continued, "There are things here that I have in stock, but many of these items won't be stocked in St Louis. I'll need some time to get everything. When do you need this?"

"We'll need to have everything no later than the middle of March," Lud told him.

"That shouldn't be a problem. Do you want me to get everything and make delivery when it's all here, or do you want some things earlier?"

"You have on hand everything we'll need before spring."

"All right. You must understand that it'll cost me the going price for everything, plus I have expense for going after it and bringing it here, and I expect to make a profit. On an order of this size, I'd be able to sell it to you for a third more than what I pay for it in St. Louis. I assure you that I'll negotiate the best possible price there, and I'll absorb the other costs. I'll show you the invoices for each item, and we can divide that by three and add that to the cost. That's what you'll pay me. You'll take a risk that I can get a good price, and I'll take the risk of going after it and bringing it here."

"Can we arrange to take delivery some place other than in Santa Fe?" Lud asked.

"I can deliver it any place along the trail we follow. I wouldn't be able to go very far off that trail."

"That'll be fine. We prefer to do it where the Army can't see what we're doing."

"How will you pay me?" he asked.

"With gold. We've melted some into bricks and have some in bags that we extracted without melting it. We have no accurate way of weighing it. We'd need to either go with you and sell the gold ourselves or trust you to handle that, too," Lud said. "You have a good reputation, and we aren't afraid to have you take care of that, too. We'll also need quite a bit of money from the sale of the gold. We'll be hiring a crew to go with us, and they'll need to be paid in cash."

"I'll take gold directly and have the equipment needed to weigh it accurately. I also buy gold. Since I take gold all the time, the Army never pays any attention to that part of my business. What kind of money would you want? I can get Spanish, British, or French coins. I keep a good supply of Spanish money on hand. How much will you need?"

"We'll need enough to pay a hundred men for a year. I'm sure Spanish coins'll be best."

"That'd take one hundred five pounds of gold. I charge five percent for converting gold to money."

Lud said, "I guess that's about right. It must cost you something to get rid of it."

He smiled and said, "I keep as much of it as I can. I'd rather have gold than money."

"All right. We need to discuss this with our partners, but I think we can make a deal," Lud said.

I said, "Can you give us an estimate of the total cost of the things on that list?"

"Of course. I can have it for you by noon day after tomorrow. Will that be soon enough?"

"That should be fine. Either Carlos or I'll come and get it."

"Good. This is a big order. I assure you I'll do everything I can to make it good for you."

I picked up the estimate at the appointed time and took it to the barn. He had done us a favor by pricing things in quantities of gold. The total for the order was three hundred thirty pounds. We'd used another two hundred pounds for the burros, and the rancher would be given ten pounds for caring for the burros.

I said, "Let's see what the total is. The wages for the crew will take one hundred five pounds, the order three hundred thirty, another two hundred ten for the animals and their care. Are we going to take any ourselves?"

Lud said, "I need some clothes and other things, and I'm sure we all need something. Why don't we each take two pounds and have the trader change it to coin? If he charges five percent that'll still give each of us more than a year's wages. Does anyone need more than that?"

We all agreed on that amount, so the total we'd need was six hundred fifty-five pounds. That would pay for everything for the coming year, and our remaining store would still be in excess of six hundred pounds. That meant each of us had more than a hundred pounds of gold.

I said, "How much would it take to buy the place we're renting?"

Juan said, "I think if we offer the owner twenty-five pounds of gold, he'll take it in a minute."

"It's worth more than that, isn't it?" Ben asked.

Pierre said, "It's probably worth twice that. We couldn't replace the building and corrals for that, and the land's worth quite a bit. When you consider the fences and other things, it'd take a lot more than that to replace it."

Lud said, "Something's worth what one man's willing to give and another man's willing to take. Let's offer twenty pounds and see if he'll take it. We can negotiate up to twenty-five if we have to."

Ben asked, "Who's going to talk to him?"

I said, "Let's have Juan invite him to the barn, and we'll all talk to him."

Juan said, "I like that idea. I'll go see him right now. When do you want him here?"

Lud said, "Let's not get in too big a rush. What if he doesn't want gold?"

I said, "We know what it'll cost to get coin for the gold. We can negotiate in coin and offer him gold if he wants it."

Juan said, "That's fine. You'll have to give us the numbers. I sure can't figure it out."

"All right. I'll have the numbers in both gold and coin by evening. Let's see if he'll come tomorrow at ten o'clock. Who's going to be our spokesman?"

I asked Juan, "Do you want to do it?"

"No. I'd like for either Lud or Pierre to do it."

Ben asked, "Do either of you know him?"

Since neither man did, we chose Pierre. Lud suggested that, and no one objected.

When the man arrived the next day, Pierre opened the conversation by pointing out every shortcoming of the facilities and suggested that the owner should improve them. The owner admitted to each item but said he couldn't afford to spend anything to correct them.

Pierre then said, "We don't want to spend the money to improve your property, but we need to have those things fixed. We might be able to do it if we were only paying half as much rent. Could you do that?"

"No. I need the amount you're paying now in order to pay my bills."

"We need to have it in better shape. We may have to move."

"I'd hate to have you do that. As I said, I need the rent to pay my bills."

Juan had told us that the owner looked and acted like a weasel, and that description fit him. He got a funny look on his face and said, "Why don't you buy it? Then you can fix it up the way you want."

Pierre said, "I don't know. We'd need to buy it at a low price so we could justify spending all that money on it. What do you think about that?"

That remark was directed to us. We all acted as though that was an entirely new thought.

I said, "We need to talk about that. All those repairs and improvements are going to cost a lot. Can we go outside and discuss this?"

We went out and walked around the barn twice, talking about what a sleazy man we were dealing with.

Juan said, "Let's cut the price we offer him. I think Pierre has him ready to take our lower figure. Cut that bottom number by ten percent."

"Can you give me that in a hurry, Carlos?"

"Sure, that's no problem. Give me a minute, and I'll write it down for you."

Pierre made our offer, and the owner said, "You're trying to steal it. I couldn't possibly take that. I think you have some gold. Give me twenty pounds of gold, and the place is yours."

Pierre said, "That's a lot of gold. How'll we weigh it so we're sure we don't give you too much?"

"You can take it to the trading post, and he'll weigh it for you, and it'll be accurate."

I said, "We've already paid rent through April. We should get a refund for that."

"How much would that be?" Juan asked.

"It'd be a little more than fifty Pesos. I'd be willing to settle for fifty."

The owner said, "I'll do that. You give me twenty pounds of gold, and I'll give you the place and fifty pesos. When can we complete the transaction?"

Ben said, "Carlos will write all this down, and we'll all sign it. Then we can go to the governor and complete the deal whenever he has time to do it."

I did it, and we all signed it as buyers, with the owner signing as the seller.

When we were alone again, Lud said, "Kid, you're about the slickest horse trader I've ever seen. Who'd have thought to get that rent money back? I'm proud of you."

"I just did what I thought he'd do if he had the opportunity," I said. "I wouldn't have done that with most people, but I kept thinking of Juan's description of him. It fit so perfectly that I couldn't resist."

"You may grow up to be a real man after all. You might even get to the point that we can say you deserve Molly."

That brought a chorus of groans. No one thought I'd ever deserve her, and I had no argument.

Molly and I had an abundance of help choosing the location for our house. She did most of the planning for the construction. She proved again that she was brilliant. Her design was inventive and practical. The only homes she remembered, with the exception of my grandparents', were tipis. She was able to design a home that included almost everything that would be wanted.

She also was responsible for supervising most of the construction because I was at the mine during the summer months. Grandpa and my uncle built it, and there was nothing lacking in that area. We didn't rush the construction, since we'd not occupy it until after our wedding. Grandpa told us that there were plenty of other jobs, but they were glad to work on our house when there was a slack time.

Molly wanted a kitchen that would meet the demands of a chef. Years of cooking over an open fire left her with a desire for convenience and efficiency. We were blessed to be able to demand what she wanted without concern for cost.

I designed my office. It was along the west wall, with one door that opened into a hallway. The north wall was covered completely by bookshelves. The south wall was covered with a striking Indian blanket. It appeared to be attached to the wall but was mounted so it could be moved aside on a cleverly designed track. A huge door was behind the rug. It had brass hinges that allowed it to open with no sound. It opened into a stairway that went down into a cavity excavated in solid rock. Our gold and other items we wanted to have stored in safety were placed directly under the office. The walls of the cavity held shelves of two inch planks supported by six inch posts. The door to the safe area contained a lock that would be all but impossible to force, and the handle was recessed, which allowed the blanket to hang with no evidence of the presence of the door. The wall of a dining room served opposite the office wall. A careful measurement of the rooms would've been required to learn that there was a stairway between the two rooms.

We had chosen a spot for the house where bedrock was three feet underground, so the vault was actually mined from solid rock. All work on it was done after the outer walls were in place, so no one outside our small group was ever aware of it.

We made a similar arrangement in the barn, where we stored the gold prior to making any distribution. We also kept our explosives there along with things we wanted to keep safe while we were at the mine. When Grandma and Molly had the responsibility of paying the wives of our crew, we stored the coins at the barn and they'd go to the barn to make the payments. We often saw evidence of people forcing their way into the barn, but the vault was well hidden, and no one ever discovered it.

We had a wonderful Christmas celebration at my grandparents' home. We had every reason to celebrate because each of us had accepted Jesus. Before we sat down to the marvelous meal Grandma and Molly had prepared, I read from the letter to the Galatians where we're told that we're all children of God in Christ Jesus. Molly had made me a suit of rich wool and a shirt of silk. She also gave me a beautiful pair of boots made of bull hide that was complete with a pair of silver spurs sporting rowels so big they touched the floor and jingled when I walked. A tooled-leather belt with a silver buckle completed the outfit, which fit me to perfection.

Pierre said, "She's got you all rigged out for a wedding. When is the date?"

I replied, "I'm ready right now, but we've agreed to go get her mother first, so we'll save all of this for at least a year. Molly, this is a wonderful gift. Thank you."

Her eyes sparkled, and her smile was like a diamond in bright sunlight. I gave her a handgun, the best and most highly decorated firearm I could find. It came with a holster of heavy cowhide. It was later, after we had eaten, that I took her outside and presented her with the real gift. It was a three-year-old filly, a bright sorrel with flaxen mane and tail, the best I had ever seen. She was an Arab, which was seldom seen at that time, and I had spent enough time training her to be certain she was ready for Molly, which meant she knew how to behave in polite company. I had slipped away immediately after our meal, saddled her, and tied her and the *grullo* in front of the house.

When I thought it was the right time, I said, "Molly, I want to show you another gift. If you'll put on your coat and join me outside, I'll give it to you."

She looked uncertain but allowed me to help her with her coat and followed me through the door. When she saw the filly, she said, "Where'd you find her?"

"It wasn't easy. She was north of Taos on a sheep ranch. I was really fortunate to be able to talk the owner into selling her. He planned to keep her for his daughter, but the Lord blessed, and I persuaded him to let her go."

"She's *perfect*. May I ride her?"

"Of course. She's never been around dresses like yours, so we need to be careful when you mount her."

"Will you help me so I don't frighten her? I want her to like for me to ride her."

"All right, hold your skirt so it doesn't fly around much when I lift you. That's fine. Now let me help you lay it over her back. That should be fine. I'll mount up, and we'll see if she knows anything."

We rode for over an hour, and they seemed to become friends quickly. Molly fell in love immediately, and the filly was soon completely at ease. By the time we came back to the house, the two of them were obviously a pair.

"Now you may have your stallion back. You've given me a perfect replacement. I'll never be able to thank you enough."

"Watching you enjoy her is all the payment I could ever want. I'm truly happy that you like her."

"The term *like* is hardly adequate. I think I love her, and now I have another reason to love you. You're wonderful, darling."

"Thank you. It gives me great joy to make you happy. I'll take a small show of appreciation later if you like."

"If you'll take me where we can have some privacy, I'll give it right now."

"We can go unsaddle and give the horses some corn, and there's a place out there where we can handle that."

"I'll race you," she said and took off at a run.

That *grullo* wasn't going to be left behind, and we were neck and neck at the barn. I lifted her down, and we were immediately embracing and kissing. The coats we wore gave some protection, and we were both careful to stay within the bounds we had set. It was the first time we had given ourselves that much freedom for over three months.

"I'd like to do this at least a hundred times every day but am grateful that we can give our love this way on Christmas Day. You're the greatest gift God's ever given me. I love you more every day. No, it's every time I see you. You're my sweetheart."

"I could never want more than this, my darling. Thank you for making me the happiest girl in the world."

"I thank God for you. Now, let's take care of the horses and go where it's safe."

The final gift was when we kissed the way we really wanted to later. Even then we were able to maintain a safety factor. Among the many things about God that I don't understand is the reason he chose to give me Molly. She has made my life complete.

CHAPTER TWENTY-SEVEN

We met the trader's wagons a three hours' ride east of Santa Fe on the fourteenth of March. We transferred the items onto burros. It took the rest of the day to complete the delivery. The trader was an excellent business man, and we were glad that he had handled everything. He had managed to negotiate a good price for the order, so the cost was less than we had expected. We all agreed that we'd give him all our future business.

We had managed to get our crew to the ranch by having them appear at the barn in groups of twenty-five, which we then moved to the place where the burros were held.

We left for the mine March 28 and reached the hot springs four days later. Molly was with us, and she and I went to the Ute camp the day following our arrival at the springs. The usual greeting was extended upon our entrance to the camp. The youngsters recognized us, and as a consequence, Smart Coyote and Fawn Heart were outside when we got to their tipi. The greeting was a lovely thing to watch. It was apparent that Molly was a daughter returning home. I was truly happy that I was allowed the privilege of watching. When they had greeted each other sufficiently, the chief said to me, "Dark Dog told us he killed you."

"We knew he thought that. We didn't want him following us any farther. God took care of me so that his bullet did no damage."

"He said he saw you fall off your horse and lie on the ground dead. He said the others rushed to help you, but you were already dead, so he left."

"We knew all of that and wanted him to believe it. I was protected, though. Can you arrange for me to talk with him in private?"

"Yes. Where would you like to meet him?"

"Where would you suggest?"

"Why don't you meet him in the horse pasture?"

"That's fine. Dawn on the Mountain'll need to be there to translate, but everyone else should be kept away from us."

"What do you want to do?"

"I want to tell him that God protected me and that his bullet couldn't hurt me. I'll warn him that if he tries again I'll ask God to turn his bullet around so it kills him instead. I'm convinced that I was protected, or he'd have killed me, and that God will do more than that if I ask him to. We need to meet with both of us unarmed."

"Would you object to my being there when you talk?"

"Not if it's all right with him."

"I'll arrange it that way. I'll go talk to him."

Smart Coyote was gone longer than I had hoped. Molly and Fawn Heart were talking up a storm, so I went outside and unsaddled the horses and picketed them at the edge of the pasture. When there was still no sign of the Ute, I made sure the tipi I had always used wasn't in use and moved my stuff into it.

Smart Coyote was gone at least an hour. When he finally returned, he said, "We're to meet immediately. Do you need to do anything before we leave?"

"No."

"Do you have any idea how long we'll be gone?"

"It depends on Dark Dog's response. If he's agreeable, we can be back quickly. If not, there's no way to estimate how long we'll be."

"He wouldn't believe that he hadn't killed you. There was no doubt in his mind that you were dead. That's the reason I was gone so long."

"When he sees me, a man he was sure was dead, it may cause him to agree to my suggestion."

"We should go now. He was on his way to the meeting when I left him."

We walked together toward the pasture. Molly said, "Dark Dog hates you. How can you accomplish anything by talking with him?"

"The Lord told me to arrange this meeting. Maybe it'll be like the times Jesus told the apostles what would happen to them. He said that they were to not worry about what they'd say when they were brought before kings and other officials but that the words they were to say would be given them at the time."

"Your life may be at stake here. How can you possibly want to meet with this man when you don't even know what you'll say to him?"

"I'm trusting the Lord. I don't know of any weapon to use. I'll wait and see what God does. Please don't worry. The God who gave me back my sight and showed me Dark Dog when he was trying to shoot me is able to handle this situation. Please join me in asking God to give you some of Jesus' faith. You don't need to just depend on your own."

"You amaze me. When did God tell you to do this?"

"After we were in the tipi when we got here. Do you think I wouldn't have told you if it had been earlier?"

"I thought you would and am glad it wasn't earlier. Please always tell me when these things happen."

"I intend to do that."

"Can we stop and pray?"

"I think that would disturb the chief. We can pray silently. God hears our thoughts."

"If you'll do that, I'll talk to the chief."

While they spoke, I asked for specific wisdom when we met Dark Dog. I thanked Jesus for telling me to arrange this meeting, for having Dark Dog agree to meet, and for Smart Coyote wanting to be at the meeting. I also prayed for Molly. She'd know how my enemy was reacting before I did, since all discussions would pass through her. That placed her in a position of great responsibility, and she'd need the peace of God to handle it. I was able to resist asking for the words to say in advance, trusting him to give them in his own time.

Dark Dog was pacing back and forth under a tall pine tree when we reached the pasture. He stopped pacing when he saw us and waited as we approached him. He stared at us, a scowl on his face. When we were close to him, he walked slowly toward us, his eyes locked on mine. "I killed you!" he exclaimed.

He scowled fiercely as he waited for Molly to translate. He waved his arms and walked in a circle until she spoke to him. He repeated those actions each time as he waited.

I replied, "My God showed me where you were. I saw you shoot, saw the bullet coming toward me, and God threw me off the horse so I wasn't hit. He made it appear to you that you had killed me, but the bullet didn't even come close. I saw it fly over me and strike a tree on the far side of the meadow. God told me to act as though I was dead so you'd not try again. My God made you think I was dead."

"I saw my bullet hit your head, and then you fell to the ground and were no longer alive. I saw it all," he said in a loud voice.

"My God made it look that way to protect me. He was also protecting Dawn on the Mountain from you. I know that you planned to make her your squaw, but my God doesn't want that. He's planned for her to become my wife, and he'll do what's needed to make that happen. Your medicine is powerless before my God,"

"If you're not afraid to meet me with a knife, I'll show you my medicine is strong!"

"My God isn't afraid of your knife. I don't trust in weapons but in the power of my God. He's the one who made the world we live in and is a strong right arm for those he's chosen. He's telling me what to say to you now. You wouldn't be fighting a man you can see. The one who'd fight you is able to make your arm like a broken willow and your leg like a burned weed. He caused your bullet to miss me, and he'd make your knife dull. It would bend like a twig in a high wind. You shouldn't consider coming against me with any weapon."

His face was a picture of fury as Molly translated. He leaped into the air and threw dust while he waited.

"I'll fight you without a weapon in a bare-handed battle to the death. I'll show you whose medicine is strong. Fight me now, right here."

"I don't want to fight you. I'm not angry with you. I'd like to be your friend, but I must warn you that you'd be fighting the God who protects Dawn on the Mountain and me. Even if you should kill me, he'd never allow you to have her. Why should we fight? You'd be facing someone you can't see, who's more powerful than any man. It wouldn't be equal in any respect. I'm under his protection, and you'd be overwhelmed. I'm not trying to frighten you, nor am I trying to avoid a fight because I fear you. I want you to understand who you'd face in battle. Please at least wait until tomorrow morning and think about this tonight."

I've never seen a person as agitated as he was. He strutted around, waving his arms and grunting loudly. He finally stopped, facing me.

"Meet me here at daybreak tomorrow. Come with your knife, and I'll show you whose medicine is weak. Your God is not my god. I'll trust my Dark Dog spirit to make me able to spill your blood. I go now."

He turned and stalked back toward camp, his head thrown back, his walk a picture of anger.

Molly said, "What'll you do? You surely won't fight him, will you?"

"We'll pray and trust God. Remember David and Goliath, Daniel and the lions, and his friends in the furnace. Our God is able to handle any enemy. Think about how the walls of Jericho fell when God's people did what he told them to do. Man's weapons are truly useless against God."

"I'll not be able to sleep tonight. How can you face an experienced fighter when you've never fought anyone?"

"I was trained for a while by a man who was an expert in hand-to-hand combat. If it's needed, I can use that training. I'm confident that God'll handle it in some other way. I have no way of telling what he'll do, but he's taken all fear from me. Please let God take away your fear. In fact, I'll ask him right now.

"Lord, you know how this situation is frightening Molly, and you understand that, as well. I ask that you'll give her your peace. Please touch her spirit so she'll be able to rest in you and sleep well tonight. I thank you for that, because I believe you have already done it. Amen."

She had come into my arms as I prayed. She whispered, "Thank you. I feel like God answered that already. Kiss me."

It was a sweet kiss. We walked on to the tipi, where we separated for the night.

It's one thing to tell someone how to trust the Lord. It's another thing to practice it. I lay awake long into the night, demonstrating to God and myself that I wasn't practicing what I had assured Molly she should do. When I did fall asleep, it was to be tormented by dreams. I didn't dream about anything related to the upcoming encounter but about falling off cliffs, being thrown off horses, and being chased by a pair of grizzlies. It wasn't a restful night, so when I walked out to the pasture in the morning, I was feeling weak and unprepared for any kind of challenge. As I prayed silently, God brought to my mind his assurance to Paul that his strength is made perfect in our weakness.

Smart Coyote accompanied me, but we couldn't understand each other and were therefore silent. Dark Dog was alone, pacing back and forth in the center of the field. He had painted his face and upper body in the manner of Indians who were facing combat. His hair, which usually was an unruly mass similar to a pile of brush, was braided, greased, and hung down his back. He wore only a breech clout and moccasins that reached to his knees. It appeared that the soles of his footwear were of heavy leather, which would give him better footing than the usual soft-soled moccasin. His knife was in a sheath attached to a thin leather strap around his waist. The blade was about eight inches long with a leather-covered handle almost the same length. The sheath indicated that it was a blade that would serve best by penetrating the body rather than cutting flesh. I was sure that he was experienced in the use of it as a lethal weapon.

I wasn't surprised at his appearance and had painted a red Christian cross on my chest, tied a soft strip of deer hide around my head, and wore only buckskin trousers and the boots I wore when I was working at the mine. My knife was a gift from Grandma and was made of Toledo steel. It was sharp enough to shave with, was a foot long, of which eight inches was steel that held an edge like no other knife I had seen. It was an impressive weapon, but I hoped to not need to inflict many wounds.

When we were twenty feet apart, Dark Dog took his knife out, brandished it and motioned with it toward his heart then pointed with his other hand toward me. He danced in a circle, chanting what was undoubtedly a form of prayer for victory. He completed the dance by dipping down and picking up a handful of dust, which he threw into the air between us.

I drew my knife and took it in my left hand. That's not my primary hand. I didn't want to win by cutting him. We circled, each of us feinting, looking for openings in the other's defense. He struck toward my throat, and as I dodged, my blade slid along his arm above his knife. It opened a gash half way between his wrist and elbow that was six inches long and half an inch deep. Blood spurted out in the cadence of a heart beat, indicating that an artery had been cut. My knife was sharp enough that he seemed to not be aware of the cut until he saw the blood. His gaze lingered on his arm, giving me the opening I had hoped for. I struck the bloody arm just above the wrist, using a karate chop that made the wrist and hand numb, rendering his arm completely useless. The knife dropped to the ground, where I was able to retrieve it easily.

With no weapon and an arm spurting blood, Dark Dog was virtually helpless. He said something to Smart Coyote and started a wailing chant while walking slowly away from us. Smart Coyote motioned to me that we should also leave. I wanted to talk with him but was forced to wait until we were at his tipi. He was surprisingly solemn, and I wondered if I had violated some tribal practice. We were fifty feet from the tipi when he started a chant in a loud voice. The flap flew open, and Molly burst out. When she saw us, she ran at top speed to me.

"You killed him. How'd you do it so quickly?"

The chief said, "Dark Dog isn't dead, but he was defeated and is disgraced. He'll not trouble you again. His medicine had no strength against Carlos. He understands now that if he bothers you, your God will destroy him. He'll not let you see him again and will never so much as speak to you. Your man has strong medicine and a strong God."

"Carlos assured me of that, but it was hard for me to believe. Now I know it's true." She then spoke to me, "I'm proud of you. I'll learn from Smart Coyote what you did. It's enough to have you back safely. I know you must leave soon, so we'll talk of happier things in the time we have."

"Please remember, whatever he tells you, that it was the Lord who did it. I was privileged to watch him. I was afraid even though you may have thought I was confident God would take care of me."

CHAPTER TWENTY-EIGHT

I left the stallion again and rode another horse up to the mine. It showed again that no other horse was equal to the *grullo*, but it was all right because I got the better part of that bargain.

The other part of the crew traveled much slower than I did. I had the mine open and ready when they arrived. The winter hadn't damaged anything, so we were in operation the next day.

That evening as we were sitting around the fire, Ben said, "We need to send somebody down to find that storage site. Whom shall we send?"

I said, "You can't go. We need you to train the crew. I'm the least valuable in the mine, so I'll go if that's all right with everyone."

Juan said, "You aren't familiar with this area. How'll you figure out where to look? We need someplace that's well hidden but where we can get to it in the winter. It needs to be where we can excavate a hole big enough to hold a lot of ore. I don't think you can do it alone."

I replied, "The Utes know this country better than anyone. I'll go and ask Smart Coyote for help. He can either tell me where a good spot is, or he may send someone with me to show me a place."

"That makes sense," Lud said. "If there's a good location, the Indians'll know of it, and none of us could do better. The kid knows that chief well enough to get his help, and no one else does. I say we let him try it."

"Besides, Carlos is already lonesome and needs to see Molly," Pierre added with a smile. "I'd want to see her if I was in his place. I vote for him."

Ben said, "Can we trust him to look for a spot rather than stay there with Molly? Maybe one of us should go along and make sure he doesn't just stay and play with her." The smile on his face said he was joking.

"I'll put together a pack and take that mule again. If I leave in the morning, I'll be in the Ute camp tomorrow evening and can be looking for a spot in a couple of more days. I'll take enough food for three weeks. If I can't find a spot by then, we'd better send someone else."

Lud said, "Take enough for ten days. We need to be digging that hole in two weeks. We need to decide some things about it, too. It needs to be where we can reach it as we go toward Santa Fe. We don't want to go clear out of our way to reach it. It can't be too close to the main trail, but I don't think we should have to go more than five miles away from the trail. We want a place we can reach from that big park this side of the hot springs so we can come back in the winter and get what we store there. I'd say we should figure on taking off from the trail close to where we cross the Piedra and come back to it in the lower end of that park."

"That narrows it down a lot, but it still needs to be somewhere that folks won't find if they're deer hunting. We need a place that's not easy to get into," said Ben. "I suggest that you find a couple of spots, and two or three of us can go look at them and make a decision about which one we want."

◆◇◆◇◆

I rushed off that mountain, leaving at least an hour before the sun was up. I ate a cold biscuit in the saddle and stopped only to drink from the creek. I was in the Ute camp by early afternoon. I had been there often enough that the kids knew my name, so Smart Coyote, Fawn Heart, and Molly were outside when I reached their tipi.

"We didn't expect you back this soon," Molly exclaimed. "Is there trouble?"

"No. I need some advice and perhaps some help from Smart Coyote. I'm looking for the place to make our cache and want to see if he can help me find it."

"I'm sure he'll give you as much help as he can. Let me tell him why you're here."

"I'll help," the chief said. "Come and eat, and then we'll talk."

The Utes rarely talk during a meal. I have occasionally been on a hunt with them, and when the men are alone, they'll often talk. They almost never do when eating with women present. Molly had become used to the way we did things in Santa Fe, so she asked some questions while we were eating.

"Is everything all right at the mine? Was it damaged during the winter?"

I observed that Smart Coyote looked at her with a surprised expression, so I answered by shaking my head and glancing at the chief.

"I'm sorry," she said. "I was impolite. I'll wait until we've eaten and the two of you have talked."

The Ute grunted and gave her a nod.

When we were through with the meal, he said, "You want something. Tell me what you need."

"The mine'll be producing more ore than we can take with us this fall. We need to find a place where we can make a hollow in a canyon or a steep hillside in which we can store the ore and return in the winter and haul it to Santa Fe. It'll need to be down much lower than the mine so we can reach it after there's too much snow to go to the mine. We'll need to have a place where there's rock underground. We don't want to use a dirt hole that'll need to be supported by timbers. We'll use dynamite to break the rock and make a large hole that'll hold as much ore as two hundred burros can carry. It needs to be close to the hot springs so we don't need to go far off the trail to the mine. We should be able to reach it from that grassy area northwest of the springs. We want to make a trail to it that'll start close to Piedra River where we cross it going to the mine. Do you know of a good place in that area?"

He sat silent with his eyes closed, rocking on his buttocks, humming softly. This continued for several minutes, the only sound being his humming and an occasional grunt. He spoke at last.

"I think of a spot that's hard to reach from the grassy area but can be reached easily from the creek crossing. I think there's rock under the ground two or three feet under the dirt. The canyon's small, but you should be able to make the hole as big as you want. I'll take you tomorrow so you can see if it's what you want. We'll need to stay there overnight. It's too far to see it and come back in one day."

"Is that the only place you know about?"

"It's the best place. There may be others, but that's what you need."

"Are there others in the tribe who might know of other places?"

"Why should you know of others when this is the spot you want? You white eyes always want more than is needed."

"I apologize. You're right, of course. We'll look at it tomorrow. I have food and camping gear, so we'll be able to stay overnight without anything other than a couple of blankets for each of you. We'll need to stay in the same tent. If that isn't all right, we'll need another tent."

"We'll be fine in the same tent. Dawn on the Mountain stays in our tipi, and it's all right."

"Good. How early will we leave?"

"Sunup is a good time to ride. We'll leave then. I'll go sleep now. You and Dawn on the Mountain want to talk. I'll see you tomorrow."

"Thank you. I hope you sleep well."

When he left, Molly and I walked down to the river.

"I thought there was a possibility that he'd tell me of a place, but it's really nice that he'll show it to me. It'll give us some time together, too. Will you be troubled by sleeping in the same tent with me?"

"Of course not. We'll need to be careful about modesty, but we've never had a problem from the three of us sleeping together here. It's common among all the tribes."

"That's fine. I can sleep outside if it'll be better."

"We'll see," she commented, smiling. "Are you troubled by the thought of being together all night?"

"We wouldn't dare let anyone know about it if we were in Santa Fe. Grandma would be shocked at the thought. I'll see how it feels tomorrow night. If it bothers me, I'll stay outside."

"You are *funny*. All we need to do is pretend there's a wall between us and act as though it's there. I'll feel quite safe. I think it'll be nice. It'll be exciting, too."

"I'll be excited, all right. I'd probably sleep better outside."

"If that's what you prefer, you should do it. I'd rather be excited."

"I'll ask Jesus about it and will do whatever he tells me is better."

"I'll be interested to see what he says. I don't think he had a situation like this. How'll he know what it's like?"

"Remember that he designed us, so he knows exactly how everything affects us. He knows precisely how we feel and what's best. I'll do what he says to do and won't question his decision. I'm glad I can depend on him. If I had to make decisions like this by myself, I'd often make mistakes, but he never does."

"I think he must be telling us we should go to bed. I love being out here with you, but it isn't safe. Let's go back."

"I don't want to, but you're right. May I have a kiss first?"

"Just one careful kiss."

We were as careful as possible then strolled back and parted at the tipi. I lay and imagined what it would be like in a couple of years. Sleep didn't come soon.

We ate while it was still dark. I had brought our horses from the pasture while the meal was being prepared and had things ready to leave before first light. Smart Coyote said, "We're leaving earlier than I planned. I may have time for a nap later."

We were about five miles from camp when the sun stuck its head over the eastern horizon. It was another hour before we were warm enough to unbutton our coats, and we took them off a short time later. There were a couple of small clouds in the southwestern sky, but it looked as though we'd not be bothered by rain. I was riding my stallion, and Molly was on her Arab filly. They were both frisky, and it was apparent that they'd enjoy going for a morning run, but Smart Coyote's horse and that mule made that a bad idea, so we held tight reins and let them prance. They were still frisky when we reached the mesa west of the hot springs. Smart Coyote told us to head toward Black Mountain, northeast of us.

We reached the far edge of the park and rode into the foothills with Smart Coyote leading the way. When we were close to the top of a primary ridge that ran off to the northwest, he turned onto a game trail and followed it. We rode several miles along that trail before he left it and rode down to the left. The slope was gentle for a quarter mile then became a small, steep canyon. There was a small stream in the bottom that was fed by a spring. The slope where we rode was gentle but changed abruptly and fell off to our left. The chief dismounted, so we did, as well.

"This is the place. I'll show you where you should dig your opening."

He scrambled down toward the bottom. When he was halfway to the stream, he stopped on a grass-covered ledge.

"You can make a hole here," he said, indicating the entire hillside. "There's solid rock here. You can make your hole as big as you want. Nobody'll come here for any reason, so it'll be safe."

"This is exactly what we need. Does that trail go over to the river?"

"Yes. It may not go exactly where you want, though. We'll eat, then we'll ride over, and you can see where it goes."

Smart Coyote put a fire together quickly while I took out my coffee pot and filled it from my canteen. Molly went to some bushes nearby and gathered a hatful of berries that were ripe to perfection. The berries made the jerky and coffee an enjoyable meal. The spot where we ate was almost level and extended far enough to serve as a camp site for a sizable crew —another positive feature of the location.

After we had eaten, Smart Coyote said, "I'll rest. You should follow this down to the park and see if there's a way to reach this spot without coming the way we did. That trail we followed will be covered with snow in the winter. If you want to come here in the winter, you'll need to come another way."

Molly and I rode along the upper slope of the canyon and found that the first half mile was easy going. Then it was too rough to attempt on the horses. We followed beyond that point on foot and were able to reach the edge of the park.. We followed the edge of the slope for a half mile in each direction but found no access that would allow the use of horses.

"We'd be forced to pack the ore using men. While that'd be hard work, it actually makes the spot better. Nobody'll be apt to go there unless they can ride, so the ore will be safe from discovery. Smart Coyote is right; this is what we need. I could have wandered around for weeks and not found this."

"God's blessing you, isn't he? Smart Coyote wouldn't do this for anyone else. I can't imagine him coming out to show another person this spot."

"You're right. Let's stop now and thank God for it. Father, we realize that you have given us a very special gift in causing Smart Coyote to show us this spot. We thank you with our whole hearts and ask that you'll give Smart Coyote the ability to understand that you're the one and only true God. We want him to become not only our friend, but we want him to be your child in Christ Jesus. If there are things we should say to Smart Coyote to help him reach that point, please give us those words. You're able to speak through a willing person. We want to be available for your use in every way possible. If he'll listen to Molly better than he will to me, please use her. I know she wants him to come to know you. Her love for him may be the instrument you can use. You know our hearts, Lord. Please show us exactly what you want, and we promise that we'll do it. We ask this in the name of Jesus. Amen."

Molly continued, "Lord, you know how much Smart Coyote and Fawn Heart mean to me. If you can use me in any way to make them believe in Jesus, I want to be your tool. Please use me."

"God'll answer that prayer, sweetheart. That was a beautiful prayer, and I know God was as pleased to hear it as I was. Let's draw on the faith of Jesus and expect to see him answer soon."

"Do I know enough to show them the way?"

"God knows everything, and he'll either give you the words, or else he'll actually speak through you. Be prepared for a wonderful experience. He won't disappoint. He's faithful."

"I love you, darling. This is another blessing. I was missing you terribly after two days, and then you rode into camp. I could hardly believe what the children were saying as they announced your arrival yesterday. Now we have this time, here in this beautiful spot, in the very presence of God. I've never felt this close to him before."

"Let's stay here and enjoy it. We may not have this experience many times in our lives. I'm so glad we're together now. What a privilege it is for me to be with you when you're being blessed. I've wanted this for you, and now you have it. Thank you, Lord. You're wonderful."

She was more beautiful than I had ever seen her. Her face was almost glowing and was a picture of joy and wonder. It's something to be savored and held onto with adoration when you realize that you're in the very throne room of the universe, being blessed by almighty God. To be there with the person I love more than life itself was a thing too wonderful to describe.

"Oh, Carlos," she said softly. "I'm so *happy*. This is the most wonderful thing that has ever happened. I'm so glad you're here with me now. It wouldn't be nearly as good if you weren't here. Thank you, Lord. I want this to last forever."

It was a marvelous time. She came into my arms, and I held her gently, sharing her joy. I can't put into words the wonder of those moments. I held her with her arms clinging to me and came to a realization that it was perhaps even more special than I had thought.

"Jesus tells us we're in him," I whispered. "We're together in him right now, and it's wonderful beyond words. Can you feel that, too?"

"Oh, yes. It's like nothing I've ever known. I wish it would last forever."

"The unbelievable part of it is that it does last forever. This is part of having eternal life. It's his allowing us to truly sense that he never leaves us. What a blessing this is. When we have it together, it is perfect."

"It wouldn't be nearly so special if we weren't together. Do you think he's placing a special seal of approval on our relationship?"

"I think he just revealed to you what he's doing, sweetheart. We can safely accept it that way."

"Thank you, Lord."

"I feel like I'm sort of floating in a pool of God's love, and he's placed you here with me. I suppose we can keep the feeling while we go back up that hill. We may just float up there, but we'll probably need to climb it. Smart Coyote will soon wonder where we are, so we need to go back."

"We must do it, I suppose. Kiss me before we start."

"You'll never need to ask me twice, darling. You weren't going to get loose without being kissed, but I really like it when you ask."

The climb was strenuous but not really difficult. I enjoyed helping Molly over some of the more difficult spots. She was fully capable of climbing without help, but why would anyone pass up a chance to hold her hand or give her a loving boost? We laughed often and expressed our love in other ways frequently. It was apparent that we were in the special presence of God all the time. It was a time to recall with wonder and made a difference when we weren't together.

The chief was awake but still resting when we reached him. He was quick to mount his horse and lead us back to the trail. We followed it to the Piedra. We were a mile upstream from the crossing we used to reach the mine, but it wouldn't be difficult to find an alternate way from that crossing. We followed down into the park, which we reached just before the sun disappeared behind the western hills. We each went to work and soon had the tent up and a meal cooking. The moon was climbing the eastern sky when we started eating. It was just shy of a full moon, so we needed no light.

"You've given me a great gift today," I told Smart Coyote. "You were right when you said you knew the best spot. I thank you, and my partners will be very grateful for your assistance. I could have never found that without your help."

"I'm glad to share with you. You're Dawn on the Mountain's man, so I'll help you whenever I can. It's good to see her with you. How long will she stay with us?"

"We'll need to go to Santa Fe for supplies in about a moon. She'll stay with you until then."

"That's good. Will you come for her?"

"Yes. I plan to go with the crew who will bring the supplies. I don't want her traveling alone."

"That's also good. You must care for her well."

"That's apparent to me. I love her more than I can tell you. You can rest assured that I'll care for her with my very life. I'm honored that you allow me to take her from your home."

We retired early and all used the same tent. Our afternoon had removed any reluctance I had. We were up early the following morning. Smart Coyote tended the fire while Molly prepared the food, and I took care of the horses and mule. I had them ready when Molly called us to eat. The chief put out the fire and cleaned up the area while Molly and I went to get the horses.

"Do you need to hurry back to camp?" I asked Smart Coyote.

"There's no need to hurry. Why do you ask?"

"If you want to see how I find gold, this would be a good time."

"How long will it take?"

"We can probably do it before we'd eat the next meal."

"I'd like to do it."

I cheated some since we were a half hour from a spot I knew held a nice deposit of ore. I led the way, and we rode to the area of our first mine. I remembered the location close to that mine which I had marked because of a strong signal from my nugget. I hadn't told anyone about it and had never had time to do anything with it. It took but a few minutes to reach the area. I stopped fifty yards away. We left the horses and mule grazing and prepared to start the search.

I said, "I can show you how I do it, or if one of you'd like to try, I'll teach you, and you can find the gold."

Molly said, "Can you teach me how to do it?"

"I'm sure I can. Would you like that?"

"I'd *love* it. Let me ask Smart Coyote if he wants to do it. If he does, I can wait."

She and the chief talked briefly. "He wants me to try. What do I need to do?"

It took but a few minutes to teach her how to handle to equipment. We were soon following the creek toward the place I had found the previous year. It was soon apparent that something had caused to creek to change course. It now followed a way twenty feet west of its previous path. I was surprised but knew that the gold hadn't moved. We were twenty feet from where I knew the gold was when Molly got the first signal.

"Why is the nugget swinging differently?"

"It's showing you something. Keep on walking like you were and let it show you more."

It was soon evident that the nugget was responding to something to her right. I told her how to interpret the actions until she was standing with the nugget swinging in a complete circle.

"You're standing directly above the gold. Stay right there, and I'll get a shovel. This is going to be easy. I expected to have water to contend with, but the creek's changed course. We'll be working with dry material."

We were further blessed when I discovered that it was only two feet to solid rock. The deposit was lying on that base. It was a cluster of nuggets, arranged like a hen's nest full of eggs. I estimated the total was five pounds of beautiful chunks of gold.

"There it is, sweetheart. You're a dowser."

"I didn't do anything. The nugget did it all. I just carried it and watched."

Her face showed the wonder she felt, and it was a marvelous thing to watch as she realized how God had done what no one else could possibly do.

"This has been a special time. I'm thrilled that God used you. This was much better than if I'd done it. Now Smart Coyote can see that I have nothing other than what God gives me. He'll find it easier to believe."

"Oh, Carlos, thank you for letting me do that. It was wonderful. I have another reason to love you now," she said, her lovely voice barely more than a whisper.

"I was given the privilege of watching God use you, sweetheart. The gold is yours. You found it."

"This nugget looks like it's been two pieces that fused together. That'll remind me of us and how we'll become one when we're married."

"What a wonderful thought. You're not just beautiful to look at, you have a beautiful mind. I'll cherish that thought when I'm lonely."

"Enough," said the chief. "We must eat and go."

I tried to make the meal last, but it seemed as though it was only a few seconds before it was time to part.

"I'll try to slip away and visit you at least once before we leave to go to Santa Fe. In the meantime I'll enjoy the memory of yesterday and today."

"I miss you terribly but I know we must be apart for now. Please come as often as you can."

"I'll look for opportunities. You can be sure I won't miss any chance to see you. This is going to be a long summer."

"I love you. Kiss me."

We walked slowly to meet Smart Coyote.

He was already in his saddle and was leading Raton toward us. I'd take Molly's filly so the stallion could go with them.

"Go dig your hole. I'll enjoy having my daughter until you return."

We parted there, they to the Ute camp and I to the mine.

My partners were skeptical when I informed them of the single place. We had agreed that I'd find two or three and we'd decide which of them was best. When they learned where it was, they were almost convinced.

I finally said, "Smart Coyote's right. He said we always want more than is needed. He said he knew the best spot, and I feel he's right about that, too. There's an area that'll be good for a camp, a trail that goes from there to a mile from the crossing of the Piedra, and it'll be easy to make a trail from the crossing to the existing trail. The spot can be reached on foot from the park about five miles from the hot springs, but you have to leave horses down at the park. When we move ore in the winter, we'll have to bring it down to the horses. That lack of access will keep the site from being discovered by anyone hunting or just passing through.

"There's plenty of room to make our cache in what appears to be solid rock. It'll be easy to hide the opening because there's grass over the entire area. By removing sod in a manner that'll keep it growing, we can put it back in place when we leave. There'll be nothing to indicate any digging. We'll need to haul the rock from the excavation to a rock slide so that evidence is gone. The place will be more secure than the mine."

Ben said, "It sounds good. Maybe that Ute does know what he's talking about. I hate to assume that somebody who's never done any mining knows that much about something this important. I want to go see it tomorrow. Who wants to go along?"

Lud said, "We can't all go. Why don't you and Juan go and look it over. If you agree, we'll do what you say is best."

Pierre said, "I'd rather trust them than try to decide myself. Let's get it done so we can start working on making a hole."

We were able to examine the site and return to the mine before the moon was up the next night. We gathered for the evening meal and prepared to discuss our findings.

Lud started by asking, "What'd you find?"

Ben shook his head and replied, "That Ute took Carlos to the best spot we could ever hope to find. I tried to find something to complain about but could only find one thing. It's half a mile from the hole to where we'll need to leave the burros. The ore will have to be carried by men that far. It'd be nice to have the spots closer to each other, but it won't work. Other than that, you couldn't design a better location. I'm ready to have us start on the hole right now."

Juan said, "We looked really hard and couldn't find any other problem. I think we gained a couple of weeks by getting that spot given to us by that Indian. We owe him a lot. If he didn't like Carlos, we'd have searched a long time to find that spot, if we could have done it at all."

Pierre asked, "All right, so we've got a spot. Who handles digging the hole?"

Juan said, "I could take Carlos, and we can find out how deep the soil is. Then we can put the entrance in place. That would give Carlos some experience with dynamite so he can be sure the crew's doing things correctly. We'll also learn how that rock breaks up and can design the main excavation. We'll need a cavity that has a ceiling tall enough to walk in without any problem, but it'll serve no purpose to make it deeper than that. What we need is a hole that goes as far as possible straight into the hill and as wide as possible so we can put a lot of ore in it. I think we can do all of the design and entrance work in a week."

Ben said, "If you can do all that in ten days, I'll be happy. While you're doing that, we'll select the crew we'll send there and get the gear ready to haul down. We'll need to plan on a couple of days to get things in place and ready to start working. We should be able to put them to work there in two weeks. I figure we can start putting ore in there a month later. We'll probably haul quite a bit down there before we can put it underground, then we shouldn't have any trouble. We'll need to keep track of what we do with the ore. We'll need to have a full pack train of ore at the mine when we close up this fall. We'll take that load to Santa Fe and come back later to get some from the cache."

Lud said, "I guess your mule will get to go with you again, kid. He seems to like it, though. We'd better get a pack together so you can leave early tomorrow."

"I didn't use much of what I took the other day, so it won't take long to add what Juan'll need."

Juan said, "I'll get my things, and you can put it together in a hurry. We'll leave here as soon as we finish breakfast. I hope we can have things ready to start on the entrance before we bed down tomorrow night."

We were all in bed within a few minutes, and it seemed as though I had barely gone to sleep when I heard sounds of a fire being put in place. I was surprised to find that it was light in the tent. We were soon up and ready for another day.

Juan and I left soon after sunup and didn't pause until we were at the new location. After a cold meal, we took shovels to the spot Smart Coyote had said was the place for the entrance.

I started carefully cutting the sod and removing it so we could replace it in the fall. We took enough soil so the grass would continue to grow and put it on the ledge about fifty feet away. We removed a section about six feet square and then dug down to rock, which was about two feet underground. We had decided to remove about six feet of the rock straight down from there and then make a tunnel six feet wide and the same height ten feet into the hillside. At that point, we'd raise the roof height to eight to ten feet and would try to continue that depth until we had a cavity a hundred feet square.

As we were eating breakfast the sixth morning, Juan said, "We'll spend today looking for a rock slide. We've done enough here to be sure this is good, solid rock, which'll be good for our storage hole. I want to go back and let the others know what we've done and make our recommendations. We should be able to bring a crew next week and have this job underway within a few days.

"I'll ride off to the east and you can go north. We'll meet back here for a noon meal. If either of us has found a slide we think will handle our rock, we'll both go look at it. If neither of us finds a good slide, we'll split up again. We can spend tomorrow looking if we need to, but I think there'll be something suitable fairly close."

When I was a half mile from the diggings, I encountered a steep slope that ended in a mesa five miles long and the same distance wide. There were steep slopes on every side, and there were sizable rock slides at three spots. Each of the slides appeared to be too small to handle the amount of rock we'd produce, but the total area of the three should be large enough. I found a fairly easy slope on the northwest side of the mesa that would give us access to the top. I tried to ride at a speed that would approximate the gait of a burro. It took less than a quarter hour to reach the excavation, which was an acceptable distance.

It lacked quite a bit of being the time we were to meet, so I picketed my horse and walked the way we'd need to carry the ore during the winter trips. I followed the course of the stream, looking for an easy way to bring water up to our camp. I was about half way to the place where the way became too steep to use horses when I found what I was seeking. There was a break in the rim I was following. A ledge sloped down to ten feet above the stream where it became a gentle slope forty feet long that extended into the water. The stream bed widened at that point until the water was an inch deep. That continued downstream until the slope steepened and the water flowed over the edge and disappeared. I walked to that point and discovered a steep deer trail. Following that took me to a spot forty feet above the level of the park. I continued down and decided I'd try riding my horse down the way I had gone.

Juan was back when I reached our camp, so we ate while I related what I had found. He had found only a half dozen small slides that wouldn't serve our purpose. I gave him a map that should take him to my mesa and slides. We agreed that I'd continue to look for a way to use burros to pack the ore down to the park.

I spent the afternoon looking for a way to get animals from the park to the ledge. I discovered one spot where we might be able to assist them, but wanted Juan to look at it.

When Juan looked at it, he said, "We can attach a rope to the horse we want to help then bring it up around the tree and take it back down to another horse. That second horse can pull the rope, and it'll help the other horse climb up here. There should be no difficulty getting several horses up here . We can go around and try it if you want, or we can wait and do it next winter."

"We can surely find time to try it later. We both think it'll work. What do you think about the rock slides?"

"They should work fine. I think we've made lots of progress. Let's go back to camp and get things ready so we can leave early tomorrow."

CHAPTER TWENTY-NINE

We took a crew of ten miners plus a cook and his helper to the cache. When they had completed twenty feet of hole, we added twenty more miners. The completed cache was a hundred feet square, with passages five feet wide around two areas for storing ore. The storage areas were within walls eight feet high, with an opening in each to allow access.

I went to the mine after all three crews were functioning and arranged for the men and animals needed to remove the material from the lower workings. I also completed the plans for the trip to Santa Fe for supplies. The pack train would leave in a week. I'd accompany them and take Molly back to my grandparents' home.

Ben had been making a map of the mine and marking the area with tree blazes. He wanted to do the same thing at the cache, so he'd replace me there while I was on the trip to Santa Fe. I arranged to meet the pack train at the hot springs and went directly from the mine to get Molly.

I left at least an hour before sunup and by pushing hard was in the Ute camp by just after noon. Thanks to the usual greeters, Molly, Smart Coyote, and Fawn Heart met me at their tipi. Smart Coyote said, "You haven't come for almost a moon. Is this when you'll take Dawn on the Mountain?"

"Yes. I'm sorry that I haven't come earlier. There were too many duties. We're digging the hole where you showed us."

"When will you leave?"

"Tomorrow."

He gazed into my eyes a full minute, and I could see the emotion he was experiencing.

"We'll talk later. You may walk together until we eat."

"Thank you. We'll go to the river."

"It's been difficult to stay away," I said. "There were so many things to do that I couldn't leave. Have you enjoyed your visit?"

"Yes, but I've been terribly lonesome."

"I've been busy, so the days have been bearable, but the nights were long. This is the last year I'll do this. I'll not be separated from you like this again. The single thing that made it bearable was the memory of that afternoon we had together with the Lord."

"Yes, that made a difference. I could think of that and almost think we were together. I agree that this should be the last time we're separated. We also need to go find Mother."

"We'll plan to do that next spring."

We had reached what had become "our spot" at the river. I made certain that we weren't visible to anyone and took Molly in my arms for a much-needed kiss. We then sat on a nearby log.

"Molly, darling, I want you to be my wife. Will you marry me after we return from getting your mother?"

"Oh, Carlos, you surely know that I can hardly wait to have you as my husband. I can think of nothing that would be more wonderful than bearing your children," she whispered, her eyes glistening. "I love you more than I ever thought I could love anyone."

"I'll have an engagement ring made while we're in Santa Fe. We'll have a party."

"I don't need a ring or a party. My life is complete already now that we're to be married. I love you, sweetheart."

"You're my life. Without you there's nothing. Please never doubt that I love you, darling. I'm sorry I didn't ask you earlier."

"It was marvelous to hear you ask me. I'd have asked you if that was proper."

"You're the most important person I'll ever know. My life is wrapped in you."

"I look forward to riding with you to Santa Fe. We'll be able to ride ahead of the others, won't we? I want some privacy with you."

"We'll be a mile ahead of those burros within a few minutes. I'll need some kisses that we haven't allowed ourselves. I hope you know how much I've missed you."

"I can only assume it was the way I missed you. The difference may be that I wasn't busy, so I missed you all the time. The nights were worse, with nothing to fill my mind but thoughts of you."

"That'll end, Molly. I can only imagine what it'll be like when we're able to be fully together. We should go back. Do you know what Smart Coyote wants to talk about?"

"No. It'll be important. He rarely has private conversations."

"Do you think the need for a translator bothers him?"

"Not when I'm the one who does it. Our relationship is such that he doesn't mind saying what's on his mind in my presence."

"I know, and that makes it so special that he's willing for you to go with me. I'll make sure he agrees that we should marry."

"He's told me what an extraordinary man you are. He assumes that you bought me so you could have me as your wife. He'll be pleased that you ask for his permission."

We ate venison and berries and drank an herb tea. It was a much more solemn meal than any I had shared with them. The four of us sat in a circle in the tipi, and we didn't move when the meal was finished.

"You have too many men and animals," Smart Coyote said. "We can't allow you to bring that many into our territory. Others will follow, and we'll soon have no place to hunt and our horses will have no pasture. You must *not* bring that many again. The council's agreed to allow you to keep that many this summer, but if you bring that many again, we'll drive you away."

"I apologize. I warned my partners that it was too many. I'll not come next year."

"What'll you do?"

"We're planning to go free Dawn on the Mountain's mother from the Sioux. We hope she's still where she was. I want to talk with you about that. We'll appreciate your help in finding the camp."

"It'll be good if Dawn on the Mountain has her mother. She has room in her heart for both Fawn Heart and her mother."

"You're truly a father to Dawn on the Mountain. I've asked her to be my wife, and she has accepted. I now ask for your permission to marry her."

I've never known another man who was able to show less emotion. However, his face displayed a flood of thoughts as he considered my question. He said nothing for such a long time that I was almost ready to suggest that he wait until morning to answer. Molly was intently watching both of us. She apparently perceived my thought. She shook her head and touched her lips to indicate that I should say nothing. Smart Coyote hadn't looked at me while he was considering my request. He finally raised his eyes, and I felt as though he was trying to see into my soul.

"Dawn on the Mountain has left no doubt that you're already her husband in her heart. I have tested you in ways that you don't know. I'm happy she's chosen you. I see that she'll only be happy when she's your squaw. You have come to me again to gain my approval. This is strange, but I like it. Fawn Heart and I have talked about this, and we want you to be her husband. Dawn on the Mountain is our daughter, and her husband will be a member of our family. I tell you that our hearts will be full when she makes you part of our home."

His eyes remained locked on mine as Molly translated. I held his gaze until her voice broke. I looked at her, and tears were flowing, but her expression was one of pure joy. I smiled at her and looked back at the chief. He was aware of her emotion but didn't look at her. Fawn Heart placed her hand on his, and he grasped it tightly. While his eyes remained locked on mine and his expression didn't change, tears started creeping down his cheeks. Soon we were all in the same condition.

Molly said, "Just say thank you."

"Thank you, sir. I'll go now."

"Yes. We'll have this night with our daughter."

We left with no fanfare at dawn. We were able to allow our horses to set their own pace, which was actually the speed at which Molly's filly wanted to go. Raton adjusted to her way of going with no direction from me. I never knew of his doing that with any other horse, but he did it every time we rode together. We reached the hot springs late in the afternoon.

The two men with the burros were there and had things ready for the night with a meal on the fire and a tent erected. I put up a tent for Molly, and we were soon eating. The next morning we were on the trail within minutes after sunup. The burros set the pace for the others, so Molly and I were soon out of sight and could ride with privacy.

We had no plans to do anything; we just wanted to be alone. Last winter with us living in the same house and being together almost all day three times a week had spoiled us. We needed some make-up time. I told her about the storage excavation and locating the rock slides and gave her a detailed description of all we had done. She appeared to be interested in all of it, so I gave her the full story.

"I understand why you weren't able to come see us during that time. I wish I'd been that busy. I just looked for you and wished we could be together."

We rode and talked until we reached the place the pack train would stop for the night. We were a pair of teenagers and acted the part. We picketed the horses and walked hand in hand along the creek. Molly picked a bunch of flowers, which she scattered where we pitched her tent. I gathered a plentiful supply of firewood, and we did all we could to make things easier for the men when they arrived. I had some line and fishhooks in my saddlebag, so we cut some willows and caught a dozen trout.

The next two days were memorable because we were together. We discussed our plans for the house, the number of children we'd have, the beauty of a particular cluster of flowers or the shape of a rock, how the sun reflected off a lake, what a cloud reminded us of, and other important things. Molly found beauty in commonplace things I'd have not noticed. An ancient log peeking out from a pile of snow, the way a vine twined up a rocky crag, an abandoned bird's nest clinging to a limb high up in a dead tree. They became treasures because she saw them and called them to my attention. I fell more deeply in love with her as she widened and deepened my world. We'd have enjoyed the day if it had been raining torrents. Since the day was particularly nice, we knew the Lord was blessing us.

The third day was similar, but the fourth was when we knew the men and burros would reach Santa Fe, so Molly and I were able to travel as fast as we wanted to. We reached home in the middle of the afternoon. After greeting my grandparents, I went to the trading post and placed our order. It'd take two days for them to get everything ready, which is what we had assumed, so it wasn't necessary for me to contact the men with the pack train. They had been instructed to leave the burros at the barn and spend a couple of days with their families.

I found Molly and Grandma in the kitchen, working together as though there had been no interruption in their routine. I was always amazed at the way they became a team.

Grandma said, "I'm sure glad you brought her back. This place echoed. It was so empty with nobody here but Grandpa and me. It's truly a blessing to have her home."

Molly said, "You have no idea how wonderful it sounds to hear you say, 'have her home'. I missed you. I feel like I *am* home."

"I had some concerns when Carlos told us about you and said he wanted to bring you here. As soon as we met, you were part of our family. Has he done anything to make certain you'll always be ours?"

"Yes," she said, her voice becoming almost a whisper. "He's made my life full. We'll wait until we go after my mother, but then there'll be nothing to prevent a wedding."

"Good. I always knew that boy had a good head on his shoulders. Now we can start planning."

"Oh, Grandma, I'm glad you approve. That makes it almost perfect."

"What will make it perfect, dear?"

"Having Mother here."

"Of course."

"We hope Smart Coyote will help. I'm praying that God will cause him to want to take us."

"Do you think that's possible? It'd be wonderful if he'd help you that much."

"If he has the idea without my asking him, it'll be better, won't it?"

"You're going to be a *great* wife! You've discovered the secret to getting what you want, especially from a man. I can see that you'll never have a problem getting what you want from Carlos."

"I suppose you've practiced that with Grandpa," I said. "He's always seemed to enjoy doing what pleases you. What you propose may not work with others."

"It'll work better than any other approach. Everyone likes to think he's the originator of anything."

"So it isn't just men who're that way?"

"No, but men are much more that way than most women are. I'm sure any couple would benefit from both the husband and wife practicing that."

"Molly, we've just had our first lesson in keeping each other happy. We need to pay attention. Grandma's an expert at getting what she wants."

"I'm listening closely; I'll try to learn many more things from her. I have no other person to learn from."

"Grandpa and I have had a good marriage, and I want the same thing for you. If we can help you avoid some of the errors we've made, it'll be wonderful. Now, let's get this meal ready."

It was the best meal I'd eaten for over a month, as were all of the others we had the next two days. Then it was time to leave—the time we had known would come but wanted to avoid.

It took a full hour to get everything packed and head back to the mine. People were moving at the Army post when we passed it. There was no logical way to avoid passing the post, and I was afraid the size of our string would bring questions. Grandpa had heard about the need for sending troops into the San Juan Range to try to discover any mines that might be operating there. Our string could trigger that sort of thing.

As soon as we arrived at the mine, I met with the partners and voiced my concerns. Lud was immediately in favor of my idea and said, "We need to post someone where he can watch that hot spring so we'll know when anyone comes. We don't dare let the Army discover what we're doing. The lower operation's especially apt to be discovered. We have a lot more going on up here, and we have people moving around over a lot of country. We're really exposed when we move ore to the cache. We need to know the minute they get here. If they don't come, having a lookout there won't cost much."

We had an older man on watch three days later. We had a very short time to wait for the payoff. A squad of troops led by a lieutenant camped at the hot spring nine days after the watchman was in place. We immediately transferred all the men from the lower site back to the mine and discontinued all activities except those within half a mile of the mine. We used only charcoal so there was no smoke and ceased all activity that would be heard beyond the area within which we continued to operate. We posted more watchmen so the troops were under scrutiny at all times and maintained a group of riders who brought word of all activity to us at the mine. Lud took charge of the observation team.

The patrol spent the first week in the valley northeast of the hot spring. We started to worry when they reached the big park below the cache. They worked along the ridge above our camp site without seeing anything. When they found the trail leading to the mine we took fifty burros a mile from the mine and led them from the trail to the mine onto a game trail that went into the course of Vallecito Creek. We dusted the tracks on the mine trail for one hundred feet, so it appeared that the other was the way all traffic had gone. After the burros had followed in that direction for ten miles, we took ten onto a rocky slope and did the same in four other spots until there was no evidence of the trail having been used by burros.

I had been skeptical of the plan. The Lieutenant in charge of the patrol was inexperienced, and we avoided detection. The patrol followed down the drainage and ended up at the Ute camp. We assumed the chief had successfully feigned ignorance. We continued to watch the rest of the season.

We resumed our operation at both sites. The Army leadership was seemingly satisfied. We were careful to never give them a reason to investigate further. All future orders of supplies were delivered out of town so the army personnel didn't see our pack trains again. We entered Santa Fe in strings of ten burros and approached from several directions so there was no reason for the military men to suspect anything when we came down for the winter.

The trips for supplies allowed me to see Molly four more times. Each time we parted was more difficult. Molly was at the age when many girls married, and the life she lived had robbed her of a normal childhood. At sixteen, I had for three years been in a position of responsibility greater than most men ever experience.

Our love was a mutual and growing thing. We developed not only a deep love for each other, but became very close friends. We were also both developing a deeper relationship with God, which increased our ability to understand and appreciate each other. I'd have done anything to fulfill her every desire. She showed the same concern for me. Grandma told me many times that Molly put my needs above everything except her relationship with the Lord. The hollow spot in my heart was bigger each time I left. That same spot was filled to overflowing when I was with her.

We were visited by the Army on three other occasions that summer. The next year was reportedly worse, with a patrol in the area almost all summer. We established a camp in a basin at the top of Wolf Creek Pass and used it as a base for the watchmen we continued to use. I continued to go with the supply pack trains and was the first to know of the Army patrols. We were inspected at least once each time we came from Santa Fe. We carefully placed everything except food in the bottoms of the packs. When they opened the packs, they saw food and nothing else. That satisfied the inspectors, who seemed to have little interest in making any discoveries.

In August I was followed—supposedly in secret—after an inspection. I took the train to the camp on the pass and unloaded everything. As soon as those who followed us were gone, we reloaded everything and took a circuitous route to the mine. The Army men thought they were hidden, but after dealing with the Utes for almost three years, their efforts seemed obvious. I had several good laughs because there were at least three braves watching them continually—without once being spotted by the patrol.

The patrols were never able to find anything that would allow them to interfere, but they were a nuisance. We felt a need to be constantly vigilant. Their presence hindered our mining. If the mine was discovered, we knew the results would be severe.

The worst incident was in early September. I had made a trip from the cache to the mine and was returning to the cache when I met a patrol. I was alone and had nothing but my saddle horse.

The officer in charge was the youngest I had encountered. It was soon apparent that he was quite impressed with himself.

"What are you doing?" he demanded.

I had been watching the patrol for the past half hour, and that's plenty of time to get ready.

"I'm going to inspect an owl's nest."

"What?"

"I'm going to inspect an owl's nest."

"Why would you do that?"

"Did you ever see a nest of baby owls?"

"No."

"Come along—I'm sure you'll find it worth the ride."

"Where are they?"

"A mile or so over that ridge. It won't take long."

"Why would I want to see them?"

"It's something you won't see very often. I've been in this country all my life, and it's the only owl's nest I've ever seen. Come on—you'll like it."

"All right. Sergeant, I'm going with this man. We'll be back soon. Let the troops rest."

We rode over the ridge and down to a tiny, spring-fed creek. The nest was in a cottonwood tree.

"We'll need to be really quiet, or the mother will make sure we don't see the babies. Whoa! One of them is almost to the end of that third branch on the left side. Do you see it?"

"No."

"Move over here. Look out toward the end of the third branch on the left. There, he just moved."

"I see him! He's a cute little thing, isn't he?"

"He sure is. Let's ride closer. Be careful. If the mother gets scared, she'll hustle them out of sight."

"I see another one! And there's another one. How many are there?"

"I saw seven the other day."

"Really?"

"Yes. I often see five."

"How long do you have to wait to see that many?"

"I was here over an hour the day I saw seven. I often see four or five in half an hour."

"Are you in a hurry?"

"I need to get to camp before long. Why don't you stay and see how many you can spot? We may meet again, and you can give me a report."

"I'm going to do that. I'll stay until dark. Would you please tell that sergeant what I'm going to do, so he won't get concerned?"

"I'll be glad to do that. I'd better go. I hope you see all of them."

"I really appreciate you showing me this. I've got something exciting to write home about, now."

"It was a privilege. I enjoyed it, amigo."

Not all officers were so easily diverted, but that's a good memory.

CHAPTER THIRTY

Before we had completed the excavation of the storage site, I had the crews begin placing ore in the north section. We were able to place a lot of ore while the hole was being completed.

When the north section of the cavern was complete, I had that crew start making charcoal. As soon as we had a decent supply of charcoal, we set up the melting equipment and heated the ore to extract the gold. We soon needed another string of burros to remove the slag from that operation.

I trained a crew at the mine, too. We melted one hundred ninety gold bricks that summer. A burro could pack six bricks, each of which weighed about forty pounds. Each brick required as much ore as five burros could pack, so each animal that was packing bricks was handling the equivalent of thirty burros with loads of ore. We made only one trip during the winter to get all the ore we left at the storage site. We retained a crew during the winter to handle the melting and enough others to go back and get the ore from the lower site.

We used a rope around the tree, as planned, and got twenty burros up to haul ore from the cache. It required a full week to get all of the ore to the park, after which we used the rope around the tree to assist the burros down from the upper level and loaded the entire pack train for the trip to Santa Fe.

We managed to slip into town by splitting the train into small groups and entering town from different directions, so there seemed to be no special notice taken by the army.

We retained five of the foremen to melt the ore that was taken to Santa Fe. We hauled the slag away at the rate of five burros every other day. That job was completed by December twentieth, and we had a storm that night, bringing six inches of snow. We all rejoiced that the storm hadn't come earlier. Now we could relax because we had finished all that we had planned for that year.

CHAPTER THIRTY-ONE

We all met at my grandparents' home to celebrate Christmas again. This year my uncle and his wife, along with their son and daughter, joined us. Grandma, Molly, and my aunt shared the kitchen duties, and we sat down to a feast. There was wild turkey, venison, squash, mashed potatoes and thick gravy, bread fresh from the oven, butter from goat milk, honey, beans, and corn. Later we enjoyed cake, pies made of mince meat and pumpkin, a plentiful supply of coffee strong enough to satisfy the miners, hot tea for those who wanted it, and cocoa for the youngsters.

We exchanged gifts during the time between the meal and the dessert. After three successful years at the mines, we were all generous. The main gift was an engagement ring for Molly, along with a teardrop nugget a full inch long on a gold chain. I gave her the nugget when we were with the others and reserved the ring for a later private time. Because it was so cold, we didn't ride but found a way to be alone at the end of the day.

When all the partners had arrived I managed to get their attention and said, "I'll not be going to the mine next year. Molly and I are going to rescue her mother from the Sioux. I'll appreciate it if we can have a division of the gold."

Lud said, "I'm leaving, too. I can't let these kids go up there alone. I'll take my share and be mighty happy."

Pierre was next. He said, "I'm homesick. If you'll give me my part, I'll head for France. I'm like Lud—we've achieved more than I'd hoped for. Now it's time to go see my family."

Juan said, "I'll miss all of you, but I plan to stay at this until we find the end of those veins. How about you, Ben?"

"I'll be with you when the gold's all mined. I'm hoping for at least two more good years up there."

I said, "Smart Coyote said the Utes won't allow that many men up there. I think you should take it seriously."

"They don't have any right to tell us how big a crew we can have. We'll take at least as many as we did this year," said Juan.

Lud said, "That chief has been a friend to us, and we've not been bothered. I don't want him for an enemy, though. I'll bet he can tear things up if you get him riled. I wouldn't want to ignore his warning. He kept the tribe off us this year but said, 'No more.' I'd recommend taking him seriously."

"What're they going to do if we take the same crew?" asked Juan. "We can give rifles to twenty men, and there's nothing they can do against us. They don't have a single rifle. We can put a handful of men in key spots and keep them from ever getting to the mine."

I said, "I don't know how many rifles they have, but Dark Dog used one to shoot at me. You'd still have to bring stuff down from there. There're plenty of places they can lie in wait for you. I doubt that you could make it off the mountain much less all the way here. Your supply trains wouldn't make it, either. You'll be facing a man who has fought in that country all his life, and he knows it like the back of his hand. His bows and arrows aren't as powerful as rifles, but there are places you'll pass where he can wait that'll put you within thirty feet. He can pick you off as easily with his weapons as he could with cannons. Your rifles will only be better if you stay in the big parks where they'll give you an advantage. You can't get here by staying in parks. They could cut you to pieces before you get to the parks."

Lud said, "You don't understand how much difference there'll be if Carlos isn't with you. That chief'll do things to help Carlos that he'll never do for you. He thinks the kid's big stuff, and has no reason to even try to keep the other men off you. With Carlos out of the picture, he'll probably be as stirred up as any of the others. I've never seen an Indian act like he has, and I'm sure it's because of Carlos and Molly."

"We'll find a way to handle it," Juan declared. "He's not such a big deal. I want the rest of that gold, so I'm going back for it. We can't get it without a crew like we had this year."

We discussed the situation for an hour. Ben and Juan were sure that they could negotiate with Smart Coyote. Ben and Juan hadn't dealt directly with the Indians the way Lud and I had and were convinced they could handle the situation.

Molly said, "This is terrible! You're all discussing this as though the Utes are enemies. Most of them are friends of mine, and you are, too. I can't stand the thought of two groups of my friends killing each other. I'm sure Smart Coyote'll do what he said he would. If you take the same crew next year, he *will* attack you. You'll be putting the entire group at risk. What'll happen to the families of the miners if the husbands and fathers are killed?"

Ben said, "What can we do? If you can help us figure out how to mine without a big crew, we'll do it."

"Let's all pray about it. God has the solution and will give it to us," I suggested. "There's time to decide. My situation hasn't changed. When can we divide the gold?"

Pierre said, "Why don't we get together tomorrow and do it? We've worked all the ore, so there should be no problem about splitting it."

"That sounds good to me. I'll use some of the mules so I can bring my part back with me."

Lud said, "Can you handle mine, too? If it's all right with you, I'll store mine at your place."

"That shouldn't be a problem."

We were rather casual about the way we divided the gold. There was a need to pay the men for January and February, and we each had a share of ownership in the land and barn plus the animals and equipment. It took us a couple of hours to negotiate a settlement of those items, but it was settled in a manner that pleased all of us. We agreed that there were some differences in the weight of the individual gold bricks, but none of us felt there was a need to weigh each of them.

I negotiated an exchange of some bricks for the gold we were able to extract without melting it. That allowed me to keep all of the nuggets. None of the others were interested in the nuggets, so we exchanged on the basis of an estimated weight of the nuggets. We each had over four hundred pounds of gold when we completed the split. We had a short prayer meeting and arranged for Molly to join us in a final meal.

The meal lasted until after it was dark, so Lud and I borrowed mules and packed our shares home that night. We felt we had more privacy that way, and it was easier to get the gold into the house quietly. Our former partners accompanied us and assisted in the transfer from the mules. We finished with a time of prayer when each of us prayed. It was a special time of unity and peace.

Molly concluded the meeting when she said, "Only the Lord could make a group of men who're so different into a team of friends like you've become. I'm privileged to be a part of it because God brought you into my life and made me the most blessed woman since Mary, the mother of Jesus. I'm thankful beyond words. When we're able to bring my mother to Santa Fe, I hope all of us will be able to have another party. You all know that I love Carlos and want to be his wife. The rest of you're wonderful friends who've added to my joy."

Pierre said, "I'm tempted to wait until after that party before going home. Molly, if God has someone a little bit like you for me, I'll be the happiest man in the world."

She was obviously pleased and embarrassed by his praise. She said, "Be sure she knows Jesus, and he'll bring you exactly what both of you need."

"That's part of what makes you so special," he responded. "You're always able to hit the exact center of the target. Carlos, you're the most blessed man I've ever met. God has opened heaven and poured it on you."

"Thanks, Pierre," I said. "Let's take another minute in prayer."

When everyone was ready, I said, "Lord, I feel that you're preparing Pierre for a truly wonderful lady. Give him your ability to recognize her when he meets her. Amen."

That pretty much put a finish to the evening. When we were alone, Molly said, "Have you ever seen a person's face change as much as Pierre's did after your final prayer? He suddenly realized what you had asked the Lord to do for him, and it almost overwhelmed him."

"Yes. I hope we learn who he's given. I think he's changed more than any of the men, and it's been a great thing to watch. The really great thing is how he's worked in Lud's heart. He's become a second father to me and is going with us to get your mother."

"Every one of them is special. I hope Ben and Juan are wise. I'm concerned for them. Smart Coyote's serious about not allowing them to take as many men as they are planning to. I'm thankful you're not going with them,"

"I'd never agree to take that many men. We're blessed to have the chief as a friend. He's an unusually powerful man, or the other men would've attacked us this past summer. He won't try to restrain them again. I'm afraid Ben and Juan will suffer, and the crews will, too."

"We'll not be forced to watch it, and I'm glad for that."

"Yes, I am, too. I hope it doesn't get too bad before Ben and Juan realize that the Utes're serious. Let's pray that they'll decide to take fewer men. We'll have our hands full getting your mother free. I want to go see Smart Coyote as early as possible and see what help he'll give us. Did you ever talk with him about that?"

"Yes, but I didn't ask for help. I said I'd pray that Jesus would give him the idea of helping us. Was that wrong?"

"No. Now Jesus can show you how important it is to believe and allow him time to answer. At the same time, he'll prove the power of prayer. We need to continue what you're doing. Let's plan to pray for that together every day. We'll go see Smart Coyote on our way to get your mother. I believe he'll go with us."

"That would be a wonderful solution, wouldn't it? I really like the idea of praying together. Shall we start now?"

"I like the idea of doing anything with you. I believe by this time next year, we'll be married and living in our new home with your mother here. Then there should be nothing to prevent us from doing anything together."

"The very thought of that sends shivers down my back. I want it in less time than that," she said, her voice a husky whisper.

"There're times I can hardly breathe when I think of it. Do you have any hint of how much I want you as my wife?"

"I hope you want it as much as I do, sweetheart. I want it more than anything in this world."

"You're the most desirable woman in the world, my darling. I'm on the brink of doing something we'd regret later."

"I know, but it'd not please God. We'll be able to rejoice later if we obey him now." Her voice was so low pitched and intimate that I thought of the siren song I had heard of. Was it Ulysses who tied himself to the mast of his ship to keep from being overwhelmed by the sound?

I took her hand and said, "Jesus, we want to please you with our behavior. Give us the strength to resist the urge to disobey. I thank you for Molly, and I want to do only things that'll benefit her and please you. Please touch our minds with your peace in this storm that's raging in our bodies. Amen."

I prayed long into the night. When I had finally told the Lord how much I wanted to make Molly my wife *now*, and how hard it was to wait, and told him several more times, I was able to stop and see if he had anything to say. He didn't speak, but it was only a few minutes before I knew what he wanted. It was clear beyond any doubt that I could make Molly my wife whenever I chose. We could also have Molly's mother. But if we were to have both, we must rescue her mother before we married. I still don't understand, but that doesn't matter. I didn't hear any voice. He left me with no questions. I was absolutely certain it was that way. I received peace of mind and a confidence in our rescue that surpassed any previous experience. I could hardly wait to tell Molly.

I was up earlier than usual and had our horses saddled and tied outside when we finished breakfast.

"I need to tell you what God did last night," I said. "Can we go for a ride?"

"Right now?"

"If you can, that would be nice."

"All right. I'll be ready by the time you get the horses."

"They're ready."

"I'll get my coat on the way out. Let's go."

We rode out of town before I said anything. Molly looked at me often, but said nothing until we were half a mile beyond the last house.

"Are you going to sit over there and tease me all day?"

"No, I want to go some place where we can sit or walk or hug each other in complete privacy."

"Please find a place soon. This must be serious."

I told her about my time with the Lord and left out nothing. As I was finishing we found a place that would be suitable.

"Let's stop here."

I lifted her down, hugged and kissed her, then led her to a log.

"We now know what the choices are. We can marry immediately, but if we do, we can't get your mother. If we wait, we can have both."

"We really have only one choice, don't we?"

"Yes. We'll get your mother, and then we can have our wedding."

"Does that bother you?"

"Absolutely not. You know how much I want you to have your mother. This is what we've planned. It's great that God is assuring us that we can have both, but we need to do it his way. We can do everything with total confidence that God will cause it to happen."

"Are you sure? Did he actually tell you this?"

"It was somewhat different than it had ever been, but there is no question that God gave me the message. There was no voice, he just made it clear in my mind that this is what he wants and how we must act."

"So what do we do now?"

"We wait until spring; then we go talk to Smart Coyote. I think he'll go with us, and we'll go get your mother, come back here, and get married. Pretty simple, wouldn't you say?"

"All except the waiting. If that's what God requires for us to have everything, we'll wait. I still have trouble understanding how God talks to you, but I no longer doubt it. When he talked to me, he let me hear his voice. He talks to you several ways. I just haven't had the same experience, but everything you've said he told you has been right. Isn't he *good*?"

"He's at least that. In fact, I'll say he's *great*."

"We could keep adding descriptions and never say it all, Darling. I keep wondering why he chose to do it to me."

"I don't wonder about that. I think he'd be less than wise if he treated you any differently. Of course, I love you almost as much as he does."

"I can't imagine anyone loving you more than I do."

"We'll never understand the complete, unchanging, unconditional love of God; we just get to enjoy it."

"I think I can understand better if you kiss me. Surely we can allow ourselves to express our feelings now."

We did, and I was totally pleased with the results. It was even easy to stay within our limits.

"I sort of think Raton feels like I do. Let's race back to the first house."

"You'll win. I don't *want* to get away from you."

"You'll never have a chance, so don't try. I love you more than life, sweetheart."

"Show me again."

"You're a brave woman. I may never let you go."

"That's not scary. You'll have to threaten to get rid of me if you want to scare me."

"Somebody's been teaching you how to thrill me with words."

"It must be the Lord. I just say what I feel."

"He does good work! I'm completely under your spell. You're the most beautiful, desirable, enticing woman God has ever created. Now that he's made the perfect woman, he can just copy you and never change a thing."

"I've fooled you completely, haven't I? You'll change your mind after living with me a while."

"I can hardly wait to see. I think it'll be at least a hundred years before I find a single thing to complain about."

"I'll remind you of that when I see you looking less than pleased with me."

"You'll have to watch full time. When I see you looking at me, it melts me down into my boots. Complaining is the last thing that would come to mind."

"I think we'd better have a horse race if we want to get Mother. I'll be dangerous if we stay here any longer. *Don't touch me!*"

"Look at me, wonderful woman. I want you to see what a man in love looks like."

"Please take me home. We're more dangerous than dynamite."

She made sure I won the race, but Raton almost refused to run ahead of her. I could only get him to win by a nose.

CHAPTER THIRTY-TWO

Molly, Lud, and I left March tenth and arrived at the Ute camp the evening of the thirteenth. We had an extra saddle horse for each of us, two more horses, and an extra saddle for Molly's mother as well as two pack horses.

It was immediately evident that Molly was no longer a member of the tribe. She was lavish with her expressions of love for Smart Coyote and Fawn Heart. They were accepted but not returned by the Indians. It was only a matter of minutes before she was aware of her error. She was then back into the role of Dawn on the Mountain, and her actions were much more subdued. She became an Indian princess, "*Daughter of the Chief.*" She's never ceased to amaze me with her gracious spirit and desire to fill the special need of the person she's with.

It was the third day before we felt free to discuss our mission with the chief. Fawn Heart was cooking our noon meal while Lud and I showed Smart Coyote the horses we were using. He took advantage of that to show us his latest crop of foals. Molly was with us to interpret.

"I don't see a bad one in the whole bunch," I said. "Raton's left his mark on all of them."

"The mares you gave me have the best young ones," Smart Coyote replied. "The others are good because of your stallion. We're indebted to you."

"I'm completely satisfied. I have Dawn on the Mountain. She's more valuable than anything I could ever give you."

"Our entire tribe's benefiting from the use of the stallion. You have one thing, but what you gave is helping all of us.

"Is she your squaw now?" he asked.

"No. We agreed to wait until her mother can be at our wedding. We're on our way to get her and are here to ask for your assistance."

"How can I help? I'll do anything I can to help Dawn on the Mountain."

"We'd like to have someone go with us. It should be a person who was with you when you took Dawn on the Mountain from the Sioux. If that's not possible, we'll appreciate your drawing a map so we can find the camp."

"I'll think about this and will tell you tomorrow morning after we eat. You shouldn't wait. She's already your squaw in her heart."

"We're doing it for her mother. It'll make a great gift for her if she can be present when we marry. We think it's important enough to wait and give her that gift. We're doing it for her mother."

"You're a strange man. I don't understand the reason but am happy that you want to do a special thing for a person you've never seen."

"Jesus died over seventeen hundred summers ago to make it possible for me to go to the perfect place he's made for me. This that we do is a small thing compared to that."

He didn't respond for at least five minutes. Then he said, "I like what he did, so it means that I should approve what you're doing. It's good."

We were allowed complete freedom in the Ute camp, so Molly, Lud, and I made an opportunity to slip off for some privacy. We used the time to pray that God would guide Smart Coyote. Molly specified that she wanted him to decide he'd go with us. It was a night when I had difficulty sleeping. Would God be able to put his thoughts into Smart Coyote's mind? I confess to having some doubts.

"I'll go with you," he said. "There's no one else who can help as much as I can. I'll enjoy another victory over those Sioux vultures.

They used to be like a thorn in our foot. I've chosen three braves to go with us, men who were with me when we stole Dawn on the Mountain. When do you want to start?"

Lud said, "We want to go as soon as you think it's all right."

"There'll be a celebration tonight. There'll be much dancing, and Star Gazer will put his good medicine on our trip. If you like, you can join and ask your God to help by adding your medicine." This was addressed to me.

I said, "We've done that every day for three moons, but I'll be honored to join Star Gazer. May I have Dawn on the Mountain with me so she can interpret?"

"Of course. Everyone assumes she'll be with you when you're here. It'll not be necessary for any of us to understand what you say to your God, but there'll be no objection to her remaining with you." He added, "We'll leave early tomorrow."

The drums started as soon as the sun disappeared, and braves were soon arriving, dressed and painted for dancing. The youngest men came first, and they danced with great enthusiasm and abandon. As the age of the dancers increased, the dancing became more intense, the body movements more controlled. Some of them were attempting to mimic the actions of a bird or animal. Several of the oldest men were obviously representing the coyote. If Smart Coyote had joined he'd have danced so that those who were watching would've almost heard the howl of the little animal.

Soon after the final old man had joined the dance, the youngest man danced his way out of the circle. This continued until only the ten oldest braves remained. At that time Star Gazer moved into the center of the circle of dancers. He wore a skirt of coyote skins with one skin that extended up his back with the pelt from the head, including the ears, nose, and upper lips fastened to the top of his head. The bottom of the skirt was a complete circle of coyote feet.

His dance started slowly even though the drummers had steadily increased the tempo of their beat. He made a move every time the drummers struck the drums five times then moved on the fourth beat. This type of change in his speed continued until he was in exact rhythm with the drums. He continued increasing his speed until he was dancing four times as fast as the drum beat. His next move was a dizzying spin that caused his skirt to flare until the coyote feet were straight out from his waist. He spun ten times and came to a complete stop. The stop was so sudden that the skirt continued to whirl. The drummers stopped at exactly the same time he did. The only sound was when the feet on his skirt were wrapped around his waist and dropped down around his legs.

He emitted a yell that was a startling imitation of the coyote. The silence that followed was dramatic and continued as every eye was locked on Star Gazer. He remained frozen in place for so long I wondered if he had injured himself. He then assumed a pose that left no doubt that it was a coyote sitting and howling at the moon. He remained in that position and sang what was surely a supplication to his god. He finished at last, stood, and turned to me. He was an exceptional showman. He bowed and extended his right arm with his hand cupped. He then swung the arm in an invitation to join him.

I had asked God for wisdom but had received no guidance. I felt that there was no way to avoid giving some demonstration of our faith in God. I silently asked the Holy Spirit to control my movements and my thoughts. No direction was forthcoming, but I knew that if I walked toward Star Gazer, I'd learn what to do and how to do it.

I walked toward him until we were facing each other about two feet apart. I bowed and made a motion that was intended to express my appreciation for the invitation. I then turned toward the drummers and swung my right arm up and down while moving my left arm in a motion to indicate the striking of a drum. A drummer started beating in time with my right arm. I nodded and smiled. The other drummers joined, one at a time, until all the drummers were beating. I raised my hands toward the sky and began a dance around the circle, trusting God to give me the proper movements. My movements were given to me as the dance progressed. I danced in a circle around Star Gazer, my body spinning slowly. My knees lifted above my waist in each step, with my arms lifted so the elbows and shoulders were the same height. My hands moved continually from touching my shoulders until the arms were straight, then back to the shoulders. The cadence remained the same all the time. I continued for several minutes then lifted both arms straight up, threw my head back, and shouted, "Jesus!" as loud as I could. I then quickly brought my whole body down and ended on my knees with my head bowed. The drummers stopped as they correctly interpreted the move. I slowly raised my head until I was looking straight up, raised my arms, palms up, and shouted, "Jesus Christ, Lord and Savior."

I held my arms in the same position as I rose to my feet. I spun slowly, shouted, "Amen!" and walked slowly to where I had been seated by Molly, bowed to her, then turned to face the center of the circle and sat down.

Smart Coyote said something, and the Utes rose and departed. Molly whispered, "You were *Magnificent!* Where'd you learn that?"

"I didn't learn it. It was God's answer to our prayers. I hope I never doubt him again."

"You mean he gave you that as you did it?"

"That's the only explanation. I had no idea what was coming next. I just let him have my body. It was no effort because he did it all."

"Most people would never believe that God would do that."

"I'm sorry for them. It's wonderful to know that God is doing what he said he'd do."

She was quiet for several moments, and then she said, "I get so many blessings just by being with you when you're doing what

God tells you to do. Everybody who saw you knew that you were asking Jesus to bless our trip."

"He's given us some special things today. We need to praise him continually. Thanks, Lord, for all you've done today."

CHAPTER THIRTY-THREE

The seven of us rode back toward Santa Fe two days then swung east just north of the Sangre de Cristo Range. The reason for the swing back to the south was to avoid the snow that still covered the higher elevations. We didn't miss the snow altogether. We swung back to the north as soon as possible, which led us to the San Luis Valley. We crossed the Rio Grande River in that valley. Within a month, it'd be swollen and difficult, if not impossible, to cross. We swung east and rode beside sand dunes, which seemed completely out of place in that high mountain valley. We rode across LaVeta Pass. There was still a lot of snow on the pass, but we managed to circumvent the really big drifts and rode down to the prairie that extends northward from Raton Pass east of the Rockies.

We rode for half a month. The weather was typical of springtime. The buffalo grass that covered those plains was just starting to turn green, but there was an abundance of feed left from the previous year. We were rained on frequently, snowed on four times, and were almost constantly riding in wind. That wind came off the eastern foothills with a force that increased as we moved to the north. We all agreed that we'd never want to live where that wind blew. We had three comfortable days during that part of our trip.

Elk, deer, antelope, and buffalo were almost always visible, and there was little fear of us when we were on the horses. I was sure that would change if we were to dismount. We had no need of meat most of the time, so the animals were left undisturbed. It was a beautiful sight to see herds of each species that would number in the hundreds and often thousands.

We crossed the Arkansas River where it roared out of an impressive canyon, which was eventually named the Royal Gorge. We were climbing from the river when Smart Coyote signaled for us to stop, remain quiet, and make sure our horses didn't make any noise. He had arranged the signal soon after we started the trip. It was a band of Comanches—twenty-two of them. They were not expecting trouble, as evidenced by the laughing and chattering that we heard clearly. We were barely able to see them through a line of trees along the river bank. There was no indication that we had been spotted. They crossed the river fifty feet downstream from where we had traveled.

"They'll see our tracks if they find the trail we used," Lud said. "We're a puny bunch compared to them. We'd better find a place where we can hide and wait."

"There's a pocket not far from here. If we can reach it before they find our tracks, we can hold them off," said Smart Coyote.

He wasted no time. He left the trees and led at a gallop across an open plain. We were hindered by the need to handle the extra saddle horses and pack animals. When we were all at full speed, Molly managed to ride to me.

"Those Indians are following," she shouted.

I said, "Pray!"

"*Pray?*" she said, and I laughed.

"Have we ever needed God's help more? He loves a good fight. What a time to watch him!"

"You're *enjoying* this?"

"This is Old Testament action. What a time to watch God at work. We get to be part of it."

"This is *serious*, Carlos. I can't believe you think this is fun."

"He just told me he has everything under control. What more could we want?"

She rode beside me, looking back most of the time. I continued to watch her. After we had gone another hundred yards, she looked at me again. I released a Ute war cry at the top of my voice. She started to smile and laughed with me. I knew Raton would follow Smart Coyote's horse. I had to keep his speed down to that of the animals I was leading.

The chief slowed and turned to his right then rode through some gigantic, broken rocks into a sunken area with a pool of water and grass. A spring flowed from the base of a steep rock slide. We could have done very little to improve it as a place of protection. We were almost completely surrounded by rocks. The smallest of those that made up the outer wall was five feet high. The biggest stood twenty feet tall.

Smart Coyote and Lud assigned each man a spot. I asked if Molly and I could have a location higher than any of the others. It would give us a view of the entire area and was farther from the outer wall than any other spot. Molly would be safer than in any other location. I wanted to keep the Indians from seeing her. Twenty-two Comanche braves traveling alone would make every effort to capture her if they saw her. They would fight harder and continue longer if she was seen. When I thought of the possibility of her being in their hands, it increased my desire to do battle.

"Don't shoot until you're sure of hitting someone," Lud cautioned. "I plan to wait until Smart Coyote shoots. If you see one of them in a position to shoot one of us, go ahead and put him down. Otherwise, hold off as long as you can. Make every shot count. Each of us needs to take care of three or four of them. Are you worried about killing someone?"

"He's *enjoying* this!" Molly said. "I'm scared to death, and he's been *laughing*."

"God assured me that he's already given us an overwhelming victory. I can't keep from laughing."

"Don't let it keep you from being careful. Try to kill one of them every time you shoot. We don't have enough ammunition to waste any. We have the only guns, so we'll be able to handle braves farther out than the Utes will. Leave as much of the close fighting as you can to them," Lud cautioned.

I led Molly through a jumble of rocks to a spot thirty feet higher than our horses. The others were in position before we reached our spot. We were behind the others of our party and would be able to tell if any of them were in danger from an enemy. I was able to clearly see two hundred yards in every direction.

"This is an ideal spot," I told Molly. "We'll be able to watch every move they make and can make every shot count. If a battle can be fun, this should be the one."

"I still don't think it's fun. I can't imagine enjoying this."

"The part I enjoy is waiting to see how God handles it. He sees everything lots better than we do and knows what each of the Comanches is going to do. He even knows what they are planning and can make sure it doesn't work. I want to watch *him* take care of them. When he wants me to do part of it, I'll be ready to act. He's giving us the privilege of watching and also participating. Lord, please let Molly understand all of this."

She was still for a while then poked me in the ribs and said, "How can I keep from enjoying it when you tell me things like that? I *think* I understand now. Thank you, Lord, for giving me this man."

"We need to stay hidden as much as we can. I'd like to be the secret weapon. We have the best spot and can do more if they don't see us. I didn't see any guns when they were close, so they probably don't have any. They'll need to be close to do anything, so we can wait until we have really good shots. Don't shoot at anyone who's moving. We'll get plenty of shots when they're standing still or barely moving."

"Do you want me to shoot?"

"Only if you want to. I'd like it if you'd reload for me."

"That sounds good to me. I'm not sure I could shoot one of them."

"You shouldn't need to. If you do want to, let me know. I don't want to be surprised."

"You are the most *amazing* man! I'm actually looking forward to this. Can you kiss me?"

"I think I can find an extra kiss around here somewhere," I said, laughing. "There, how's that?"

"Thank you, Happy Warrior."

"You're welcome, Sweet Woman. I got the best part."

"Do it again so I can catch up."

"I've got to get ready to take care of that fellow who's sneaking up to Lud."

"What? Oh, my! Can you kill him? He's going to shoot!"

I was already squeezing the trigger, and the bullet went true. Half of his throat diappeared, his arrow went almost straight up, and he was no longer a threat. Lud looked up and raised his hand.

"I didn't see that Indian," Molly said. "If you hadn't been here, he'd have killed Lud. That was *great*, sweetheart."

The battle was lop-sided from the start. Molly shot three, I took care of eight, Lud wiped out five, Smart Coyote sent three to the happy hunting ground, each of the other Utes accounted for one, and the battle was over. Lud got one and I two as they were trying to leave the scene. We gathered in the bottom next to our animals.

"This is where I planned to camp," Smart Coyote said. "I think we'll find another place. I don't want to sleep surrounded by enemies, even dead ones."

Although there were many creeks flowing down from the foothills, the only other rivers were the South Platte and the Poudre. We rode far enough north to escape the foothills, and enjoyed a day of calm. That was followed by a flat, featureless stretch where the wind blew at us all day and all night. I was ready to believe we were trapped in a place where the wind never stopped. Smart Coyote finally turned to the east. We were soon riding into the Black Hills, the home of the Sioux, Dakotas and Lakotas.

Smart Coyote said, "No talking. We're approaching the Sioux camp. We'll ride single file with me in the lead and Lud at the rear. Dawn on the Mountain will be in the middle, with Carlos just behind her."

"How soon will we reach the camp?" I asked.

"If we can travel without interruption, we'll be very close tomorrow, but we may need to travel very slowly. We're close enough to require much care. We may need to stop for quite a long time."

We stayed on game trails that ran along the upper reaches of the hills and stopped frequently. The pauses enabled him to listen for any sound that would indicate the presence of people.

Twice that day we spotted parties of riders moving on trails below us. We all dismounted and made certain that none of our horses neighed. We had nineteen horses, so it wasn't easy to watch all of them, but we never had a mishap. Late in the day we saw eighteen Indians walking. They were going in the opposite direction from that being taken by the parties of riders.

"Those were Sioux. We're close to their camp. They'd not be going to camp this late in the day unless it's close," Smart Coyote stated. "We'll not have a fire tonight, and we must be very quiet. We dare not get too close. Tomorrow, some of us will locate their camp. We'll then decide how to find Dawn on the Mountain's mother and get her away from them."

"Do you recognize this area?" I asked.

"Yes, but we didn't travel these trails. We were a large party, so we didn't need to be so careful. I remember the mountains and streams but want to be certain where their camp is."

We crossed a tiny stream, watered the horses and filled our canteens, then rode until we could no longer hear the water and stopped. The horses were picketed in a small meadow, and we each selected our spot to bed down. We gathered for a cold meal. It wasn't yet dark when we had eaten, so Smart Coyote, Molly, and I walked to a promontory.

There was a huge rock just below the crest of the hill that offered an excellent view of the entire area. We settled down to look at the region. We saw nothing until it was completely dark, then the light of fires was visible.

"We'll need to get closer before we'll be able to see how the camp's arranged," Smart Coyote said. "From that next ridge, we should be able to locate the place where the women are held, and we can determine how much freedom they have. If they're allowed to walk alone, we can locate the mother. We'll need to get close enough for Dawn on the Mountain to talk to her. Then we'll arrange a time for the escape. Do you want to expose Dawn on the Mountain to that much danger?"

Molly answered, "I'll do whatever it takes to free my mother. God will protect me."

The chief said. "We'll be up there as soon as it's light enough to see. The three of us will watch until we know how to plan to get your mother free. We also must have a plan for escaping. If we can get half a day head start, they'll never catch us."

"Are we too close to their camp?"

"They won't expect an enemy this close."

We returned to camp and arranged the schedule of keeping watch before we all turned in. Molly and I spent a few minutes alone.

"I've never been this excited," she exclaimed. "We might get Mother and be on our way tomorrow."

"I guess that we won't do that until the day after tomorrow."

"I'll be delighted if we're able to do it that soon. Won't it become more dangerous every day?"

"Yes. However, if we're really careful, the danger may not increase. I trust Smart Coyote and Lud to make good decisions."

"At least we'll know what they're planning. They can't communicate without me."

"They may plan something that we'd never consider doing. We need to trust God to give them wisdom and then put his cover of safety over all of us. He's assured us that he'll get us home safely with your mother."

"Oh, darling, this is so *wonderful*. I'd have never hoped for this. Now we're doing it. I love you more every day. Thank you, Jesus."

CHAPTER THIRTY-FOUR

We were on that hill an hour before the sun was up. The only activity in the camp below was an occasional dog barking. Smoke was coming from several of the tipis, and horses were grazing. There were at least forty dogs. We saw where the lookout had been stationed, which was a valuable piece of information.

We were located so our view was through trees, and we could move carefully without exposing ourselves. We found places that would allow us to each see a different part of the camp. Molly determined that the building housing the prisoners was unchanged. It was almost noon when women emerged from that building. They went to the stream that flowed along the east side of the camp. They bathed and washed clothing. They then separated and went in different directions.

It took Molly several minutes to identify her mother. When she did, she wept silently. She turned toward me and came into my arms.

"She looks wonderful—just the way I remember her. I want to rush down there and shout her name."

"That'll soon be possible. Which one is she?"

"The one with the white dog behind her."

"She seems to be in good health and is walking easily. I think she's fine."

"Yes. Isn't she beautiful?"

"It's almost like watching you. Yes, she *is* beautiful."

"I can hardly breathe. I wish we could rush down there and get her right now."

"I feel the same way. I hope she walks a long way from camp. If she does we may be able to contact her today."

She continued walking until she was almost out of sight. She was alone except for the dog. She left the trail she was on and went into some trees. The trees had no leaves yet, or we wouldn't have been able to see her. She walked to a big fallen tree. She sat quietly on the log then rose and turned to face the log. She knelt and appeared to be praying. After a half hour she rose and walked back to the house.

"I think she does that every day," I said. "We can slip to that spot and wait for her tomorrow. It's far enough from the camp so we should be able to talk with her safely."

"If this is something she does every day, we'll not have much trouble doing that," said Smart Coyote.

We had no difficulty getting back to our camp. We slipped to the other side of the ridge and were completely hidden from their view. We went over a ridge and settled in where a small creek came in from the north. We followed a trail that took us to a clearing hidden by a cluster of aspens. We picketed all the animals in the clearing and prepared our morning meal over a fire you could've covered with a small sombrero.

We spoke only when it was necessary. The fire was extinguished as soon as our meal was cooked. We all moved to the farthest point of the clearing for our planning session.

Smart Coyote said, "Do you think your mother will do every day what she did today?"

"She spent time in prayer every morning. She was never allowed to move around as she did today, but she never failed to pray. I think she *will* go there every day if it isn't raining."

"Do you think she'll need to get anything before she leaves?"

"I imagine she'll be willing to leave everything."

"All right. We'll plan accordingly. You, Carlos, and I'll be in the trees near the place she prayed. We may need to wait half a day. You'll get her attention and will tell her what we plan. If she's willing, we'll bring her with us, and we'll leave. The rest of you'll need to have everything ready so there'll be no delay."

Lame Lion, one of the braves, said, "The Sioux will send out parties as soon as they realize she's gone. We know a way that looks as though there's nothing but open ground even though we'll be able to ride as safely as if we were in heavy timber. Our chief can take us through there with little danger."

I said, "I trust him to lead us where we'll be safe."

Smart Coyote said, "We need to send someone ahead to choose the trails we'll use during the first day. He'll find the water we'll need and the place we'll camp the first night and will learn where we can ride fast without being seen. Lame Lion knows this region better than I do, so he'll do that. Carlos, you'll find the best place for those who'll wait for us while we get Dawn on the Mountain's mother."

"I'll look for a place close to her prayer spot where we can leave our horses. The sooner we're on them, the faster we can get away." I said.

"I'll help you," Molly said. "I'm too excited to sit here."

I asked the chief, "Will that be safe?"

"She'll be safe with you."

"Let's go."

We took food for our noon meal as well as two canteens. We had long since made certain that our clothing had nothing metal that would reflect the sun's rays.

We had no difficulty traveling the first half mile and were able to walk beside each other and hold hands. Then we crossed over a ridge, and were where we could more easily be seen. We had no trouble until we reached the spot from which we had watched Molly's mother.

We paused where we had spent time that morning, and looked for a way down the hill. Molly looked at me, asking the question with her eyes. I shrugged and held out my hands.

I whispered, "Did you see anything this morning?"

"I never took my eyes off Mother. I'm sorry."

"I didn't either. I saw Smart Coyote looking to our left. I'll sneak over that way."

"I'm going with you. I won't stay here alone. Smart Coyote said I'd be safe with you."

"I'll go ahead a short distance then signal you to follow. We have to find a safe way out of that clearing down there."

"Does it have to be a way that comes through here?"

"Why didn't I think of that? We don't care where the safe trail goes. It just needs to get us out of that clearing safely. You're a wise woman." I pulled her close and kissed her.

"Are you glad you agreed to let me come with you?"

"I'm glad you wanted to come, Sweetheart. I wish I could shout it."

Later, we found what we had come for. It was a roundabout way that went away from the camp at a lower level but was entirely shielded by trees as it sloped gradually up and over the first ridge. We found a good place for the main part of our group to wait.

There was a small pocket a quarter mile from the place we'd wait for Molly's mother where we could leave five horses. That would allow us to leave several minutes earlier than if we walked.

Molly and I followed the trail to the prayer room. I used all of the ways Lud had taught me to remove footprints. We paid attention to where we walked, so there were no crushed plants or broken twigs. I sifted dust over each footprint we made.

When we were away from the Sioux camp, I said, "We can talk now, but quietly. It wouldn't be unusual for some of them to be over here."

"Will it be all right to stop and eat something? I'm really tired. I was tied in knots all the time we were on the other side. I kept thinking someone would spot us. If you hadn't been so calm and sure, I'd have never made it."

"Can you wait until we find a level spot where we can get off the trail and sit down?"

"Yes, if it comes fairly soon."

"I remember a place up ahead that should be great."

My memory served well, and we were soon seated, leaning against a smooth log and having our meal.

"I'm sorry I didn't stop for this earlier. You mentioned that I was calm, but I was as nervous as a cat. I hope we don't have to go there more than one more time. The critical time will be when you first contact your mother. If she makes any loud noise, we could be wiped out in a minute. I hate putting you in that kind of danger."

"We must pray that God will enable her to understand that we're not dangerous to her. If she knows we're friends, she'll not make any loud sounds. I trust God to touch her with his understanding. He's proven that he can do whatever's needed. We must trust him now, and he'll not fail."

"You're teaching me, now. Thank you. I needed that."

"You're always so close to him. I'm amazed that you ever doubt that God will do what's needed."

"It's much easier to believe he'll do what you want than it is when I want something. I'm ashamed that I don't always have confidence in him, and I apologize to him often because I can't seem to draw on him like I should."

"What does he say when you apologize?"

"He told me that he designed me, so he knows how I feel. He said that I shouldn't worry about it."

"So why don't you just do what he tells you to do?"

"I figure he knows that he made me. I think he knows he'll just have to put up with me the way he made me."

"I'm sure he's delighted with you just the way you are."

"I suppose even that's possible. Just like I'm delighted with you."

"When you have to put up with me day after day, you may find things you don't like."

"It won't happen for at least a hundred years. By then I'll be so used to it that it won't matter."

"I won't find anything wrong until we've been together forever. Will we still be married in heaven?"

"If we aren't, it'll be because there's no marriage there. I won't give you up."

"You'll never get rid of me, either. I'm going to pray."

She knelt with her head on my thigh and said, "Please, Lord, give us success tomorrow. You know how much I've missed Mother, and we've tried to do what you've directed us to do. Give her understanding so she'll not do anything dangerous when I call to her. Watch over us and protect us as we escape. We need your wisdom as we talk with her. We ask for direction as we ride back to Santa Fe. Amen."

"Lord, thank you for the way you're leading. Please enable us to believe we have what we're praying for. You tell us that if we do that, you'll give it. We need your faith for that. You know we can only accomplish what we want if you go before us and come behind us. We ask for that. Amen and Amen"

Molly's face was a thing of beauty as she gazed up at me—her face snuggled against my leg. I lifted her onto my lap and drew her against me. We didn't need words to express our emotion; it flowed freely between us and surrounded us in an extremely intimate way. It was also a time of worship in which we were again together in Christ.

"Thank you, Lord, for Molly. Please give her mother to her tomorrow. She's a choice child of yours and deserves a special blessing."

"Thank you, sweetheart. May I have a kiss?"

"Not the kind of kiss I want to give, but, yes, I happen to have one that I can spare."

We managed to separate before it became the kiss I wanted to give her. "We must go back, darling. The sooner we rescue your mother, the quicker our wedding will occur," I forced myself to say. "Then we can remove the restrictions, and I'll demonstrate how I want to kiss you."

"I can hardly breathe, just imagining it."

We both heard it at the same time. As she was rising, we heard horses on the trail. I grabbed her by the waist and tossed her then leaped over the log. I dropped to the ground and praised God for the size of the log. It was a long time before the horses reached us. They passed without any comment by the riders. The trail curved fifty feet from us, which allowed me to see the backs of the horses and riders. I counted eighteen.

We remained where we were for fifteen minutes, neither moving nor talking. When I was confident that all of them were gone, I stood and helped Molly get up.

"That was too close for comfort. There was no indication that this trail had been used for a long time. We need to tell Smart Coyote about this. I'm sorry I treated you so roughly when I threw you over the log, Honey. I was afraid they'd see us."

"You threw me gently. I was scared half to death."

"I'm glad you weren't hurt. There may be others coming along here. We must be quiet so we'll hear them if they do come. This makes our entire plan more difficult and dangerous."

We walked as fast as we could. It was necessary for me to match my stride to Molly's, but she didn't hold me back very much since she's tall and has long legs. She took my hand and occasionally pulled on it to slow me some. I tried to walk slowly enough to prevent her from needing to breathe hard, which would add some noise.

When we had traveled about a half mile, I slowed down and whispered, "We're probably all right now, so we don't need to hurry so much. We're almost to our camp."

"Good. I'm getting tired. I don't think I could continue at that speed very much longer. You don't know how hard it is to keep up with you."

"Please tell me when I go too fast. I don't want you so tired you can't run if we need to."

"I didn't think of that. I could still run."

"I promise to pay more attention in the future. Please forgive me."

"You are doing what needs to be done, and it's all to get my mother for me. I'm sorry for making you feel that you did something wrong," she said. "I think I should apologize to you."

I took her hand and led her into a nice clump of trees where I took her in my arms and kissed her soundly.

"I hope we can always settle our differences as easily as we did that one."

"This is a nice way to do it, isn't it?" she responded and kissed me again. "I may make you think you need to apologize often if we can end it like this."

"I agree, but we had better get back to the business at hand. This will do very little to get your mother free."

"Kiss me again, and you can run the rest of the way if you want to."

"If I kiss you again, we may not ever get to camp. As much as I want to, we need to get there as quickly as possible."

"All right, but you owe me a kiss."

I grabbed her hand and pulled her back onto the trail. "You're too tempting. I love it, but we must wait. I'll pay my debt, with interest, as soon as it's safe."

We were close to our camp, so we walked slowly and whispered as we walked. Brown Bird, one of the Ute braves, was the only person there. He had been left to watch the camp while everyone else was away. Red Arrow, the other brave, soon returned with the things we had left at our first camp in that area. He hadn't seen any Sioux. Lud was the next person to return. He had gone completely around the camp and hadn't seen any parties except a group of eighteen that returned in early afternoon. We decided it was the bunch Molly and I had seen.

Smart Coyote came into camp just at sundown. He had gone to the spot from which we had viewed the camp the first evening. He said there were almost no men in camp, so we knew that there'd be war parties traveling throughout the region.

"We should have little trouble close to their camp, but we'll be in greater danger of meeting some of them as we travel," he said. "The party who came into camp this afternoon will be tired and should spend tomorrow preparing to go out again, so they'll not be a problem. Any parties that are gone won't usually be close to camp until late tomorrow. If the women follow the same pattern they did today, it'll be midday before we meet Dawn's mother, so we could contact a party at any time after that. We'll need to be especially careful as we leave, so we can gain that first half day travel before anyone realizes she's gone."

Lud asked, "Does this mean we need to change our plans?"

"No. We now know better how we should plan," was Smart Coyote's response. "We're probably better able to do what we plan than we originally thought. We can move with less danger here but will need to be especially careful after that. Let's discuss what each of us learned today. Carlos, we'll start with you."

I said, "We found a trail that'll take us to and from the place we plan to make contact and a good place to keep some horses about halfway down on the other side of that ridge. I suggest we take an extra man and five horses to that spot, which will have a horse for Dawn, Smart Coyote, me, whoever stays with the horses, and Dawn's mother. We can then ride to where the others wait with the horses and equipment, which will get us away from here faster than if we have to walk all the way. The trail we found will allow us to approach and leave the place the mother prayed today with almost no danger of being seen. We saw eighteen braves on the trail we used to return here. I think it was the party you saw going into the camp. We also found a good place to have those who aren't involved in the rescue wait with the rest of the horses and gear. It's only about a quarter mile from where we'll cross the ridge after the rescue.

"None of the trails we followed showed any sign of being used recently, but then the party of braves came along the one we followed home. We heard them coming and were able to hide. There was no indication that any of them saw us, and we had been extra careful to not leave any evidence of our using the trail."

Smart Coyote nodded his head and said, "That's good. Lud, what did you discover?"

"I was able to go completely around the camp. There are four trails that're used heavily, and all but one of them showed that the last travel was away from camp. The other one was used by the party we all saw. Those were the only men I saw. We chose a good time to come as far as safety close to the camp is concerned."

"Lame Lion's not returned yet. I think we'll not have a problem getting Dawn on the Mountain's mother and leaving this area. We need to wait and learn what Lame Lion says. He may know where some of the braves have gone, which could make our travel safer or more difficult," Smart Coyote commented. "We'll cook our meal while we wait for him."

We made another hatful of fire, using dry wood that would produce almost no smoke. It was placed under a tall pine tree that would filter the small amount of smoke so that almost none would appear above it.

We waited for Lame Lion long after we had eaten, but there was no sign of him. He was still not with us the next morning.

"What do you think happened?" I asked Smart Coyote.

"There are many things that could have caused him to delay. We may see him coming soon, and he may never come. There are many ways a man's life can end, but not being in camp one night doesn't mean something bad has come to him. We'll know more tomorrow."

Lud said, "Will you go the way you planned if he doesn't come?"

"It's the best way. It's the only way to reach the rest of the way we'll go. If Lame Lion returns, we'll know more about that way. If he doesn't, we'll not have that knowledge, but we'll know to be especially careful as we go. The loss of a good man doesn't cause us to change our direction, but it may change the way we walk as we go there."

The Lord impressed me with the thought that I should remember his last comment. It was a concept that could apply to many situations.

CHAPTER THIRTY-FIVE

Lame Lion hadn't returned when we left the following morning. We felt it was necessary to proceed as though we'd be able to leave with Molly's mother that day. Accordingly, we broke camp and were ready to leave the area soon after the morning meal. We left soon after the sun was visible in the east. I led the party to the spot we had chosen for the main group to wait. When everything was situated so that nothing would hinder our hasty departure, we prepared to split up.

Smart Coyote said, "I've decided that only Carlos and Dawn on the Mountain should go meet her mother. Lud'll go with them and care for the horses needed there. I'll go to the high point and watch the camp. There'll be fewer close to the Sioux camp, which means there's less of a chance of discovery. The mother will be less afraid to come if she doesn't see an Indian. I'll be able to see any danger. If I see anything, I'll be able to signal Carlos. We'll have a long wait if she follows the schedule we saw yesterday. We'll each take food and water."

He continued, "Please be careful to not make noise, especially when your mother first sees you. Try to get her to go with you into the trees where you'll be hidden before you talk. Leave that spot as quickly as you can. Those who stay here must move as little as possible. Lud knows what he needs to do. We'll be away from here today if our medicine's strong. I believe it is. I go now."

Molly, Lud, and I left immediately after that with Lud leading the horse intended for her mother. I led the way, and within a matter of minutes, we had crossed the top of the ridge. I left the trail and dismounted where we'd decided to leave our horses.

We left Lud and walked down toward the prayer room. All of this was done without a single word being spoken. Molly hugged Lud, and I shook his hand. He clapped my shoulder as we parted.

Pine forests are the home of a special squirrel that loves to bark at anything that invades his territory. We heard several when we were in that area the previous day. They had apparently contacted all the squirrels within twenty miles. Every time we moved, one of them barked. Only a deaf person would have been unaware of our presence as we walked, or more accurately, crept, to the spot we had chosen to wait.

We were barely in place when three Sioux braves appeared on the trail we were watching. The barking continued, but it came from a considerable distance east of us. The braves were moving fast but were watching the hillside where we had been. The squirrels stopped barking. The braves were obviously concerned and made a thorough search of the area. The barking resumed, so we were able to follow their progress. It was quite a while before they came back. We had been careful to leave no evidence of our use of the trail. They were talking as they went past our hiding place.

"They've decided it was a deer or some other animal that disturbed the squirrels," Molly whispered. She was trembling, so I drew her close and hugged her. She placed her mouth close to my ear and said, "I love you. Please pray that I'll know exactly the right way to get Mother's attention and the right words to say to her."

"All right. Jesus, you already know what's going to happen here today, but we don't. We ask you to use us to rescue Molly's mother and get home safely. Please enable Molly to do and say exactly what will be acceptable to her mother. Only you know what's needed. We can plan and hope, but you can actually bring it to pass. We're confident that we're following your instructions. Please enable us to rescue Molly's mother. You know it'll bring great joy and will complete the family. We worship you and believe you for these things. Now we wait for you to give them. Thank you. Amen"

Molly said, "How do you *do* that? You make it seem as though we already have what you asked for."

"Remember the portion in the Gospel of Mark where Jesus said we're to believe we *have* what we ask for and we'll *receive* it? He even gives us the faith to do that."

"I remember, but it's difficult to practice."

"It's easy to talk as though I'm always confident, but you should know that I'm not always the way I sound. However, what we're doing now is definitely something God's led us to do, so we can be absolutely certain he'll give us success."

"Please help me, Lord. I want this so much it hurts, and I'm confident it's what you want. I want to be as sure as Carlos is. Please touch my heart with your faith."

"Thank you, Lord. I know you've given Molly what she asked for. Now, let her feel it, too."

She snuggled a little closer and pressed her cheek against mine. It seemed like just a moment before she breathed deeply and said, "Thank you."

I felt her whole body relax. She sat quietly, saying not a word. It was several minutes before she placed her mouth against my ear so I felt and heard her say, "It's happened. I *know* he's given us Mother. All we need to do is wait until we see it."

It was a truly lovely day to be out with hardly a cloud in sight. We could stay where the sun warmed us or get in the shade if that was more comfortable. There was a grassy slope that was free of rocks where we could sit with our backs resting against a log and watch the place where her mother had prayed. We had food and water, so we could be comfortable for quite a long time. We had decided that we'd barely whisper if talk was necessary.

We waited until the sun was almost at the midpoint of its travel. We ate some berries and jerky. When we were putting things away, we both spotted her mother. She was on the trail leading to the place she had used the previous day. I prayed silently and was sure that Molly did as well, and we almost quit breathing until we saw her come out of the trees and walk to the log she had used before.

Molly stood up and walked out toward her mother. When she was out of the trees, she stopped and waved her right arm while looking at her mother. Her mother looked back, and an expression of wonder came to her face. She rose from the log and started walking toward Molly, who ran to her. They met, and the older lady said, "Molly?"

"Yes, Mother, I'm Molly."

They hugged for a long time, and I could see tears flowing from the mother's eyes as she sobbed softly. Molly was facing away from me, but her body shook from her sobs.. The clearing they were in was well hidden from view except from a place higher than we were, so I didn't bother them for quite while. Molly finally released her mother. She took her by the hand and led her to our hiding place.

She continued to whisper. "Mother, this is Carlos. We want to take you to Santa Fe with us. We're with others who're helping us rescue you. Can you go with us right now?"

"Oh, yes. I'll never let you out of my sight again if I can help it. What do I need to do?"

"Just follow Carlos. He'll show the way, and I'll be right behind you."

I had picked up everything, so I turned and led back up the trail to our horses. When we got there, I said, "This is Lud, and this is Molly's mother. Can you ride in this saddle, dressed as you are? If not, Molly has something you can change to."

"I'm not dressed for riding. What do you have, Molly?"

"I made a dress like mine. Let me show you how it's made. See, there are leggings underneath the skirt. I can ride and still be modest and comfortable, too."

"That's wonderful, if it'll fit me."

"It won't fit perfectly, but I made it fairly large, so you'll have no trouble getting it on."

"Where can I change?"

"Lud and I'll go over there and look the other way. Molly can let us know when it's all right."

She made quick work of the change, and we were mounted and riding to meet the rest of our party in a short time. I motioned for Lud to lead, put the mother next, and then Molly directly ahead of me. As I helped Mother mount, I said, "We're with some Ute Indians, so please don't be frightened when you see them. They're our friends."

We met Smart Coyote just before we reached the rest of our party and were headed east within a few more minutes. We'd be able to travel four hours before stopping, which should give us a good lead on any pursuit. Mother had told us that she'd probably not be missed by the Sioux until well after dark, so we could expect no attempt to take her back until the next day.

We resumed our positions with Smart Coyote leading, Lud bringing up the rear, and me in the middle with Molly and Mother just ahead of me. The chief knew where he was going even though he had sent Lame Lion ahead yesterday. We went rather slowly for ten miles, then he stepped up the pace. He continued until it was almost dark, at which time he veered to the left and rode into a heavily timbered area. After a quarter of a mile, we reached a sort of hollow where two ridges met, forming a hidden pocket surrounded by trees with an abundance of dead trees and brush. That would prevent anyone from approaching quietly.

We were soon settled in with a small fire cooking our evening meal. We erected a tent for the ladies while we men spread our beds around the perimeter of the camp. There was almost no danger of anyone coming near without at least one of us knowing about it. In less than an hour we were all in bed. We had discussed our plan for the next day, and the first thing was that we'd be mounted and underway before sunup.

Coyotes and wolves filled the night with their howling. I heard owls twice just after I woke the next morning. The stars told me it was almost morning, so I rolled my bed and was starting the fire when Lud joined me. He got the coffee pot ready and put it on the fire.

"Well, kid, we pulled it off. Molly's mother sure looks a lot like her, doesn't she?"

"Yes. I told Molly it was almost like seeing her. She's a beautiful lady."

"I didn't get to talk with her much, but she seems nice, too."

"Molly's told me things about her that makes me think she's a very smart lady, as well. She's may be almost as sharp as her daughter."

"That's a lot to expect. She may be pretty special, like Molly. If she is, I could get excited about getting to know her well."

"You better be careful. You'll be hogtied and branded if you keep thinking like that."

"If she really is like Molly, I could be happy with that."

"I'll bet you could. Don't push for a while, though. She's not apt to be interested in much except getting acquainted with her daughter. They've a lot of catching up to do, and anyone trying to step in the way of that could be pretty unpopular."

"All right. If you see me pushing too hard, will you tell me?"

"Yes, but please remember that you asked me to do that."

"All right, just be gentle, but don't let me get out of line. I don't want to lose out by doing something foolish. I need you to be my teacher again. If you'll also pray for me, I'd like that."

That request really touched me in a special way. I said, "Let's pray right now."

"You lead off."

"Lord, Lud needs your wisdom so he'll be able to do and say the right things when he's with Molly's mother and with Molly. Lud's attracted to the mother and wants to do things that'll cause her to like him. If this pleases you, we ask that you'll enable him to become a man she admires. You're the only one with the knowledge to direct everyone's thoughts, so your will is what will happen. Lord, you know that I'd like for these two people to become close friends, and maybe more than that. We want to be sure of what you want. I ask you to place in each of their minds the things you want for them. I ask it and thank you for it, in Jesus's name. Amen."

He followed with, "Jesus, I already like this lady a lot and have an idea she's the one I have looked for all my life. Show me how to make her love me, if that's a good thing. Amen."

We each got a cup from the now boiling pot of coffee and walked out to check the horses. We continued to talk quietly so we wouldn't disturb the others who were still sleeping—but also for safety. We were still in Sioux territory.

"Do you think we're safe from the Sioux?" I asked.

"If someone discovered right away that she's gone, they'll be after us as soon as they can find our trail. There's no way we could keep from leaving a trail that any Indian kid could follow. We've got too many horses to hide our trail. Being at the back, I can't tell if we used trails that're heavily traveled or if we were on one that isn't used much. I could see that most anyone could follow the tracks that were on that trail by the time I had gone by. If we followed where lots of others have gone, it wouldn't be easy. I'm guessing that the chief used trails where we aren't apt to meet anyone, so our trail's probably plain. I imagine we'll start using regular trails before much longer, and then it'll be hard to follow. We traveled pretty fast yesterday and have maybe a half-day lead, which can be a big advantage if we're able to start using trails where our tracks aren't easy to follow. I trust Smart Coyote. He's a cagey one and knows what he's doing. We're lucky to have him leading us."

The horses were all quiet, some grazing and others still sleeping. We had made our camp with the animals between us and the trail we had followed, trusting them to warn us of anything approaching. Since there was no indication of that, we returned to the fire where the others were now gathering.

Molly and her mother were holding hands, smiling, and talking quietly. Molly saw me and motioned for me to come to her and to bring Lud. We headed over to meet them.

She reached for my hand and pulled me close. "Mother, we didn't have an opportunity to say much yesterday. This is Carlos, whom I'll marry soon after we reach Santa Fe. This is Lud, who's been a partner with Carlos and some others in a gold mine. He's also our very special friend and has become almost a father to us. You know that this is my mother. Her name is Maureen."

I said, "We've looked forward to this for three years. You have a wonderful daughter. I love her and am wonderfully blessed to be the person she's chosen to marry. We've waited until you're with us before we had our wedding."

Lud added, "These two are really special, and I'm glad we were able to get you away like we did. I'm glad to meet you. If there's any way I can help, just let me know."

"Molly's told me lots about you, Carlos. I'm glad you came for me, and I welcome you to our family. If you're half the man she thinks you are, she's extremely fortunate to have you. Lud, Molly's been lavish in her praise of you. I look forward to getting to know you well," was Mother's reply.

Molly said, "Carlos is the one who thought of coming for you. I had never even dreamed of it, but he decided to do it soon after we met. God has given me a man who stands above anyone in my mind. And Lud wouldn't hear of our coming without him. I hope you know, Lud, that I love you, too. You and Smart Coyote are my foster fathers."

Smart Coyote joined us, and Molly said, "Mother, this is Smart Coyote. He and his squaw, Fawn Heart, have taken me into their home and treated me like a daughter. He is the man who made your rescue a success. Please cherish him in your heart. He's a truly wonderful man."

She continued, speaking to the chief, "You're aware that this is my mother, Maureen O'Hara. She's grateful for the way you've cared for me and thanks you for your help in getting her from the Sioux."

He said, "I welcome you. Dawn on the Mountain is the name we gave your daughter, because she's been that to us. She's filled a spot in my heart that would've been an emptiness without her. My squaw and I will keep her in our hearts forever. We're glad you're with her now. We'll share her."

Mother's eyes were filled with tears when she answered. "I can never thank you enough for giving Molly a home and your love. You've blessed me by what you have done. Thank you for helping in my rescue. I'm truly happy for the first time since they captured us and killed my husband. I can see that you've been a father to Molly and have helped her become a beautiful lady. Thank you."

"Enough," said Smart Coyote. "We must eat and go."

CHAPTER THIRTY-SIX

We lined out in the same formation as the previous day with Smart Coyote leading and Red Arrow leading the spare horses for the four Utes followed by Molly's mother, Molly, and me. I led the extra four saddle horses we had brought from Santa Fe. Brown Bird, who was leading the pack horses, was next, and Lud was the last in line. When we were strung out, there were over fifty yards between Smart Coyote and Lud, and the only place where two men rode together was at the front of the line. Lud, Molly, and I had the only rifles and handguns, while the Utes had only the usual bows and arrows common among Indians. It'd be unusual to encounter any rifles among the Sioux, so we were probably better armed than anyone who might attack us.

Smart Coyote and Lud were in the most dangerous positions, and we were depending on the chief to guide us to safety. The women were in the places most easily defended, and I was placed with them because of our relationship.

Smart Coyote led at a trot for the first ten miles. Raton walked as fast as the other horses most of the time, shifting to the single-foot occasionally when it was needed. He seldom needed the faster gait. Molly's filly switched back and forth between a walk and trot, since she walked considerably faster than all the others except Raton. We were apparently on a trail Smart Coyote was familiar with, which enabled him to travel at that rate. The next few hours were covered at a slower pace because of the terrain we covered. In order to stay where we weren't easily seen, we took trails that went along some rather rough country, but even there, he slowed down only slightly, and by the end of the day, I estimated that we were fifty miles from our previous camp. We stopped three times and watched parties of warriors moving below us. None of them saw us, although it seemed to me that we weren't very well hidden any of those times. The fact that we were above them and weren't moving made the difference.

When the sun was fairly low and was almost directly behind us, Smart Coyote dropped down off the ridge we were following and crossed a shallow valley. He then turned so we were riding back toward the west and followed a low place into a pocket surrounded by pines with brush growing thickly between the trees. He led us slowly through some fallen trees into a low place with about an acre of grass. He dismounted, and we all were happy to follow his example. We had been in the saddle for a long day with no stops. The only times we hadn't been traveling were when we watered the horses in three creeks and the pauses when the Indian parties were in sight.

I hurried to help Molly. She was so tired she almost fell into my arms. After making sure she was safely down, I turned to go assist her mother. Lud was there ahead of me and was handling the situation better than I could have. I turned back to Molly.

"Lud thinks you mother is a special lady. Don't be surprised if he spends a lot of time with us."

"She's impressed by him, too, so he'll be welcome."

"Really?"

"She's seen nothing but Indians for all those years, and a nice white man's rather impressive. She asked about him last night. You know that I think he's special, so he got treated favorably."

"I cautioned him to not push very hard for a while. I thought she'd want quite a bit of time alone with you before she'd welcome any other attention."

"That's probably right, but she's certainly noticed him. Things like his helping her will be quite welcome, I'm sure. He should proceed fairly slowly."

"All right. Will you help me advise Lud as we watch developments?"

"Of course. I can't think of anyone I'd like more for her to be interested in. I don't want to try to push her into anything, though."

"I agree. You must be exhausted, and she will be, too. I'll let you help her while I help with making camp,"

The Utes had a fire going, and the coffee pot was heating. I gathered firewood and erected a tent for the women then took care of our horses. There was plenty of good grass, and all the horses were soon picketed and grazing. We men each chose a spot and spread our beds so the area was given a perimeter of safety.

Molly and Brown Bird were soon busy preparing our meal, which was ready soon after the other chores were done. As I looked at our party, I observed that the only person who seemed to have suffered much was Molly's mother. She was noticeably stiff and more tired than any of the others. I was certain that none of us was used to riding as long without interruption as we had that day, so we were all weary. Mother wasn't used to riding at all. The excitement of being rescued and re-united with Molly would also drain her strength.

Lud had done his share of the work, but he had done it a bit more quickly than he might have usually. He then hurried to Molly's mother and looked for ways to help her. I made sure that Molly was aware of what was happening and remained quiet. I asked the Lord for wisdom for all of us and asked him to guide Lud in his conduct. I admit to doing it with a smile because I liked the potential of the situation.

We were soon seated on logs, eating our meal of venison, dried berries, and dry biscuits. Hot coffee completed the meal, which was very welcome. We hadn't eaten since early morning before we left camp.

Smart Coyote said, "I think we'll go east another full day before we ride south. We'll be out of the mountains then, and travel will be easier. It'll take another day to reach the point where we go back west. We should be in the hills south of that flat, windy country three days after that. We can go slower then, and we may even stop and rest a day or two."

"Have you gone this way before?" I asked.

"No. Why do you ask?"

"I really don't know. I just wondered."

"If you have doubts, please tell me. The way I've gone before is farther east than the way I mentioned, but we have no reason to go that far before we turn. We'll be out of the mountains, and our travel will be easier if we go east. If you think we should go another way, I want to know that."

"I'll ask my God tonight and will tell you what he says after we sleep. Will that be all right?"

"I'll also seek wisdom, and we'll talk tomorrow., Does anyone else have ideas?"

No one responded, so we all started getting ready to go to bed. Molly and I went to the side of the park and knelt in prayer.

I began by saying, "Lord, I think you gave me that question, but I don't know what you mean by it. If you want us to go a different direction, please make it plain. Thanks, Lord. Amen."

Molly said, "Thank you for guiding. We know you'll do exactly what we need. I rejoice that you've given me Mother. Thanks for Carlos and Lud, and for Smart Coyote. You've been wonderfully gracious to me. I love you, Lord."

I stood and helped her stand, as well. We walked to the tent where her mother and Lud stood talking.

I said, "It's been a long, hard day, and tomorrow will probably be another one. We should all get a good night of rest. I trust you'll all have a good night." I gave Molly a very light kiss and went to my bed. They all returned my wish.

I was asleep almost immediately and didn't awaken until it was almost time to get up the next morning. I began praying as soon as I was awake and quickly became aware of a definite uneasiness in my spirit. When no peace came after a lengthy period of prayer, I got up and walked quietly to the edge of the grass that was farthest from the area where we had slept. I found a convenient log and knelt beside it to seek an answer.

I had told God everything I knew to say, so I just waited there on my knees. It seemed like a long time with no response, but I was absolutely certain that I needed to stay where I was, and that if I did, the answer would come. It seemed like at least an hour with nothing happening when I heard someone approaching. I didn't move but was soon aware that it was Molly. Her scent was easily recognized—a special, precious one that I would never fail to know. She knelt beside me and brushed my cheek with her lips.

"Jesus told me you were here and said I should join you," she whispered. "He said we're to wait a little longer, and the answer will come."

I reached for her and she came quickly into my embrace. "I love you more than you can imagine, sweetheart. Thank you for coming," I whispered in her ear.

"We must wait a bit and listen. He'll tell you what you need to know. I love you."

It was but a few minutes before I knew we were to go back and that the answer would come.

I stood up, helped Molly to her feet, kissed her softly, and gazed into her beautiful eyes. "I love it that Jesus spoke to you and led you to join me."

"It was wonderful. I didn't hear him, but he caused me to know that I should come and tell you. I can hardly wait to see what he says."

"He's doing it differently this time. I'm glad he's using you like this. It's even better than when he speaks just to me."

"Yes, I feel like he's given me a precious privilege. He knows we're almost a single unit. I love sharing this with you," she said. If her mouth hadn't been touching my ear I'd have not been able to hear, her voice was so quiet. There was an extra huskiness to her voice that seemed to vibrate through my whole body.

I took her hand, and we almost ran across the meadow. Smart Coyote was standing at the fire, watching as we approached.

"Do you have an answer?" he asked.

It came to me then. "We should follow along this range far up on the second ridge from the flat land to the east. It'll take three days to reach the point where we're to turn west. Tomorrow we'll encounter a war party that has captured Lame Lion. It'll be shortly after the sun reaches its high point, and we'll kill seven Sioux warriors and get Lame Lion free. None of us will be harmed. We'll be told where to wait for that party so we can do all of this."

The chief looked startled, and then his face changed to an expression I could only interpret as wonder. He said, "I've never had a message like that. We'll do as you say. You will lead us."

I had no idea what would come out of my mouth when I started talking, and I had no plan about how we should go. I walked into the trees and prayed desperately for a few minutes and returned completely confident that God'd lead me as I led the party. When we were all mounted, Smart Coyote and I changed places, and I felt like Abraham must have when God told him to leave his family and go to the promised land. We soon crossed the trail we had been following when the chief had turned off toward the place we had spent the night. We were going across an area in which no trail was visible, and it was a half mile before we saw any path. I turned onto it and rode up a brushy hillside. The opening through the brush was so narrow we were touched by branches on each side. It suddenly broke out of the thick vegetation onto a slope covered by yellow pines, the tallest I had ever seen. The trail was barely identifiable, but there was no doubt in my mind that it was the proper way to go. The ground was covered with a layer of pine needles that made almost no sound as we traveled over them. We were hidden from view in every direction.

We followed the dim trail across a ridge and down the east side a hundred feet, where a game trail crossed our path. It appeared to continue at about that same level for a considerable distance. I could see it for well beyond a quarter mile. We were on the second ridge from the flat area to our east, which is where we had been instructed to travel. It seemed logical to follow it, so I did, confident that I'd be given some sign if that wasn't correct. The trail was easy to follow and allowed us to go at a fast pace. I kept to the normal walk of the *grullo*, which caused all the other horses to trot most of the time, and we were able to continue without interruption all morning.

When the sun showed that it was midday, I heard running water and signaled for a halt. I dismounted and walked forward until a small stream came into view. I walked carefully until I was able to see almost a quarter of a mile in each direction along the stream. There was nothing in sight, so I called to the stallion and motioned for the others to follow him. We all drank from the icy stream, watered the horses, and found places to sit, eat, and rest. Our meal was jerky, pemmican, and coffee.

The trail we followed continued along that ridge until it blended into a mesa, where it held at the same altitude along the side of the mesa for the rest of that day. When the sun was almost touching the western horizon we found another game trail leading to the mesa top where we found an excellent camp area.

Red Arrow had killed several blue grouse, which were soon roasting over the fire, while Molly had discovered berries, so we enjoyed a welcome change in our fare. Even though we had rested an hour or so at noon, we had covered a long distance.

Although we were relatively safe from discovery because of our high location, we continued to make as little noise as we could. The mesa was about a mile from side to side and stretched at least ten miles to the south. After we had eaten, I saddled my spare horse with the intention of riding along the edge of the mesa for some distance then crossing to the other side and riding back. I assumed that I'd be able to see any other camps as soon as it was dark. That knowledge could be valuable as we continued our travel.

"Why are you doing that?" Molly asked.

When I told her, she asked, "May I join you?"

"Aren't you tired of riding?"

"Not so it'll keep me from going with you if you want me to."

"I can't imagine not wanting you with me."

We waited until it was dark before leaving and rode several miles south without seeing a fire. We rode across the mesa and followed the eastern edge back toward our camp. We soon spotted a fire close to the bottom of the slope that led up to where we were. It was a tiny blaze, which caused us to assume it was an Indian camp. We followed along that side until I thought we were almost straight across from our camp and turned west. When we saw our fire it was about one hundred feet to our right.

"How'd you know how to come this close to camp?"

"It was partly a good sense of where we were, but this horse told me he wanted to head this way."

"You could have easily taken full credit, but you're too honest for that. You're continually amazing me. I think most men would never give a horse credit like you did. I'll never doubt anything you tell me."

"Promise?"

"Yes, I promise."

"Stay with me after we have put the horses back on grass, and I'll test you."

It took only a matter of minutes to handle that chore, and it left us quite a distance from the rest of our party. I took her into my arms and said, "You're the most wonderful, exciting, and beautiful woman God has ever created. I love you more than any man has ever loved a woman. I'll never stop wanting to have you in my arms. You'll bear lovely daughters and strong, handsome, wise sons. God will continue to bless us until our lives end. Please tell me you don't doubt a word of that."

"Oh, Carlos, right now I don't doubt it at all. I can't tell you how much I love you. Please tell me you don't doubt that."

I kissed her as gently as I could, which was almost more than it should've been. We were both breathless when we separated and walked slowly to the fire.

When I woke the next morning, I felt ready to face whatever came. I rolled my bed and searched out a place to pray.

I was able to lift praise and adoration to God in a way that was more complete and free than had been true for days. It was but a short time before Molly was on her knees beside me, her hand in mine. I said, "Thank you again for this marvelous woman."

CHAPTER THIRTY-SEVEN

We were ready to leave before the sun was more than a brightness in the eastern sky. We all rode our spare horses. Our better mounts had allowed us to travel at the speed we did. Today would be different not only because of the difference in our horses, but we'd be slowed by the encounter with the Sioux party.

I rode diagonally across the mesa toward the spot from which we had seen the fire, and we were soon able to look down on the Sioux camp. There were eight men, of which we were sure one was Lame Lion. Smart Coyote, Lud, Molly, and I waited to see where the party below us would travel. The Sioux were quite leisurely in their breaking of camp.

"They had a horse or mule for their meal last night," Smart Coyote said. "They're full and lazy now. That will make it easier to take them by surprise."

"I'll be glad for any advantage we have," Lud commented. "I've never been in a fight that was too easy."

I said, "We'll learn where they go and will plan accordingly. God said he'd tell us where to wait for them, but it'll help to know which direction they go."

They rode south along the base of the mesa. Lame Lion was afoot in the middle with a rope around his neck. He was led by the fourth Sioux, who was less than gentle in the way he treated the Ute brave. If the rope was allowed to grow taut, Lame Lion was jerked forward in a manner intended to jerk him off his feet. He was often running in order to avoid that treatment. He couldn't maintain that pace all day.

I said, "We'll ride fast enough to get ahead of them. We'll be told where to wait and how to attack."

We rode south for twenty miles. We came to a trail leading off the mesa into a dense growth of mixed pine and oak brush. I had no doubt about following it. Our cover continued as we followed a gentle way toward the base of the mesa. We came to an area where the growth of brush thinned, and the trail went into a cup with a spring flowing into a pool fifteen feet across. It was surrounded by a lush patch of grass. There was a huge rock overhanging the southeast corner with a shady area under it. The shade would cover a larger area as the sun traveled toward the south.

The eastern rim of the cup was a series of large rocks which would offer protection. All that was lacking was the enemy. I crept to the rim and looked through some weeds. The trail passed twenty feet from where I stood.

I chose the highest point along the rim and asked Red Arrow to go to it and watch for the other party. I assigned each man a spot. I placed myself and Lud in the middle so we could take out the brave who was leading Lame Lion and the one directly behind him. Smart Coyote knew the Sioux language, so he was given the spot to the far right. He'd order the Sioux leader to surrender. When that order wasn't obeyed, we'd each aim to kill the man directly in front of us. There'd be only two remaining. Lud and I would use our handguns on our first shots, which would leave our rifles for the remaining braves.

We had everyone in place when Red Arrow gave the signal that the enemy was coming. Smart Coyote rose and shouted the demand for surrender. We all watched so we could follow his lead. When he released his arrow, the rest of us rose up and located our man.

My man was almost directly in front of me, and the same was true of everyone. The two extra braves were at the rear and presented almost no danger. Within minutes, five Sioux braves were laying inert before us. Lud and I shot the final braves.

Lame Lion had removed the rope from his neck before the last shot was fired. His neck was bleeding, but he wasn't injured seriously. The braves hadn't been as interested in torturing him as in gorging on mule meat, but another day would've undoubtedly been Lame Lion's last.

Smart Coyote looked over the scene and ordered Red Arrow and Brown Bird to join Lud, who was catching the Sioux horses. He turned to me and said, "I want to know this God of yours. I've never been this successful in battle before. Everything was exactly like you said it would be. Can you show me how to know him?"

"I'll have Dawn on the Mountain ride beside you now so she can tell you everything you need to know."

Molly looked at me a long time before she translated that comment. I smiled and said, "You deserve to have that privilege. I'd like to be there when you do it, but that isn't necessary."

She told him what I had said and he nodded his head and looked into the distance, a sign that he was thinking deeply.

"I'll hear her, but I want you there. She's learned from you?"

"She's learned some, but she's known him since before she came to your home. She knows him very well now and will make sure you're introduced properly."

"It's good. We'll do it that way. Where do we go now?"

"You must lead us now. My message was for the time until now. You're our leader."

"I'll follow you if you want to lead. You have medicine strong enough to take us home with no trouble. You may lead or ride beside me any time."

"I thank you, but I can't lead as well as you. Please take the position you deserve."

Molly said, "He says I have a good, wise man."

Molly rode beside him, with me positioned so that I could hear them talking. I had never doubted that she'd do an excellent job but was all smiles when she handled it as she did. She told him simply that God the Father, God the Son, who is Jesus, and

God the Holy Spirit are together as one God just as he and Fawn Heart are one. They, God, loved all of us so much that Jesus was sent to make a perfect sacrifice in payment for all the bad things we've done and for all the things we will ever do. In order to receive the benefit of that, we must accept Jesus as our Savior. When we do that, the Father makes us a part of his family, and the Holy Spirit comes to live in us. From that time on, the Spirit can talk with our spirit and take our requests to the Father. Jesus is talking to the Father also, telling him things that we need and reminding him that we're his in Jesus. It was a rather simple explanation but covered the major points effectively.

The chief listened carefully and asked, "How do I do all of that?"

"You simply tell God that you believe that Jesus died to pay for the things you've done that he didn't like and that you want to accept his offer of forgiveness. You ask him to come into your heart and live there and ask him to guide you."

She then asked, "Do you want to do that?"

"I want to know the God Carlos serves. If this is the way to know him, I want it."

Molly related that to me, and I said, "That's the way I came to know him. Jesus said in his Word that he's the way, the truth, and the life, and that there's no other way to the Father. It really is that simple."

"I do that now," said Smart Coyote, thereby proving his name was right for him.

"You're now a child of God," Molly assured him. "We'll come as often as possible and help you get better acquainted with the Father."

"Good. I'll tell Fawn Heart of this and invite her to join me."

"That will make Jesus happy," Molly told him.

He was an excellent horseman and did what it took to make his horse prance.

We saw eight more parties of Indians as we proceeded into the flat country where the winds blew, but we managed to avoid being seen and had no further contacts. It took us five days to get into the north edge of the mountains we had skirted coming north from Raton Pass. We rode beside a creek swollen by melting snow from the peaks that ranged on either side of us. The valley we rode through ended in a huge grassy plain that ran up to a fairly high pass, which we finally recognized as Rabbit Ears Pass.

We continued in a southwesterly direction across that pass into a valley dominated by a river that stretched to the west between mountains on both sides. We broke out into an area of lush grass that stretched as far as the eye could see. We turned toward the south and rode along the western edge of the range we had just skirted. The mountains had been on our left, and as we turned south they were still there. We followed to the southwest, staying fairly close to the mountains for three days of easy travel with fairly long midday stops.

The mountains became smaller, and the vegetation changed as we continued south. We were almost constantly following a flowing stream. When we left one, it was never long before we came to another. We saw many deer and enough elk to tell us that we were in an area with lots of game animals. When we saw antelope, they were usually in herds of several hundred. It was the time for fawns, and the young antelope were a joy to watch. When they were just a few days old, they could run faster than any horse and seemed to delight in racing away from the herd and back again in groups of fifty to seventy-five. Sage grouse were busily mating, and the cocks were a sight to behold as they strutted and puffed. Tom turkeys also put on displays of proud marches with their wings stretched down along their sides, scraping along the ground in an effort to impress any hen in the area. When we rode through brushy hillsides, we were sometimes given the privilege of sighting a deer's fawn hidden away, still as a stone, pretending to be another rock or bush. We never bothered them because to touch them was to risk the doe's rejection when she encountered man smell.

We rode around a camp of Northern Utes along the White River. Our Indian companions rode into the camp and powwowed with their counterparts. We whites rode slowly along and camped a couple of hours later in a sheltered nook. The next day we came to the biggest river we had seen on the entire trip. We were on the north and west side of it, and it roared through a canyon that offered no possibility of crossing. We stayed close to the river and were barely able to remain in the canyon until it broke out into a valley that was obviously fertile. Twenty miles into that valley, another river joined the one we were following and added at least another third as much water.

We continued along the big river, searching for a safe crossing. We were finally able to spot a place where the stream bed widened, and the flow was low enough for us to attempt a crossing. I put Raton into it, and he waded almost fifty feet before he had to swim, and it was but twenty more feet until he was walking again. We went back to the other bank, where Lud and I went with Molly and her mother while the Utes brought the rest of the animals across. We soon found a sheltered area and stopped for the night.

The next morning Lud, Molly, Smart Coyote, and I rode to a high point to attempt to find the best way to go. The choice was to cross the mountains to our south or follow the river in a generally westerly direction and avoid the higher elevations. The mountains were still white with snow almost down to the level where we were, so we elected to follow the river until we found a suitable place to leave it. The river was roaring and as muddy as any I had ever seen. It came close to filling the canyon in many places, which forced us to cover some rather rough country. We traveled along it for six days. When we left the river, we rode south through formations that surely had been centuries forming. Rocky spires rose from bases that stretched for miles.

Rocky canyons ran among the buttes that were in varied shapes. Some of them were truly beautiful while others were ghostly and grotesque. None of us desired to spend much time there, so we pushed through but not fast enough to tire our horses. It was a forest of huge, rocky goblins with meager vegetation and almost no decent water. Our path through that region forced us fairly far west, but we finally broke free and headed south again.

We rode south for another six days before Lud and Smart Coyote agreed that we should turn and go east. We reached the Ute's camp after another four days of riding. Lud told of ancient cliff dwellings in some of the canyons south of the way we rode. He said, "I spent six months roamin' those canyons and climbin' cliffs to see the cliff houses. I don't know who put 'em there, but whoever did it sure knew how to put a house in a spot that was hard to get to. I had to crawl through some purty small holes to reach some of them. They left all kinds of stuff, like baskets and vases, along with ears of corn and dried vegetables. Some of the houses were on top of a mesa. There was nothing but adobe brick used to build with. They used cedar poles in the roofs and in the floors of houses that had more than one story. It's worth the ride to see it. I saw plenty of places big enough to hold several hundred folks. I wonder what happened that caused them to leave."

There was a celebration the night of our arrival at the Ute camp. It was to celebrate the success we had enjoyed. We learned that it was proper for everyone to participate in the dancing this time, so Molly and I joined in it together. There was no design to any of the dances, but it seemed that each person allowed his or her body to move in joy. Grandma had taught us some Spanish dances, so we did a couple of them together. It was certainly a joy to dance with her, and the tempo of the drums was suitable.

It truly became an expression of worship, and our Indian friends praised us for helping them celebrate.

We were free at last to continue homeward. Molly, Lud, and I joined Smart Coyote in a final circle in his tipi. While Fawn Heart didn't participate, she was present this time. At the conclusion I asked the two of them if they'd consider coming to our wedding.

"When will it be?"

"We've not decided a day for it, but we'll make sure you know fourteen days before. It'll be no later than two moons from now."

"We'll come."

"We'd also like for the three braves who went with us and Star Gazer, along with their squaws, to come with you."

We headed for home the next morning. Our horses had rested for six days, so we each rode our favorite the entire trip, which lasted only three days. We had no heavy packs, and all the animals were fresh and knew they were going home. We let the extra saddle horses run free, and Lud and I each handled a pack horse, which was almost no trouble. Raton and Molly's filly were soon quite a ways ahead of the other horses, so we rode in pairs most of each day. We managed to observe Lud and Mother several times the first day. It was apparent that they were enjoying that manner of traveling, so we left it the way it was. Molly and I were pleased to have the time alone.

Our welcome in Santa Fe was enthusiastic, to understate it considerably. My grandparents and uncle's family joined us to celebrate the success of our trip and to get acquainted with Mother. We managed to spend a couple of hours with Father Manuel and discuss our wedding plans. Grandma had spent some of the time we were gone making a wedding dress for Molly. I didn't see it until the wedding, but Molly was delighted and made sure I knew it was a beautiful creation and that it fit her perfectly.

It was the fourth evening before my grandparents, Lud, Mother, Molly, and I were alone together for almost the first time since our return. I mentioned that we wanted to set a date for our wedding.

"If it's all right with you, Maureen and I want to have our wedding at the same time you have yours," Lud announced.

Molly's husky voice would never be considered a squeak, but it was as close as it'd ever be when she cried, "Mother! Are you serious? This is wonderful. Why didn't you tell me?"

"I couldn't ask him, could I? He waited until today to ask me. I lost thirteen years of my life, and when Ludwig finally worked up enough courage to ask me, I jumped at the chance. I don't intend to waste a single minute if I can avoid it," Mother declared. Her face was a picture of joy.

I said, "Lud, I'm afraid I'd have given you bad advice if I hadn't been so busy handling our affairs, but you did fine without me. Congratulations for doing the right thing at the right time. We'll be happy to share our wedding day, won't we, Molly?"

"I'll be delighted if you're willing to marry soon. We're not going to delay very long. It's seemed too long already. How soon can you be ready?"

"You can name the date, and we'll adjust to it," said Lud. "It can't be too soon."

I said, "We promised Smart Coyote we'd let him know at least two weeks before the date, so we need to set a time and inform him. We really want him and Fawn Heart to be here, and I'm sure you do, as well."

They agreed, and we decided to set up a meeting with Father Manuel as soon as possible and make decisions. The four of us met with him the following Monday and arranged for a wedding the fifteenth of June, which was less than three weeks from that day. Molly and her mother made that decision, and it was a time that would allow us to do everything we needed. None of us was willing to extend the time beyond that date. I hired two young fellows to make the trip to tell Smart Coyote when the wedding was to occur. They returned with assurances that all ten of those we had invited would be in Santa Fe five days before the wedding.

Molly, her mother, and Grandma gathered in Grandma's sewing room to make a dress for Mother and a suit for Lud. We agreed that the suit Molly gave me was suitable. Lud and I erected five tents at the partnership barn in preparation for the Utes' arrival. There was nothing else suitable as housing for them. We covered the floors with hides and rugs and built a good fire pit where there was easy access from all the tents. We had constructed an outhouse for the use of our party who stayed there during the winter, which was suitable for their use and was close enough to be convenient.

Lud knew a rancher who had a couple of cabins that were only a couple of hours from town. We rode out and examined them and then made arrangements to rent them for our honeymoons. There was fifteen miles between them with a good trail so we could visit some if we wanted to.

"Don't plan to come over too soon," I warned Lud. "We'll be occupied trying to catch up for all the delays of the last three years and won't be looking for company for a few days."

"I reckon I can find something to do for a while. I never planned on anything like this until I met Maureen, but she's the one I've always been hoping would come along. I don't think there are two fellows as blessed as we are."

Grandma had Grandpa as busy as a one-armed man in a canoe, getting things ready for the crowd she was certain would show up for the celebration. He and I built a fire pit where we'd roast a pig and a deer. Lud helped us get tables and benches ready. Grandma was sure there'd be at least seventy-five people to feed, so we bought or borrowed dinnerware for one hundred. All of these preparations were made at our new home, which we had furnished but hadn't occupied. There was plenty of space, and most of the ground was covered with grass, so we thought it would serve well.

Lud, Mother, Molly, and I went to check everything a week before the wedding. The ladies had a few suggestions, which were reasonable and easy to accommodate. They were generous with their praise, and we took the opportunity to show Mother our new home.

"I'm amazed," she said. "My Molly has a palace. You've given my girl more than any woman should expect. I'm happier than I ever hoped to be. Ludwig and I may never have a home like this, but we'll have a home together, which is a blessing beyond my wildest dream."

Lud said, "You can have whatever kind of house you want. You'll need to wait a while because I had no use for anything like this until you came along."

"We'll not even plan for a while. I need to get my bearings before we make decisions like that. I'm still getting used to being free and haven't started to think of the future. The three of you have turned my world upside down, and it's still spinning pretty fast. It's enough for now to see Molly and Carlos enjoy what they have. I had no hope of doing that a month ago."

Lud said, "Kid, you better bring the Lord into this."

He reached for Mother with one hand and Molly with the other, and we all joined hands.

I sought the exact words that fit the occasion. "Lord God, we really don't know how to say it the way it should be said, but we're overwhelmed by what you've done and are doing. You've given each of us what we asked for and went beyond that. When we set out to free Mother, we hoped only to do it without injury, and that she'd still be healthy. You led Smart Coyote to help us and gave us victory over the Sioux, returned Lame Lion, and brought us safely back here. Now you've caused Lud and Mother to recognize in each other the person who'll fill their lives with joy. We can only lift praise and adoration to you, God and Savior, precious Spirit, and Father. Please enable us to recognize and appreciate fully how greatly you've blessed us. I pray a special blessing on Lud and Mother. They're precious in our sight, and I know they are in yours as well. Enlarge our hearts so we can completely embrace your blessings. We ask it in the name of our Lord, Jesus. Amen"

"Thank you, Lord," Molly said. "My heart's bursting with joy for what you've done. Only you know what a blessing it is to have Mother here. You've given me more in Carlos than anyone could ever ask for. I ask you to enable me to be the wife he deserves. You've already given us things no one could hope for on those occasions when we've been together in you, being blessed in ways we don't fully understand. I have all I need. Thank you." That wonderful voice filled my senses as nothing else will ever duplicate. Molly turned and put her arms around me.

Lud and Mother were also embracing. Lud said, "God, we haven't been friends very long, but I have more than any man could ask for. You know I want Carlos and Molly to have everything you can give them and you know that seeing what they have has made me want it, too. You're giving me Maureen, and now we have it. I didn't even ask for it first—you just gave it. I don't deserve it, but I thank you with all my heart."

Mother added, and I could sense the tears, "Jesus, all those times I asked you to care for Molly were answered even though I couldn't see it happen. I never dared to ask that you'd give me freedom, and you gave it anyway. And you added Ludwig. I'm like Molly; I have all I need. Thanks."

There was no need for more. We stayed there in the presence of God in joy and tears with no sense of time. I was enveloped by Molly's love mingled with the love of God. She brushed my ear with her lips and whispered, "He did it again, didn't he? We're together in him. I love you, sweetheart. No one else could ever be here with me."

"Yes, Molly, darling, He's taken us into the Throne Room of the Universe. I give you a new name: *Handmaid of the Lord*."

"Thank you, *Prophet of God*. You're my one and only. I love you so much it won't stay inside me."

"My love for you exceeds all other human emotion. Without you I'd be less than nothing. We're once again allowed to enjoy a thing that's seldom granted. Our love is pure and holy and is being blessed by the one called *Wonderful Counselor*."

"What will it be like when I can give you my love without reservation? I almost melt just thinking about it," that husky, stirring voice whispered.

"We'll know in a week. After all this time, we won't need to wait any longer," I whispered back. "I'm glad we've waited, but even seven days seems like an eternity now."

"Yes. But the end of our wait's almost here. Let's enjoy every minute of this time. It's the only time we'll do it. What a wonder it is that we'll have almost all of the people who're important to us here in a couple of days. I'm really glad the Utes are coming."

"Isn't it usual for the father of the bride to walk her down the aisle?"

"Yes. I hadn't thought of that."

"Whom will you have be your father?"

"Smart Coyote's the logical one, isn't he? Do you think he'd do it for me?"

"He'll do almost anything that would make you happy. Let's ask him when he comes. I can't think of anyone who'd be more appropriate for that honor."

"We'll have all the Utes in our family group with him and Fawn Heart in the front row. They've been my parents for all this time, and Mother won't be there. They'll sit with Grandpa and Grandma. I can hardly wait to introduce them. What a marvelous time this is going to be." She was no longer whispering, and Lud and Mother were smiling broadly.

"I agree, dear," said her mother. "I want them to be counted as members of our immediate family, too. Isn't it great that we can have them in our wedding? I've wondered why you asked for the medicine man to come, though."

I said, "I'll try to explain that. He's helped us a lot and in several ways. He traveled a long way to help me when I was shot and hurting terribly. He invited me to participate in a ceremony when he was putting his blessing on our trip to rescue you. He's an extremely wise man who cares deeply for his tribe. I want to introduce him to the Army doctor who took care of me when we got here. They'll be able to help each other."

"You know the details of that, so I'll trust you to tell me all about it, Ludwig," she said. "It sounds like an exciting tale. I didn't even know you had been shot."

Molly said, "That was a *terrible* time. His own father shot him in the head. I didn't know if he was well for over six months, and it almost killed me. I was so worried. It'll take Lud a while to tell the complete story. I think you should wait until there's lots of time, so he can give you every detail."

"There's so much that I don't know that it'll take years to hear it all. I'll probably wear you out just asking questions," she said. "I want to hear every detail."

"I suppose my voice'll last through it all," Lud said.

"If you get him started, he can tell some pretty exciting tales," I told her. "Half of them may just be stories, but he'll make it exciting."

"You don't mean that he'd tell me things that aren't true, do you?"

"If he thinks something would sound better if he changed the facts, he might stretch things."

"Don't listen to him," Lud pleaded. "Molly, did I ever tell you anything that wasn't true?"

"I wasn't able to find out if some of your tales were fact or fiction, so I really can't answer that."

"They're just fooling, Maureen! I'll never lie to you about anything. I guess Carlos is trying to pay me back for some of the times I kidded with him. Is that what you're doing, kid?"

"We're just having fun with you. I think you can believe him… most of the time."

"I don't care. I've fallen in love with him, and I want him just like he is. He's told me he knows Jesus, and that's the most important thing, anyway."

"Well, if you're going to get all serious about it, Lud's been almost a father to me. He's taught me more than any other man, and he wouldn't let us come after you without him. If he didn't have any other good quality, he loves Molly as much as if she was his daughter, and that would cover a lot of shortcomings. I could never want a better friend, and I'm truly happy that you've chosen to marry him. You could look for years and not find a man as good as he is."

Molly added, "Yes, Mother, you've chosen well. Lud's been wonderful, and I'm truly delighted that you'll be his wife. He's already almost a father, and he soon will truly be my daddy."

Lud said, "Let's get out of here before you start telling *good* things about me that aren't true. I'm already embarrassed."

CHAPTER THIRTY-EIGHT

The Utes came two days later, and we spent a couple of hours getting them greeted properly and settled into the tents we had prepared. That was followed by a tour of Santa Fe, particularly our home and the central square. I managed to arrange a meeting at a later time between Star Gazer and the doctor who cared for my head injury. Molly and I were there so she could interpret, and I was pleased when the Army man obviously understood most of what the medicine man told him. He saw the reason for almost everything the Ute told him. When he asked for the ingredients in the painkiller I had been given, it raised him several more notches. Star Gazer was impressed by the equipment his counterpart had, but that was the extent of his interest. He was willing to answer every question, though.

The captain in charge of the Army post extended an invitation to the Utes to join him in reviewing the troops when they did their drills. All of the men, plus Fawn Heart, accepted that invitation, so Molly and I accompanied them. It was interesting to watch Smart Coyote try to figure out the purpose of the display.

"How often do you do this?" he asked.

Captain Rivera said, "Every day. It keeps the men ready for action better than any other process we've tried."

The chief smiled as he looked at me. I smiled and shook my head. We both knew that his braves needed nothing to keep them ready. However, if there was time for it, the Utes would spend a full night of dancing and painting before they went into battle. I wondered which effort was the more effective. The Utes had no need of paying special braves to take part in their battles, while the people in Santa Fe would've not been able to survive if the Army left. I wasn't sure which group came off better in that comparison.

The Indian women were impressed by our home, but the men were much more interested in the things outside. We had a barn sufficient to handle twice the number of horses we had. It consisted of stalls, a tack room, a loft for storing hay, a granary, and a blacksmith shop. The adjoining corrals were similar to the setup at our partnership property with separate sections and sheds along with more storage for hay. We had completed two small homes for the families of employees who'd be hired in the future, and there was provision for more homes if they were needed.

Smart Coyote said, "This is more than our entire camp. I thought maybe you had learned, but you still want more than you need."

"I didn't learn everything you tried to teach me," I agreed. "We'll use most of this, and as our family grows there'll be a need for more of it. Part of this is done in preparation for the future. Our children will need horses, and we'll have room for them. The house'll have room for the children and for guests who visit. We want you to come and use one of those extra rooms. Dawn on the Mountain and I will begin living here after our wedding, and we'll want you to visit often."

I was pleased as I watched as that thought progressed through his mind. When he seemed to fully grasp what I was offering, it brought a full smile, which was extremely rare. "You'll want Fawn Heart and me to stay in this house?"

"Yes, we will. We've stayed in your home, and you'll *always* be welcome in ours," Molly stated.

She placed her hand on his shoulder as she spoke, and he reached up, took that hand and her other one, and looked into her eyes. Her face was showing the obvious love she felt for that special man, and she pulled him close and managed to hug him and kiss his cheek. That broke through his reticence, and he pulled her close and gave her the only embrace I ever saw him give anyone. His eyes were sparkling with tears, which he tried to hide.

"Enough," he said.

Molly showed her Indian training. "Enough," she echoed and released him. She came to me, her tears flowing freely. I was happy to take her in my arms and wipe them away. What a special lady she is.

The town filled up during the next few days as ranchers came from their grants to their homes in town and others traveled from other areas. I soon wondered if Grandma had underestimated the number of guests we'd have, but there were so many other things needing attention that I decided to let someone else worry about it. Neither Molly nor I had attended a wedding, so we had lots of things to learn. Both Mother and Grandma were well acquainted with the proper way to do things, so all we needed to do was listen and ask questions. Our problems involved the portions where we were offered options such as the number of attendants. There was no shortage of people with opinions, which really didn't make it easier. We prayed together often, which was extremely pleasant, and the results were satisfactory. Lud and I were pleased to leave most of the decision making in the hands of our brides.

We discussed the matter of dress for Smart Coyote since he had accepted the responsibility of bringing Molly down the aisle. I said, "Why don't we trust him?"

Molly said, "I agree. He has such wisdom I think we'll offend him if we ask what he intends to wear. He'll do something that's better than any of us could suggest."

Lud said, "I'll say that's the best thing we can do. I reckon he'll do something special that we may not expect, but it'll be good."

Mother insisted that the wedding ceremonies make it clear that ours was the main event. We allowed her to arrange the order of service, and it went well.

CHAPTER THIRTY-NINE

The wedding was scheduled for ten o'clock Saturday morning, June 15. It was a rarely beautiful day with hardly a cloud in the sky and no wind. We had asked all those who'd have a part in the wedding to be at the church an hour early so we'd have time for the ladies to go over things with the priest, look over the church, and get dressed. I had arranged for a pot of coffee in the kitchen, so we men would have something to keep us busy.

The Utes arrived as a group, and that was worth seeing. Smart Coyote was in his full regalia complete with an outstanding headdress of mixed eagle and goose feathers. The alternating dark and light feathers, each of which was barely shorter than the one just above it, stretched across his forehead, around his head, and down his back to just below his waist. His jacket and trousers were of fringed white buckskin, as were his moccasins. The jacket was adorned with porcupine quills, bear claws, and elk teeth in depictions of coyotes. The moccasins were also decorated with quills and red leather. We could have never asked for better clothing. Molly was overjoyed.

Star Gazer was dressed in similar clothing, which was red but had his coyote skirt and cape over the jacket and trousers. He also carried a buckskin bag and a small drum. His headgear was the coyote head and a beaded headband of black. He tapped the drum in the proper cadence when the chief and Molly walked the aisle and again when she and I went back up at the end of the ceremony. He didn't accompany his and Mother's walk down the aisle. The drum was attached to his arm with a quill-covered strap. The presence of the two Utes was probably startling to some, but we rejoiced that they had agreed to participate.

Things proceeded on schedule. Father Manuel, Lud, and I were in place, waiting for the brides, promptly at ten o'clock. When Grandma started playing the wedding march on her guitar, it surprised me. I hadn't been aware of that plan.

Molly was absolutely stunning in a marvelous white silk dress with a train that must've been at least ten feet long and a veil that reached to her breasts. Her Indian background was expressed with a white headband with a delicate, blue outline of a coyote above each of her eyes, which was the single bit of color. Walking beside Smart Coyote in his dramatic regalia, she was beautiful beyond description. I had difficulty breathing. She couldn't have held everyone's attention more completely if the place had been totally dark and she had been in a bright spot of light. Star Gazer's drum was in perfect rhythm with Grandma's guitar but added a dramatic touch as perhaps nothing else could have. Her eyes were locked on mine, and her smile was her crowning glory. A murmur swept through the church just from the drama of the occasion. She was absolute perfection.

The single bit of direction we had given Smart Coyote was regarding the way to answer the priest when he asked, "Who gives this woman to be wed to this man?" At that moment the chief raised his left hand, which held a short spear, and brought it, point up across his chest, and then he pointed to Fawn Heart. She nodded vigorously. He then took Molly's hand and led her to the steps leading to the altar. I met them there, and he placed her hand in mine and walked to stand beside Fawn Heart.

Mother was escorted by Star Gazer, and while it was a wonderful sight for those of us who were involved, it was almost muted in comparison with the vision that preceded it. There was no missing the fact that the brides were related. This dress was also a work of art with a brilliant blue upper section, a gray skirt, and very light, gray veil. Star Gazer's clothing was striking but almost subdued beside Smart Coyote's. All of this was intentional so that Molly would be the star of the show, according to Mother's wishes. This bride's face showed the same measure of joy that Molly's had, but it seemed to not hold the same double-distilled beauty in my eyes. I was sure Lud would disagree and was extremely happy for him.

When Star Gazer handed Lud his bride, the priest went at once into the ceremony of marriage for Lud and Maureen. He was concise and efficient in the performance of the rites, and as soon as he had pronounced that they were wed, he turned to us then seemed to remember something and waited.

Grandma had played the wedding march from her place in the front row of seats. She now came and stood beside me and played and sang two appropriate wedding songs. Her voice was in great form, and she was a wizard on the guitar. It was a tremendous bonus that neither of us had expected. The songs were about a deep, strong love between a man and a woman. I suspected that they were songs that represented times in her own life that she was sharing with us. They were nearly the most significant part of the ceremony. Her voice was precisely right for the songs. When she finished she turned and gave Molly a lengthy hug. I saw her saying so softly only Molly could hear, "I love you." She then returned to her seat. I doubt that there was a dry eye in that church, and every single person knew that Molly was welcome in our family.

I confess that, except for listening closely enough to avoid missing a required response, I spent most of the time exchanging silent messages with Molly. She was without doubt the most beautiful of God's creation, and her magnetism was so strong I could barely stay in the place assigned me. It was evident that she was feeling the same things almost as strongly. We had waited, and the Lord had finally brought us to this moment when we could unleash all of our love. I heard the priest tell of the ways Molly and Mother had been captured and of the years of separation. He gave the Utes full credit for their part in the ultimate victory and told a little bit about how God had intervened in our behalf.

We had an absolutely perfect wedding for several reasons, but it'd have seemed that way if it had been in a dingy, broken-down shack with Molly, the priest, and I the only people present. When it was complete, we were man and wife, for which we had waited and prayed. When he finally declared that we were married, I almost gave a Ute war cry. But I didn't—yet. Instead, I offered Molly my arm, and prepared to lead Lud and Mother toward the back of the church.

Molly stopped at the foot of the altar. Smart Coyote came and stood facing us. He removed his beautiful headdress and placed it on me. He placed a hand on each of my shoulders and said, "My son." He moved to Molly, assumed the same position, and said, "My daughter." He moved until he could place one hand on Molly's shoulder and the other on mine. "I bless you," he said. All the declarations were in Spanish.

Tradition was important to Grandma, so we stood for an hour as folks we barely knew gave us their wishes for a successful marriage. Mother knew none of them, so it must have been especially tiring for her. She maintained her smile to the end, as did Molly. Even Grandma had reached the limit of her endurance when the last well-wishers had passed and we were able to go change our clothes and go to the reception.

We had assigned a room in our new home to each couple who was in the wedding party. We had reserved for ourselves the bedroom that would be ours. We spent some time learning about expressing our love with no restrictions, and when we finally arrived at the reception, enough time had passed to bring smiles to several faces. We'll never tell whether they were right. We were married and had no reason to report to anyone.

We were able to join the celebration and enjoy it fully. There was an orchestra, and we had prepared a place for those who wanted to dance. It was soon apparent that no one was going to dance until the four of us did, so I requested Molly's favorite song and we led off with Lud and Mother joining us almost immediately. Star Gazer danced alone, as did Red Arrow.

Remembering our few moments of privacy, I whispered, "A sip of the nectar of heaven was absolutely wonderful, but it brought a thirst beyond description. I need a deep, sweet drink as soon as possible."

I had thought we were dancing closely, but she drew me even closer and breathed, her voice deeper than I had ever heard, "My cup's overflowing, sweetheart. I didn't know what love was until now. You'll never drink deeply enough, my love."

"I'm blessed beyond anything man has ever dreamed. You're my world, my beautiful wife, my very life."

Then words from the Song of Solomon came into my mind. I placed my lips against her ear and quoted,

> Behold, you are beautiful, my love, behold, you are beautiful! Your eyes are doves behind your veil. Your hair is like a flock of goats leaping down the slopes of Gilead. Your teeth are like a flock of shorn ewes that have come up from the washing, all of which bear twins, and not one among them has lost its young. Your lips are like a scarlet thread, and your mouth is lovely. Your cheeks are like halves of a pomegranate behind your veil. Your neck is like the tower of David, built in rows of stone; on it hang a thousand shields, all of them shields of warriors. Your two breasts are like two fawns, twins of a gazelle, that graze among the lilies.
>
> Song of Solomon 4:1-5 (NKJV)

I was thrilled when she moved so her lips touched my ear, and that exquisite voice quoted from the same passage, "Let my beloved come to his garden, and eat its choicest fruits" (Song of Solomon 4:16b, NKJV).

We may have danced well beyond the end of the song. We needed no music beyond that which was playing in our hearts.

CHAPTER FORTY

Lud and I were almost certain the man we had rented cabins from would quickly spread the news and arrange some tomfoolery. We made sure that almost everyone knew we were leaving the reception, and rode our horses away from the party. We made certain that no one followed us. The ladies and I left Lud when we were at the front of our house, and we hurried inside while Lud continued, leading our three mounts. We had made arrangements to hide the horses at a place half a mile away. When Lud had the horses safely hidden he returned along a way that wasn't often used.

The party had run until it was almost dark, and there was no likelihood that anyone would come into the rooms we had chosen, so we felt that we were reasonably safe from detection. We were very quiet and were able to hear when the others who had changed in the house earlier came and retrieved the clothing they had left. My grandparents had been given the responsibility of closing and locking the house. When we were sure they had left, we notified Lud and Mother, and we all met in the kitchen for a meal. It wasn't yet dark enough to require a light.

We learned later that more than twenty men were disappointed when they made the ride to the cabins and learned that we weren't there. As far as we were able to learn, they never did find out where we were, and we enjoyed some precious privacy. As Smart Coyote had mentioned, we had more house than we needed, so Lud and Mother used a room in the opposite end of the house, and we had the privacy we sought. We each found pure delight in our mate. It was a time when reality exceeded any dream.

We encountered Lud and Mother the following afternoon, and there was no doubt that we were all in the situations we had hoped for. We agreed that our God is wonderful beyond description.

I awoke the next morning while it was still dark. Molly was sleeping peacefully, her wonderful face completely relaxed, a hint of a smile on her lips. I slipped out of bed without disturbing her, got some clothes, and left our room. After dressing quietly, I hurried outside and went to get our horses where Lud had left them. No one was apt to see me while it was dark. I was back before the sun had put any color in the eastern sky and was back beside Molly before she woke up.

I managed to be awake and watching when Molly opened her beautiful eyes.

"Good morning, Dawn on the Mountain. What do you see on your mountain today?"

"Oh, sweetheart, it's a wonderful sight. My doe and her fawn are there, and a marvelous buck's joined them. Raton and Mary are there with a *grullo* colt. A huge bull elk and his cow and calf just walked into the picture, and there's a trio of bears. It's a beautiful scene, completely beautiful."

"I think I see a lake with some trout jumping, don't I?"

"Oh, yes. You promised me that, didn't you?"

"Yes, that first day. Look up on that mountain. See that Bighorn ram and his gorgeous mate—and there's the lamb!"

"Aren't they wonderful? What else do you see?"

"The full moon's resting exactly on that western hill, and the single cloud in the eastern sky is painted a bright red by that sun, just peeking over the mountain. That's a miraculous sight that could only be given by God himself."

"What a wonderful sight. Do you think we'll ever see it again, darling?"

"It'll be better every time I wake up and find you here beside me, sweetheart."

"Oh, yes! I'll love you more every time I see you, Carlos, my Man of God."

"You have so many names now, but may I add another?"

"What name would you add?"

"Beautiful Wife. No one has ever been given beauty like yours, my darling."

"The name *wife* by itself is enough. My beauty will fade, but the name *wife* will grow into something truly beautiful."

"It's already beautiful, and so are you. The Lord's blessed me beyond all that can be thought or asked. He promises that he'll do that, and he's done it for me. I love you more than words can express, my *Gift from God*."

"Oh, my husband, you will never know how much I love you. I give you that same name. Can we share it?"

"You may have anything that I'm able to give you, sweetheart."

"Give me another of those kisses we waited for so long. They take me into a world I had never dreamed of."

"And I get to go with you."

"Mmm, thank you. My heart's singing now."

"Kiss me again, and I'll sing the harmony."

"Are you hungry?"

"I have hungers I didn't know existed, but yes, I 'm ready for some breakfast—as soon as I kiss you again."

"Only one."

"Why?"

"You might have to wait until noon if you kiss me twice."

"I can handle that."

"Only one, hungry man."

"Well…all right, delicious woman."

"I love you."

"I love you."

We rode to visit the Utes before they left, riding a circuitous route to avoid people. Our friends were pleased to have been welcomed as they were and invited us to visit soon. We gave Molly some privacy with her foster parents, which was obviously a tender time. We returned after it was dark to avoid being seen by any potential pranksters.

CHAPTER FORTY-ONE

We enjoyed a wonderful summer. Lud and Mother lived with us most of the time In early August they asked us to help them choose a location for their home. We spent several days looking at spots, and they chose an area similar to ours half a mile southwest of us. Molly and Mother had discussed the design of their home, so it was only a short time before my uncle and Grandpa were at work on it. There were many similarities to our house, but they each had some special things they wanted so it was definitely their home. The outbuildings were also similar but arranged to utilize the location to the best advantage.

We expected that our former partners would appear no later than mid-September and often rode north, hoping to intercept them and learn about their season. Molly and I each had a sense of urgency the morning of the tenth, so we left town early and let our horses work off the morning friskiness by allowing them to run for almost a mile. When we were ten miles out, we met a group of miners. They were exhausted. Each of them tried to tell us what had happened. I was able to select one man and get the others to remain silent as I questioned him.

He said, "The Indians attacked us when we left the mine. They caught us where the trail goes through that first draw and killed the owners first. The men who had rifles resisted and were also killed. We ran."

"When did this happen?"

"Five days ago. We've hidden a lot and traveled only when we were sure none of them was around. We've eaten almost nothing and are in bad trouble."

"Do you know if any others escaped?"

"No. We hid every time we thought someone was near."

We each had a full canteen that we left with them and told them we'd go try to find horses to bring back for them. We rode swiftly back to Santa Fe, where Molly hurried to tell Lud what we had learned. I began borrowing horses, and within an hour we had fifty of them. Molly and Mother insisted on going with us.We put bridles on all the horses and drove them as fast as possible back toward the miners.

We mounted two of them on each of five animals and sent them south. They were instructed to release the horses in the pasture at the partnership barn, go home, and return to the barn in ten days. We continued north, looking for more survivors.

We discovered thirty-six more thirty miles above that spot. All of them were in good shape, so we left them with enough horses to enable them to ride home, two on each animal. We rode on and met no more survivors that day. We camped and spent an hour in prayer, which was undoubtedly the reason I was able to sleep.

The sun was barely causing a red glow in the east when we mounted and continued our search. It was almost noon when we found the next group. They were all in good shape except for their fear. They had been in hiding almost continually, afraid to have a fire, and creeping along in the deep forest. We assured them they'd encounter no trouble if they took the easiest trail and went home. They had killed a deer with a bow and arrow they had found so weren't in need of food.

We continued our search and found nothing until two days later when we found where the battle had taken place. The Utes had chosen the spot well and had apparently waited until Ben and Juan were together. Their bodies were still easily identified, even though birds and animals had been busy. We counted forty-five bodies, but there were many more that were so messed up we weren't able to count them. The packs had been removed from the burros and were lying around the area.

There was no possibility that we could bury all the bodies, but we took care of Ben's and Juan's.

Lud said, "What can we do now?"

I said, "At least one of us needs to go see Smart Coyote and make sure this is the end of their rampage. We also need to get horses, mules, or burros up here and pack the gold to Santa Fe. I imagine that Molly and I should deal with Smart Coyote."

"How long can we use the horses we have now?"

"Probably not more than a couple of weeks. While we're here, let's check the cache. If there's room there, we can bring a small crew and put most of this in there."

"That's a good idea. Let's ride over there."

Mother said, "Is there no way we can bury the others?"

Lud answered, "It'd take us a week to get a hole big enough to hold that many bodies. The coyotes, wolves, and bears, along with birds, will have the bones picked by then. I don't like it either, but other things are more important."

That conversation took place while we were riding toward the cache. When we arrived, it appeared that there had been no activity there. It took a half hour to remove the sod and other dirt and logs from the entry way. I dropped down and entered the cache. It was as empty as a church at daybreak on Tuesday. It appeared that there had been no activity since we had cleaned it out the previous winter.

"We can pack everything here that we don't have horses enough to take to Santa Fe. I think a crew of ten can handle the job," I said. "If you'll go and get that many men together and bring them and the horses back, we'll go talk with Smart Coyote."

"Why don't I bring fifteen men? The hard part of this job'll be handling the ore here. We don't want to be delayed because we don't have enough help."

"That's fine. We need enough help to get this done as quickly as possible."

"We'll do things as fast as we can, but I doubt if we can be back in less than a week. We'll need supplies and food for everybody plus cooking gear and stuff for camping,"

"We have camping and cooking gear stored here, but we need food. If you can be back in a week, we should be all right. Be sure you have a cook. Nobody will work if we don't feed them well."

"All right, we'll get on our way."

Molly said, "Aren't we going to pray about this?"

I said, "Of course we are. Will you lead us, sweetheart?"

"Lord, we're really sorry about what's happened, and we ask you to lead us now so we'll do only the things you want us to. Please watch over Mother and Lud as they go home and back and give Lud wisdom as he selects the men. Carlos and I need direction as we go talk with Smart Coyote. We're trusting you for that as well as for safety. We don't know how angry the Utes may be, so we ask you to cover us with your protection. We ask for this in the name of Jesus. Amen."

Mother said, "We can't ask for more than that. Be careful. We don't know what kind of reception you'll get."

"We'll be fine after we're in their camp," Molly assured.

"Smart Coyote would say, 'Enough.' We need to get underway," I said.

Molly and Mother hugged and we headed in our separate directions. We were on Raton and Mary, so we were able to reach the chief's tipi before he and Fawn Heart had eaten the evening meal. They were uncomfortable, but nothing was discussed until we had eaten and were in the position to smoke. Smart Coyote and I went through the required three puffs each, and the pipe was placed on the floor.

The chief said, "Did you see what happened when the miners started to take the ore to the cache?"

"We saw. Has it ended?"

"We'll not do more, if no more miners come. The council would wait no longer, and I had no way to oppose them."

"Lud, Dawn on the Mountain, and I tried to convince them that they shouldn't bring so many. We're sorry it happened."

"What will you do?"

"Lud will bring fifteen men and fifty horses. We'll take as much ore as we can in one trip to Santa Fe. We plan to put the rest of the ore in the cache before we leave. If we leave the ore where it is, the story will be told, and there'll be a rush of people to pick up what was on the burros, and they'll also be like a swarm of ants over these mountains. They'll be trying to find the mine. Did you fix it so it'll be difficult to find?"

"That gully's half full of rocks. Nobody will be able to tell that there was a mine there."

"We'll leave it like that. We may come back next year and get the stuff we put in the cache, but we won't bring a big crew. We'll talk with you first if we decide to do that."

"I'll like that. You're of our tribe, and we don't want to be against you."

Molly said, "We came to make certain that you're not still angry and to tell you that we'll not bring a large number of people. We don't intend to work the mine again."

"Do you also speak for Lud?"

"Yes. He and Mother agree with us completely."

"I told you he's a wise man." He motioned toward me.

"Enough. We're sorry that our friends caused this problem. You've taught us that it's foolish to want more than is needed. We value our relationship with you more than gold."

"It's a thing the others didn't learn. We have no reason to fight with you. It's good that we have this talk. There's no wall between us."

There was nothing we could do at the cache, so we decided to stay with the Utes another five days. I awoke early the fourth morning and went to check our horses. I planned to make certain they were doing well and come back within a short time. Raton was favoring his left foreleg, so I went to investigate. He had a rock caught in his hoof, which will cause a serious limp if not cared for. It took a few minutes to extract the stone, and I spent some more time watching to make sure there was no lingering pain.

As I was returning, I heard a muffled cry close to the tipi. I walked swiftly to check and be sure it wasn't Molly. She wasn't in the tipi. I immediately lifted a prayer for safety for her and wisdom for both of us. There was a frightening certainty in my mind that Dark Dog was involved. The cry I had heard had come from north of the tipi, which was an area covered with dense brush. I went outside and around the tipi, watching for anything that would tell me where they had gone.

Molly had dragged her foot where there was loose soil, dust, twigs, or grass. She had stepped on a short clump of brush where they had left the trail and had managed to continue leaving signs of her passage clearly through the brush. I could follow at a fast walk. I wasn't far behind them. If her captor discovered what she was doing, it'd almost certainly bring some punishment and the trail would disappear. At the worst that punishment would be death or injury. At the least it'd be a blow to her face.

The trail she left was plain until they left the brush and went into a grass-covered section. Most of the grass wasn't tall, which made it difficult to follow. Molly still managed to step on a tall clump of grass and kick at a twig so it would appear disturbed. She stepped on every blooming plant and was quite inventive. I had no idea where she was being taken. We were beyond all of the tipis and were traveling away from the river. When it was apparent that they had gone into another brushy area, I pretended to lose the trail and hurried past that area.

I had spotted a distinct trail about one hundred feet ahead of me that went into the brush. I went to it and followed it until it intersected another trail that would take me back toward the place I had passed. I slipped quietly along, watching and gauging the distance. I didn't want to go back farther than the place where they had gone into the brush. When I was certain I had gone beyond that point and had seen no evidence of their having crossed the trail I was on, I turned back and found a place where I could safely watch the trail.

It was only a few minutes before I heard a man's voice. I didn't understand what was said, but the voice definitely had a mocking tone. I assumed it was Dark Dog telling Molly that he had succeeded in eluding me. When they appeared, Molly had a piece of leather tied over her mouth. Her hands were tied behind her waist and she was being pulled along with a hair rope around her throat. Dark Dog was forcing her to follow by jerking the rope. The tone of his voice had changed and sounded threatening. I assumed that he was telling Molly what he intended to do to her.

Smart Coyote had told us that some of the braves were afraid that I'd attempt to learn who had killed the men at the mine and would attack them. He had suggested that I not carry any firearms. It seemed like a reasonable request, so I had complied. When I discovered that Molly was gone I had no weapon except my knife. Dark Dog had a bow and a quiver of arrows and was carrying a spear. His knife hung at his waist.

The Ute turned onto the trail rather than crossing it. He came toward my hiding place but was looking back at Molly most of the time. I drew my knife and stepped onto the trail while he was looking away from me. When he looked toward me, we were ten feet apart.

He dropped the rope, raised the spear, and squatted in anticipation of a battle. He jumped toward me, the spear ready for attacking me. When he was almost where the spear could be driven into my body, he drew it back and then struck toward my belly. I stepped aside and tripped him with my foot. He fell into the brush and dropped his spear. While he was retrieving his weapon, I went behind Molly and cut the strap holding her hands. She started removing the gag, and I moved toward the

Ute. I asked Molly to move into the brush, which would not only give her some protection but would give me more freedom to move.

When Dark Dog faced me again, I asked Molly to tell him that I warned him that his medicine had no strength against my God. He'd be wise to admit that fact and leave us. His response was a raucous war cry and another attack almost exactly like his previous effort. I assumed that he'd be expecting me to also repeat my defense, so I stepped the other way. He did what I anticipated by pointing his spear where he thought I'd step. I grasped his right wrist, stepped under his arm, turned so my back was against him, and threw him over my head. He lay on his back, gasping for air.

I was overcome by anger because of his treatment of my beloved wife and went berserk for a bit. I've never been so angry, before or since. I still had his wrist in my grasp and jerked him to a standing position facing me. What followed was not planned and left me dazed. I drove my knife blade into his chest just under his chin then jerked the blade through his rib cage and on down to his crotch. He collapsed at my feet. I opened his chest and removed his heart by severing everything that extended from it. I jumped to my feet and threw his heart as far as I could into the brush then knelt beside him and wiped his blood from my hands and knife on his clothing.

I stood, completely overwhelmed with passion. Molly came to me, her arms outstretched. I gathered her into a gentle embrace and touched her throat where the rope had left scratches.

"Did he hurt you?"

"He hurt my arms and my neck. My wrist and face are tender, but those are minor things. I'm fine now. How'd you get ahead of him?"

"I'm sure the Holy Spirit led me. You did a great job, leaving marks that I could follow easily. I saw where he had gone into the brush, but at the same time saw a trail one hundred feet farther along. It took me to this trail, which I followed to this point and knew this was the place to wait. His medicine wasn't able to deal with the power of God."

"He'd have taken me to a place where I may have never been seen again. I was sure you'd rescue me, so I made a mark every time I saw an opportunity. He was too excited and never saw a single track I left."

I kissed her softly and removed the rope that was still hanging loosely on her shoulders. "Let's go tell Smart Coyote about this."

"I'm so weak I can hardly stand. That was *terrible*."

"I'm sorry, darling I'll run and get your horse."

"Don't even *think* of leaving me. I'll crawl if I have to, but don't leave me."

"All right, I'm not going anywhere. I'll carry you," I said and picked her up.

She was apparently at an emotional state of complete release after a terrible time of tension. She put her head on my shoulder and closed her eyes. "You have no way to know how horrible that was. He planned things too awful to even think about. If he had been able to do it, you wouldn't have wanted to see me if he had ever turned me loose. I can't even talk about some of the things he told me he was going to do. You're certainly the answer to my prayers."

"He never had a chance. You're more precious to Jesus than you are to me, if that's possible. He heard your prayers along with mine and took care of him. It was the Holy Spirit who gave me the ability to know in advance what Dark Dog would do."

"I praise God, but I can feel you. That's more than anything else I could want. I love you more now than I did yesterday. This showed me, as nothing else could, how much you are part of me. We're truly one flesh, aren't we?"

"Yes, sweetheart, never doubt that without you I'm less than nothing. God is the only one who's as much a part of me as you are. I think you're my very life. I couldn't breathe, and my heart stopped the moment I knew you were gone. If God hadn't intervened, I might have died then."

"I had no life until I saw you step onto the trail. I knew the moment I saw you that I could still live. You're a true gift from God. If you'll let me stand, I'll show you how much I love you, and we can walk together."

We were able to continue sometime later. Our kisses were sweeter and our love deeper than ever before. It was like receiving her back from the grave.

Our union that night was more complete than I had ever dreamed it could be. We were each able to give our love so fully and at the same time receive love from the other in the same measure that it could only be the result of God making us absolutely one. Neither of us thought until later that it was the time we usually avoided to prevent pregnancy.

When I realized what we had done, I prayed, and then said to Molly, "Do you know what we did? We made a little girl last night."

"No, we made a little boy. God told me he is giving me another man."

"Get ready for twins, sweetheart. He's never been wrong, and he said he's giving me another *you*."

"Oh, goodness! Do you think so?"

"We'd better be prepared for that. What a wonderful way to finish that experience! *What a God we serve!*"

"Amen to that. I suppose he'll get me ready for two babies at the same time. Oh, my! *Oh, my!*"

"Only God could make another you. I can hardly wait. He surely won't make you put up with someone else like me, though."

"Nothing would please me more, Perfect Man. Do you think you can handle two of me?"

"No, that'll never happen. If he gives us a daughter like you, he'll also give us what's needed to avoid being overcome with joy.

You'll need another name; Queen Mother, and I suppose she'll be Perfect Princess."

"*Enough*! I need some time to get used to this. I can hardly wait to tell Lud and Mother."

"We need to tell Smart Coyote and Fawn Heart, too, before we leave."

"Oh, my! This brings so many things with it, doesn't it?"

"I may need some new shirts. I'll strut so much the ones I have will bust wide open."

"I guess there'll be some changes in me, too."

"Enough! I love you the way you are."

"You'll need a good memory, 'cause I'll change."

"We'll make some memories."

"*Don't touch me!*"

"We will, though."

"I love you, you big galoot. Kiss me."

"I love you, Big Mama."

"I'm not big yet. Come here!"

"Remember, you invited me."

"I surely did, my darling. Oh, yes. Yes. *Yes!*"

"Mmmm. You're wonderful."

"I love you"

"I love you."

CHAPTER FORTY-TWO

We met Lud and Mother as we had arranged. Lud said, "Maureen insisted that she and Molly can serve as cooks, so I let her have her way."

Molly said, "That's a great idea. I wondered how I could help. You did right."

It took six days to get one hundred fifty of the packs into the cache. On the seventh day, we rested, and I led in a study of the third chapter of the letter to the Philippians. The Holy Spirit, through Paul, tells how much more precious our relationship with Jesus is than anything this world offers. We allowed the men a day of rest, and the four of us rode to investigate the mine site. There wasn't a single trace of our work, which pleased us greatly. It had brought us riches but had caused much trouble.

As we stood looking at the spot that had brought such joy and sorrow, I said, "Lord, we need your wisdom again. You want to tell us something. We'll wait until you tell us what it is."

We had joined hands while I was praying. We stayed like that for several minutes with our heads bowed, waiting.

I felt Molly sink to her knees. She pulled her hand from mine. I couldn't resist looking. She was in the position I had seen only once before, her face toward heaven and her arms extended upward, palms up. It was a beautiful position of worship. There was a smile on her lips, and her face almost shined with pure joy. It seemed like a long time, but she finally said, "Thank you, Lord," and opened her eyes. She reached for my hand, and I helped her stand and took her in my arms.

"He said that we're to make the cache secure and take the remaining packs to Santa Fe. We're to melt the gold from the ore and use it and the bricks in the other packs to pay for the use of the horses and to care for the families of the miners who were killed. We're to pay the miners who survived for the full year they were hired. Those funds will come from the gold stored in the barn. The balance that remains, plus the property where the barn is, belongs to us. Neither Ben nor Juan had a family."

Lud said, "You've definitely become a part of Carlos. How can we argue with those orders? He didn't leave anything unanswered. Nothing could be more fair, either."

Mother found a place to sit. She was smiling and shaking her head.

Molly went to her and said, "Is something wrong?"

"I'm overwhelmed that my little girl has that kind of relationship with Jesus. I've never seen anything like it. You and Carlos may not realize what God's done for you. I can hardly wait to see how he works in the lives of your children. This sort of thing passes on to the next generations. Please seek God's wisdom when you're given those youngsters."

Molly reached for her mother's hands, helped her stand, and gave her a tight hug and a kiss on her cheek. "Thanks, Mother. You were given that message for us. We're all here together in what Carlos calls the throne room of the universe with Almighty God."

Lud said, "He even let me be a part of it. I say again that I've never heard of a better deal."

The spell was broken when Raton tossed his head and came to nudge me with his nose. We all laughed, and I said, "All right, so you aren't impressed. We'll come back to earth and go let you graze. You're saying, 'Enough.'"

CHAPTER FORTY-THREE

We celebrated Christmas in Lud's and Mother's new home. Grandma, Grandpa, my uncle's family, and fifteen children of the miners who were killed gathered with us for a feast. The children ate at a separate table in the same room with us. They were each clothed in items Molly and Mother had given them. The ladies had gifts for each of them, which were distributed after we had eaten.

We exchanged gifts as well, but that was a minor part of our celebration. Each of us had become more aware of the real reason for the occasion and the fact that Jesus was the one whose birthday we were celebrating. We enjoyed watching the children. Each of them received at least three gifts. Lud had made a sleigh that was capable of carrying all the children. He and Mother had it decorated for the season, and the team he used was fitted out appropriately. The trip to and from the dinner was the best part of the day for many of the youngsters.

Lud insisted that Molly and I stay to eat leftovers. It was apparent to me that he had something serious on his mind, but he waited until we had eaten before he told us what it was.

He said, "We're wondering about something and need to get it cleared up. Did you check the packs to see what was in them before we filled the cache?"

I said, "No. I asked the Lord to arrange that. Are you surprised about the way it worked out?"

"Yes, we are. All but eight of the packs we brought down here were full of gold bricks, which meant they contained about eighteen times as much gold as the others. Each of the families of the men who were killed got enough to buy a nice home and live comfortably for years. We're happy about that but wanted to know if you did anything to cause it to happen that way."

I said, "I suppose we did but not the way you may have suspected. As I said, we asked the Lord to handle that, and he did. We might have had all the packs filled with bricks, but God did enough to satisfy us."

Molly said, "I appreciate your asking us about this. We should always do this when we have questions. Otherwise we'll have things that cause us to doubt each other. Carlos and I have pledged to each other that we'll never fail to talk about anything that we don't understand fully. We want our love to flourish and stay in full bloom forever. That won't happen if we allow anything to go unresolved."

Mother said, "Ludwig and I have done the same thing. We're starting with many more things in our past. If we don't deal with them, they'll become problems. Thanks for allowing us to discuss this."

I said, "Ben drew a map of each of the locations. I've copied them and had Molly compare them. She could find no difference in them. Here's one of each of them. We'll not use ours. Some of our children, or others down the line further, may need them, so we think they're worth keeping."

Lud said, "That's exactly the way we feel about it. Let me see them." He and Mother examined them closely. "These are really accurate. I could find either spot easily using them. I imagine it'll be more difficult after a couple of hundred years and trees have died. Some of the rocks will move, and frost will bring changes, but these may be really important to some of those who follow us. Thanks for making copies and sharing with us."

Molly said, "Let's pray. Will you lead, Lud?"

"I want to get on my knees. I read this week that every knee will bow and every tongue confess that Jesus is Lord of Lords and King of Kings."

"Lord, I can't imagine why you've chosen to put us in front of the spout where you make the blessings come out, but you have. We've talked about a few of them, but when you chose to bless me with Maureen, it went past anything I ever wanted. That's the best thing except when you taught me about Jesus, which came from Carlos. You made us rich with that mine, gave us Ute friends, kept us safe from the Sioux, and fixed it so we could help the families of the miners who were killed. I could take another hour and not even touch the rim of what you did. I'll like it a lot if you keep on doing nice things for us, but there's a special thing I'd like. If you'll give us a baby, I'll be even happier."

Mother followed with, "Jesus, I've known you a long time, but not like it's been the past year. To be here with the man I love, with my precious Molly and her Carlos, in a home I had never even hoped for, free of fear and able to kneel and know you're right here with us, is beyond my dreams or prayers. I'm still trying to find out how you work with Carlos and Molly and am flabbergasted every time you do it. I don't care if you never work through me that way, but please let me keep watching you do it in them. You know what I want to say, Lord. I said it before, and it's still true. I have all I need."

I felt Molly start crying early in her mother's prayer, so I went next. "You've given me so many things that I thought were the best things you could possibly do, but you've kept doing something better. I thought you had done the best thing when you brought Molly into my life, but you've taken us into things that are better because we've done it together. It does make Molly still the best, though. I know you have more things to teach us and to give us that exceed anything we can imagine or dream. We want children and we trust you to provide them. There's really nothing I need, but I ask you to place your hand of blessing on Molly."

Molly waited quite awhile. I was almost ready to ask if she wanted me to close for her when she said, with her voice breaking, "Lord, you've already given me so much that I can hardly believe it. I have Carlos and Mother, and you've even talked with me and let me be a part of what you're doing. We were able to watch children who recently lost their fathers enjoy your birthday party. We're here in your presence, talking with you right now. What more could I *want*? I want to bear children with Carlos. That'll be the greatest honor you could give me. I want to see Lud and Mother's baby. I want to see many folks accept Christ as their Savior. I want to see the foal from Raton and Mary. I want to learn to worship you the way you deserve. But really I can still say that I have all I need. Thank you, Lord."

There was no need to move except to turn to my precious, beautiful wife and take her into my arms. When I looked, Lud and Mother were in a similar embrace. I touched Molly and showed her, and she hugged me tighter and smiled. I enjoyed it until it was almost too much and then said, "Enough. Merry Christmas."

We all smiled, shook hands, or embraced, and Molly took me to her "castle." We wandered through Solomon's garden that night, eating of its choicest fruits. It's a wonderful place!

As I lay with her in my arms, I said, "Solomon didn't have anyone like you."

"Flatterer."

"No, I can prove it."

"How?"

"He'd have had only one wife and no concubines if there was anyone like you."

"You're right. I'd have either killed him or run all the other women off. Don't ever get any crazy ideas."

"How about this?"

"Mmm. That's not a crazy idea. Oh, yes. I love you, sweetheart. Oh, yes."

"There's never been anyone like you, my wonderful, gorgeous, delectable wife. I love every beautiful inch of you."

"Oh, oh, oh, Darling, yes."

"My cup's overflowed."

"No, it's my cup that overflowed. Merry Christmas, my darling."

"It is a merry Christmas, my beloved, wonderful, precious sweetheart. I love you."

"Show me again."

"Give me a minute. Those horses are still out there with their saddles on. Don't go anywhere. I'll be right back."

"Hurry, darling."

"I'll sure do that."

"I love you."

"I love you."

You have captivated my heart, my sister, my bride; you have captivated my heart with one glance of your eyes, with one jewel of your necklace. How beautiful is your love, my sister, my bride! How much better is your love than wine, and the fragrance of your oils than any spice! Your lips drip nectar, my bride; honey and milk are under your tongue; the fragrance of your garments is like the fragrance of Lebanon. A garden locked is my sister, my bride, a spring locked, a fountain sealed. Your shoots are an orchard of pomegranates with all choicest fruits, henna with nard, nard and saffron, calamus and cinnamon, with all trees of frankincense, myrrh and aloes, with all choice spices—a garden fountain, a well of living water, and flowing streams from Lebanon. Awake, O north wind, and come, O south wind! Blow upon my garden, let its spices flow.

Let my beloved come to his garden, and eat its choicest fruits.

Song of Solomon 4:1-16 (ESV)